THE ACCLAIMED
SHOW BUSINESS NOVEL

Curtain

"Michael Korda is the
consummate storyteller."
—*Jackie Collins*

⸱⸰⸱⸰⸱⸰⸱⸰⸱⸰

"A real page-turner . . . a vivid depiction
of life in the theatre . . . I couldn't
put it down!"
—**Patricia Bosworth, author of**
Montgomery Clift

⸱⸰⸱⸰⸱⸰⸱⸰⸱⸰

"Fascinating."
—**Dominick Dunne**

⸱⸰⸱⸰⸱⸰⸱⸰⸱⸰

more . . .

"A rattling good storyteller."
—*Cosmopolitan*

"An unforgettable drama of sound and fury, of tempestuous love, soaring talent and shattering tragedy. As this *Curtain* rings down, you'll find yourself rising up in applause."
—*Literary Guild Magazine*

ABOUT THE AUTHOR

MICHAEL KORDA is the nephew of Merle Oberon and the great Alexander Korda, and the son of movie art director Vincent Korda and English actress Gertrude Musgrove. Educated in Beverly Hills, New York City, Switzerland, and England, where he graduated from Magdalen College, Oxford, Mr. Korda served in the RAF and then wrote for many years for the *New York Times*, *Vogue*, *New York* magazine, and *Glamour*. He is the author of such bestsellers as *Queenie*, *The Fortune*, and *Power!* He lives in New York with his wife, Margaret.

BY MICHAEL KORDA

CURTAIN*
THE FORTUNE*
QUEENIE*
WORLDLY GOODS
CHARMED LIVES
SUCCESS!
POWER!*
MALE CHAUVINISM

*Published by
WARNER BOOKS

Curtain

MICHAEL KORDA

WARNER BOOKS

A Time Warner Company

WARNER BOOKS EDITION

FOR MARGARET
WITH ALL MY LOVE

"All the world's a stage,
And all the men and women merely players."
—As You Like It

Curtain

PROLOGUE

Rain poured down out of a cold, gunmetal-gray sky.

Despite the blazing fire, and central heating set so high that moisture ran down the inside of the windows, Lord Vane was shivering, his lips and fingernails an alarming blue. His hands shook so badly that he had great difficulty holding his knife and fork for his first meal downstairs in many weeks.

He had been dying for months, breaking his own cardinal rule: "When you've finished what you're doing, get offstage as soon as you can."

Even the press was bored waiting for England's first theatrical peer and greatest actor to make his exit. Vane's obituaries had been prepared for ages, along with all the feature articles and photographs that would accompany them. A week ago an equerry had arrived from Buckingham Palace bearing a handwritten note from the Queen herself, informing Lord Vane that her thoughts, and those of the entire Royal Family, were with him, but even this unprecedented honor had failed to make up his mind.

Indeed, the message seemed to have had a contrary effect. To everyone's surprise, he had rallied, perhaps only to spite his doctors. His breathing improved, he was allowed out of bed to sit for an hour at a time, then to take a few faltering steps, supported by his nurse. Finally, he expressed his desire—his *intention*, to be more accurate—to come down to luncheon, despite the doctors' warnings on the subject.

Cook had labored long and hard, but Vane hardly touched a thing. He sipped at his wine and made a show of moving the food around on his plate, but it was as if merely *looking* at it was as much as he could manage.

Lady Vane, who had been opposed to the idea from the very beginning, hardly even bothered to conceal her impatience. Guillam Pentecost, Vane's collaborator, theatrical adviser, and confidant for nearly forty years, ate heartily, as he always did. The three of them were seated at one end of a long dining table that could hold—had once often held—eighteen people. The effect was rather like that of a meal in an officers' mess the day after a battle, the survivors dwarfed by the room and the table.

Vane slumped in his chair at the head of the table, exhausted. Even in distress, his dignity was immense. With his snow-white hair, the short beard he had grown in old age, the famous dark blue eyes, and his majestic profile, he might have been playing Lear in modern dress. He waved away the butler, who was holding a silver sauceboat full of custard. "Tea," he said weakly. "A cup of tea, with a drop or two of brandy."

Lady Vane frowned. "Is that a *good* idea, Robby, darling?" she asked.

"It seems like a bloody good idea to *me*." Vane glared at the butler, who glanced toward Lady Vane. She sighed and nodded her head. After all, there was no point in contradicting him now. "Did Guillam tell you how well the exhibit is coming along, darling?" she asked, raising her voice. Vane refused to wear a hearing aid, but on the other hand he didn't like being shouted at, which made it hard for those around him to know how loud to speak.

The exhibit was being held in the National Theatre to mark Lord Vane's eighty-fifth birthday, and many of his mementos, carefully selected by Pentecost, would be on display there. Originally it had been intended that Vane himself would open the exhibit, but that plan had long since been shelved, and Lady Vane was to replace him.

Vane closed his eyes—the eyelids were pale blue, almost transparent, the skin so pale and tightly stretched over his bones that he might already have been dead—and thought for a moment. "I think so," he said at last. "Don't give a damn. I shan't live to see it."

Pentecost spoke up with false cheeriness. "I'll bet you *do*, Robby. My money's on you to cut the ribbon. It's going to be fascinating, you know . . . your costumes, your note-books, your prompt copies, hundreds of photographs. . . . There'll be television sets all over the place playing scenes from your films. 'Multimedia,' they call it, whatever the hell that means."

"I *know* what it bloody means." Vane took the cup of tea laced with brandy from the butler's silver salver and held it to his lips with trembling fingers, blowing on the surface. When he judged it cool enough, he took a couple of noisy sips. They seemed to revive him. His skin was as pale as ever, but there was the hint of a sparkle in his dark blue eyes. "And Felicia's portrait will definitely be there?" he asked slyly.

Pentecost and Lady Vane exchanged glances, his apologetic, hers furious. Any mention of Felicia Lisle, the *first* Lady Vane, was bound to offend the second and present Lady Vane. Pentecost thought it was tactless—even hurtful—of his old friend to mention Felicia's name, particularly after all the trouble Lady Vane had gone to over the lunch.

The portrait was a sore point in any case, since Lady Vane had strenuously objected to its inclusion in the exhibit and had been overruled. Felicia Lisle had been the most famous actress of her time, more famous than Vane, in fact, and for nearly fifteen years the two of them had been the most celebrated and romantic couple of the theatre, legendary lovers on stage and on screen, though after the war they never acted together again—which had always puzzled Pentecost.

As if that were not enough to make the present Lady Vane envious, Felicia Lisle had also been one of the most beautiful women in the world, the epitome of glamour, charm, style, and talent. It was impossible to exclude her name—or her portrait—from the exhibit, as Pentecost had been obliged to use all his tact to explain.

"It's going to be there, Robby, of course," he said soothingly, hoping to get the subject out of the way as fast as possible.

Lady Vane's expression would have done credit to Medea, whom she had once played. She was—or had been—a striking woman and a modestly successful actress, which only made it that much harder for her to accept a lifetime role as the successor to a legend, for Felicia Lisle had been a star of the stage at twenty and had won her first Academy Award at thirty, conquering Hollywood in one leap. There was a bronze star with her name on it set in the pavement at Hollywood and Vine, her handprints were preserved in concrete outside Grauman's Chinese Theater, theatres on Broadway and in London's West End were named after her, the sorrows and triumphs of her life had been the subject of innumerable magazine stories and biographies. Her death twenty-five years ago of pneumonia aggravated by heavy smoking and drinking had been an occasion of national mourning on both sides of the Atlantic.

Vane's tea had cooled to the point where he could gulp it. "I want to see it before it goes."

"*Really*, Robby! Surely that's not necessary?" Lady Vane snapped.

"I want—to—see—it," Vane repeated petulantly, like a child, emphasizing each word. Many people thought he was senile, but Pentecost knew better. Vane was the greatest of actors, even in extreme old age. He was quite capable of making people think he was senile to get his own way, and never more likely than when he thought he was going to be thwarted.

"It's *too* bad!" Lady Vane said, dabbing her eyes with her napkin. "After all the trouble I've been to about this *stupid* luncheon . . . and everything I've had to put up with these past few weeks . . . you might at least have the decency not to flaunt her to me now."

"I merely expressed a wish to look at her portrait." Vane's

energy seemed to be ebbing again. For a moment Pentecost thought he was about to give in to Lady Vane, but the old man visibly summoned what remained of his strength and shook his head stubbornly, his eyes blazing. "I want it put up in my room," he said. "Where I can see it. At once." He directed his orders at Pentecost, not at Lady Vane, knowing very well that she wouldn't carry them out, while Pentecost, however reluctantly, would.

"Oh, do as you please, the two of you, damn you!" Lady Vane shouted. "You've given me a headache!" She balled up her napkin and threw it in Vane's direction, rose from her seat, and bolted from the room in tears, slamming the door behind her.

Vane stared at the crumpled napkin, which had landed on his pudding. "Magnificent!" he said, wheezing and chuckling softly. "If only she'd been as good as that onstage!"

Pentecost directed the butler to see to the painting, then lit a cigarette. Lady Vane was a vehement nonsmoker, and prohibited tobacco in her presence. Felicia Lisle had been a chain-smoker, and her death had been enough to frighten Vane into giving up smoking for good.

"Robby, that was a perfectly bloody thing to do," Pentecost said.

"For God's sake, Guillam, if a man can't do what he wants when he's dying, whenever *can* he?" Vane was beginning to breathe in short gasps, and his voice had dropped to a whisper, so that Pentecost, who towered over him, had to lean forward to hear what he was saying.

It was obvious to Pentecost that coming down for lunch had not only been a mistake on the marital front—it had also been too much for Vane to take. The doctors spoke of his heart and lungs with awe, having predicted their failure long ago, but it looked to Pentecost as if the doctors were about to be proved right at long last. "Robby," he said, "I think we'd better call the nurse and get you back upstairs for a nap."

Vane shook his head feebly, but his protest was clearly not intended to be taken seriously. He had come down for luncheon, as he wanted to, made his point, whatever it was, to Lady Vane, and now he wanted to get back to his bed as fast as Pentecost wanted to get him there.

"Why?" Pentecost asked, pushing the button that summoned the nurse. "Why bring up the portrait now?"

Vane's eyes were cloudy. He seemed to be having trouble concentrating, as well as breathing. He looked around the dining room as if he were no longer sure where he was. The flowers caught his attention. "She loved flowers. Always had scads of 'em. In the house. In the garden. Had a Jap gardener when we were in Hollywood, you know, the year Lisha won the Oscar. She was happy as a lark chatting away with him, though neither of them understood a word the other said."

"Happy? In Hollywood? In 1939? I thought that was when she first went mad?"

"That was later," Vane said irritably. "In San Francisco, I believe." He fell silent. He looked as if he were asleep, except that his eyes were open. Pentecost had a panicky feeling that he might be dead, but then Vane looked at him as if he were surprised to find him there. "I loved her," he said, by way of explanation. "Still do. Always will. I promised her that once upon a time." He made a choking sound that might have been laughter. "Not sure it wasn't a kind of curse, you know. Loving somebody till you die, even long after they're dead. Well, it's not something you'd *choose* to do, is it?"

"Perhaps not."

"Oh, count on it, dear boy. Anyway, I want to see her face once more before I go, it's as simple as that. I owe her that, at least, you see." He closed his eyes. "Weak as a kitten," he complained. "Where *is* that confounded nurse?"

She appeared, her expression making it clear how strongly she disapproved of her patient's behavior. Together she and Pentecost somehow managed to get Vane out of his seat and into a wheelchair. It wasn't a question of his weight—he seemed to weigh nothing—so much as the fact that his body was limp, fragile, awkward to handle.

Pentecost let the nurse do most of the work. Moving Vane

around was too much like handling a corpse for his taste—the corpse of someone he loved and admired.

"I'm having a painting sent up to hang in Lord Vane's room, Sister," he said.

Sister sniffed, as if to say that they would be lucky if Lord Vane lived to see it. She wheeled Vane at a brisk pace out into the hallway, where the butler held open the gates of the small lift. It had been installed over Vane's fierce objections after his first heart attack, when it became obvious to everyone except him that he would never manage the stairs on his feet again.

It had sometimes occurred to Pentecost that if Vane had ever had any hope at all of a happy marriage to the present Lady Vane—and he surely must have had some, or why do it?—he doomed it from day one by keeping this house.

He wondered how Lady Vane could bear to live here surrounded by the memories of her predecessor—for this was the famous house they had bought after the war, their present to each other, their *home*, the decoration and restoration of which had occupied Felicia off and on for years.

He bent his head—his height made going from room to room in the house a hazardous proceeding—and went off to see that the painting was brought down from the attic and hung in Vane's bedroom.

"I can't understand the hold the woman has on him still, after all these years," Lady Vane said plaintively. She was "resting" in her own bedroom, a damp cloth over her eyes, in the first stages of one of the migraines she suffered from.

Pentecost made a sympathetic noise. "Anything I can do?" he asked, but he knew there wasn't. The poor woman was exhausted from week after week of watching Robby's fragile health crumble, and the best thing to do was to let her sleep, if she could. He closed the door gently and made his way down the corridor to Robby's bedroom.

He opened the door, tiptoed in, and stood for a moment.

The room was hushed, the heavy curtains drawn against the dying light of an English winter afternoon. A single lamp on a bedside table illuminated Robby's face. His eyes were closed. A white plastic oxygen mask, obscenely out of place in a room that had been built in a more elegant century, now covered his nose.

With his usual concern for staging, Robby had decided months ago to die in his own bedroom beneath the eighteenth-century painted ceiling of nymphs and cherubs cavorting at the marriage of Bacchus. The ceiling had been plastered over as indecent in Victorian times, then uncovered and restored by Felicia Lisle, at great expense. Now its bright celebration of the flesh seemed once more indecent by contrast with the pale skin and labored breath of the man who lay beneath it.

Pentecost guessed that Robby had imagined a Victorian deathbed scene—the mourners grouped at the foot of the bed for the last words, straw outside on the cobblestones to muffle the sound of the horses' hooves, the fire flickering in the grate, but the doctors, irritated by his refusal to go to a hospital like a sensible man, had cheated him out of all that once he was too weak to resist.

He lay in his own bed, but beside it were all the paraphernalia of modern medical technology—an oxygen tank, a monitor that recorded his heartbeat, a chrome stand with a drip bottle of saline solution. Sister had again hooked him up to all this bedside machinery. But Robby looked much worse than he had downstairs. Pentecost had expected to find his old friend sleeping, dozing restlessly, perhaps, but he seemed to be in a coma, hardly breathing at all despite the oxygen. He raised an eyebrow at Sister, who shook her head. "He's very weak," she said. "I've sent for the doctor."

He sat down beside the bed, opposite Sister. The portrait of Felicia had been hung above the fireplace, as he had instructed, replacing a picture of the old Duke of York Theatre. Once upon a time, Felicia's Renoir, a present from the American impresario Marty Quick, had hung there. After her death, Robby had sold the painting at Christie's despite everybody's advice that he hold on to it. It was as if he had simply wanted the Renoir out of the house as quickly as possible, which had mystified everyone except Pentecost, who knew the reason only too well.

He looked again at Felicia's portrait with the enigmatic smile that was at once innocent and deeply sensual, and the jade-green eyes that bewitched men throughout her tormented life. The painting had been given to her after the war by her Uncle Harry—a man Robby had particularly disliked, Pentecost remembered. Laszlo, who painted only beautiful women, had outdone himself, capturing Felicia's beauty at its zenith—though, in fact, she had aged hardly at all in the years between the time Laszlo had painted her and her death.

Pentecost shook his head at the memory of all those years. Only a man as strong as Robert Vane could have survived them, he thought. *"O, she doth teach the torches to burn bright,"* Robby had murmured when he first saw the painting, but in the end they had burned too brightly for Felicia Vane. He thought not only about what had happened to her, but also about her daughter's untimely death in a riding accident.

He glanced at the other familiar paintings on the walls: Burbage as Hamlet, Kean as Shylock, the portrait of Garrick as Richard III which Robby had always had in his dressing room as his good luck charm, Sir Henry Irving as Lear. The most competitive of actors, Robby still respected talent in others, which perhaps explained why he kept on his desk signed photographs of Sir Toby Eden, his old friend, as Peer Gynt, and Sir Philip Chagrin, his greatest rival, who had closed a lifetime of competing with Vane by dying before him.

A few of the souvenirs of a lifetime were neatly arranged beside the photographs, among them the Oscar Vane finally won twenty-five years after Felicia won hers, and a Degas bronze of a ballerina, a gift from Randy Brooks and his wife Natalie, both long since gone. Poor Vane, he thought, so many deaths . . .

It was warm in the room. The gentle hiss of the oxygen and the hum of the monitor made it hard for Pentecost to keep his eyes open. He felt his chin touch his chest, and dozed uncomfortably, his mind hardly able to separate the portrait of Felicia from his memory of her as Cleopatra, eyes blazing as she made her entrance hand in hand with

Robby. . . . He had been twenty when he saw them acting together for the first time. Now he was nearly sixty-five. . . .

He woke with a start at the feel of a hand tugging at his sleeve. "I don't like the look of things," Sister whispered. "His pulse is bad. His breathing's worse. The doctor's on his rounds, but I asked his secretary to find him and say it's urgent."

"Yes, yes, quite right." He fought an overwhelming desire to go back to sleep. He tried to remember how much he had to drink at lunch. The days were long since gone when he could put away a couple of cocktails and a bottle of wine and go right back to work.

One glance at Robby was enough to wake him up for good. "My God," he said. "Is he going?"

Sister pursed her lips as if to say that it was not her job to give opinions to a layman. "It's hard to know," she said, increasing the flow of oxygen. "It could be another false alarm."

He nodded. There had been many false alarms in the past few weeks. He wondered if he should fetch Lady Vane, but decided against it. Sister examined the monitor carefully, watching the green line oscillate, though it could surely not tell her anything more than she already knew, which was that the patient was hanging on to life long past the point where it could do him any good.

She leaned over to feel Vane's pulse with her fingers, as if she didn't trust the sophisticated instrument. A look of surprise crossed her face. "I think he's trying to speak," she said.

"Are you sure?"

"*Quite* sure," she said frostily, not accustomed to being contradicted.

She removed the oxygen mask. Pentecost put his ear so close to Robby's lips that he could feel his breath. He thought he heard two or three words, but he couldn't be sure. One of them might have been "Nile." Was he reciting from *Antony and Cleopatra*?

"I can't hear you, Robby," he whispered, then, realizing that it made no sense to whisper simply because Robby was unable to do anything else, he repeated what he had said more loudly—*too* loudly.

Robby opened one eye a fraction. "File," he croaked hoarsely, with great effort.

"File?"

"Desk. Drawer." Robby fought for breath. Pentecost caught the words "You bloody fool!" Then: "Stop shouting!"

"There's a file in the desk drawer?"

Vane did his best to nod, a tiny, abrupt jerk of his head that seemed to exhaust him. Sister brought the oxygen mask back to his face. He waved it away with a feeble, impatient movement of his hand.

His fingers were short and blunt, with big, square nails, the fingers of a tradesman, not an aristocrat. He was proud of them, for he regarded acting as a craft, a trade, to be learned and perfected. It was *work*, he liked to say, like making a table or building a ship, and damned hard work at that. "I'm just an ordinary chap—I read the lines and try to put myself in the other chap's shoes," was all he would ever say about his genius, like a magician afraid to give away his secrets.

Pentecost pulled at the desk drawer obediently. It was locked. He hesitated, reluctant to pry it open. "Box," he heard Robby whisper urgently behind him. He puzzled over that a moment, then saw, on the desk's gleaming leather surface, the silver cigarette box, with its engraved inscription:

> *For Robby and Lisha—*
> *Friends and neighbors*
> *Randy and Natalie Brooks*
> *Los Angeles, October 15, 1939.*

The lid of the box was scarred, as if it had been attacked with a sharp instrument in an attempt to obliterate Randy Brooks's name. Pentecost had often wondered how that had happened, and why Robby kept the box among his more treasured possessions. He opened it and found a small key, with which he unlocked the drawer.

Wedged at the back, he saw a plain manila folder, the edges torn and frayed. A faded label read "Marty Quick Productions, Inc.," with a New York address. Behind it was a bundle, wrapped in a stained piece of silk.

He glanced toward the bed. Both Robby's eyes were open now, as commanding as they had been onstage in his prime.

Pentecost brought the file over to the bed and held it up so that Robby could see it without moving his head. Robby stared at it for a moment, his face expressionless, then nodded, sighed gently, and closed his eyes. "Burn it."

Pentecost lifted an eyebrow. "Now? *Here*?"

Robby opened his eyes again and focused them directly on Pentecost's. Years ago, Pentecost had learned that he could argue with him or question him only up to a point—until those dark blue eyes made it clear his patience was at an end. "Oh, quite," he said. He looked at the fireplace, but it was empty—another victory for the doctors, who had pointed out that oxygen was far too flammable to allow a fire in the room while it was in use.

"I'll just burn this in the fireplace, Sister," Pentecost said. "I won't take a minute."

"You'll do no such thing," she snapped, with a look that would have frozen most men in their tracks.

Most people were taken aback by Pentecost, whose towering height and sheer ugliness had long since made him something of a landmark in the English theatre. He had made his reputation as a critic and an intellectual gadfly before becoming Lord Vane's closest—indeed his *only*—collaborator, with the special responsibility of doing all the unpleasant things that Vane hated to do, like saying no to people. He knotted his immense bushy eyebrows in a simian frown and glared at her. "You heard him, Sister," he said firmly. "That was his express wish."

"His lordship is in no position to express his wishes. He's a patient—a very sick one."

Pentecost knew there was no point in arguing with her. "Lord Vane may be ill, but he knows what he wants," he said quietly. "I intend to carry out his wishes. If you won't turn off the oxygen, so be it. We'll all go up together, in one big blaze." He bared huge teeth in a smile, as if he were looking forward to the prospect.

She bit her lip, hesitated for a second, then tightly screwed down the knob on the oxygen regulator. The hissing sound to which Pentecost had grown so accustomed grew fainter, then stopped.

He hurried over to the fireplace, opened the flue, and holding the file in both hands, tried to tear it in half. It was thicker than he had supposed. He felt a slight flush of embarrassment, conscious of Sister's eyes on him. No doubt, *she* could have torn the damned thing into shreds!

He took a deep breath and tried again, this time successfully. A scrap of paper fell at his feet, part of a photograph. He recognized the young Vane, handsome and smiling, sitting by a pool. There was a man's hand on his shoulder, as if somebody was sitting close to him, his arm around Robby. Whoever it was, he wore a gold identification bracelet on his wrist, the lettering picked out in diamonds. Pentecost scooped the fragment up, dumped the pile of torn papers on the grate, lit a match, and set fire to the edges.

The flames joined together in a bright blaze, the fragments of burning paper rising in the draft. Robby raised his head slightly to watch, his face lit by the glow, so that he appeared for a moment almost healthy. Then the file blackened, turned to ashes, the glow faded, and the impression of life left him. "Well done, Guillam," he whispered gratefully, his voice ghostlike, a ripple on a pool of silence.

Pentecost went back to the desk. He reached into the drawer, took out the bundle and began to unwrap it. He could see now that the piece of silk was a pale beige scarf, the same color as that of an American officer's tie during the war. Here and there it was spotted with dark brown stains, like rust. The initials "MQ" were embroidered at one end, so he had no difficulty in guessing that it had once belonged to Marty Quick—though what it was doing *here* was more difficult to explain.

He gasped in astonishment as he uncovered the object inside it—the most famous artifact in the history of the English theatre, missing for almost forty-five years, the where-

abouts of which Robby had always refused to discuss: the
Shakespeare dagger!

Pentecost knew almost everything about it—what student
of the theatre did not? It had been a gift from Shakespeare
himself to his friend, collaborator, and leading player, Richard Burbage, then passed from one great Shakespearean actor
to another across three centuries. Garrick had owned it, as
had Kean, Irving, and, more recently, Philip Chagrin. The
dagger was at once a link to the past—to the very origins of
the English theatre—and a symbol of theatrical greatness,
the acting equivalent of a monarch's crown.

Pentecost held it reverently. It was plain, except for a few
decoratively engraved squiggles on the guard and the silver
wire braid entwined around the hilt. Burbage had carried it
as a weapon, as well as wearing it onstage, in an age when
men commonly went armed, so the point was needle-sharp,
the gleaming edges honed like a razor's.

There was a stain on the point that might have been rust,
but otherwise the dagger was as good as new. Pentecost had
not seen it since the day Robby and Felicia were married,
when it had been the cause, he remembered vaguely, of some
trouble. . . .

He felt a small surge of triumph and relief. For years he
had been making an inventory of everything that touched on
Robby's career—for quite apart from the forthcoming exhibit, there were plans to build a museum in his honor at the
National Theatre, as well as to memorialize his name by a
new theatre, and a chair in Elizabethan Drama at Oxford, not
to speak of innumerable other worthy projects throughout the
British Commonwealth and the United States. At each of
these there was a demand for some object which had belonged
to Robby. He and Robby had spent many hours, particularly
in the past few weeks, drawing up lists of items and deciding
where each of them should go after his death—but on the
subject of the Shakespeare dagger, Vane had remained obstinately, even angrily, silent.

Pentecost eventually came to the conclusion that Robby
had probably mislaid the relic and was embarrassed to admit

it—which seemed to be the case, now that Pentecost had found it. He brought it over to the bed, so that Robby could see it. "Thank God," he said. "I've found it at last!"

But Robby's expression was so horrified that Pentecost almost dropped the dagger on the bed. His eyes opened wide in fear, his lips parted in a terrible grimace, he clenched his teeth, his fingers dug into the blanket. Sister hastily produced a syringe and began to fill it.

"Put it *away*!" Robby wailed, his voice louder now, though distorted with what Pentecost realized was real terror.

"It's nothing to be afraid of, old chap," Pentecost said soothingly. "It must be in the exhibit, of course. It was the one thing that was missing. . . ."

Robby's expression silenced him. Sister was already wiping down his arm with a swab of cotton wool, but he brushed her hand away sharply, his strength returning suddenly, if only for an instant. "Wrap the bloody thing up again," he said sharply. "I want it buried with me."

Pentecost puzzled over this. "Buried? With you?" He couldn't believe his ears. It was a three-hundred-year-old theatrical tradition, the most precious object of the theatre. In a manner of speaking, the dagger belonged to the theatre, to the nation—not to one man, however great. "You can't *mean* it, Robby," he said, pleading.

But Robby's eyes were fierce, unyielding. "Promise," he commanded harshly.

Pentecost nodded. "I promise."

"Thank you. You've been a good friend. Hold my hand, please." His eyes closed, and he let out a long sigh, as if he had completed any business he had left to do on earth and was ready, at last, to go.

Pentecost was not given to physical gestures where his old friend and mentor was concerned, for there had always been a certain reserve between them. Besides, he had never been at ease with the hugs and kisses theatre people lavished on each other, and he knew that Robby, too, avoided them whenever possible. Still, there was nobody else to do it. He gently took Robby's hand in his own and held it.

He felt Robby's fingers grasp his with surprising strength, as if he were holding on for dear life. Was he reaching for one last touch of human comfort?

The silence was unbroken now, except for the ticking of the clock and the hiss of air as the nurse unscrewed the valve on her machine. Robby's breath, if any, was inaudible. At least he's going quietly, Pentecost thought, eager to disengage his fingers from a grasp that was growing increasingly unpleasant.

But he was not yet dead. His lips moved ever so slightly, and Pentecost bent to listen. "Lisha," Robby muttered. His eyes opened. For a moment, Pentecost thought the dying man was staring into space, but then he realized that he was staring at Felicia's portrait, as if he had just noticed it. There were tears in his eyes now, beginning to run down the sunken cheeks. *"More sinned against than sinning,"* he muttered, though whether he was thinking of himself or of Felicia was impossible to guess.

And why quote *Lear*, the play in which he had made his farewell performance onstage, at the age of eighty? Did he *see* himself as Lear? It was the appropriate choice, certainly, for old age and death. . . .

He felt Robby tighten his grip, his nails digging into Pentecost's palm, heard him whisper urgently, "Lisha, don't go! Kiss me!"

Pentecost hesitated. The notion of kissing the dying man was deeply repugnant to him. He nerved himself, bent low, closed his eyes, and kissed Robby's forehead quickly. He could taste the sweat on his lips, and fancied for a moment that he recognized, like Lear, the smell of mortality.

"Forgive me!" Robby cried. Then he took a deep breath, and in the voice that had filled the house for sixty years, reaching without amplification (which he despised) "to the gods," as theatre people used to call the cheapest seats in the balcony, a voice so powerful that the darkly paneled bedroom could hardly contain it, he exclaimed, *"Thus with a kiss I die."*

His head fell back against his pillows, and his fingers relaxed their grip on Pentecost's. His eyes were still open, fixed on Felicia's portrait, but there was a faint film on them now.

Sister held the mask against his mouth briefly, then put it down. She seemed shaken, not so much by the presence of death as by the sudden, last-minute renewal of Lord Vane's powers. "He's gone," she said.

Pentecost nodded. He did not need the nurse to tell him that Robby had spoken his last line, delivered with all the strength and artistry of a lifetime on the stage, then made his exit. For a minute he stood in silence, his head bowed, searching for the right gesture, the appropriate words. If Robby had been a religious man, Pentecost might have said a few words of prayer, but he had not been. Both of them put more faith in Shakespeare than in the Bible.

Then Pentecost realized what was missing, and although he was in some respects the most conventional of Englishmen, he clapped his hands together, hesitantly at first, then in loud, enthusiastic applause, indifferent to the shocked glare from Sister, indifferent to his own embarrassment, indifferent to everything but the sound that Robert Gilles Vane had sought all his life, and had probably heard more often than any other actor.

Pentecost clapped until his hands stung, and kept on clapping, the tears running down his cheeks.

ACT ONE
A Muse of Fire
1940

1

There was a hush in the theatre as the world's most famous lovers embraced.

Arms around each other, lips almost touching, they stood gazing into each other's eyes in the bright spotlight, high above the darkened stage on a narrow balcony. They were placed so that the audience saw them in profile, hers turned upward adoringly toward his.

"Farewell, farewell! One kiss and I'll descend," he said, his voice low, infinitely soft and gentle. As they kissed, a sigh rose from the audience—from the women in it, anyway—even though the theatre was less than half full.

This was what they had come to see—not just Shakespeare's *Romeo and Juliet*, but Robert Vane and Felicia Lisle—who only a few months ago had won the Oscar for Best Actress in her first Hollywood movie—*playing* Romeo and Juliet.

Slowly, reluctantly, he drew away from her, running his fingers gently over her face, as if he wanted to fix her beauty forever in his mind, then, with an athletic leap, he swung himself over the low railing and hung from the balcony, looking up at her.

There was a long silence—so long that there were a couple of coughs from the audience, then a titter. Those in the front

23

rows could see Vane's lips moving, as if he was whispering something, but Felicia Lisle's face remained impassive, the only sign of life a wild look of terror in her eyes.

For what seemed like hours, Vane remained suspended above the stage, dangling from the balcony, waiting, like the audience, for Juliet to come to her senses and say good-bye, then, with a look of fear that was clearly genuine, and had nothing whatsoever to do with acting, he lost his grip and fell heavily to the stage, landing in a heap with a cry of pain.

There was a moment of silence, while Felicia Lisle stared down at her co-star and lover as if she couldn't imagine what he was doing lying on the stage. Then she started to laugh.

She was still laughing when the curtain came down and at last, mercifully, hid the actors from the audience.

"Thus with a kiss I die."

The words were written in careful, elaborate, over-scale letters on the back of a postcard, intruding into the space on the right that was intended for the addressee. His own name was written in a minuscule version of the same familiar hand, squeezed into a corner. He wondered if there was any significance to the fact.

He read them aloud, the words echoing in the hot, still air, the voice rising above the hum of the ventilating fans and the noise of carpenters making yet another last-minute adjustment to the set on the sound stage next door. Outside it was probably ninety degrees and sunny, but here it was like being inside a submarine—the air smelled of stale cigarette smoke, sweat, machinery, electricity.

"Come again?"

Robert Vane did not look at his companion. He had turned his attention to the front of the postcard, a tinted photograph of a building not unlike a miniature version of the Beverly Hills Hotel, in the same garish pink stucco, surrounded by palm trees, with a roof of Spanish tiles. The windows were heavily barred, but with such an exuberance of Southern California wrought-iron fantasy that they might have been the whim of an architect or a decorator. On one of the upper

windows a large cross had been drawn in ink, as if the oc-
cupant of the room were calling for rescue. He felt the familiar
combination of guilt and fear grip his stomach, and winced.
"Romeo and Juliet," he explained, a trace of impatience in
his voice. "Romeo's last line. After he's killed himself, the
silly twit."

Vane sat in front of his dressing table, smoking. He wore
an elaborate frilled shirt, tight buckskin breeches and full
makeup. His hair was long, the Hollywood style for romantic
heroes of the eighteenth century. He had removed his riding
boots, which had been made for Ronald Colman, who apparently had smaller feet, and which pinched like the blazes.
Jackets, shirts, and breeches could be altered by the costume
department overnight, but when it came to hats and boots
you had to take what there was and make the best of it. He
put the card down and massaged his feet with a sigh. "God,
I hate the waiting," Vane said.

"Hey, the pay's the same, acting or waiting. Why not take
up knitting, pass the time?" the other man said. He took up
a pair of imaginary knitting needles, moving his hands with
frenzied precision. When Vane didn't laugh, he shook his
head. "Feeling sorry for yourself isn't gonna help, pal."

"Really? Apart from drink, it's my only comfort, at present."

"People aren't supposed to feel sorry for themselves here.
It's against the rules, like walking at night in Beverly Hills.
'You gotta start off each day with a smile,' " he rasped, in
an imitation of Jimmy Durante that would have convinced
Durante himself, but which was wasted on Vane, who had
never heard of him.

Randy Brooks had the clown's gift of using every bit of
his face to express himself, which was hardly surprising, since
he was, at the moment, the most famous comedian in the
world. Slumped in a canvas director's chair facing Vane, he
wore the local costume: white trousers, a flowered Hawaiian
shirt, sunglasses, and Mexican sandals. Despite the clothes,
there was something about him that suggested he was not a
native Californian—not that many people in Hollywood

were—a big-city street urchin's quickness in his speech, a pale, freckled skin that burned pink in the sun instead of tanning.

Brooks was not handsome by Hollywood leading-man standards—his face was too sharp and angular for that, and his bright red curly hair made him look a little clownish even when he was trying to be serious—but there was a boyish liveliness to him which made him seem younger than his years. Like Vane, he was in his early thirties. Unlike Vane, he was one of the dozen or so names on anybody's list of Hollywood's top stars.

"Christ, pal, I'm just trying to cheer you up. I mean, I finished *my* work today, you know. I could be home, sitting at my pool, reading about myself in *Life* magazine."

"I don't *want* to be cheered up," Vane said glumly. "I can't imagine how life could be worse. Job was better off, boils and all."

"You made a deal with Marty Quick and you got fucked," Brooks said cheerfully. "You should excuse the expression," he added quickly. Brooks seldom swore, and always apologized when he did, perhaps because so many of his fans were children. "Welcome to the club. It's not the end of the world, for Christ's sake."

"Thank you," Vane said, with a grave irony in his voice that was lost on Brooks. "I am well aware that I'm not Quick's first victim. I'm also aware that Felicia has had a breakdown, and for four weeks has been under the care of a high-priced quack whom I can't afford. Not to speak of the fact that any moment Hitler may land in England, while I'm sitting here on my ass waiting for this idiot of a director to make up his mind. I should be home in uniform, fighting. And all the bloody doctor will say is that Felicia is 'making progress,' whatever *that* means."

"She's gone through a difficult time, Robby," Brooks said, choosing his words carefully. "It may take a lot longer than you think."

"We've *both* been through a difficult time," Vane snapped. He took another cigarette out of a gold case, tapped it, lit it with his lighter, and breathed out a plume of smoke with a deep sigh.

Anybody who had seen Vane's early films, the dashing, romantic ones he had made in England in the thirties, would have recognized the gesture instantly. Vane had made it something of a trademark, along with the fedora he wore cocked rakishly to one side, and the polo coat thrown over his shoulders. "Did you know," he asked Brooks plaintively, "that in England they actually named a cigarette after me? No, really! 'Vanes'! The advertising slogan was, '*Every inch a great performance!*' " He gave a mournful laugh. "Lisha always used to say that *any* man would have trouble living up to that billing! Typical of her to notice a *double-entendre* where nobody else had. Christ, after she said that, I nearly went mad! I mean, there it was, this bloody ad, with my picture, on the sides of buses, in the underground, pasted up on walls and hoardings all over the country! I began to think the entire female population of the United Kingdom must be having a laugh at my expense."

Brooks looked envious. He was a star himself, one of the biggest, but he had never been a sex symbol. "You should have looked on the bright side, Robby," he said. "A lot of them must have wanted to find out if it was true!"

"I suppose so," Vane said thoughtfully. "I never thought of it that way. Between Penelope, my wife, and Lisha, I had as much in the way of women as I could handle, then . . . *more* than enough, in fact."

"I'd say you still do."

Vane nodded gloomily, then ran his hands over his face, as if thinking about the past had exhausted him. "*Christ*, Randy," he groaned, "the point is, I was a star there! Everybody in England knew who I was. Here I'm just another bloody British actor. Nobody gives a *shit*!"

"Come on! You had a big hit in your last picture. So did Felicia." Brooks left it tactfully unsaid that Felicia's had been bigger by far.

Vane gave a wry smile. "That's the irony of it, isn't it? A year ago, you might have thought we had it all. I mean,

who would have *believed* Lisha would become the most famous Southern belle in history and win an Oscar first time
out?'' The thought seemed to cheer him up momentarily.
''She showed *everybody* in this bloody town! She had her
Oscar, I was nominated for one—would have *won* it, too, if
it hadn't been for Mr. Gary-fucking-Cooper. We were rolling
in money and happy as larks. . . .''

''I thought you told me Felicia wasn't happy, even then?''

''Well, she was and she wasn't,'' Vane said cautiously,
narrowing his eyes. ''It's sometimes hard to tell, frankly.''

Brooks crossed his eyes and gave a high-pitched cackle,
his trademark, and launched into one of the rapid-fire mon-
ologues that always brought the house down when he performed onstage. ''You think *you've* got troubles? You're not
married to Leo Stone's daughter, pal, Hollywood royalty,
born with a silver caviar spoon in her mouth. Imagine having
a *gonif* like Leo as your father-in-law, pal! The Napoleon of
Culver City, runs his studio the way Hitler runs Germany,
except in Leo's case the Jews are on top.''

Brooks's expression was one of manic glee, though a close
observer might have noticed a hint of malice in his eyes, for
it was well known in Hollywood that Leo Stone disliked
Randy and thought Natalie had married beneath her. ''And
how about Natalie's *mother*?'' Brooks cried, giving an instant
and remarkable impression of Mrs. Stone, one of the movie
community's more glittering snobs. ''Did you know she accused Leo of trying to make her perform an unnatural act on
her wedding night? Yes, it's true! Leo asked her to take off
her jewelry before coming to bed. . . .''

Brooks's patter was delivered at such high speed that it
threatened to outrun his tongue. He could go on like this for
minutes at a time, building from laugh to laugh, talking so
fast that audiences waited breathlessly for him to run out of
steam or miss a word, but he never did.

He stopped to see if Vane would laugh, or at least ask what
a *gonif* was, but since neither was forthcoming, he dropped
his voice back to a normal pitch. ''Listen, Robby, *bubbi*, I'm
your neighbor. Natalie and I *care* about you guys.'' He took

off his sunglasses and wiped at his eyes. Tears came easily to him, as they did to most people in Beverly Hills. "I know what you're going through," he said. "You feel guilty, right?"

He did not pause for an answer. Out here, most questions were rhetorical, as Vane had learned. There was no such thing as conversation, in the English sense of the word— people talked until they were tired of talking, without expecting a reply or an interruption. When they were through, *you* talked, while they thought about something else. Vane closed his eyes, waiting for Brooks to finish analyzing his problems.

"Up to a point, that's *healthy*. Okay, maybe you should have known better than to dive straight into *Romeo and Juliet* when Felicia was so tired. And sure—it was a mistake to make a deal with Marty Quick. Maybe you should have paid more attention to Felicia, too, but listen, that's the way it is here, everybody's busy with his own career. If there's one thing I've learned in analysis, it's that you've got to forgive yourself. That's Step One. And you've got to forgive *her*. That's Step Two."

Brooks's expression was rapt, as it always was when he gave advice. Brotherhood, forgiveness, and love were part of his act. "You want my advice?" he went on, without waiting for Vane to say whether he did or not. "Go see her, whatever the doctors say. You'll feel better. Hell, who knows? Maybe *she'll* feel better."

Vane appeared to consider this. Even here, in his modest dressing room—Brooks's, across the hallway, was grander by far—there was something regal about him, as if many years of playing kings and princes had given him a dignity beyond his youth—even beyond his appearance, for he was in fact small and slight, his face raised out of the ordinary only by his dark blue eyes, almost the color of lapis lazuli flecked with gold. "The problem is," he said at last, "I'm not sure I want to see *her*. It's all my fault, you see. I was *relieved* when the doctor told me not to come. I'm not sure I can face her."

"That's not so terrible, Robby. Of *course* you don't want to see her in some goddamned rest home, or whatever they call it, looking her worst. It's nothing to be ashamed of."

"That's not what I'm ashamed of. Randy, doing *Romeo and Juliet* was *my* idea. *I* sunk all our earnings into it. It seemed such a marvelous thing to do——bring Shakespeare to the masses, tour the country the way Booth did in the nineteenth century. . . ."

Vane bared his teeth in a grimace that almost passed for a smile, but didn't quite make it. "The masses certainly showed us where we could shove Shakespeare!" His teeth were not nearly as white and regular as Brooks's. His refusal to have them capped had caused major problems with closeups in his almost-Oscar film, leading him to complain that Si Krieger, the producer, didn't know the difference between acting and dentistry. Krieger retaliated by complaining that he couldn't understand Vane's English accent, so that every scene had to be shot over and over again. It had been this experience, as much as anything else, that had made Vane decide to do *Romeo and Juliet* with his own money——and Felicia's.

"Hey," Brooks said, "it wasn't a bad idea. You just had lousy luck, that's all. And the wrong partner. Hitler would have been a better choice than Marty Quick."

Vane did not seem to have heard. "And I, of all people, should have known how tired Lisha was. She's delicate, you know." He paused. "Fragile," he added, as if the concept of delicacy might not be one with which Brooks was familiar.

Although he had lived in the United States for nearly eighteen months, Vane still spoke very slowly, separating each word carefully, as if he feared the natives might have difficulty understanding the mother tongue when it was properly spoken. This was partly the result of six months of trench warfare with Si Krieger, who had once screamed at him, in front of the entire crew, "*Fuck* the King's English! This is Metro, not Windsor Palace. I decide what's English around here!"

"Felicia has always lived on her nerves," Vane went on.

"I should have realized she was exhausted, after all that work and success. Certainly in no state for a tour. And Juliet's not an easy part."

"I guess not," Brooks said vaguely. His knowledge of Shakespeare was sketchy, though, like all comedians, he had aspirations to be a "serious" actor.

"It's not just the part. It's hard enough for a mature woman to strike a balance between sensuality and innocence, but for a pair of 'world-famous lovers' "—he shook his head sadly—"as the bloody press insists on calling us, what could be more dangerous than *playing* the world's most famous pair of lovers every night onstage, and twice on Wednesdays and Saturdays!"

He stubbed his cigarette out savagely. "The audiences came to gawp at us as if we were a pair of circus freaks. Come one, come all, see Robert Vane and Felicia Lisle, the most famous romantic couple since Edward and Mrs. Simpson—and almost as great a scandal! *She's* about to lose custody of her child! *His* divorce has been going on for years, with no bloody end in sight!"

He closed his eyes for a moment. "What a *farce* we've made of our lives. And nothing to show for it but debts."

"I wouldn't say that. You're both young, talented, famous. . . ." Brooks groaned comically. "Come to think of it, you're right. You're up shit creek."

"If we were married," Vane continued, as if he were talking to himself, "at least we could get on with our lives. Lisha misses little Portia dreadfully. She feels desperately guilty for having left her behind."

"I love kids," Brooks said, and it was true. He liked to be surrounded by children, was never happier than when clowning for them.

Vane nodded. "So do I. I grew up in a big family, and I've always wanted one of my own. So does Lisha. But we can't very well make a start until we're married, can we? We've got enough problems as it is, what with the bloody gossip columnists and the Legion of Decency. Do you know, the studios made us rent two separate houses when we came out here? Couldn't let the great American public know we were living together 'in sin,' as they say. What a bloody *stupid* country this is!''

"Hey, go easy, kiddo. It's my country. Anyway, I don't suppose the two of you could have a baby in England without a scandal.''

Vane shrugged. "True enough. But nobody at home threatened to picket the theatre because we were living together.''

"Listen, movies are big business. This isn't the theatre, and don't you ever forget it. Public opinion *matters*. That's why there's only one rule here: *Don't get caught*!'' His voice dropped to a whisper. Nobody in Hollywood was cleaner than Randy Brooks, whose study was covered in awards from the Legion of Decency, and who was always in demand for speeches about "wholesome" entertainment. "Well, no,'' he added, "there's another rule. When you're knocked down, get up off the floor and keep fighting, or you're out for the count.''

"Somebody once told me much the same thing,'' Vane said. "My father, actually. When he entered me in the school boxing competition.''

"What happened?''

"I got knocked down. Took a bloody nose. 'Get back up on your feet and fight, Robert!' Father said.''

"And did you?''

"Oh, yes. Scared shitless, and hated every moment of it, but I did it.'' He massaged his nose as if he could still feel the pain. "The next day I joined the theatre club. It met on the same day as the boxing, you see, so I couldn't do both. I didn't fancy acting much, but I knew I never wanted to box again, and I never did. Funny thing, isn't it? I wouldn't have become an actor if I hadn't taken a bloody nose my first time in the ring.''

"There you are—proves my point! Christ, when I was a kid, I grew up in East Harlem. That probably doesn't mean anything to you, but it was a tough neighborhood—maybe the toughest. Me and my family, we were the only Jews, so I got beaten up by the Wops once a day. Twice, if it was a saint's day. I think they got a saint for every goddamned day, you know.''

''And did you fight back?''

''Are you kidding? I learned how to make them laugh at me instead. That's how I got to be a comedian.''

Vane tried to imagine the scene—Randy Brooks surrounded by his tormentors, desperately telling jokes and making fun of himself, a skinny, wild-eyed kid, funny-looking enough to begin with, no doubt, with his orange-red hair, his bright green eyes and his pale, freckled skin, the colors, more or less, of the Irish flag. It was an oddly touching picture, a scene straight from Dickens. He wondered if any of it was true.

If Brooks hadn't told him he was Jewish, Vane would never have guessed it, but Brooks was always mentioning it as if he were afraid people might think he was trying to hide his origins because he had changed his name. There was nothing Jewish about his face, to Vane's eye. Brooks had strong cheekbones, a firm jaw, and a big nose, long, straight, and bony, with a strange lump at the end of it, which gave his face a curiously mournful look when he wasn't smiling, and made him look funny when he was—the perfect nose for a comedian. With the help of a little putty and a touch of makeup, it would have been a good nose for Cyrano, and it occurred to Vane that Brooks would probably be very good in the part if he could be taught not to milk it for laughs.

Vane wondered vaguely why he was devoting so much thought to Randy Brooks, and decided that it was simply easier to think about Brooks than about Felicia or his own financial problems. Thinking about his finances gave Vane a headache. He had been brought up to take money seriously, to look after the pennies, to scrimp and save. His father had kept up middle-class appearances on a schoolmaster's meager salary—''Making Do'' might have served as the family motto, from the bath water, which every member of the family shared modestly, one after the other, so that by the time young Robert had his bath, the water was always stone-cold and covered with soap scum, to the Sunday joint, which Mr. Vane carved in slices as thin as airmail paper and served only after everyone's appetite had been blunted by a large helping of Yorkshire pudding and mashed potatoes. "Neither a borrower nor a lender be," had been drummed into Robert—yet here he was, five thousand miles from home, head over heels in debt.

Thinking about Felicia was even more painful. Sometimes he lay awake in the hot California night, listening to the infernal sound of the bloody water sprinklers, trying to work out in his mind what had gone wrong between them, and why. No two people had ever been drawn to each other by such passion; surely no two people had ever shared so much—he and Felicia were not just lovers, they were *partners*. Yet there was a rivalry between them onstage that Felicia had always refused to acknowledge and to face.

There was a knock at the door. Arnie Bucher, the director, stuck his face in. "Ready soon, Robby," he said gruffly, then, seeing Randy, he smiled, as if he were in the presence of royalty. "How goes it, Randy? How's Natalie?" he asked. Randy kissed his fingers, to indicate that everything was well at home.

"We fixed the set, Robby," Bucher said. "Opened up the staircase to give us a better angle, yes?"

Vane shrugged. He knew perfectly well that the change had been made because producer Si Krieger thought the angle wrong for Debby Darvas, Vane's bosomy co-star. "The audience is paying to see Debby's tits," Krieger had howled when he saw the rushes, "not that Limey actor's fucking face!" Most of the day had been spent rebuilding the set while Vane cooled his heels in his dressing room.

"Wouldn't it have been better to fix the *script*, Arnie?" he now asked.

Bucher faltered uncertainly, not sure how to respond, and afraid of losing face in front of Randy, who was Leo Stone's son-in-law. He apparently decided the best way to handle it was to pretend Vane was joking, and gave a mechanical chuckle, the effect spoiled by the venomous glare he gave Vane through his thick, steel-rimmed spectacles. "I love that

English sense of humor," he said, jaw muscles tense. "Don't you, Randy?"

"Me too, Arnie. Slays me every time." Brooks stared at the door as Bucher slammed it behind him. "There's a third rule," he said quietly. "Don't piss off a director until the picture is in the can."

"Bucher's an idiot."

"No argument. But watch out. Once he gets this picture into the cutting room, he's going to louse your scenes up every chance he gets. The audience is going to see you futzing around in the shadows for two hours, *bubbi*, with all the lights on Debby's tits."

Vane turned to the mirror. Like most stage actors, he preferred to do as much of his own makeup as possible. That, too, had made problems, not only with makeup men, but also with directors and cinematographers, who thought that he came across on film as too "stagy." He picked up a stick of Leichtner's and darkened his eyebrows. "What I hate about this business," he said, "is being told what to do all the time. I *know* what to do. I'm an actor."

"A *stage* actor, pal. Being a movie star's a whole different thing. You think the camera is like the audience. It isn't. It's a machine, and you have to learn how to use it. And to trust the guy behind it, even if he's a shmuck like Arnie Bucher. Now you take Felicia, *she* got the idea, right away."

"Lisha doesn't *mind* being told what to do, provided she's the center of attention. That's part of her problem, you see."

"No, not really."

"She lives to do what some male authority figure tells her to. Excluding me, of course."

Brooks laughed. "Of course! The husband!" He feigned a courtly bow. "After you, Prince Myshkin."

"I'm *not* the husband."

"You don't have to be married to be the husband, *bubbi*. It's a type, a role. Some people are born husbands, that's all."

"Lisha and I used to think of ourselves as *lovers*," Vane said sadly. "I still do."

"That's a role, too, but it doesn't last. Take it from me, women need a husband a lot more than they need a lover. It's their husband who makes them feel superior to men—every time!" He gave a quick peal of laughter.

Brooks had a disconcerting habit of touching a raw nerve, Vane thought—several raw nerves. After eight years of living together as lovers, he and Felicia enjoyed—hardly the word!—all the disadvantages of marriage without any of the compensations.

They had moved mountains—flown over them, at any rate—to stay together, and fought being separated even when their careers seemed to depend on it. Because they refused to do plays unless they were together, each of them had been obliged to turn down plum roles; because neither of them wanted to make a film without the other, they missed countless opportunities. Which was why when Felicia finally had been offered the most glittering movie role of a lifetime in Hollywood, he had accompanied her, an unwilling satellite, rather than spend a few months alone. . . .

The telephone on the dressing table rang—a soft buzz, unlike the strident ambulance-bell clangor of the English telephones he was still used to. It was funny, he thought, how often the little things reminded him that he was in a foreign country: tea bags, the big, bulbous, brightly colored cars, Jell-O and cottage cheese on salads. No matter how hard he tried, he remained hopelessly homesick in the land of peace and plenty.

He picked up the telephone, listened, and suddenly felt his stomach cramp with fear and surprise. It was warm in the dressing room, but he could feel cold sweat running down his back. In the brightly lit mirror, he saw his own face turn pale beneath the dark makeup. "Darling," he shouted, with desperate, hearty make-believe enthusiasm. "How *are* you?"

"You can't understand. The very *idea* of seeing her frightens me." He was pacing the length of the dressing room.

"Hey, how bad can it be, pal?"

Bad, Vane thought to himself. When she had collapsed after the debacle onstage in San Francisco five weeks ago, the doctors had talked cautiously of many months to "recovery," of shock treatment, new drugs, extended therapy —yet here she was, as bright as a button, begging him to come and see her, apparently with her doctor's blessing. "Do you know," he said, "I haven't the foggiest idea what to *say* to her? Or what to do?"

"It's not a play, Robby. There aren't any lines to memorize. You go, you put your arms around her, you take it from there. It's not going to be easy, okay, but nothing like this *is* easy."

Vane found himself envying the comedian. Natalie Brooks was hard as nails, and it was difficult to detect the slightest sign of any passion between her and Brooks, but at least they weren't rivals in the same profession. Natalie's life—that part of it which wasn't devoted to social climbing and shopping—was spent burnishing Brooks's image, with all the ferocious, single-minded energy she had inherited from her father. Randy's fame was her life-work, and God help anyone who voiced even the mildest criticism of him.

Theirs was what was usually described in Hollywood as a "good" marriage, meaning one that paid off at the box office and played well in the columns. The "good" marriages— the ones that lasted more than a year or two—were based on mutual interest, not on passion. That was something which Felicia could never understand. She, a victim of insomnia, would never consider separate beds, let alone the separate bedrooms Randy and Natalie had. When they traveled or toured, elaborate instructions had to be sent ahead to ensure not only that their suite had a double bed but also to inform the management that Miss Lisle would be bringing her own sheets and pillowcases, without which there was no hope of her getting even an hour's restless sleep. Vane, on the other hand, fell asleep the moment he was stretched out.

"Come on," he heard Brooks saying, "it's like diving into the pool in the morning. The longer you think about it, the harder it is."

Vane nodded. At home the Brookses' pool next door was just visible from the bedroom window, but he had never seen Randy swim in the mornings, although on weekends he sometimes invited underprivileged boys and girls over to use the pool, and would clown in it for them, his pale white body gleaming as he stood on his head at the shallow end, while Natalie stood on the flagstone border, making sure the photographers from the newspapers and wire services got plenty of pictures.

"Just tell her she looks great and you're glad to see her, and it'll all be okay, take my word for it!"

"You're quite right," Vane said, in the tone of a man facing the firing squad. "I'll go." He paused. "And thank you, Randy. You've been a true friend, listening to me like this."

Brooks shrugged. "I told you—you and Felicia, you're family."

Vane stood up and glanced at his watch, partly to cover a mild feeling of embarrassment. The easy, overabundant emotions of Hollywood made him nervous. "Should I call first, do you think?" he asked.

"Nah. The doctors will just give you a hard time. Surprise her. That's my advice."

"I'll bring some flowers. Though her room must be full of them—I've been sending flowers every day."

"Get going," Brooks urged. "When you get back, come over to the house, have dinner, tell us all about it. Or tell *me*—I think Natalie is going to be out, having dinner with her dad. Is that a deal, or what?"

"It's a deal," Vane said, wondering by what strange twist of fate Randy Brooks, of all people, had become his adviser and confidant, or how he had ended up in a place where everything was a "deal."

Brooks gave him a searching look. "What's keeping you, Robby?" he asked. "I mean, is there another problem?"

Vane sighed. "Yes," he said. "It's stupid, but the worst of it is that I owe them for Lisha's stay there. They're patient enough, but I can tell they want their money. Of course, when it all happened, Marty said to send all the bills to him. Ha!" Vane frowned, stuck out his jaw, narrowed his eyes, and put on a New York Jewish accent, a gravelly tough-guy's voice that went with Quick's street brawler's heavy-shouldered crouch. " 'Don't worry about a fuckin' thing, Robby,' " Vane growled, " 'everything's gonna be taken care of. Leave it all to me!' "

He bared his teeth in a ferocious, lopsided grin, lips parted to accommodate the giant cigar that Marty Quick usually kept in his mouth while he talked.

Brooks laughed—with a trace of envy at Vane's performance. "And he welshed?"

"Of *course* he welshed, the bastard. I should have known better than to trust a man who wears a bloody great diamond ring and cuts his initials into his champagne glass at Chasen's to prove it's real."

"Listen, Robby, pal, neighbor, genius—how much do you owe for Lisha?"

Vane put his hands over his eyes. "Two weeks. Around ten thousand dollars. 'Ten grand,' as Marty would say."

"Robby, that's *bupkis*—chickenshit. A week's salary."

"A week's salary if you've got it to spare, old boy, yes. But I don't. Lisha's problems have scared off the studios—including your father-in-law, by the way."

"Robby, I'll pay Lisha's bill, okay? Go, take care of her, leave the rest to me."

Vane stared at him, amazed and embarrassed by his generosity—which he was in no position to refuse. "That's very kind of you, Randy," he said, wishing he could manage not to sound quite so English. "Are you *sure*? I don't know when I can pay you back."

"Forget it. You'll pay me back when you can." Brooks tucked his sunglasses into the pocket of his shirt, swung his sandaled feet onto the floor, stood up, and took Vane's hand in both of his, clasping it tightly. On his left wrist he wore a massive gold identification bracelet with his name spelled out in diamonds. He stood close to Vane, his eyes misting over with tears. He kept one hand on Vane's, then put an arm around his shoulder, giving him a firm, manly squeeze, as if he were a trainer congratulating a successful athlete after a race.

Vane—who was not fond of the human touch—could hardly back away from his benefactor.

"I can't tell you how grateful I am," he said, a little stiffly. He was conscious that in moments of emotion he had a tendency to sound exactly like the kind of pompous Englishman Americans detested, something Felicia often pointed out to him—conscious, too, that Brooks probably expected a "thank-you" on some higher scale of Russian-Jewish emotionalism.

Vane was no anti-Semite. At worst, he shared the mild prejudices of his class, attenuated by twenty years in the theatre and film world, where even in England many of the cleverest people were Jewish. His view of life was Shakespearean: old age was *Lear*; jealousy, *Othello*; Jewishness, *The Merchant of Venice*—which he had played with such an excess of passion and emotion that the critics had accused him of changing Shylock into the hero, making him something of a hero to many people in England, who read into it a condemnation of Nazi racial politics.

Whatever emotions he unleashed onstage, however, he kept them tightly to himself in his private life. He was moved by Brooks's offer, but he would not play a tearful scene of gratitude for his benefit. "Thank you," he said softly.

Brooks patted the back of Vane's neck, his hand dry, but unpleasantly warm. He let it linger there for a moment.

"Forget it," he said. "What are friends for?"

2

"He's *not* 'my friend,' Doctor."

"What would you prefer me to call him?"

"I don't know. Robby, perhaps. Anything but 'Your friend, Mr. Vane,' if you don't mind."

"How about 'Mr. Vane,' simply? So?"

" 'Mr. Vane' will do."

"Why does the word 'friend' make you uncomfortable? You and Mr. Vane *are* friends, surely?"

"We're lovers. If we *ever* get our divorces, we'll be husband and wife, I suppose."

"So lovers can't be friends?"

"I have no idea. Friends are surely the people one falls back on when things are going badly with one's lover. Or one's husband. Are you friends with your wife, Doctor?"

"Mrs. Vogel and I *are* friends, yes. We discuss things together. We enjoy doing things together, also . . . tennis; bridge; and so on."

"I'm pleased for you both. Mr. Vane and I are *not* friends, however. I do not play tennis. He does not play bridge. We are lovers. There are times when I'd like to kill him, as a matter of fact, and that's not what one thinks about one's friends."

"Yet you tried to kill *yourself*? Not Mr. Vane?"

"We've been through that a hundred times, Doctor. I did *not* try to kill myself! I was tired, I couldn't sleep, I kept forgetting my lines—*nothing* makes Robby angrier than when I dry up onstage, not that it happens often. I had a drink or two too many, and when my sleeping pill didn't work, I got up and took another. . . ."

"Only one?"

"Perhaps two, I don't remember. In any case, I was *not* trying to kill myself. If Robby hadn't panicked and called Marty Quick, and if Marty hadn't sent for an ambulance, I'd simply have slept late and woken up with a hangover."

"Isn't it possible that Mr. Vane's reaction was not panic but concern?"

"No. Robby can't stand unpleasantness. He particularly can't stand it when *he's* been unpleasant, and he was perfectly bloody to me after the performance. So, naturally, when he couldn't wake me up, he jumped to the wrong conclusion because he felt guilty. As if I'd kill myself because he shouted at me! But if you're doing *Romeo and Juliet* night after night, you get used to the idea of people killing themselves. Romeo kills himself. Juliet kills herself. So, you see, it's a perfectly natural mistake."

"Mr. Quick didn't think so. Neither did the doctor in the emergency room."

"Marty Quick loves drama. Lives for it. The first time I met him he told me he'd just taken a girl to the hospital who tried to kill herself on Si Krieger's yacht by eating a champagne glass. Marty would set your house on fire just for the pleasure of rescuing you. The only reason the doctor in San Francisco thought it was a suicide attempt was that Marty told him so. It wasn't, and that's that."

"So. I see."

"There's really nothing the matter with me at all, Dr. Vogel. I feel like a malingerer, in fact. I'm quite rested."

"Yes? Well, of course rest is certainly important. You've been sleeping well, too."

"Wonderfully! It's so peaceful here. No nerving myself up to do *Romeo and Juliet* every night—how I've come to *hate* that play! No photographers or reporters hiding behind every tree. No screaming fans tearing my clothes. . . . I feel like a new person, thanks to you."

"No thanks to me. You were removed from your problems by this unfortunate—accident, shall we say? The problems are now to one side, so you feel better, yes? What worries me is that we haven't *faced* these problems, Miss Lisle, hmm? They're still out there, waiting for you. Rest and isolation are all very well in the short term, but they aren't a cure. I can't cure you if you won't talk about what's wrong."

"*Dear* Dr. Vogel, I've nothing to be cured *of*. I'm ready to go back to work."

"To acting?"

She raised an eyebrow, with some annoyance. "Well, of course, acting," she said with a show of patience. "What else?"

"With Mr. Vane?"

She nodded.

Vogel smiled—a skeptical, weary smile, like a man bearing bad news. "It's a great strain, surely? Acting with the man you love?"

"Strain? Whatever do you mean? There isn't anybody even half as good as Robby." She didn't say that acting with him was what she lived for, that from the very first moment she had seen him onstage she had known that their careers must be as intertwined as their lives, that if she couldn't act with Robby she didn't want to act at all—would rather be dead, in fact. The only tiny glimmer of doubt that afflicted her on the subject, sometimes in the middle of the sleepless nights, was the fear that Robby might not feel the same, but she refused to think about it in the daylight. "I'm ready to work," she said brightly, putting her all into her smile. "The sooner the better!"

Vogel nodded glumly, clearly not convinced. "So," he said. "And are you ready to see Mr. Vane yet, do you think?"

"Why do you ask?"

"Because he's downstairs in the lobby waiting, with a dozen roses."

"God damn him!" Felicia Lisle said; she had already forgotten she had called for him. "It's about bloody time!"

And damn Dr. Vogel, too! she thought, sitting at the dressing table in her bedroom, examining her face.

When writers tried to describe Felicia Lisle's beauty, they almost always fell back on the word "feline." She had read, sometimes with amusement, countless descriptions of her "catlike" eyes, her "feline grace," her "kittenish charm" (that vanished when she "bared her claws"), until it sometimes seemed to her that the critics and magazine writers would not be satisfied until she grew fur and whiskers. Her own father had been in the habit of referring to her as "my kitten," or "my puss," when she was a little girl, and even then she had not been able to see the resemblance, nor, given her feelings about cats, to feel flattered by it. Cats were lazy, vain, and distant, and she was none of those things, whatever people thought.

Still, her eyes *were* her best feature—huge, luminous, dark green, the color of good jade, with lashes so dark and thick that she had never needed false ones, even for close-ups here in Hollywood. Her cheekbones were high and perfectly molded (Who had ever heard of a cat with cheekbones!), her face heart-shaped, tapering sharply down to a determined little chin.

Her nose, which, too, inspired rapturous praise ("Miss

Lisle's nose is one that Helen of Troy need not have been ashamed of,'' wrote George Christy in the *Los Angeles News* on her arrival in Hollywood), had always seemed to her a bit ordinary, small, pert, "a shopgirl's nose," as her vile Uncle Harry had once told her. . . . Damn Harry, too, she thought.

She had no complaints about her lips, which were formed in a Cupid's bow of sensuality, nor of her complexion, which, despite years of harsh theatrical makeup, was still the pale ivory of an English rose, nor of her neck, which was long, slender, swanlike, and at the age of thirty-one, unlined. Hundreds of thousands of words had been written and set in type to describe the perfection of the face that she stared at now in her dressing-table mirror.

How much of her life had been spent before a mirror! How many times had she sat in the harsh light of her dressing room, making herself up as Cleopatra (heavy eye shadow, dark complexion, exaggerated eyebrows, scarlet lips), Desdemona (the palest face paint, almost dead white, to make the contrast between her complexion and Othello's more striking), Ophelia (a virgin's rosy cheeks and a blond wig), Juliet (she shuddered at the thought)—not to speak of a hundred, perhaps a thousand, lesser parts. . . . For Cleopatra she always wore a crown in the form of a gold snake, its head raised above her forehead, with green stones for eyes that matched the color of her own; for Cordelia, a modest coronet; for Desdemona, a diaphanous veil, worn as a head scarf, with which Othello would eventually suffocate her; for Ophelia, a circlet of wildflowers (artificial, since real ones made Vane sneeze onstage).

She concentrated on her eyebrows, then on her lips, trying not to think about Robby pacing back and forth downstairs, no doubt embarrassed to be there.

Well, he had a lot to be embarrassed about, not all of which she was about to share with Dr. Vogel! There was much that Felicia liked about California, but not the local passion for baring one's soul to psychoanalysts. Randy and Natalie Brooks, for example, hardly made a move without consulting their psychoanalysts, and not only talked about their sessions, but actually invited their doctors to dinner parties!

Felicia believed in solving her own problems, in *facing* facts, not talking about them to doctors. Her father had brought her up to be tough-minded. And tough-minded she had needed to be, she told herself, thinking for a moment of her father, handsome, dashing, hard-drinking, who had come tumbling down the social scale from the lofty heights of the peerage (where as the second son, he had had to watch the title and the land go to his brother, Harry) to end his days as a white hunter in Kenya, tracking down lions for his wealthy clients to kill, and seducing their wives, while Felicia's mother, beautiful, remote, and mad, went from one scandalous love affair to another, on her way to a death that seemed to everyone, even Felicia, like a blessing.

She searched her mirror-image for signs of age, found none for the moment, and sighed. Her dressing table, like everything else in her life, even here, away from home (But where *was* home? Certainly not a rented house in Beverly Hills!), was neatly organized, spotlessly clean, arranged with loving care exactly as she wanted it to be, the jars, bottles, and tubes of makeup precisely aligned.

To one side of the table was a folding picture frame in silver, displaying the three photographs that she carried wherever she traveled. The first was a snapshot of her parents, taken at some brief, remote moment of happiness before she was born, her father dressed in his elegant riding clothes, a devilish grin on his handsome face, her mother holding onto him as if for dear life.

In the middle of the frame's three panels was a photograph of Felicia's daughter, Portia, at the age of five, in a sweet little dress Felicia had bought for her over Nanny's objections, a child's version of something that Marie Antoinette might have worn to a rustic picnic at Le Petit Trianon. It was a mystery to Felicia that her daughter had inherited neither her fine bones nor her graceful features. The child stared into the camera unsmilingly, plump-cheeked, her face screwed up in an unbecoming frown.

Portia's hand was raised to hold onto her father's, but Felicia had cut her husband, Charles, out of the photograph with her nail scissors, leaving only his fingers behind, the wedding ring clearly visible.

The third photograph was of Robert Vane as Hamlet—the first play in which they had appeared together—his hair cropped short and bleached blond, his expression unlike that of the gloomy prince who could not make up his mind—for Robby had chosen to play a forceful, energetic, Machiavellian Hamlet, whose relationship to Ophelia left no doubt, in the minds of more knowledgeable members of the audience, that he and Felicia were already lovers in fact, as well as onstage.

"I could a tale unfold," she whispered to herself, looking at the photograph. Nothing in her life had mattered—not even her success as an actress—as much as possessing Vane. She had sacrificed her marriage, given up Portia, shocked her family and friends, without hesitation, knowing that it was what she wanted, beyond her control, fate. . . .

Yet, here she was, taking sanctuary in Dr. Vogel's luxurious establishment, the kind of place where wealthy and socially prominent drunks went to dry out, when, only six months ago, she had been so anxious to be back onstage with him again! "It will be like the old days, darling!" she remembered saying to him over a bottle of champagne.

But it had not been like the old days at all. In fact, it had been so bloody awful from day one that she had begun to question whether the old days had really been so wonderful after all. And *that* was the kind of thinking that led to sleepless nights, to missed cues, to the final horror of standing onstage in the sudden, awful knowledge that her lines had vanished from her memory, lost beyond any hope of recapturing them.

> *"Give me some present counsel, or, behold,*
> *Twixt my extremes and me this bloody knife*
> *Shall play the umpire. . . ."*

She wondered why she could remember her lines here, where she didn't need them—why, when she had stood on the balcony in San Francisco, her mind had been a complete blank. Remembering your lines was basic, something no serious actress ever thought twice about. *Real* actresses might forget their children's names, their lovers', their husbands', even their *own*, but given the right cue, whole speeches came to them, line after line, as effortlessly as if the mind contained a recording machine. It was as natural as walking, and when it failed her, she felt as if she were paralyzed, her limbs unable to move.

Not more paralyzed than was poor Robby, she thought— with a certain satisfaction. *"Farewell, farewell! One kiss and I'll descend,"* he had called, hanging from the balcony, ready to take that great athletic leap which was his trademark, down to the stage below, a drop of twelve feet which he took like a gymnast or a ballet dancer, sailing out into space, in full flight, arms spread.

"Art thou gone so?" she was supposed to respond, of course, but instead she had stood dumbly on the makeshift balcony, staring into his eyes, watching her own panic suddenly reflected there.

His expression had been that of a man whose parachute has failed to open in midair—an analogy which was all too appropriate, for suddenly he lost his hold on the flimsy balcony and fell to the stage heavily like a sack of coal, with a terrible cry of pain as he landed, spraining his ankle so badly that he had to be carried off the stage.

From the balcony she had seen Robby's face clearly. He was biting his lips against the pain, but his eyes were focused on her, and she had no trouble in reading, even from a distance, the anger there—which made it all the worse when she started to laugh hysterically, uncontrollably, a soaring, high-pitched laughter that wouldn't stop, that reached to the highest rows of the balcony, that poor Robby could no doubt hear all the way up to his dressing room, hardly muffled by the mercifully descending curtain. She did not stop until Marty Quick, their producer and backer, appeared from the platform behind her with astonishing speed and agility, grabbed her by the arm, pulled her from the balcony, and gave her one quick slap—hard enough to bring her to her senses. "You can cut that shit out now, Lisha, the party's over," he had rasped, in the sudden silence.

It was only later, when she had a chance to think about it,

that she realized Quick's slap was the work of an expert. He had something of a reputation for hitting women—for beating them quite severely sometimes, in fact. For Felicia the real shock had come from seeing the brief flash of pleasure in Marty Quick's eyes as his hand smacked her cheek.

She tried to reconstruct the disastrous evening once again in her mind, as she did countless times a day, and most of the night.

She had come to the conclusion—which she had not shared with Vogel—that if Robby hadn't been so bloody *forgiving*, she might not have taken the extra pill—well, to be honest, the extra *pills*. If only Robby had at least lost his temper, she told herself, it might have cleared the air between them, but by the time they had returned to the hotel after the quick trip to the hospital to have his ankle bound, he had turned his anger inside out, or whatever it was he did so that it didn't show. It was *his* fault for pushing her too hard, he told her, though she knew he didn't believe it, *his* fault for taking the play on tour. . . . He had sat wearily, stretching out his injured leg, a martyr's expression on his face, and said gently, "I don't want you to blame yourself, but I think we'll have to cancel the tour."

"Then cancel the bloody thing, Robby," she had snapped and gone off to the bedroom with her drink to prepare herself for another sleepless night.

She powdered her face—she was fast running out of her favorite Chanel powder, with no hope of getting more, given the war in Europe—brushed her hair, put a drop of Schiaparelli's Scandale behind each ear—with the Germans in Paris, that too would soon be impossible to find—and slipped off her dressing gown.

Life at Dr. Vogel's institute was supposed to be "informal," but on the rare occasions that she saw her fellow patients (she refused to think of them, or of herself, as "inmates"), they looked as if they were dressed for a weekend at an expensive resort. She preferred to eat alone in her room, because it was something of a relief not to have to dress or make up her face.

She caught sight of her reflection in the full-length antique pier glass. Dr. Vogel had gone to some pains and expense to make his wealthy clients feel at home, and she rather liked her small suite of rooms.

The figure in the pier glass did not hold her attention as much as her face did. Felicia was a realist about her assets. She was thirty-one in a city full of seventeen-year-old blond girls who seemed to spend half their lives on the beach, and in an industry where long legs and a big bosom were so common that the girls waiting on tables in the studio commissaries would have caused a sensation anywhere else.

"This is flesh city," Marty Quick had growled, soon after she arrived, meaning to be kind. "Never forget, what *you* got is face, talent, class. For that, this is a seller's market. Tits and ass here are a drug on the market."

Marty Quick's judgment about women's figures was like that of a first-class racing trainer's for good horseflesh. His career had begun with girlie shows, and in the view of most people in the industry he had never risen above them. It was Marty Quick who had sold Billy Rose on the idea of the aquacade, Quick who first put a chorus line on roller skates, Quick who guaranteed his audiences exactly one hundred beautiful girls ("Count 'em!"), each a long-legged beauty and every one personally chosen by Quick, who boasted that he had never given a job to a girl he hadn't fucked.

Oh, Quick knew girls all right, girls and show business, which were pretty much synonymous to him. Who else would have brought chorus girls to air shows, twenty of them, in abbreviated spangled costumes, dancing on a platform suspended from two blimps high above the crowd? Who else would have put together a team of doctors and anthropologists from distinguished universities to draw up the specifications for the perfect young American woman, then sponsor a nationwide contest for the girl who most closely met the ideal measurements and marry the winner? Felicia Lisle relished Quick's stories about himself and liked him enough to nickname him, only partly in jest, "Caliban."

Still and all, she told herself, she had nothing to apologize for, even if she did not come up to the measurements of

Quick's ideal American beauty—whom he had divorced within six months. Felicia's legs were slender and finely formed, her waist so small that it was hard to imagine she had ever given birth to a child, her breasts, while small by the standards of the motion picture industry, perfectly formed and still firmly defying the effects of gravity.

There was not an ounce of superfluous fat on her. She liked good food—she would have been content with a diet of oysters, caviar and champagne—but was blessed with a small appetite. She turned slightly to admire her boyish bottom and slender thighs. What was there was more than good enough for any man, in her opinion, and the only question was why it no longer seemed to interest Robby Vane. . . .

She slipped on her bra, her garter belt, her panties, all of them scented from the pomander balls she always placed in her lingerie drawer. Her fastidiousness was legendary. Everything she owned was neatly folded in lavender tissue paper, her lingerie laid out for her neatly under a piece of antique lace every night, ready for the morning. It had taken her a day or two to train the maids here in her demands, but that, too, was one of her gifts: servants adored her and quickly became accomplices in her pursuit of perfection.

She fastened her stockings and inspected them for wrinkles. In the old days, Robby had loved to watch her dress, and not infrequently interrupted the process to make love, which meant that she had to start all over again. They were, as a result, very often late for lunch or dinner invitations, which once prompted dear Guy Darling to begin his lunch at The Ivy without them, complaining that "He wasn't going to have *his* appetite spoiled while Robby and Lisha satisfied *theirs*!"

Then, their appetite for each other was a well-known and much-discussed fact of London theatrical and social life. Robby made love to her in her dressing room or in his, before the curtain; they left the luncheon table early at country-house weekends to retire to their room; they touched each other constantly, in public and in private, so much so that Guy once asked if they were rehearsing for a part as Siamese twins. At meals, they took off their shoes and groped for each other's toes under the table. Once, slightly drunk, she had stroked Toby Eden's leg by mistake, with disastrous consequences, for he was ticklish and had dropped his glass of wine into his lap, shouting, "I say, Lisha, steady on, you're feeling up the wrong fella!"

She raised her arms and put on her slip—here in California, semi-nudity was the fashion, but Felicia clung to the habits of her youth because they suited her. She did not like "casual" clothes, or anything else that was casual, for that matter.

She chose with care a suit that had been made for her by Chanel in Paris, the year before the war began, when she and Robby had done *Antony and Cleopatra* at La Comédie Française, with enormous success. They had been hailed by the Parisians not only as romantic lovers but also because their performing Shakespeare in English at France's oldest and most distinguished theatre was seen as a symbol of Franco-British solidarity against Germany. Every night the audience rose to sing "La Marseillaise" and "God Save the King," the theatre was draped in tricolor flags and Union Jacks, and she and Robby were acclaimed with such patriotic zeal that the German ambassador to France had been reprimanded by Hitler for attending a performance and sending her flowers.

There had been a party after the theatre every night. She had been feted by Sacha Guitry, Maurice Chevalier, and the President of the Republic, and a dish had been named after her by the chef at Maxim's. She and Robby had spent long afternoons making love in their suite at the Ritz, visited Picasso in his studio, lunched with Cocteau in his garden. . . .

For a moment, wearing the suit she had tried on at Chanel while Robby sat in a flimsy gilt chair, chain-smoking through the fitting, she wanted to cry. Now the hated *boches* were in Paris: some monocle-wearing, fat-necked German general was probably sleeping at this very moment in the bed at the Ritz where she and Robby had made love, bombs were falling on her beloved England, she could no longer remember how long it had been since she and Robby had spent an afternoon together in each other's arms. . . .

She held her tears back—she was not about to ruin her makeup—and fastened a diamond brooch to the collar of her suit, a present from Robby the night they had opened together in *The Loving Couple*. She placed a large picture hat on her head, a pink chiffon scarf wound around the crown, the broad brim curled down to frame her face perfectly. She took out of her jewelry case the diamond-and-pearl earrings—her "lucky" earrings—given to her by Uncle Harry on the opening night of Guy Darling's *Mayfair Madness*, her first starring role; she pinned them on, gave herself a last-minute inspection, and went to the door.

Beyond it, in her sitting room, Robby waited—had been waiting almost exactly an hour, just as she intended him to. Oh, how she loved him! And oh, how it drove her mad!

Curtain up! she told herself. It was time to make her entrance.

3

Robert Vane was an ogre for punctuality. Nobody knew that better than Felicia, so he concluded that she was either punishing him or still in the grip of madness. On the whole, he thought it was more likely that she was punishing him, particularly since he was obliged to wait for her with Dr. Vogel, who had expressed some reservations about the wisdom of their being alone together. "There are tensions, you see," Vogel explained, rubbing his pipe against his nose. "There is a potential for a setback, yes?"

Vane was in no position to argue against medical authority, and besides was secretly relieved at not having to face Felicia alone. He paced the room, still holding his flowers, hating every moment of the wait as if his time were being wasted, although in fact there was nothing much he had to do.

The sitting room was small, comfortably furnished, elegant, and everywhere there were the telltale signs of Felicia's occupancy: framed photographs of her in various roles, as well as of the two of them together; her favorite afghan—

knitted by some long-forgotten admirer—neatly folded at the foot of a chaise longue so she could cover her legs when she lay down to have her tea and read a book; stacks of the latest best-sellers on the floor. On a chair lay a piece of petit point embroidery, which Felicia worked on spasmodically to calm her nerves, and which, like Penelope's weaving, she never seemed to finish. There was the faint scent of Schiaparelli's Scandale, potpourri, and lavender that accompanied her everywhere, and, of course, flowers, for she could never have enough.

As an alternative to conversation with Dr. Vogel, Vane examined the flowers. There were cards from Marty Quick ("Come out of the corner fighting, Lish, my money's on you!"), Randy and Natalie Brooks, Si Krieger, most of the studio heads and major stars, and all of the more important agents, but those he had been sending for at regular intervals were nowhere in sight.

"How is she, then?" he asked Dr. Vogel.

"As I have told you, she is making progress."

Vane sighed. He had disliked Dr. Vogel at first sight, and nothing since had caused him to change his mind. Polite as the doctor was, Vogel clearly blamed him for what had happened to Felicia without even having heard his side of the story. Besides, Vogel reminded Vane of a bad actor playing the role of a psychiatrist, with the phony Viennese speech pattern that he seemed unable to keep up consistently, the neat little Freudian beard, and a shaggy tweed suit with suede leather patches on the elbows. Vane particularly hated the affectation of the patches, for the suit was clearly new.

Vogel was tall, thin, stooped, given to making small, snuffling snorts from someplace deep within his nasal passages. He smoked a large, curved, dark-briar pipe like Sherlock Holmes's—or rather he played with it as a prop, lighting it, banging it out against ashtrays, poking around in its bowl with a small silver instrument like a miniature hoof-pick, cleaning out the stem with a pipe cleaner from what appeared to be an inexhaustible supply that he carried in his pockets. Vane decided he would have played him without the beard, disarmingly jolly, with only a certain shrewd gleam in his eyes to show the audience that he knew what was going on in other people's minds.

It was an exercise Vane performed constantly without even thinking about it—looking at people for small touches he could use in his own performances, or wondering how *he* would play them if he were acting their parts. He had been delighted to find in Marty Quick, for example, all sorts of elements he could use—the transparent cunning, the unconcealed pleasure in manipulating people, the facile charm with which he won you over even while he was betraying you. Vane hadn't been in his company for more than a few hours before he had conceived, in his mind's eye, a Richard III based on Quick, right down to the heavy eyebrows, the long, twisted beak of a nose, the fighter's crouch.

Felicia was the one person who understood what Vane was doing when he suddenly showed an interest in some otherwise ordinary person or a stranger in the street. When she noticed him absorbed in a taxi driver's face or a dinner guest's conversation, she would take one quick look and whisper, "He'd do for your Falstaff," or "He looks just like Astrov in *Uncle Vanya*." She always guessed what was on his mind; sometimes—when she was in a good mood—she even pointed out models to him, whispering, "Look at the man on my right with the sad eyes and the brave little mustache, he's got the perfect face for Edgar in *The Dance of Death*," or "There's a nose over there, do you see, that would do you just right for Malvolio."

Often his own behavior was modeled on the characters he played, as though the line between acting and real life was so thin that he could not always be sure which side of it he was on. Felicia, however, *always* knew—for in the heat of their love affair she had discovered the real Robert Vane which he had been at such pains to hide.

"Progress," he said, dismissing the word with a wave of his flowers. "Is she happier? How does she look? How does she feel about me?"

"Happiness is a relative concept," Dr. Vogel said placidly, retreating behind a cloud of pipe smoke. He made a few unpleasant puffing sounds before the pipe went out with a gurgle. "We have to walk before we can run, yes? Here, we can only lay the basis"—he pronounced it, to Vane's annoyance, "bah-zees," as if he were speaking German—"for future happiness, not *achieve* it. In the meantime, Miss Lisle is relaxed. It helps that alcohol is not available here. And of course there is an absence of stress. Both of those things, however, will be there when she leaves. As for her appearance, she looks well enough to me. She is a beautiful woman, even without makeup. . . ."

"Without makeup?"

"She has been living very simply. We do not run a nature cure here, you understand, but there is no need for cosmetics and fashionable clothes. Miss Lisle has been resting, taking a little air on her balcony, reading. She swims daily in the pool, when there are no other—ah, guests—there." He fiddled with his pipe, lit a match, held it over the bowl, then gave up and blew it out. "A great beauty does not need artifice," he said in an oracular tone.

Vane tried to imagine Felicia going ten days without makeup or a hairdresser, and failed. Guy Darling had once said that if Felicia had been on the *Titanic* she would have stayed in her cabin to do her face and to dress before taking to the boats. If she was slopping around Dr. Vogel's clinic without makeup, then she must be even more ill than he had supposed, Vane thought, alarmed. "Does she talk about me?"

Dr. Vogel shrugged, like a stork rearranging its feathers. "Constantly." His mournful expression made it seem that he had heard as much about Robert Vane as he cared to.

"And what exactly does she say?"

"I can't tell you. Miss Lisle is my patient, yes? But there is much strong emotion. And I would say, a certain degree of, ah, ambivalence."

"For Christ's sake, man," Vane said, "who the hell *isn't* ambivalent? Does she still love me? *That's* what I want to know!" It astonished him that he had managed to ask a question like that of a comparative stranger.

Dr. Vogel didn't seem surprised. He even managed to get

his pipe lit momentarily. "My dear Mr. Vane," he said, "that's not the question at all." He gave Vane a shrewd look through the smoke. "What we have to know, I think, is this: Do you still love *her*?"

"Don't be a bloody fool, of *course* I love her," Vane shouted, and it was true. Whatever the problems between them, despite the disappointments and the guilt that had blighted their happiness in America, it was the one thing besides his talent that he believed in absolutely.

Vogel nodded wisely, as if Vane's answer was just what he expected. "Enough to give up acting with her?"

Vane stared at Vogel as if he were mad. "Why on earth would I do that?"

"Because it may be too heavy a burden for the relationship to bear. Lovers, partners, rivals—because you *are* rivals, you know, you compete for attention, praise, the spotlight, and so forth . . . That's a lot of roles to play."

"You don't understand, Dr. Vogel," Vane said, rather more loudly than he had intended to, "Felicia would never give it up. It means more to her than anything else between us . . ."

Vogel nodded cheerfully, as if Vane had confirmed his point. "Yes," he said, "I can see that. But does it mean more to *you* than anything else?"

Vane glared at Vogel with such fury that he did not hear the door open. He *felt* Felicia's entrance, with an actor's instinct. "Hello, Lisha," he said, without turning. "We were just talking about you."

"Of course you were, darling!" Her tone suggested that it was unthinkable they would have been talking about anything else. "Though shouting is more like it, judging from what I heard. How do I look, Robby, darling?"

He turned to face her, and blinked. He had expected the worst. After all, this was a woman who only weeks before had tried to kill herself. Yet here she stood, as glamorous and beautiful as if she were about to make her entrance at the Colony in New York for lunch, standing at the top of the stairs just long enough to make sure everyone saw her.

He knew he should have been pleased, relieved, at any

rate, but instead he felt instantly depressed. An abject Felicia, pale, wan, and suffering, would have sparked off his concern, but Felicia looking as beautiful as ever——*more* beautiful than ever, if that was possible——and perfectly dressed, only made it clear that nothing had changed between them. She had put him through hell, made him look like a fool, and yet here she was, the very picture of health and beauty, artfully silhouetted in the doorway as if expecting applause. "You look very well, indeed, my love," he said, knowing it wasn't the compliment she expected.

"Thank you," she said coldly. " 'Praise from Sir Hubert is praise indeed.' I don't think it's against the house rules to kiss me, Robby."

"Of course." He walked over to her, holding the flowers in front of him like a shield, and gave her a kiss on the cheek. Now that he was close to her, he could see the familiar signs of tension——the glitter of fear deep in her eyes, the vein in her neck, just below the ear, that always pulsated when she was upset, the slight tremble to her lips, which most men found sexy, but which he knew was a sign of nerves. He felt a surge of irritation with Vogel's know-it-all complacency. If Vogel thought that Felicia was rested and relaxed, then he didn't understand a damn thing about her. She had simply put on a performance calculated to persuade him that she was better. Vane knew exactly how good she was at this kind of scene——he had played it with her a hundred times onstage. *She's an actress, Vogel, you fool! A better one than you can ever know. The best.*

He despised himself for spoiling her scene——for that was exactly what it was, a well-planned scene, with improvised dialogue that had gone wrong because he had misread his cue. He sighed, put his flowers down, and took her in his arms, kissing her gently on her lips. "You've never looked lovelier, darling," he said, putting his heart into it. "*God,* how I've missed you!"

"That's better." She sat down gracefully on the sofa and patted the cushion for him to sit beside her. Dr. Vogel remained standing, reduced for the moment to a bit part. "Tell me what you've been doing, then."

He sat beside her obediently. Felicia curled herself up on the sofa, displaying as much leg as she could, playing the temptress to perfection. Part of him applauded her performance, part was nauseated by the whole spectacle. Well, he told himself, there were no miracle cures. She was what she was, and so was he. "Not much," he said. "Moping. Taking most of my meals with the Brookses—who send you their best. I've eaten enough avocados to last me a lifetime. And you?"

"I've been having a *divine* time. Such lovely chats we've had, haven't we, Doctor?"

Vogel beamed and nodded on cue. She opened the nearest pack of cigarettes and waited while Vane extracted his lighter, lit hers, then lit one for himself. "The Japanese gardener bows to me every morning, and asks after 'Missy Rile,' " he said. "Or at least I think that's what he's saying. He misses you, too, I think."

She laughed. "Dear Mr. Fujita. Such a sweet little man, always bowing and hissing like one of the chorus in *The Mikado*." She smiled brightly to Dr. Vogel, as if bringing him into the conversation.

"Randy says he's probably a spy. Natalie fired *their* Japanese gardener and hired a Mexican instead."

"How perfectly beastly of her! I don't believe anybody who's as good with flowers as Mr. Fujita could be a spy. And why would anybody in Tokyo want to spy on *us*? Or Natalie, I ask you? Any work on the horizon?"

He shook his head. "I had lunch with Aaron Diamond, but he wasn't hopeful. The story around town is that you're exhausted and resting, but you know what the studios are like."

"Well, I *was* exhausted. And now I'm rested and ready to work again. Aren't I, Doctor?"

Vane glanced at Dr. Vogel, who gave him a quick shake of the head, scattering tobacco ash on his tweed waistcoat. Clearly this was a subject to be avoided, which was just as well, since, in fact, the whole town was full of rumors, ranging from a suicide attempt to a lovers' quarrel involving a triangle of himself, Lisha, and Marty Quick. Some people whispered that Felicia was an alcoholic, others that Vane had beaten her so badly that she required plastic surgery, still others that she had caught Vane with another woman and tried to kill him. Under the circumstances she was unemployable, despite her Academy Award, and he scarcely less so.

"No need to rush it, darling," he said quickly, watching Dr. Vogel nod approvingly, like a prompter from his prompt box. "I've had a few offers for myself, but they're mostly slim pickings, I'm afraid. The latest is a part as a foppish English lord with a beautiful young wife. They get captured at sea by Errol Flynn as a pirate, and he falls in love with my wife. I get killed in a duel, and Errol gets the girl, of course. I'm thinking about it."

"Not seriously, I hope."

"Seriously enough. It's the best Aaron could find for me, so you can imagine what the others are like. I have a few nice scenes as a fop, and you know I always do fops well."

He plucked an imaginary snuffbox from his sleeve, took a pinch of snuff, made a monocle with his thumb and forefinger and gave Dr. Vogel a stare of withering contempt. Felicia applauded.

"Errol gets to prance about bare-chested, of course, and has all the good lines," Vane said. "Still, beggars can't be choosers."

"Surely we're not beggars, darling?"

"Damn near. After what, ah, happened, in San Francisco, Marty Quick did a midnight flit—flew back to New York to put on another of his tits-and-ass shows, cured for the moment of his fatal passion for the classic theatre—leaving *us*, my love, in Queer Street, up to our necks in debt. No, we need the money, and if I have to play the bad guy in a pirate melodrama, so be it."

"Poor Robby." She patted his hand. "And your ankle? How is it?"

"Not too bad. A sprain. I'm hardly limping at all now. Thank God it wasn't a break."

She patted his hand again. "I still don't know what came over me, drying up like that. The look on your face! And then, when you slipped and fell—I thought, my God, Robby *can't* fall. . . .''

He raised an eyebrow. "I· didn't fall."

"Of course you did."

"Lisha, don't you see? I *let go*! It was the only way I could think of to bring the bloody curtain down. By God, I thought, there's nothing for it now but to have an accident. So I let go and dropped."

She pulled off her hat, leaned over, put her arms around him, and gave him a kiss. "*Dear* Robby! And I thought you were so angry with me that you lost your footing."

"Well, I *was* angry with you, Lisha. Furious, if you want the truth."

She snuggled closer to him, ignoring Dr. Vogel as if he were a piece of scenery. Vane felt a tinge of embarrassment. Felicia's skirt had risen, showing the top of one stocking, a tab of her garter belt, several inches of pale thigh. He told himself that Vogel was a doctor—human flesh was presumably his stock-in-trade. He had examined Felicia on her arrival here, after all, placed his stethoscope on her bare chest. A quick glimpse of Felicia's thigh was small beer compared to the view Vogel had already had of her body. Still, Vane was uncomfortable, as if he were a part of a pornographic tableau, with Dr. Vogel the voyeur, puffing away on his bloody pipe.

Vane tried to move a little farther away on the sofa, but he was already against its side, while Felicia, inch by inch, pressed harder against him, slipping an arm around his waist. He could feel her fingers digging into his side, playing with the buttons on his braces—"suspenders," Americans called them for some reason. "You might have *killed* yourself, my poor darling," she whispered in a throaty voice.

"That did not occur to me," he said. He had only intended to make a dramatic fall and fake an injury and had been astonished when he landed clumsily so that his howl of pain was genuine. The theatre was like war—it required courage, cunning, discipline, an occasional act of desperation, the willingness to take risks. One look at Felicia's face had been enough to tell him that the play was over and that the only way to save her reputation—*their* reputation—was to stage an accident.

"It was a very courageous thing to do. And you did it for me!" She kissed his cheek. "I do love you, Robby darling. You do know that, don't you?"

"I know."

"I've behaved like a selfish bitch, haven't I? No, no, it's true, don't deny it."

He shrugged, but in fact he had no wish to deny it. In the past few months Felicia *had* made his life impossible, with her moods, her tantrums, her unprofessional behavior onstage, her refusal to take into account the pressures on him —for ultimately he was responsible for the whole bloody production, forty actors, a small army of stagehands and technicians, three truckloads of scenery and costumes, all of it lumbering from city to city across the United States to dwindling houses and abominable reviews, eating up every penny of their savings on the way.

"Face it, a flop is what we got, *bubbi*," Marty Quick had announced in Chicago, early in the tour, with clinical accuracy. He had recommended closing the production then and there, but Vane had argued against it, stupidly, as things turned out. Working all night, he had cut the play by half an hour, closed it on Juliet's dying words, as Victorian actor/ managers often did—thus eliminating nearly two hundred lines and all of the moral Shakespeare wanted the audience to draw from the story—and agreed to Quick's suggestion to have Felicia wear an indecently transparent nightgown for the bedroom scene in which she says farewell to Romeo.

None of it had helped. The audience still laughed at the wrong moments, shifted restlessly in their seats during the longer speeches, and left early to catch their trains or buses home. Some spark was missing, or perhaps the whole idea of killing yourself for love seemed absurd in a world at war. "Shit," Marty Quick had said at the first dress rehearsal, apparently unfamiliar with the story until that moment, "Romeo's a fucking *dummy*, stabbing himself over a broad! You come right down to it, one's the same as another. They all got the same plumbing."

"Do you forgive me?" Felicia asked now, taking Vane's hand in hers, playing the kitten for all it was worth. He felt himself sliding down a familiar, slippery slope. Though he loved her, he did not—*could* not—forgive her, but that hardly seemed the right thing to say in front of Dr. Vogel.

In the old days their quarrels had been followed by intense bursts of passionate sex and forgiveness on both sides. Now the quarrels simply gave way to mutual exhaustion, valleys without peaks, as it were. "These things happen, darling," he said consolingly, feeling her hand clutching his, the fingernails biting deep into his skin. It was not the most generous of pardons, but it was the best he could offer.

"Thank you, darling." Her grip tightened. "I'm sorry we flopped, but now the nightmare's over, isn't it? You'll do your dreadful pirate picture. I'll find *something*. We'll muddle through somehow, won't we?"

"Of course we shall, darling," he said. "The main thing is to get you home again."

The very word gave him a sharp pain, like a knife to the heart. "Home" was stately oaks and rose gardens, not palm trees and bougainvillea; a fine misty drizzle over the Haymarket, not the sun beating down on Hollywood and Vine; quiet, patient crowds queuing outside the theatre for Shakespeare, not people who thought *Romeo and Juliet* too slow, or too romantic, or just plain silly. "Home" was England, and he longed to be there—wished he had never left, in fact. "We'll survive, Lisha, dear heart," he said. "Get a picture or two under our belts—earn enough between us to make a start on paying off our debts. . . ."

"Oh, God," Felicia wailed. "Money. How I hate the bloody subject!"

That was true enough, Vane thought. Felicia's attitude toward money was essentially aristocratic—she spent extravagantly and assumed that God would provide.

He blamed himself for not trying to control her spending, but he could seldom bring himself to confront her with it. There were enough things to argue about as it was.

"And this place—" she looked desperately around her,

as if she had personally paid for every piece of furniture herself—"must be costing a fortune!"

Vane was delighted to observe a look of alarm on Dr. Vogel's sallow face. "Not to worry, darling," he said. "As a matter of fact, Randy Brooks offered to help out, if need be."

Tears appeared in Felicia's eyes. "Oh, the dear, *dear* man. How sweet! What a wonderful gesture! We must do something for him, Robby, darling." She paused for a moment. "I know what. We'll give a party."

She was animated now, her eyes sparkling beyond the tears, natural color in her cheeks. "We'll invite *all* our friends, shall we? Make a real occasion of it. We can get one of those adorable striped tents put up on the lawn, with candles all over the place, and dear Mr. Fujita can arrange flowers everywhere. Oh, Robby, I haven't danced in years! We *must* have flowers floating in the pool. I wonder if Mr. Fujita is up to water lilies. . . ." She paused for breath. "And dear Dr. Vogel and his wife must come. Do say you will, Doctor!"

Vogel bobbed his head up and down, smiling nervously. "Mrs. Vogel and I would be delighted," he said. "Mrs. Vogel enjoys dancing."

It was on the tip of Vane's tongue to point out that an expensive party was an odd way to thank someone who had just paid your hospital bill for you, but on reflection he thought Randy Brooks would enjoy being the guest of honor and the center of attention. Besides, Felicia's notion was not a bad one. A party would show the world they were still together, and solvent. In Hollywood social life, attack was the best form of defense. Really, he thought, it might be the smartest move they could make—always assuming she was up to it.

Of course there was no telling how they were going to pay for it all, he thought, but something of Felicia's jaunty optimism had transferred itself to him. This was often the case—he saw difficulties where she saw none; her enthusiasms were instant, passionate, and infectious. Where would I be without her? he asked himself. "It sounds like a splendid idea," he said enthusiastically. "If you're up to it, that is?" He glanced at Dr. Vogel for support.

He wanted to believe that she was cured, that they would love each other again the way they used to in the old days, that the party would be a huge success. He *needed* to believe it, so he did.

He looked at her, helpless as he always was in the face of such beauty. He knew better than anyone how much she loved him. He was her life—she not only said it all the time, she *meant* it, even when she was at her worst and determined to make him utterly miserable. When it came to love, he was always in her debt, and like any debtor, he felt a combination of guilt and resentment at the fear he might not be able to repay in full what he had borrowed.

"I'm up to it, darling," she said breathlessly, eyes shining. "Aren't I, Dr. Vogel, dear? I've never felt better."

Vogel looked wary. "Enjoyment is good therapy, yes?" he said, as if he were trying to convince himself. "I can see no harm."

"There you are! But I can't arrange a party from here. I'll need to go home."

Ay, there's the rub, thought Vane, wondering if Felicia had invented the idea of giving a party simply to give Dr. Vogel a reason to let her go. She was capable of that—capable of anything, when she wanted something badly enough.

Vogel probably believed that an ambitious plan was a sign of mental health. Vane had been in too many films and plays to believe that. People in show business often committed themselves to enormous, complicated undertakings just to escape from the disorder and chaos of their personal lives. He had done that himself with *Romeo and Juliet*, and suspected Felicia was doing it now.

All the same, there was a part of him that wanted her home again. However unhappy they were at times, they belonged together, and that was that.

He knew his cue. He took both her hands in his and squeezed them, gazing down into her eyes—in which he saw now a desperate, helpless plea—and said, "Of *course* you shall come home, darling. Today! That will be all right, won't it, Doctor?"

Vogel nodded, perhaps a little overcome by how fast things were moving. Why not? Two great actors had just played a perfect reconciliation scene before his very eyes. Felicia's expression was radiant, her eyes sparkled with love and desire, two small tears trickled down her cheeks, her lips were open, as if she were inviting a kiss.

Vane felt, as he so often did when he was with Felicia, the blurring of that fine line between acting and life. Sometimes he didn't know whether he was acting out a love scene with her or genuinely making love. It was a torment to him that often he couldn't tell the difference.

His life was acting; acting was his life. There was no dividing line in himself that he could find between the actor and the man. "Of course Robby's a great actor and can play anything well," Guy Darling had once said in a moment of waspish impatience at hearing so much praise for the younger man, "but the one part he *hasn't* learned to play is himself."

Well, he was doing his best to play it today, Vane told himself. And he knew his lines. "I need you and I love you," he said in a firm, low voice. "I want you home, beside me, forever. Now."

She knew hers too. "I'll never leave you again, Robby," she said. "I promise."

They embraced, heads turned toward Dr. Vogel, as if waiting for applause.

4

Felicia lay stretched out on a chaise by the pool, carefully screened from the sun by a striped lawn umbrella. She never sunbathed, as people here were so fond of doing: tans, bathing suits, beaches, yachts, and sun worship were not for her.

When the studio had ordered her to pose in a bathing suit for the usual glamour shots, she refused. When they insisted, she put in a call to Aaron Diamond, who interrupted his weekly game of golf to come down to the studio in his plus fours and cashmere pullover to fight it out with Leo Stone himself, in Stone's imperial office with the fifteen-foot-long white-and-gold desk on its dais, the famous white leather casting couch, and the studio's twenty-one Oscars for "best picture" artfully spotlighted on the wall. "You want cheese-cake, take the fucking Super Chief to New York and go to Lindy's!" Diamond had shouted. "What you got here is an *actress*, you *shmuck*!"

Stone, who had never backed down to anyone, and who had thrown many another major agent out of his office with his own hands, gave in to Felicia's diminutive agent, and she was photographed in an evening gown instead.

Randy Brooks sat beside her chaise, a pad of paper and a pencil on his lap, working on the guest list of the party that was to be held in his honor. It was impossible, Felicia thought, not to like Randy. Having him around was like having a *cavaliere servante*, or an admiring older brother. Besides, she and Brooks had so many interests in common: antiques, interior decoration, and art. Brooks's tastes were refined and well-educated—he had a good eye for colors and fabrics, rare in a man, and knew a lot about fashion.

He clearly worshipped Robby, which was also unusual in Hollywood, where stage actors—particularly English ones— were viewed with suspicion and hostility. Robby was thought to be "stuck-up," contemptuous of the values by which everyone else lived here, an unwelcome guest. The fact that he had succeeded first time out in a Hollywood picture, missing an Oscar by only a whisker, made him even more disliked in the industry—particularly since he didn't seem to give a damn.

At this very moment, Robby was pacing back and forth across the lawn, perfecting his role in the pirate melodrama. It was an easy part for an actor of his talents, hardly requiring anything in the way of preparation, but for him there was no such thing as a minor part. He had already remodeled his nose a dozen times to turn it into a thin, aristocratic beak, shaved and bleached his thick eyebrows, given himself a sharper chin, used up pounds of putty and endless quantities of spirit gum. When he was at last satisfied, his face bore a startling resemblance to Randy Brooks's.

If Brooks noticed the resemblance, he didn't let on. "You gotta have Louella and Hedda," he said to Felicia.

"Robby hates gossip columnists. And they've both written awful things about us."

"They'll write worse things, honey, if you don't invite them. Take it from me."

"Oh, very well." She sighed, wishing she were in England and could invite Guy Darling, and dear Noel, and Toby Eden, and Philip Chagrin, instead of Louella Parsons and Hedda Hopper and a whole cast of dreadful people whom Robby despised. "Did you put Marty Quick down?" she asked.

Brooks lifted his sunglasses and propped them up against his carefully combed pompadour. "He's in New York, putting on some dumb-ass show at the Winter Garden. Marty Quick's All-Star Salute to the American Woman, I think. Betsy Ross sewing the first flag in a G-string and high heels, a hundred girls dressed in Minutemen costumes doing the high kick. . . ."

"He'll come if I ask him."

"I thought you and Robby were teed off with Marty?"

"Robby doesn't hold a grudge. And as for me, I've always found Marty—interesting."

"Interesting? Marty? He's a gangster. He's to show business what Al Capone was to distilling. Oh, hell, don't get me wrong, I like him myself. Marty gave me my first break, you know—stand-up comedy in a strip joint he was running in the Catskills." He laughed. " 'Keep 'em in their seats while the girls are changing their costumes, *bubbi*, that's all I want from you,' he told me. And I did. He was his own bouncer back then. He *liked* getting rid of drunks, breaking up fights, keeping the girls in line."

"How are you and Robby getting along?" Brooks asked, switching subjects.

"Fine," she said shortly, raising an eyebrow. She wondered how much—and what—Robby had told him.

Up to a point it was true—though she could not help wondering how much the pills Dr. Vogel had prescribed for her had to do with it. Between the sleeping pills she took every night and the ones she took during the day to calm her nerves, she lived in a kind of daze, with occasional moments of panic at the thought of what life would be like when she gave them up—for she could hardly continue taking them when she resumed working, as she soon must.

Even the war news came to her distantly, softened by the medications, which was a blessing, for she could hardly bear to think about what was happening in England. At least Portia was away in the country, safe from bombing, though that would not help much if the Germans invaded, as everyone here believed they would.

The nights seemed endless. Robby, she knew, out of guilt and the feeling that she wasn't "ready," as well as from his own exhaustion, avoided her physically, treating her as if she were some fragile object. Sex, which had once played such an important part in their relationship, had ceased to do so years ago, if she was going to be honest with herself, taking second place to their work. What had once held them together now separated them, and neither one wanted to bring the subject up, perhaps for fear of what that might lead to, or of what else might be uncovered. She ached sometimes for him to touch her, but she could not ask him to, out of pride as well as fear. Did he suffer, too? If so, he did not show it. Sometimes she wondered if their acting together onstage wasn't a substitute for sex—not even such a bad one, at that—but now she neither had him in bed *nor* onstage.

The days were a little better so that at times she was almost able to persuade herself she was happy. Robby was immersed in his role, she in planning the party. She rose late in the mornings and breakfasted in bed, as she always did when she was not working on a film, for her metabolism was geared to the stage, and she seldom retired until several hours after the curtain went down.

She could still smell the greasepaint, the flowers, the human warmth from a thousand people who had sat transfixed for three hours, the spirit gum and the cold cream. . . . Every night she dreamed that she had just come home from the theatre, and every morning she woke groggy, unable to convince herself that she had slept at all, ready for the next performance, until she realized there wasn't one.

Yes, things were fine between them, she supposed—but only as long as she did not think about the past. Robby was attentive, kind, but he treated her with a wary caution that came, she guessed, from some discreet warning from Vogel. Vogel had warned her, too, not to expect too much, not to expose herself to what he called "stressful situations" (though how she was to avoid them, he did not say), to abstain from alcohol as much as possible. She did her best. No drinking at lunchtime, that was the important thing, a single cocktail before dinner, no more than one glass of wine during dinner. She did not really miss the drinking—not nearly so much as she missed a lot of other things.

There was a gentle cough behind her as the maid came out, bearing a silver tray with the mail. It had taken Felicia weeks to break in the stout black lady who, in Felicia's opinion, had been outrageously spoiled by her previous employers. They had apparently been content to have their mail piled upon the hall table. "Thank you, Marvella," she said—the first rule of keeping good servants was being polite to them. None of the letters seemed interesting, so she put them on the table beside her. "We'll have tea, now, please."

Marvella bobbed her head, her expression unfathomable. It was always a mistake to try to guess what servants were thinking, her father—whose boys in Kenya often went unpaid for months—had told her. "It doesn't matter what they think so long as they do as they're told, and they'll do as they're told so long as you don't care what they think."

She closed her eyes and saw her father quite clearly, stretched out in the heat of the late afternoon in his folding canvas chair under the shade of a baobab tree, sipping his tea and looking into the distance in search of game—or perhaps thinking, as he often did, about the strange twist of fate that had brought him and her mother from the social whirl of London to Kenya, only to separate when they got there.

He was not a bitter man—nobody who had won the Military Cross and survived the second Battle of the Somme was likely to be bitter about anything else life had to offer—but he sometimes seemed puzzled and lonely, unable to decide at what point his life had gone wrong, and why.

She opened her eyes to see Robby smiling at her. "My gracious lady," he lisped, his face set in an aristocratic sneer. He examined her through an imaginary spyglass, then leaned over to take her hand and kiss it. "God, but I wish you were playing my bride in this bloody thing instead of some little tart who got her dramatic training faking pleasure on Leo Stone's white couch. How often does he have to have it recovered, do you think?"

Randy shook his head, grinning. "He gets a new one every year, courtesy of the studio prop department. The springs give out before the leather. He's a big man."

Felicia had been brooding for days about the fact that she wasn't playing opposite Robby in his picture—not that she particularly wanted the role of the beautiful and seductive young bride who gets swept off her feet by Errol Flynn. But she was angry at the prospect of Robby's making a film with some big-bosomed blond Hollywood star.

She knew all about "DCOL"—the Hollywood tradition of "Doesn't count on location." Mark Strong, her leading man in the picture that had won her an Oscar, had tried to take advantage of it in the hotel in Vacaville, where the more important members of the cast were billeted.

"I *always* fuck my leading ladies," he had complained, after forcing his way into her room. "It's practically in my frigging contract. Ask Aaron Diamond. Ask anyone!"

She had given him a stare that would have withered anyone but a Hollywood star with his fly unzipped. "Well, you're not fucking *this* one."

"Oh," Strong had said, standing in the doorway, all six feet two of him, his toupee slightly askew. "Do you have that word in England, too?"

Robby sat down with a sigh. "Why is it," he asked, "that

the stupid parts one plays for money are always so much harder than the good ones?''

''Because they're beneath you,'' Brooks said reverently. ''You ought to be doing something better, that's your problem. *Lear*, for example. *There's* a part!''

Vane dismissed *King Lear* with a weary wave of his hand. ''Lear's easy,'' he said. ''He's just a stupid old fart like the rest of us, completely selfish and hell-bent on getting his own way. The only trick to playing him is to find the right Cordelia. She's got to be a featherweight, you see, because you have to pick her up at the end of the play, after three hours onstage.''

The sight of tea never failed to cheer Felicia up—always provided that it was properly served. There were certain things in life that simply had to be done the right way, and tea was one of them. She glanced at the tray approvingly. She felt lazy, and guilty for it.

Every day she promised herself that she would get down to it again, have lunch with Aaron Diamond and tell him to find her a part, however small and unsuitable, or confront Robby about his plans and set some kind of rational deadline for their return home—but every day found her putting all these things off, shopping, instead, for antiques with Randy Brooks, or dozing in the garden after tea, or listlessly trying to read one of the best-sellers which she bought by the dozen at the bookshop in Beverly Hills, most of which she put down and forgot before she had even finished reading the first chapter.

She picked up the mail and handed it to Robby. Usually it did not interest him much, unless it was from England. He leafed through the letters, picked out one in a plain white envelope, and slit it open. There was a look of excitement on his face that Felicia couldn't help noticing.

''Ha!'' he shouted, slapping the folded paper across his open palm, ''I've got it!''

Randy Brooks smiled. ''No kidding,'' he said. ''That's great! When do you start?''

''Right away. I can fit it in with this film, a few hours a week, anyway. It's not as if I had Errol's part.''

"What's that, darling?" she asked, trying not to sound curious. Lately, more and more, she had the feeling that she was being kept out of things.

Robby looked a little sheepish—as sheepish as a man could look while wearing a false nose and chin, with a beauty spot pasted on one cheek. "Ah," he said, "I thought I'd mentioned it. I've applied to take flying lessons. It seems I've passed the physical—I should bloody well hope so! I can start in right away."

She stared at him in astonishment. Flying, as he very well knew, was one of the things she hated and feared most. When there was no choice she flew, but it was always a strain. She would do it only if Robby sat beside her holding her hand, which, because they were not married, had caused great difficulty when the studio sent her on a whirlwind tour of the United States to promote her last film. Felicia had firmly refused to fly without Robby, and the studio's PR department had just as firmly refused to let him accompany her—the deadlock finally resolved by Leo Stone, who persuaded Robby to get on and off the airplane separately from Felicia, so they were never photographed together on the landing steps.

Felicia would never have allowed Robby to fly alone. If there was going to be an air crash, they would both go together, hand in hand. The fact that Robby intended not only to fly but to be a pilot was as terrifying and inexplicable to her as if he had announced his intention of climbing Mount Everest. "You can't be serious," she said angrily. "I've never heard of such nonsense!"

Robby and Brooks exchanged a brief, nervous glance. "Dear heart," Robby said soothingly, "there's less risk in flying than there is driving a car down Sunset Boulevard."

"Oh, don't be bloody silly! Cars don't drop out of the sky. It's madness, Robby! If you have to take up a hobby, play golf, for Christ's sake. What makes you think you could fly an airplane anyway?"

He lit a cigarette and stared into the middle distance. His expression was ambiguous, a mixture of defiance and the embarrassment of a man who has been caught out in a lie. "Lisha," he said quietly, "I'm too old for the infantry."

"Well, of course you are, darling, but what does that have to do with it?"

"If I can get a pilot's license, Lisha, there's a good chance the RAF will give me a commission. I don't suppose they'll make me a fighter pilot, that's not a job for actors in their thirties, but I might make a perfectly good bomber pilot."

"*Bomber* pilot? What *are* you talking about?"

"I went to see the consul, here in Los Angeles. He told me to stay put—the best thing I could do for England was to keep on acting in American films. I don't see myself sitting out the war here like that, do you? So I called our ambassador in Washington, and he put me in touch with the air attaché. I can't say he sounded very keen to have me—apparently we have more pilots than planes at the moment—but in the end he allowed that if I learned to fly, the RAF would probably take me." He smiled. "As a matter of fact, his exact words were, 'We're taking all sorts of odds and sods in the RAF these days, so I suppose we can manage a bloody actor, too.' So that's it, you see. If I get my pilot's license, the RAF will take me."

"And you're going to do it?"

Vane grinned. "It can't be any harder than learning to act in the movies."

"How long is all this going to take?"

"Three months to make this silly picture. Say, three months of flying instruction." He stared into the sky, as if he were already transforming himself into an air ace, with the devil-may-care grin, the eyes fixed on the far horizon, the tone of modest, boyish courage.

She leaned over and took his hand. She could feel herself starting to cry, from pride, from fear, from love. "Oh, God," she said, "I don't want you to do it, Robby, darling. But you're going to, aren't you?"

He nodded. "Yes. I am. I'll be a frightful failure at flying, I imagine. All thumbs, or whatever."

"No, you won't," she said, and she knew she was right. He was never a failure at anything he set his mind to. He could never resist a new challenge—that was part of his strength. Other actors tended carefully to their laurels; Robby regularly tore his own up, and set out to earn them all over again.

"What about our debts?" she asked. "We owe a fortune, surely?"

"I'll find a way."

"Declare bankruptcy," Randy Brooks suggested cheerfully. "That's what everyone does around here."

Robby shook his head. "I can't do that," he said firmly to Brooks.

"Marty Quick does it all the time. It's no big deal."

"I'm not Marty, Randy. But four hundred thousand dollars isn't the end of the world, anyway, is it?"

They sat silently for a moment, now that the sum had at least been mentioned. Much as she hated thinking about money, Felicia was no fool on the subject.

Robby's going price for a film at the moment was about a hundred thousand—good money for an actor who wasn't one of the town's half-dozen top box-office stars, easily two or three times what he would get at home. She thought about the rent on this house, the cook, the maids, Mr. Fujita the gardener, the man who came to clean the pool and wash the cars, the cost of the party they were giving for Randy Brooks, not to speak of all the expenses that were inseparable from stardom, and she realized that the money from Robby's pirate picture was already gone—would only just cover their expenses for the next few months.

She tried to think of ways in which she could economize, but none came to her mind. She was crying now, in earnest. "Oh, God!" she said, "it's all my fault."

"It is *not* all your fault, Lisha. We've been all over that together. You've been all over it with damned Dr. Vogel. *Romeo and Juliet* was something we both decided to do. I was dead long before we got to San Francisco. We *both* fucked up. Now do stop crying."

But she couldn't stop. If she hadn't insisted on their doing a play together, if she hadn't convinced herself that playing lovers every night would make them lovers again, if she had sensibly left well enough alone . . .

"I could sell my jewelry," she wailed.

"Thank you, darling, but I won't hear of it. I said I'll find a way, and I will."

He stood up, came over to her chaise, pulled her to her feet, embraced her. In his arms she felt as if everything was going to be all right again—they would go home, their divorces would finally come through, they would buy a sweet little thatched cottage, close to wherever he would be flying, Portia would come and live with them, the past, with all its failures and problems, would be forgotten.

He kissed her, gently at first, then harder, his lips pressing against hers. She closed her eyes and wondered how long it had been exactly since he had kissed her like this.

The first time he had *really* kissed her was in her dressing room during the rehearsals for his production of *Hamlet* at Stratford. Ophelia had been her first "serious" role after years of dazzling, but shallow, success as the ingenue in Guy Darling's frothy comedies; Hamlet had been one of Vane's first bids for greatness; he had deliberately taken on Philip Chagrin in a knockdown competition to see whose Hamlet was the best, not two years after Chagrin's had been judged by most critics "the finest Hamlet of the century."

She had never known anything like the passion that acting with him unleashed in her. For the first time onstage, she had felt that magical electric current that ran between herself and him, between *them* and the audience, a glow so warm that she, who seldom did more than perspire, was drenched in sweat, her chest heaving as if she had just made love. When he touched her with his fingertips in their first scene together, she had jumped as if she had just received a shock, her eyes wide-open with the intensity of the feeling, an intensity which had eluded her from time to time for years as it did onstage in San Francisco, in *Romeo and Juliet*, when she thought for a moment it was there, then realized it wasn't, and froze. . . .

She had been young then, married, so determined to get him into her bed that she was not surprised when he finally

took her in his arms and kissed her. The only surprise was
that it had taken so long. She remembered that he had been
blond then, his hair cut as if someone had put a bowl on his
head and shaved around the edges, and painfully thin, for he
had decided that Hamlet should be lean and gaunt, like a
student coming home from school, and had starved himself
for weeks.

"Oh, Robby," she whispered, "I do love you so!"—and
then out of the corner of her eye, she caught a glimpse of
Randy looking at them as if this were the final "clinch" in
a movie, the expression on his face part envy, part keen
interest, but in no way embarrassed to be a spectator.

Damn you! she thought. You might at least have looked
the other way. But as she felt herself go limp in Robby's
arms, surrendering to him, it occurred to her with dismay
that it was Randy in whom Robby had confided about his
flying lessons, not *her*. Then she told herself not to be silly.
Randy was a friend, Randy had paid for her therapy, Randy
was always happy to drive her anywhere she wanted to go
in his bright red LaSalle with the top down, telling her jokes,
giving her the latest gossip, even helping her choose
clothes. . . . What could be more natural than for Robby,
who had always depended so much on friends like Toby Eden
or Guy Darling, to confide in his neighbor—especially when
she had left him alone and shaken at a moment of crisis in
both their lives?

She slipped out of his arms, made her excuses, went back
into the cool of the house, and for the first time in weeks
poured herself a stiff shot of vodka and took it upstairs to
her bedroom.

She had imagined there at the pool that Robby might pick
her up and carry her upstairs, throw her on the bed, pull off
her clothes and make love to her the way he had so long ago
in her dressing room.

She slipped out of her clothes now, put on a robe, sipped
her drink. It tasted good. To hell with Dr. Vogel, she told
herself. Robby had poured her a drink that night in Stratford,
whiskey and water, perhaps because he thought it might make
it easier to seduce her. Little did he know she had been

planning for this moment for three months, night and day. She hated whiskey, remembering the smell of it on her father's breath, a constant reminder that he couldn't face her, or his life, without a *chota peg* in his hand, but she had downed it bravely, not to give herself courage but to give *him* the confidence to break his marriage vows.

She could still taste the greasepaint on his face, smell the sweat on his body from two and a half hours of what would soon become famous as "the most physical Hamlet in living memory," feel his bones pressed hard against her body.

He had not waited for her to remove her underclothes. He *couldn't* wait! He took her the first time almost brutally, pulling her silk pants to one side with his fingers, thrusting into her as if his life depended on it, and she, who normally preferred endless preparation and slow, building excitement before making love—as Charles, her husband, frequently complained—was surprised to find she was ready for him, so wet that when she came to dress again, she had been unable to put her pants on, and had gone back to the hotel with them wadded up in her handbag, where her maid had found them the next day.

She remembered the feel of him as he entered her, triggering off, after so much anticipation, instant spasms of pleasure that arched her back and made her tremble from top to toe. He came quickly, but not before her, and instead of letting his weight slip off her and resting, as Charles always did, he slid from the sofa to his knees, kissed her thighs, her stomach, undid her garters and pulled off her stockings and balled them up, throwing them the length of the tiny room, then, turning her over, made love to her again, more slowly this time, his hand covering her mouth as she alternately groaned with pleasure and suggested they go back to the hotel, where at least they would be more comfortable.

"I don't *want* to be comfortable!" he had told her brusquely, and the truth was that she didn't, either. She had him, just as she had promised herself she would, and he was all that she had ever hoped he would be.

She was wet now, just thinking of it—and angry, too. How could he have stopped needing her? And why? And if it had to happen, why did she still need him as much as ever? It all seemed unfair, pointless even, as if the only thing that mattered to her in life had been taken away.

She gathered her robe around her and went to the window. From it she could see Robby and Randy seated side by side at the far side of the pool, deep in discussion.

She sighed and walked to the bathroom, holding her drink, to bathe and get ready for dinner—yet again—with the Brookses.

War, she decided, would be a relief, if they ever got home to it.

5

"Look, she's having a good time. What more do you want?"

Robert Vane shrugged. He wanted Felicia to have a good time, and she *was*, no doubt about it, but at the back of his mind was an uneasy question: Was she having *too* good a time? He was uncomfortably aware that every time a waiter passed with a tray of champagne glasses she took a fresh one.

She had worked hard to make the party a success, and he desperately wanted the evening to work for her. In a place where ostentation was the norm, she had managed to bring off a rare triumph of good taste, starting with herself. She wore a floor-length evening gown of black lace, exposing her perfect shoulders, a dress that Molyneux himself had made for her in Paris before the war, of such simple elegance that it made all the other women look either dowdy or overdressed. Most Hollywood parties, however glamorous they might appear in *Life* magazine, were boring—the men sat together as soon as they could to talk business, while the women huddled in a group to trade gossip and complain about their husbands. Felicia would have none of that. By sheer energy and charm, she managed to keep her guests on their feet—even made them dance, which took some doing in a town where dancing was a well-paid profession.

She had danced with Si Krieger, she had danced with Leo Stone, and Randy Brooks, and Aaron Diamond. To Vane's surprise she had even danced a tango with Dr. Vogel. The big tent on the lawn was so full of flowers, miniature orange trees, and exotic shrubbery that it looked like a Victorian conservatory. Randy had found a couple of young men who hid the canvas ceiling with elaborately arranged foliage, to which they painstakingly attached fruit, flowers, and brightly plumed fake birds, so that in the candlelight, looking up, it was like dancing in an enchanted forest. *"Le tout* Hollywood" had come, stars, producers, directors, even studio heads, partly because nobody would refuse an invitation to a party given for Randy Brooks for fear of offending Natalie and her father, partly out of curiosity to see what was really going on between Robby Vane and Felicia Lisle.

"It's a great party," Brooks persisted. "Everybody's here. Everybody's having a good time. You're going to get fabulous press. You'll see—tomorrow morning, Lisha's going to be up to her ass in offers."

Vane watched Felicia flash in and out of sight on the dance floor. "I notice Marty Quick isn't here," he said.

"I told you, Marty's in New York. You want my opinion, that's a plus. Listen, go dance with Lisha, pal. That's what everybody's come to see."

That was true enough, Vane thought, wishing he could shake off his concern. It was not that he didn't enjoy parties—he did—but everything about this one seemed false to him. These were not his friends, this was not where he wanted to be. In England he would be savagely criticized for giving such a lavish party while his countrymen were preparing themselves for the German invasion that was expected at any moment.

The newspapers at home were running scathing stories about him already, pointing out that he was enjoying life as a movie star in California while his colleagues were "doing their bit" for the war effort. The *Daily Express* had run a photograph of him sitting at Randy Brooks's pool next to one of Toby Eden in naval uniform, pipe in his mouth, leaning against the propeller of his airplane. The *Daily Mirror* had published a cartoon of him as Nero, fiddling while London burned, with Felicia beside him, a voluptuous Poppaea.

The Hollywood correspondents for the English dailies sent home a constant stream of derogatory pieces about "The British Colony" in Los Angeles, and his name, as well as Felicia's, was prominently featured in most of them.

If he felt a certain degree of patriotic guilt about the party, he felt even more about Felicia. Despite all his good intentions of spending more time with her, his life was determined by the strict demands of his shooting schedule. Promptly at six every morning a studio car picked him up, and he seldom came home until late at night. And the few hours he was not working were spent mostly above the Burbank airport, slewing back and forth across the sky in a Piper Cub, hanging on to the control stick for dear life. They called it the "joystick" in movies, but he derived no pleasure from flying at all. He felt only a dull, constant apprehension, rather like going onstage in a demanding role without being certain of his lines.

Every day he tried to make time for Felicia, somehow, and every day he failed. At night he fell asleep exhausted, partly because he was paying the price for the elaborate makeup he had invented for his role. He could never break himself of the habit of changing his features for a part, and the worse the part was, the further he went to hide himself behind putty, wigs, and greasepaint, as if he didn't want to be recognized in it. Every morning, he labored for hours to transform himself completely, and every evening he had to strip the layers of putty and gauze off laboriously—a procedure which kept him at the studio long after the rest of the cast had gone home.

He had asked Randy, who was between pictures at present, to keep an eye on Felicia, and Randy had been happy to oblige. There was nothing to worry about, Randy reported, every time they talked: Felicia was busy, happy, didn't miss him at all during the day. "Relax. She's having a great time," he said.

But if she was, she was damn well determined not to let Robby know about it. She complained that her days were empty, she nursed a simmering, low-level, jealous suspicion about his relationship with his co-star, Virginia Glad (whose reputation for pleasing older men was such that she was known throughout the industry as "The Glad Hand"), she blamed him for working when she wasn't, in much the same way that she had always blamed him for sleeping when she couldn't. Oh, how she wanted him to love her and not allow their lives to settle into humdrum domesticity!

But at least there were moments of calm and happiness, when their hands touched by accident at a party and they held on to each other, fingers intertwined, or when he woke in the middle of the night to feel her pressed against his back. Their life was a good deal better than it had been in the two years since they had left England.

Of course, Randy was right. Vane plunged into the crowd, smiling, shaking hands, greeting people he knew by name and those he didn't with cheerful shouts of "Delighted you could come, old boy," or "Darling," allowing himself to be hugged, squeezed, kissed, on his way, until he found himself on the dance floor.

Felicia—looking rather flushed, he thought—was dancing with Arnie Bucher, Vane's erstwhile director. Bucher, despite his toadlike appearance, had a reputation as a ladies' man, and Vane could not help noticing that Felicia was pressed hard against his ample stomach. Bucher's pudgy fingers were splayed out at the base of her spine, just at the top of the daringly cut dress that left most of her back exposed. An inch or so farther down and his hand would be on her ass, Vane thought angrily. Felicia's expression was that of a contented cat, eyes half-shut as she kept time to the music. Bucher had the bemused smile of a man who can't believe his own luck. Vane tapped him on the shoulder, rather harder than was necessary. "Mind if I cut in?" he asked.

"By all means." Bucher's dark little eyes flickered over the dance floor as he looked for another partner. "She's all yours," he said, as if he were handing over the keys to a car.

"I think you might ask *me* first, Robby," Felicia said, holding tight to Bucher.

Vane scented trouble. Easy does it, he told himself. No scenes. He smiled. "*May* I have the pleasure?" he asked.

"Arnie's been such a dear to dance with me. He's thinking of doing *Anna Karenina*, darling. He thinks I'd be *perfect* for it."

"It's been done before," Vane said.

Bucher shrugged. "Not by me. Not with Lish as Anna."

"*You* could do Karenin, darling. It would be such heaven to be working together again on a film!"

Vane frowned. "Vronsky, surely? Karenin's not the right part for me at all."

"No, dear, Karenin." She smiled at him sweetly. "The cold, indifferent husband who lets his lovely wife slip through his fingers into Vronsky's hands."

Bucher pulled away from her as quickly as he could. "I see Si Krieger over there," he muttered. "If you'll forgive me, I must talk to him. So many thanks . . ." He took her hand, bowed, kissed it, and vanished swiftly into the crowd of dancers.

"So much for the Frog Prince," Felicia said scornfully. "He jumped back into the pond at the first sign of a storm."

"Is there going to be a storm?"

"There will be if you don't dance with me right now, darling."

Vane put his arms around her and moved to the music. He did not much like dancing, though he had trained himself to be an accomplished dancer. An actor had to be able to do anything physical that the role required, and his early films had invariably contained a scene in which he danced with the heroine. He had once even subjected himself to a long course of ballet lessons because he felt he lacked physical grace. Still, dancing gave him no pleasure, and he had never been able to overcome a deaf ear for music. His tone deafness was so notorious that Guy Darling always claimed that the only tune Robby Vane could recognize was "God Save the King," and then only because it was always played after the final curtain. Felicia, on the other hand, loved dancing. For her, the summit of happiness was whirling around in the center of the floor, knowing everyone's eyes were on her.

They were certainly on her now, which was hardly surprising, given the rumors that had spread about their relationship since the disaster in San Francisco. He held her tightly, his cheek against hers, and guided her out onto the center of the floor, where it was more brightly lit. "Let's show them a thing or two, shall we?" he asked.

"To hell with them. Try showing *me* a thing or two, for once, darling."

It occurred to him that Felicia's speech was ever so slightly slurred—a danger signal.

He fixed a cheerful grin on his face and decided that the sooner he got her off the dance floor and made her drink some coffee, the better. He could feel her weight against his arms, as if he were holding her up, and her feet seemed to be moving just a little more slowly than his own, so that he had to take care not to tread on her toes.

"Do you remember when we used to dress up and go dancing at the Café de Paris, after the curtain, darling?" he asked. "Hutch used to play 'A Nightingale Sang in Berkeley Square' for us—'Our song,' he used to say."

Her eyes were closed. "For God's sake, Robby, our song was 'Springtime in Mayfair.' I would have thought you could at least have remembered *that*!"

He felt his stomach sink. Felicia's memory for this kind of thing, drunk or sober, was flawless. Birthdays, favorite songs, sentimental allusions were always difficult for him to remember. Felicia could remember exactly where they sat, what they had eaten, what each of them had worn the first time they had lunch together (both of them already aware that there was more at stake than just the question of whether or not she would play Ophelia to his Hamlet at Stratford), whereas the whole luncheon was a complete blank in his memory, except for the fact that she had flirted with him outrageously.

He had left the restaurant determined to let her have the part. . . . What would his life have been like if he hadn't?

He would certainly not be here, that was sure, for it had been Leo Stone's offer of a glamorous part (and an even more glamorous contract) for Felicia that had brought them to Hollywood in the first place.

They had thought it would be fun, a kind of well-paid lark ("A bit of fame, a lot of jolly, old boy," Toby Eden had said approvingly. "Of *course* Lisha must do it!"), a few months of sun in the fleshpots of Beverly Hills, then home to London, richer and more famous. But they had made the great mistake of staying here too long, just like the prehistoric animals that stopped for a drink of water at the La Brea tar pits. "You're quite right, darling," he said soothingly. "I'm hopeless with tunes, as you know."

"Tunes are the least of it. And have you enjoyed dancing with the glamorous young Miss Glad?"

"We haven't shot the dancing scene yet."

"Oh, really? Randy told me that he'd seen the two of you dancing—he thought you looked very good together."

"We were *rehearsing*, dear heart, that's all. A costume test. There was some question about whether she could dance in the costume they made for her."

"So Randy mentioned. 'Her boobs kept popping out every time she moved,' he told me. Poor you! I'm sure you helped her stuff them back in."

Vane held his temper with difficulty. As it happened, he could have had Virginia Glad for the asking, which admittedly wasn't saying much. He could not deny that he had been tempted at the thought of so much ripe flesh ("Like biting into a ripe peach that bites *back*, old man!" Errol Flynn had whispered to him, having given Miss Glad what he called "a test run" himself), but Vane was not about to compromise his dignity by locking himself up with one of Hollywood's more notorious easy lays, and so he behaved toward her with all the fussy, good-mannered correctness of an elderly clergyman counseling a pretty young parishioner.

For his pains, Miss Glad spread the word around the cast that he was "a stuck-up Limey fag," and at every opportunity made his life on the set difficult. Under the circumstances, he resented Felicia's suspicion bitterly. "It was a question of the length and stiffness of her skirt," he said sharply. "Miss Glad's 'boobs,' as you call them, were not an issue."

"Length and stiffness!" Felicia murmured in his ear, a sweet smile on her face. "I'm not up on that sort of thing myself nowadays, more's the pity."

This was no place to argue, in full view of most of the people who mattered in Hollywood, as well as of the major gossip writers. "Lisha, darling," he said, "there's nothing between myself and Miss Glad but a lot of bad temper and worse acting."

"Oh, as to her acting ability, I can believe that. I don't suppose she's ever had a *real* actor like you, darling. I'm surprised you managed to beat her off."

"I've had no need to do anything of the kind."

"How very sad for you. The one man in town Virginia Glad hasn't made a play for. Poor Robby! People will think you don't like sex if you're not careful. I sometimes wonder myself."

"You know very well I do."

"Well, I know you *used* to. With me, as a matter of fact. Of course, these days I hardly see you. You're up at dawn to go to the studio—probably all atwitter to show Miss Glad the secrets of your makeup kit. I'm sure she's *fascinated* by all that quaint Shakespearean stage lore. And you're not home until late at night, because you're either at the studio or off flying your bloody aeroplane—if that's what you're actually doing."

"You know perfectly well that's what I'm doing."

She sighed. "Yes, I suppose I do. In a way, darling, I could understand it better if you were having a sexy, romantic fling with Miss Glad. I mean, then there'd be a good reason for ignoring me, wouldn't there? So the only possible reason is that you're bored with me."

"That is simply not true."

"Oh, I think it *is*, Robby. . . . Give a nice smile and a wave to that loathsome old bitch in the funny hat, Louella or Hedda, I can never remember which is which. . . . That's it!"

Felicia threw her head back, laughing, her eyes sparkling

as if she were having the time of her life, the living picture
of romance, beauty, love, as Vane waved vaguely to which-
ever of the press harridans it was, his face set in what he
hoped was a look of smoldering passion. A flashbulb went
off. Each of the columnists had been allowed to bring a
photographer, and there was another from *Life*. Tomorrow
the world would see them dancing in each other's arms, the
handsomest couple in the world, showing how much they
loved each other for the millions of readers who were more
interested in them than in the war news.

"Things will be better once we're home," he said, but he
wasn't sure he believed it himself. It was merely a wish, like
knocking on wood.

"Then it will be the war. Or the theatre. There's always
something to keep us apart. And do you know why, Robby?
It's because that's the way you want it. It's not *me* you want,
not anymore."

She was beginning to cry now—in the middle of the dance
floor at their own party. "Kiss me, you bloody fool!" she
ordered, so loudly that he was afraid the whole room would
hear her. "Kiss me as if you *meant* it, goddamn you!"

He bent his head to kiss her, and saw in her eyes such a
depth of pain that he was terrified. He kissed her as hard as
he could, holding her pressed to him, and felt a sudden tap
on his shoulder.

"I'll take one of those," a familiar voice growled. "It
looks like just what the doctor ordered for a guy that's been
flying twenty-four fucking hours just to come to a party."

Felicia laughed. "My darling Caliban!" she cried, throwing her arms around him. "I thought you weren't coming."

"Christ, I wouldn't have missed it. Move over, Robby,
let me dance with Lish. The last time I saw her, she'd just
had her stomach pumped, and here she is, the belle of her
own fucking ball! Stick with me, Lish, I'll build a show
around you. Great love scenes from Shakespeare on ice! I
like it already."

"I can't skate, Marty."

"Nobody's perfect. Let's cut to the chase." Quick tossed
his cigar away as if it were a live hand grenade, trusting that

one of his flunkies would catch it. He traveled with an entourage of heavyset, scowling young men who looked more like prizefighters than assistants, and a couple of interchangeable blond girls who claimed to be secretaries. Like a sports team, they were trained to catch whatever he threw—when he entered a room, he sent his hat and his overcoat sailing into the air, while his followers lunged desperately to grab them before they hit the floor. It was one of his favorite tricks, like throwing coins out the window of his limousine in poor neighborhoods to watch the children fight over them.

Quick believed in competition. For years he had boasted in the press that he planned to revive the Roman circus, complete with gladiatorial games and fights between men and wild animals, and there were many who thought he was not joking.

"Fuck this slow crap," he said. "Play something we can *dance* to!" he shouted at the orchestra. There was no question of his not being obeyed, since he was not only a friend of Vinnie Pettrillo, the head of the musicians' union, but also employed bands and orchestras by the dozens. If he had ordered them to stand on their heads to play, they would have done their best to please him.

They broke into one of Quick's favorites, "When Veronica Plays the Harmonica Down Upon the Pier in Santa Monica," a song he had commissioned for his 1939 All-Star Aquacade at the World's Fair, which had first been sung by America's beloved Olympic swimming champion, flanked by two performing seals playing the kazoo. Since he had briefly married his swimming star, the song had sentimental associations for Quick, to the degree that he had any.

He danced, as he did everything, with ferocious energy, holding Felicia as if he didn't care whether her feet touched the ground or not. "How ya doin', baby?" he shouted at her over the noise of the band. He was the only person who had ever called her "baby" and it always delighted her.

"Enjoying myself, Marty."

"That a fact?" Quick grinned.

His grin was famous. It was well known that Walt Disney had drawn on him as the inspiration for the Big Bad Wolf, after a brief and disastrous experience as one of Quick's luckless investors. Even if she hadn't known the story—which Quick himself told proudly—Felicia would have seen the resemblance: the wolfish grin, the bared, gleaming teeth, the dark eyes that seemed to glitter with joy at his own evil intentions. All you had to do to complete the picture, she thought, was add pointed ears and ask him to "huff and puff and blow the house down."

His hair was jet-black and slicked back so heavily on his flat skull that it seemed to have been painted on, and although he was shaved at least twice a day, his chin and cheeks were always dark. Even the way he carried himself was threatening, in an aggressive crouch, the big head thrust forward, the arms pumping away to speed up his progress, his chest puffed out, as if he were about to crash through the nearest wall in pursuit of his squealing prey. His hands were as hairy as a wolf's paws, though perfectly manicured.

Quick was short, but his shortness was not something you noticed about him. It was, Felicia thought, as if nature had intended him to be tall, and given him the head, chest, and shoulders of a much bigger man, except that he had been in such a hurry to be born and get on in the world that he hadn't bothered to wait in the womb for the height.

She liked Quick, who seemed to get more fun out of life than most people, even if it *was* usually at the expense of others—for Quick had left behind him a trail of bankruptcies, suicides, violence, and rumors of murder.

"I hear Robby's working in some piece of shit of Si Krieger's," he growled. "Why not you?"

She caught her breath. Dancing with Quick was like doing calisthenics. "I'm considered unemployable at the moment. Because of what happened in San Francisco. The object of this party is to show that I've recovered."

"I knew *that*, baby, the moment I heard about it. Smart thinking. Your idea or Robby-boy's?"

"Mine."

"Figures. It might work, too, if you can lay off the sauce for the rest of the evening. Do yourself a favor and don't drink any more champagne." He held her in a viselike grip.

"I'm sorry I had to hit you back there in San Francisco. Has Robby forgiven me?"

"For hitting me?"

"Nah. Fuck that. He should have done it himself, Lish, baby, you had it coming. For the fact I ran out on the show?"

"He's still rather bitter about it. With good reason."

He laughed. "Business is business. A show goes down the drain, I don't stick around chewing the fat with the investors. I get out of town fast. He should have done the same, like I told him."

"Robby couldn't have left the cast in the lurch, Marty. It isn't in him."

"Christ, I once left a whole *circus* stranded. If you're not selling tickets, pack your bag and run for your life, that's my rule. You start worrying about actors in this business, you're dead. Listen, I gotta talk to him. And you, you go dance with Leo Stone. He's thinking of making one of those classy movies, some Limey novel, you know—French Revolution, hero gets his head cut off at the end of it. . . ."

"*A Tale of Two Cities?*"

"Maybe," Quick said warily. He was, she knew, surprisingly well read, but he liked to keep the fact hidden, afraid that people might think it was a weakness if they knew he read books. Felicia had accidentally discovered him reading *Bleak House* one day on tour, while one of his blond "secretaries" was giving him a pedicure, and it was the only time she had ever seen him blush.

"How do you know about Stone?" It seemed to her unlikely that Leo Stone, notorious for playing his cards close to his chest, would confide in Marty Quick, of all people, whom he loathed, as did everybody in Hollywood. Quick had spent years trying to take over a movie studio, and failing that, to dethrone one of the studio heads. "Let him go back to Coney Island and run freak shows there where he came from," Stone had once suggested, and there were few people in the industry who would have disagreed with him.

"I hear everything I want to know," Quick said—and it was true. He was a relentless gatherer of information, and had most of the entertainment journalists and gossip columnists on his payroll. "Go talk to Leo," he ordered gruffly, and since he was never content merely to tell people what to do, he steered her across the crowded floor to where Stone was shuffling vaguely with his wife, bewildered by the sudden fast pace of the music, said, "Here, Leo, your hostess wants to dance with you," and swept off into the crowd with Mrs. Stone, who did not look unhappy with the exchange.

The major producers and the studio heads might hate Quick, but he exerted an unlikely fascination over their wives, partly because he had cultivated a slew of stories about his sexual powers. There were legends about the size of his organ: women were said to go weak at the knees in fear at the sight of it when he undressed, and men who had seen him naked in the steam room at the Hillside Country Club were rumored to have been awe struck. Randy Brooks, a great spreader of Marty Quick stories—some thought that Quick actually fed him the stories—said that Clarence, the black steam-bath attendant at the club, had exclaimed he'd never seen a white man as well-endowed as he himself was until he saw Quick in the shower.

Felicia was only mildly curious on the subject, though after he had suddenly hit her in San Francisco, she had been unable to stop her mind from wandering toward him. And later, when she slept uneasily, drugged and in pain, hardly even aware that she was being moved to Los Angeles by plane, she had been tormented by grotesque erotic dreams, most of which seemed to involve being hand-cuffed to a bed in the St. Francis Hotel while Marty Quick approached her from behind, the famous penis more than living up to its reputation. In some of the dreams Robby, dressed in his costume as Romeo, watched approvingly, giving helpful advice and suggestions to Quick. She had attributed these dreams to the drugs the doctors gave her, and was careful not to mention them to Dr. Vogel, though they were exactly the kind of thing he wanted to hear.

"I hate that son of a bitch Quick," Stone said, bringing her back to reality, his sweaty hand on the small of her back. Like so many older men in Hollywood, he had gone to the expense of having his teeth capped, with the result that they were unnaturally white and large, giving him a kind of ghastly death's-head grin when he smiled. His face was tanned to the color of crisp bacon, and it was just possible, if you looked hard enough, to see the line where his toupee met what remained of his own hair.

The toupee had become famous throughout the industry when Leona Landon, tired of being pursued around his desk, tore it off Stone's head and threw it out the window of his office into the studio parking lot. He swore she would never act in Hollywood again, and she didn't. Stone was clearly not a man to cross, but Felicia was loyal to people she liked. "I've always found Marty amusing, Leo," she said.

"Amusing? I'll never understand you Brits. He stole money from you and Robby, the way I hear it. What's so goddamn 'amusing' about that?"

"He stole it with *style*," she said firmly. Grabbing a glass of champagne from a passing waiter, she downed it in one gulp, pressed herself a little closer to Stone, despite the feel of his clammy hand, and, looking up into his eyes—or what she could see of them through his thick, tinted glasses—she said, in a breathless, small-girl voice, "Do you know Dickens is one of my *favorite* writers, Leo, darling? Take *A Tale of Two Cities*, for instance. . . ."

"You take *A Tale of Two Cities*, Marty, it's perfect for the two of us. I could do Sydney Carton very well indeed. '*It is a far, far better thing that I do now . . .*' " Vane ran his finger down his nose as if trying to decide what shape he would give it for the part.

"That just shows you don't know shit about movies, Robby. First rule is, a big star never dies onscreen. The public doesn't like it. Stars get wounded, not killed. They killed Gary Cooper in a movie a few years ago, and in a lot of countries people wouldn't go to his next picture because they figured the guy on the screen was a ghost, or something. They had to send Coop on a tour of South America to prove he was still alive, poor bastard!"

Vane laughed. "So much for Shakespeare!"

Quick drew on his cigar. "Shakespeare gave the audience

of his day what it wanted, right? If he worked for Leo Stone today, he'd be writing happy endings. It's a rough world, Robby. People want to believe things work out for *somebody*, you know? They want pessimism, all they have to do is stay home and listen to the news or think about their own crappy little lives. If Leo thinks they wanna sit through two hours of the French Revolution, then watch the hero get his head cut off, he's out of his friggin' mind.''

Quick had taken over a table in a dark corner of the tent, as close to the door as he could get, his back to the canvas. Certain habits of his youth he never gave up, and one of them was that he liked to sit with his back against the wall, and next to the door—to see who was approaching him and be in a position to make a fast getaway.

He sat hunched over the table, in front of a bottle of champagne he had commandeered, with Randy Brooks and Robby Vane on either side of him. Quick placed himself at the center of things. In New York, years ago, he had boldly pushed his way into the comedians' table at Lindy's, and since he was willing to pick up the check, they had reluctantly allowed him to become a regular. Within a few months he transformed it into "his" table, and took it upon himself to decide which comedians could sit there and which couldn't, with the result that there was now a *second* comedians' table, at the rival Stage Delicatessen, though anybody who ate there was banned from Quick's shows.

"You still mad at me?" he asked.

Vane shrugged. He blamed himself for what had happened, not Quick, who in any case lived by a different set of rules. Vane believed in paying his debts, and Quick did not. "Marty," he said, "I haven't any time to waste on anger. I owe four hundred thousand dollars. I'm going to have to make a couple of films very fast, and it would help if Felicia could make one, too. The moment I've paid everyone off, I'm going home, and taking her with me. And I'm never coming back here again."

"It's a plan," Quick said thoughtfully. "It's always a good idea to have a plan. The only trouble is, you want my opinion, it ain't gonna fly."

"Have you a better suggestion?"

"Maybe." Quick glanced around him, then dropped his gravelly voice to a conspiratorial whisper. *"Don Quixote,"* he said.

"I've not read it," Vane confessed.

"Well, Christ, who *has*? But everybody knows the story. That's the point."

"What point, Marty?"

"The point of making it into a movie. It's got class, it's a world-famous book. And it has a happy ending."

Vane racked his memory. "I don't think it *does*, surely?" he said doubtfully.

"Well, we could tack one on. At least nobody gets guillotined, right?"

"Right," Randy said, bobbing his head. It was odd, Vane thought, but Randy always deferred to Quick when they were together. Quick seemed to terrify him, for some reason, though he did not behave toward Brooks any more brutally than he behaved toward everyone else. "It's a great idea, Marty, but do you think you can sell a studio on it?"

Quick glared at him fiercely. "Randy, don't be a shmuck. Who needs a studio? Do I need a studio to put on a Broadway show? No. So why do I need a studio to make a movie? I need an idea—which I got. I need a script—which I can get written. I need money—which I can raise. And I need stars, because I can't raise the money unless I can tell investors that I've got the famous Robert Vane to play Quixote, and America's most beloved comedian, my old friend Randy Brooks, to play Sancho Panza"—he paused dramatically—"and the beautiful Felicia Lisle for the role of Dulcinea! With *those* names, my friends, I can raise four, five million easy, not here, but in New York, which is where the money and brains are, anyway. Then all we gotta do is make a movie so good that we can sell it to the exhibitors *without* the goddamn studio."

Brooks looked doubtful. "They'll never stand for it," he said. "The exhibitors don't have the guts to stand up to the studios."

Quick gave him a stony glare. Everybody knew that for

years he had fought the studio heads tooth and nail. Bungalow One of the Beverly Hills Hotel, which Quick kept as his headquarters on the West Coast, was regarded with fear and loathing throughout the industry—so much so that many people took the long way round to the pool for fear somebody might see them near Quick's bungalow and suppose they had been visiting him.

For years Quick had toyed with the idea of making a movie so big, so profitable at the box office, so irresistible to the public, that the industry would be forced to accept him. His plan, hatched at regular intervals, failed every time because the studio heads whom Quick was so determined to destroy controlled distribution and were certainly smart enough not to supply Quick with a knife with which to cut their throats. Now he had apparently come up with a plan to reach over their heads and take his picture directly to the public, if it ever got made.

Brooks looked gloomy, and for good reason. As Quick's close friend he could hardly refuse to help him; as Leo Stone's son-in-law and a major beneficiary of the studio system, he was appalled at what the consequences would be, starting of course with what Natalie would say.

As for Vane, he was an actor and a foreigner—the power and the intricate politics of the studios was of no great interest to him. It was not that he didn't take motion pictures seriously—no actor could afford not to—but it still seemed to him a second-rate use of his talent.

There was a lot he had learned about technique here, but the trick was to apply that technique to something worthwhile, as he had told Marty—filming Shakespeare, or the other great theatrical classics. Studio heads didn't even want to *talk* about such things, but Quick was an altogether more complicated person, and part of him yearned for "quality." It was just this yearning that had fired Quick's imagination when Vane had proposed to take *Romeo and Juliet* on a nationwide tour, showing the classics to the American people. Vane knew Quick liked taking risks, had dreams of glory. He was convinced that Quick's talents as a showman would have appealed to Shakespeare, who after all had lived in an age when bull-baiting and freak shows took place side by side with the theatre.

Vane stared glumly at the party that would add another twenty-five thousand dollars to his debts. Under the glittering false foliage, the dance floor was crowded. People actually seemed to be enjoying themselves, which was rare in Hollywood. It was as if Felicia's nervous energy and beauty were spurring her guests on to have a good time. But then, she could make even the dullest of dinner guests feel witty and charming. When Felicia entertained, dowdy women glowed like great beauties, ugly men preened as if they were handsome, people who hardly ever smiled told funny stories.

Felicia used up her energy as if she had a bottomless supply of it, wasted it on strangers, on servants, on social occasions, whereas he had learned long ago to hoard and concentrate his own for his work. Again and again he had tried to explain to her that any actor or actress had only so much energy—or perhaps better, passion—to give, and that the whole art of acting lay in *directing* it precisely toward the character you were playing. Great actors—and how few there were, perhaps not more than one or two in a whole generation—rationed their energy like great athletes, saving it up for the moments that counted. For the athlete it was the high jump or the sprint; for the actor, it was Hamlet's soliloquy, Lear shouting his defiance to the elements, the animal cry of Oedipus when he understands, too late, what the gods have done to him.

He watched Felicia as she flashed from partner to partner, laughing, smiling, blowing kisses to people, dancing faster and faster as if she couldn't stop or rest. . . . The only way to harness that energy, he thought, was to get her back to work as soon as possible, in something they could do together, so he could keep his eye on her. Involving her in some farfetched crackpot scheme of Marty Quick's would be fatal, he decided. "I don't think it's for us, Marty," he said. "Sorry."

Opposition, however polite, always brought Quick up short. "What the fuck are you talking about?" he barked.

"What Felicia needs is something she can handle without a lot of stress. A nice, carefully planned little film like *A*

Tale of Two Cities, with a sensible director and a disciplined shooting schedule.''

"You're outta your mind, Robby. I'm talking about something that's going to be bigger than *Gone With the Wind*, bigger than *Birth of a Nation*. I already talked to Dali about designing the costumes. I'm gonna get Stravinsky to write the music. I was thinking maybe T. S. Eliot could write the script, some of it, anyway. . . .''

Quick's face glowed. His plans always included the participation of major cultural figures, some of whom he bulldozed into agreement by sheer force of personality, others by an adroit appeal to their greed. Mostly they gave in just to get Quick off their backs, trusting that in the end probably nothing would come of it, which was usually the case.

"Dali would be great," Randy Brooks said enthusiastically.

"Of *course* he'd be great," Quick snapped irritably. "He's gonna do it, too, I can tell you that right now." He gave Brooks a dark glance.

"The point is," Brooks went on, correcting his course on Quick's cue, "*you'd* be great, Robby. Don Quixote and Sancho Panza—Jesus, we could really do something terrific together! It would be like the time you played Justice Shallow to Toby Eden's Falstaff, in Bristol. . . .''

Vane raised an eyebrow. Randy seemed to know more about his career than he did himself. As it happened, he had felt at Bristol, as he often did, that Toby had stolen the show—not surprisingly, since Falstaff was by far the more appealing role. But then Toby always went for the audience's heart, while he struggled for their souls.

Still, he had to admit to himself that the idea of playing with Randy Brooks was intriguing. In his mind's eye he pictured them, himself astride a bony horse, bearded, dressed in rusty armor, with a sharp beak of a nose and unkempt, bushy eyebrows, Randy beside him on a donkey, the obsequious servant who is in fact smarter than his master, his feet more firmly planted on the ground, flesh as opposed to spirit.

In life, as in art, he thought, the real wisdom was the

clown's, for the clown always saw the truth of things—that power is a shallow pretense, love merely self-delusion, an attempt to cloak lust with some finer, more noble emotion, ambition just a series of stepping stones on the way to a ludicrous fall.

Vane had always yearned to play comic roles, but when he had tried Falstaff, he had been unhappy with his performance. "It's not the belly you strap on, dear boy," Toby had told him. "It's the belly in the *mind* that matters."

Tempted as he was, Vane stood his ground. "Toby played rings around me in Bristol," he said. "Anyway, that's neither here nor there. I can't afford to involve Felicia or myself in a long, complicated project, however interesting and ambitious. We'll dance to the studios' tune, briefly, make enough to pay off our debts, then go home. I'm flattered, Marty, but it's not the right moment."

"You're thinking small, Robby. That's a mistake. You take my advice. . . ."

Vane knocked back his glass of champagne. "I *took* your advice," he snapped back. "As a result Felicia and I are in debt to the tune of four hundred thousand dollars."

Quick grinned. "Bullshit! My advice was to close the show in Chicago. Listen, you're pissed off at me, okay, I understand that. How about this? You need four hundred thousand dollars? You got it. Better than that. I'll pay you four hundred thousand dollars *each*, if you sign with me. Up front, my friend, no screwing around."

Brooks whistled. "That's a hell of a lot of money," he said, rolling his eyes, as if Vane might not realize it.

"Yeah. And you get the same, Randy. I'll do better. I'll give each of you a percentage of the picture. That's more than Leo Stone can do. Think about *that*!"

Vane thought about it. It was an enormous sum—more than three times what either of them could hope to make from an ordinary film. All the same, he had no intention of signing himself up for what might be years of work while Quick controlled his life. "Thank you, Marty," he said, "but my mind's made up."

Quick stubbed out his cigar, took out another, bit off the end and spat it out. One of his minions appeared instantly from the shadows with a box of Swan Vesta matches.

Quick was always on the lookout for little touches that might add class to his presence. He had no doubt learned about Swan Vesta matches in England, Vane guessed, as well as Lobb shoes and Savile Row tailoring, in Paris about Charvet ties, silk underwear, and Roederer Cristal champagne. Who but Quick would have been bold enough to walk right up to the Duke of Windsor at the Colony and ask him where he got his shirts? Who else would have found out from Winston Churchill where his cigars were made, and then bought an interest in the plantation?

When John Hamilton Tree, the most august and blueblooded of New York financiers, had refused to give his blessing to Quick's marrying his daughter, Quick had made an offer for Tree's family portraits, right there in Tree's own Fifth Avenue living room, under the painting of Makepeace Tree signing the Declaration of Independence. Quick's approach to life was very much like Vane's approach to acting, and it was one of the things that made Vane warily tolerant of him, though uneasily conscious that friendship with Quick was like owning a dog that bites.

Quick patted him on the shoulder. "Hey, if your mind's made up, no sweat," he said, in a careless voice that failed to disguise his irritation. "Forget about it."

There was a roll of drums, and Vane caught a glimpse of Felicia, staring in his direction. This was a party in Randy Brooks's honor, and according to local tradition, it could not end without a salute to him.

"Hey, time for the Bar-Mitzvah boy!" Quick cried, and rising to his feet he grabbed Randy and pulled him into the center of the floor as if *he* were the host. Vane followed, a smile fixed on his face.

He put his arm around Felicia, noticing how warm she felt. Her face was flushed, her eyes unnaturally wide open. Clearly she had been overdoing it. Perhaps they could get away to Palm Springs and stay in the Brookses' house there, just the two of them. . . .

He cleared his throat, dropped his voice down an octave, as he had learned to do with such difficulty for those Shakespearean parts that required a deep voice, Othello, for example, or Lear, and grabbing a glass from a passing waiter, he held it up and said, simply and with dignity, "I want to propose a toast to our dear friend Randy Brooks."

He had no trouble making himself heard above the noise of conversation in the tent. His voice could fill a theatre without difficulty—or amplification. His diction was so precise, so perfectly articulated, that it was like listening to a great musician play a simple melody. Even this blasé audience, which had seen—and heard—everything, fell silent. In England, where speaking English properly was more appreciated, Philip Chagrin's voice was held by many to be superior to Vane's (an opinion which Vane shared), but Vane had worked hard over the years to challenge his rival, eventually managing to give his a resonant depth which Chagrin's lacked. Chagrin's voice was like a superb etching, but Vane's was rich, full of color. They listened to him as they might have watched Pavlova dance, or heard Caruso sing.

"Felicia and I"—he clutched her tightly to him and smiled down at her—"are visitors here." He paused. "But not strangers," he added. "For all of you have made us feel at home."

He looked directly at Leo Stone, an old actor's trick: Always pick out a face in the audience and speak directly to that person, as if he or she were the whole audience. "And why not? Ours is a common language, a common set of values, a common culture." He smiled. "The culture of Shakespeare. And Dickens." So much for *A Tale of Two Cities*, he told himself. He wondered if Stone would go as high as one hundred fifty thousand dollars for each of them.

"Nobody has been kinder to us here, or made us feel more at home, than Randy and Natalie Brooks, our neighbors and friends." He raised his glass high, and as he did so felt a slight tremor run through Felicia's body. For a moment, he thought she might be about to have a fit of giggling; then he decided that she was probably just shivering because she was cold after so much exertion.

He stopped for a moment to look at her, and noticed with alarm that her eyes seemed unfocused. He squeezed her waist sharply and gave her a dazzling smile. *"There's nothing worth the wear of winning,/But laughter and the love of friends,"* he said.

Randy Brooks, who had been clowning about as if he were getting ready to fend off an onslaught of jokes at his expense—he had been expecting the usual roast—seemed taken by surprise at the rich sentimentality of Vane's words—even a little embarrassed by it. For a moment he looked awkward and out of place, standing in the limelight with Quick on one side of him and Natalie on the other.

". . . *The love of friends,*" Vane went on, feeling Felicia beginning to sag a little on his arm. He paused, realizing quite suddenly how much, to his own surprise, he really *meant* what he was saying, and heard beside him a muffled giggle from Felicia, followed by a full-blown laugh that trembled delicately through the hushed tent. There was a devilish, sharp-edged quality to it.

If you had to describe it, he thought, feeling his stomach sink, you would have to call it "mocking" or "bitter." It was pitched high, like breaking glass, and brought about an instant deadly silence. Vane felt himself break out into a cold sweat, just as he had when he had been hanging from the balcony in San Francisco. From all over the room he was conscious of eyes staring at him in horror, as if he had just missed his cue.

"*Love,*" Felicia said slowly, dragging the word out, still giggling. "Oh, *tell* them about love, Robby."

He was smiling so hard now that it felt as if his jaws would break. "Love," he said wildly. "Of course. Friendship and love . . ."

But as he tried desperately to decide what to say about friendship and love, he saw Felicia's lips, exquisite and beautiful as always, begin to move, heard her voice, pitched perfectly to reach every ear from one end of the big tent to the other. "Robby, darling," she said sweetly, eyes sparkling as she looked up at him. "Tell me—*why* don't you ever fuck me anymore?"

6

He was not a great actor for nothing.

For a second or two, no more, his face had turned white and he had seemed about to faint, but it would not have been apparent except to somebody who had worked with him on-stage. He had taken the shock like a stout tree bending to a gust of wind, then instantly set his face in an expression of high good humor, as if she had just told a good joke—bawdy and shocking, perhaps, but still well-meant and loving—on him—then he began to roar with laughter, tears swelling from his eyes, while the guests, who for one dreadful moment had stood and started like people watching a natural disaster or tenement fire, decided to laugh, too, as if she had just made the wittiest remark of the year.

She lay in bed wondering how she had managed to get out of her clothes. Her head throbbed, her mouth was dry, she could feel her makeup still caked on her face. Had Robby undressed her? She had a vague memory of his doing so, silently and none too gently. She dimly remembered shouting at him, "Fuck me, then, come on, *fuck* me, why don't you?" But she was fairly sure he hadn't—which was rather a pity, she thought, since it would have been at least one thing gained from the wreck of the evening.

She tried to remember the rest of the evening. She had a faint recollection of whirling around the floor faster and faster with a whole succession of men, a stronger picture of Marty Quick, on the sidelines, giving her a warning glance—But what she remembered most clearly of all, unfortunately, was Robby's face in the instant before he managed to summon up laughter.

Bravo Robby! she had been tempted to shout. As usual, he had put on a splendid performance, and as usual he had cheated her out of what she wanted. She had reached out for him in the most outrageous way she could, with a cry of hunger, need, pain, and—as usual—had succeeded only in humiliating him. What she *wanted* was to provoke his rage, and break through from there to love, but what she got instead was long-suffering politeness, instant forgiveness, a helping hand to get her upstairs and safely tucked into bed.

She tossed and turned restlessly on the bed, smearing the damp pillows with her makeup, though usually the very notion of smudging her freshly laundered linen with traces of lipstick or mascara was intolerable to her. She would just as soon have worn dirty underwear, or put on a pair of stockings with runs in them. . . .

She looked around the room. Her clothes had been neatly placed over a chair. Robby had undressed her efficiently. She closed her eyes and tried to recall the scene. Dr. Vogel had been there, she was sure—she could remember his earnest face, sweaty from dancing, or perhaps just from thinking of the damage to his professional reputation, as he gave her an injection. She thought she remembered Randy Brooks beside her, and Marty Quick. Had they been present when Robby pulled her clothes off? For some reason, she was repelled by the idea of Brooks seeing her naked. Marty she didn't mind, but the thought of Brooks's pale face looking down at her made her shiver.

She got up unsteadily, slipped on a robe, went to the bathroom, and turned the lights on. The sight of her face in the mirror shocked her—puffy eyes, disheveled hair, smears of makeup. She washed her face and brushed her hair, and told herself she would have to find Robby and face him. There was no point in apologizing—she had gone far beyond the point where any apology would matter—but perhaps, if she said nothing, if she simply stood before him in tears, he would forgive her. She could not bear to be alone here a moment longer in this rented house that she was never able to think of as ''home.'' A series of miscalculations, errors in judgment, misfortunes, had brought them here by stages, as if they had been trying to escape from her unhappiness by moving farther and farther west, until finally they had reached the Pacific.

Alex Korda, a fellow exile in Hollywood, had told them that on an earlier trip here, at the time of The Crash, he had rented a house in Malibu and sometimes found on the beach in the mornings the neatly folded clothes and the shoes of people who had simply swum out into the Pacific to die— poor wretches who had moved west in pursuit of some dream of happiness and success, and having come as far as they could go, had failed again. Korda moved back to Beverly Hills, afraid that he might do the same one night. "The sunsets are nice," he said, dismissing Malibu, "but it's too much like standing on the edge of a cliff for me." Robby had laughed, but she had understood Korda's fear only too well.

Her mother had felt the same, she was sure, when they set out for Kenya. Had her parents supposed that whatever had gone wrong between them in London would be put right if only they traveled far enough away? It was under Nairobi's blazing equatorial sun that her father had finally been forced to confront both his incompetence as a farmer and businessman and the certifiable death of the marriage. To the end, he maintained that if they had moved farther on, to Rhodesia perhaps, or South Africa, the marriage might have survived, but it was only one of the many illusions with which he comforted himself when he had been drinking.

"A clean start," she remembered him saying buoyantly, standing amidst the piles of their belongings, as they were crated for shipment. He had a touching belief in clean starts, which Felicia had inherited, along with the inability to make them. She dreamed of going back to some mythical turning point when things had gone wrong, but the more she thought about it, the farther back it seemed to be. She had hoped to make a clean start with her marriage to Charles, and erase what had gone wrong when she came home to England to stay with Uncle Harry and his wife. When that had not worked, she determined to make a clean start when Portia was born and she became a mother. Becoming a successful young actress had seemed like a clean start for a time, and leaving Charles for Robby had been the sharpest break of all, the most dramatic way of finally starting clean—except that it, too, had been an illusion.

Dr. Vogel had urged on her the importance of getting her life under control, though he had no magic formula for doing it, but she saw her life as being too *much* controlled—controlled by the past, by her own mistakes, by Robby's, by her parents', a chain of errors, small and large, that she was unable to break.

She went out into the hallway, assuming that Robby was probably downstairs, brooding alone on the night's catastrophe. Like most big houses in Beverly Hills, theirs had been built with multiple living rooms. There was no center to it, no sense that there was one single room where a family might gather, no hearth at the heart of things. You made your way from one living room to the next until you were out the glass doors on the other side and standing by the pool. It was like walking through the lobby of a large hotel—so much so that she was sometimes surprised not to see total strangers sitting in the armchairs, reading the newspaper, or being paged by a bellboy. Was the impersonality of the house one of the things that was driving her crazy? Very likely, she told herself, calmly accepting the possibility that she was in fact *going* crazy.

She paused downstairs. The rooms were dimly lit and heavily mirrored. Large, unwieldy clumps of overstuffed furniture were reflected in the shadows. She had hated the house from the first moment they had set eyes on it, even though it was in the "right" part of Beverly Hills and had belonged to Aaron Diamond before he moved farther up into the hills to be closer to the important producers and farther away from his clients. There was too much shiny lacquer, too many surfaces with gold flecks embedded in glossy paint, *trompe l'oeil* and painted *faux*-everything wherever you looked, as if the decorator had been determined to prove that anything could be made to look like malachite, or marble, or lapis lazuli. She had no idea in which room Robby might be until she heard a murmur of voices and saw the glow of a single cigarette.

". . . laughingstock," she heard Robby whisper.

"What the hell, Robby, you're worth more than all of them put together."

She recognized Randy Brooks's voice, even though he was whispering too. Why whisper? she wondered. They surely must assume she was upstairs asleep. There was a curious intimacy to whispering—Robby himself always whispered to her when they were in bed together, even though there was nobody who could overhear them. She had always found that strange. She herself talked in a normal voice, laughed, cried out, when she made love, but Robby seemed to feel that he had to keep his voice low as if they were doing something illicit and dangerous.

Against all her better instincts she stood still and strained to listen, leaning against the bar.

"If Lisha hated me," she heard Robby say, "I'd understand why she did it. What makes it so bloody hard to live with is that she *loves* me."

"She's got a funny way of showing it, you don't mind my saying. Have you ever considered she might be nuts?"

"Nuts?"

"Crazy."

Robby drew on his cigarette, his profile emerging for a brief instant out of the dark in the red glow. He was seated on a sofa, facing away from her, so that she could see only the back of his head. Brooks sat close to him, one arm thrown over Robby's shoulder. "Oh, she's not 'nuts,' Randy, not at all."

"Then what's her problem?"

"I'm her problem."

"*You?* What have you done to her?"

"It's what I haven't done." Robby sighed. "Lisha is a very passionate woman, you see."

"What's wrong with that?"

There was a long silence. "It's been some time since we —slept together," Robby said.

"Hey, that happens."

Robby did not seem to be listening—it was as if he were talking to himself. "It's very odd," he said, "but sex never interested me much until I met Lisha. My father drummed it into us when we were children that sex was a bad, dangerous thing, and I suppose I believed him. Do you know, I didn't sleep with Penelope, my wife, until after we were married?"

She hadn't known that. She couldn't imagine why he was telling Brooks, of all people!

"Is that a fact?" Brooks asked warily, perhaps unprepared for this kind of intimate revelation. Lisha was unprepared for it herself—he'd never told *her*, and yet he was sharing this secret with Randy Brooks.

"Penelope thought it was peculiar, too," Robby went on. " 'It's not as if you're religious,' she told me. She was quite peeved. I mean, it was the twenties, you know, I was an actor, playing romantic leads, and doing very well at it. And here I was, behaving like a stuffy Victorian prig. It's not as if *she* was hesitant, either—she offered me every opportunity, damned near wouldn't marry me because of it."

"She had a point."

"I suppose she did. Then when we *did* finally sleep together, in Paris, on the way to Venice for our honeymoon, it wasn't much good for either of us. I don't know. I thought perhaps if I saved it up, you know, waited until we'd tied the knot, there'd be this marvelous explosion of passion between us, but it was really rather disappointing. Particularly for Penelope. She made it clear that I didn't come up to her expectations."

"That's too bad."

"When I was in acting school, old Elsie Donnell, the best teacher there ever was, always used to say to me, 'It's like sports, you see, you have to save all that up for the role.' It made perfectly good sense to me. I mean, sex is passion, energy, physical power, all of that, isn't it? And you have only so much, don't you? If you use it up in your personal relationships, it's gone, then you don't have enough left for your work. There's only so much passion *in* one, do you see? At some point, I think, I became actually *afraid* of passion, as if I were being sucked in, somehow—as if it was taking my strength. . . .'' He paused for a moment. "I thought my performance on stage was suffering," he said miserably. "I felt I had to make a choice."

Was *that* the explanation? She froze at the thought of what she had been deprived of over the years. Had he traded *their* lives for *his* work?

"I've never thought of sex that way," Brooks said doubtfully. Then, after a pause, he added, "It's *pleasure*, too, Robby."

"Yes, yes, of course it is," Robby said impatiently. "I'm not saying that Elsie was right, either, but the point is, I *believed* her. I still think there's some truth to it. Never mind," he said savagely, "it fucked up my marriage. Then I met Lisha, and everything changed. She was an actress, you see, a damned fine one, and she believed quite the opposite—love, sex, passion, acting, they were all the same to her, all *connected* in some way. It was sex at first sight, you know, between us, not love at all. I felt this dreadful guilt about what I was doing to Penelope—or not doing— and about getting between the sheets with another man's wife—quite a decent fellow, too, as I discovered later, not at all the pompous tyrant of a husband Lisha described to me, but then everyone lies about their spouse in a love affair. I couldn't resist her—didn't even *try* very hard to resist, now that I look back on it. I let it happen, and it was bloody wonderful."

"Well, that's good. . . ."

"I did things with Felicia that I would never have dreamed of doing with Penelope. She drew me in, somehow, made me understand for the first time what sex was about. I couldn't get enough of her, Randy, couldn't keep my hands off her. I could smell her on me in my dressing room when I was getting ready to go on, taste her on my lips, couldn't get her out of my mind even when I was onstage. . . . We used to hide away together in odd little hotels and inns, always afraid that a divorce detective might be following us. Fear, guilt, passion—what a time we had! And then, when we'd made a clean breast of it, what a relief. We could live together, act together, wake up in the morning knowing there were no explanations to invent. . . ."

"And then?"

"And then? I hardly know. Suddenly, we were no longer secret lovers—we were a famous couple. We weren't hiding away—we were displaying ourselves. And I began to think my work was suffering. Oh, not at first. On the contrary, at first I thought, she's right—all this sex *is* making me better onstage. I don't have to invent passion, I can *feel* it."

He laughed. "I gave some very sexy performances then, even in roles where nothing of the kind was called for. I remember poor Toby Eden complaining that I was playing Iago as if I were a dog trying to rub itself on Othello's leg! He was so embarrassed, Toby was, that he couldn't even look me in the eye onstage—he kept twisting his head around to avoid me. One of the critics wrote that he looked like a horse who'd seen something in the road he didn't like and was damned if he'd go near it. . . . But in the long run you can't build a role just on sex, can you? Nor a life. Felicia always wanted more of me than I was able to give."

Brooks's voice was so low that he hardly even sounded interested. Or was it an act? she wondered. Did he feel that the best way to keep Robby talking was not to argue or interrupt? "Women always do, Robby," he murmured softly. "It's the way they're made."

Felicia could hear herself breathing, surprised that Robby and Randy hadn't already noticed her. She felt a curious sense of detachment—was this what audiences felt?—along with a growing resentment that Robby was willing to share these intimacies with Randy Brooks. He hated talking about himself, always avoided it with her, yet here he was, chattering away with Randy about the very things that mattered most between himself and her. She remembered only too well the way he had drawn away from her gradually, becoming day by day—or rather, night by night—more remote. Robby had seemed to be almost frightened by what she had unleashed in him.

She had persuaded herself that it didn't matter, that their

love for each other was more important than sex, that their work together onstage would more than compensate for anything they had lost, but the hurt and resentment never left her, grew, in fact, until it began, somehow, to eat away at her life.

"Perhaps I don't know much about women. Sometimes I think I don't know much about anything, frankly, except the theatre. . . ."

He was silent for a long time, then he gave a deep sigh. "The worst of it is that I don't know if Lisha and I can ever act together again, the way we used to."

She felt her heart literally stop. She dug her nails into her palms, as if to will it back to life again.

"Why do you think that, Robby?"

"Vogel thinks it might be too much of a strain on her. I didn't like to say it to him, but I think it might be too much of a strain on *me*."

"Just because she screwed up in San Francisco?"

"No—though that's part of it. Because she expects too much out of me. I can see it in her eyes—I saw it there, on the balcony, in San Francisco, all that love, anger, need, whatever combination of emotions it is that she brings to me, and I realized that I was thinking about *her*, Felicia, not about Romeo. My mind wasn't on the part, you see—it was on her, and that's really why I fell." She heard a sound that might have been a sob.

The refrigerator began to hum noisily beside her, drowning out the conversation. She caught the words "Marty Quick's deal" and heard Brooks say, "You've got to be out of your mind, Robby." She did not pay much attention—her mind was not on deals or business. The refrigerator fell silent. What on earth was she doing, she wondered, living in a house that contained a real bar, with white leather bar stools, a sink, and a mirrored counter? She steadied herself against the bar and felt her hand touch the sharp, cold blade of a knife. It was a present to Robby from Aaron Diamond, one of those expensive handmade bar tools, shaped like a serrated dagger, with which the amateur bartender could slice lemons, open bottles, and crush ice, with a hilt made of staghorn. Robby never used it, never having mixed a cocktail in his life. She grasped it.

"I need the money, and that's that," Robby said.

She saw a flash of flame as Robby lit another cigarette, heard the clink of ice cubes as Randy Brooks sipped at his soft drink. How long had they been sitting here in the dark, exchanging intimacies?

"You shouldn't smoke so much, Robby," Brooks said gently. "It's bad for you." There was a curious tone to his voice, almost wifely in his concern.

"It's a bad habit, I know."

"The thing to do with bad habits, Robby, is to break them."

"My dear Randy, I admire your willpower, but I don't think giving up smoking or becoming a vegetarian will solve my problems."

"I guess not. You should take better care of yourself, that's all I'm saying. You worry all the time about taking care of Lisha. Try taking care of yourself for a change."

"Caring for Lisha—look what a mess I've made of that!" There was a note of agony in Robby's voice.

"Have you ever thought that maybe it's not all your fault? Everybody always worries about Lisha. Well, sure, why not? She's beautiful, she's fragile, she's talented, she's got problems. But you're a genius, Robby, the best. And I don't see anybody caring for *you*."

Brooks paused for a moment. "What I'm trying to say, see, is *I* care about Robby Vane. I worry about whether *you're* happy."

"I can't be happy if she's not."

"I don't buy that. If I sat around waiting for Natalie to be happy, I might as well be dead. Listen, you guys are a team, I understand that, and if Lisha ever pulls herself together again, you're a damned *good* team, the best. But you're also partners, rivals, you've got a whole history of who did what to whom, and who's to blame. Christ, it's hard enough to be a star without being *married* to one, as well. . . . Do what you have to do to help Lisha, but all I'm saying is don't

forget there's someone else who cares for you, very much."
He laughed mournfully. "Christ, why are these things so
hard to say?"

Felicia wanted to run back upstairs to her room, but she
stood rooted to the spot, afraid that if she moved she'd be
heard, unwilling to hear any more, but unable not to listen.
She tried to tell herself that she was imagining things—Robby
was only unburdening himself to a friend, Randy Brooks was
simply concerned. Neither of them had actually said anything
she didn't already know. . . . And yet, there was something
in their conversation, in the way they sat close together, that
made her stomach turn. She longed for Robby to express his
embarrassment and move farther away on the sofa, but he
did neither.

"I see," Robby said. "Or I *think* I do. But, my dear Randy,
I'm not . . ."

Brooks laughed mournfully. "I *know*. Jesus, we can't even
say it, can we? It isn't such a big deal, is it—I mean for you?
Let's face it, in England the theatre is full of it, isn't that so?
Look at Noel, or Binkie, or Guy Darling. . . ."

"Yes, or Philip Chagrin. I know. Frankly, though, that
seems to me rather different. There's no pretense, you see.
Philip *is* effeminate. He likes boys. Well, and grown men,
too. So do Noel, and Binkie, and Guy. They don't pretend
to be what they're not."

"This is a different world. A limp wrist is the kiss of death.
Look at Mark Strong."

"Mark Strong? But he's almost as much a man's man as
Gable. I thought he was well known for trying to get every
one of his leading ladies to go to bed with him? Lisha told
me he chased her around her hotel room when they were on
location. His wrist seems to be quite the opposite of limp."

"Mark makes a play for his leading ladies, that's true, but
that's mostly for show."

"I hadn't realized."

"Who's to realize? He's a big star. All he has to do is be
careful."

"Quite. But I've nothing to be careful *about*, Randy."

"I'm just saying that these things can be handled, Robby,

that there are ways. . . . Oh, shit, what I'm *trying* to say is
that I love you."

She waited for Robby to stand up and walk out of the
room, or to hit Randy, or to point out that the only person
he loved was her, but nothing of the sort happened. Instead,
in the dim light, she could see Randy turn and gently give
Robby a kiss.

It was as if a trapdoor onstage had opened before her and,
instead of an actor dressed as Mephistopheles, had revealed
the fires of hell, with the damned squirming in the flames at
her feet, beckoning her to take her place among them. That
Randy Brooks, beloved comedian, America's Pied Piper, and
model husband, was a homosexual, and that Robby could sit
there calmly and let himself be seduced like a stagestruck
ingenue in a star's dressing room, struck her as so improbable
that she would not, she *could* not, accept it!

She backed away to the stairs, unwilling to hear more—
but stopped when she heard Robby say, very quietly, "Thank
you, Randy."

"I was afraid you would be angry—scared shitless, to tell
you the truth. But I meant it, and I guess I'll *always* mean
it. Maybe someday you will, too, I hope so. But it doesn't
make any difference in the way I feel."

She grasped the banister, surprised that it felt as cold as
dry ice, so cold that for a moment it seemed to her her hand
was burning.

Then she stumbled upstairs, choking on her own bile,
hardly even conscious that she had reached the brightly lit
bathroom. She looked in the mirror and saw the face of a
madwoman staring back at her, the eyes wild and staring,
the mouth open as if she were struggling for breath, tears
streaming down her cheeks. And yet she felt perfectly calm,
almost detached, as if she were part of the audience, not a
player. One part of her mind tried to make reasonable plans:
She would leave Robby, call Aaron Diamond first thing in
the morning, pull every string she could to get air passage
back to England. . . .

She could picture exactly where her passport was, remember Aaron's telephone number, decide what she would pack

and what she would have to leave behind. In a week, with any luck, she would be home, she calculated—a day and a night to fly from Los Angeles to New York, an overnight stay at the St. Regis Hotel, then the long haul across the Atlantic on the Pan American Clipper flying boat, via Florida, Cuba, Brazil, the Azores and Lisbon. . . .

She had always insisted on crossing the country by train and the Atlantic by ship, but this time she would master her fear and fly—away from here, away from Robby.

She hardly even noticed her fingers opening the bottles in the medicine chest. She took a handful of pills at random and swallowed them, gagging as they went down. She poured out another handful and paused to admire their cheerful colors —the big bright pink capsules that were for sleeping, the little pale blue pills that were supposed to calm her nerves, the green heart-shaped ones that Marty Quick had given her to keep awake and alert, the white-and-blue ones for pain that she took whenever she had a problem with a tooth or a headache, so as not to be distracted while she was working, the yellow ones that Natalie had given her to help when she had a difficult period. . . .

She poured herself a glass of water and took them all, sipping the water to help them down; then she walked back into the bedroom, opened her desk drawer and took out a half-pint bottle of vodka. Dr. Vogel had been adamant about keeping liquor where it belonged, in the bar downstairs, on the theory that the farther you had to walk for a drink, the more time you had to think twice about having one. She, however, preferred to set herself a challenge: the liquor was only a few steps away from her bed, and she had forced herself not to touch it, an exercise in discipline and willpower.

She had succeeded so far, but tonight there was no point in denying herself. She splashed a drink into the toothbrush glass, paused to look at it, made it a strong double, and downed it in a long, breathless, steady gulp. She took a cigarette from the silver box on the desk, then noticed the inscription from Randy and Natalie Brooks. She saw, to her surprise, the knife from the bar downstairs, Aaron Diamond's expensive and inappropriate "housewarming" present. She didn't remember bringing it upstairs with her. She picked it up and, with painstaking care, tried to scratch out Randy's name, gouging deeply into the silver.

It was harder to do than she had imagined—she worked away at the box for what seemed like a very long time, doing considerable damage, but Randy's name was still visible. It suddenly seemed the most important task of her life to efface his name from the lid of the box. She dug the point of the knife harder into the metal until it slipped, carving a deep cut in her left hand, at the base of the thumb.

It was remarkable, she thought, how much blood the cut produced. Before she even felt any pain, the bleeding had spread everywhere. There was blood on the box, on the knife, on her dressing gown, on the floor. She dabbed at it with a tissue, and the tissue turned bright red.

She decided that she would have to bandage her hand and stood up to go to the bathroom and deal with it.

Her legs felt so weak that for a moment she wondered if she was bleeding to death, but that was foolish, she told herself—you don't bleed to death from a cut on the hand. She seemed to have no control over her feet, which felt as heavy as if she wore a deep-sea diver's lead boots. *"Full fathom five thy father lies/Of his bones are coral made,"* she sang, suddenly picturing herself walking along the sea bottom, not clumsily, but gracefully, the white sand spurting up in clouds with each step she took, the sunlight, flickering through the coral reef and gently waving seaweed fronds, illuminating the brilliant, glimmering colors of the tiny fish that swam around her, pink and blue and green and white, by some odd coincidence exactly the same colors as the pills she had admired in her hand.

She wondered vaguely why she was there, her only experience of reefs having been a brief look at one from a glass-bottomed boat at Catalina during a weekend cruise on Leo Stone's yacht, on which she had been seasick for forty-eight uninterrupted and hideous hours.

She hated the sea almost as much as she hated the air. She thought of Robby, wheeling and soaring in the air as he practiced his flying, cleaving through clouds, climbing toward the sun. . . .

Did Randy Brooks accompany him? she wondered. If she had shown more interest, gone to see him take off or land, perhaps even flown with him, would he have been grateful? Or was his flying just an excuse to escape from her, the equivalent of the polo and golf lessons which filled the weekends of people like Si Krieger so they could spend a few hours in the Beverly Wilshire hotel with some slut like Virginia Glad—except that in Robby's case it would be an excuse to be with Randy Brooks.

She felt a kind of fierce stabbing in her stomach, as if she had been knifed, but then it stopped and she felt nothing at all, which was more frightening. She realized dimly that she was no longer standing up but lying on the peach-colored wall-to-wall carpeting, splattered now with blood. She felt a fleeting moment of guilt, then decided the carpet would be cleaned or replaced. She hated the color anyway.

She closed her eyes. She saw Robby, his face blackened —it took her a moment to realize that he was made up for *Othello*—leaning over her, a frown on his face, his eyes bright against the black face paint. *"I that am cruel and yet merciful,"* she heard him say, *"I would not have thee linger in thy pain."*

She had no wish to linger in it herself. With a sigh, she let herself drift into sleep, arching her neck, to kiss him for the last time, as he ended her life. . . .

ACT TWO
The Prince of Darkness
Is a Gentleman
1942

7

"Five minutes, please!"

Robert Vane kept staring into the mirror, as if he hadn't heard the call. No need to hurry, he told himself. Shakespeare always gave his leading man a moment or two to prepare his entrance, perhaps because he was an actor himself.

Of course, there were exceptions. In *Richard III*, you had to stand there in the wings, waiting to go on as soon as the curtain rose, with no prologue, no pause while other players warmed the audience up, no time to get the feel of the house. Willy-boy wouldn't have written it that way for himself, Vane decided. He must have been angry with his friend Burbage and thought to himself, "There, go on cold, old man, before the audience has settled down, and see how you like *that*!"

This is no time to be thinking of other plays, he warned himself firmly. In a few minutes he would be Antony, another of Shakespeare's heroes who comes to grief because of a woman. Strange, Vane thought, that so many of them—Othello, Romeo, Macbeth, Antony—were undone by love. Well, no use brooding on that, either. Acting is like flying a plane—you have to keep your mind on what you are doing all the time. Let it wander, and you are done for.

It was that discipline that had kept him alive—and sane—during the year he had flown in the Royal Air Force. He had concentrated fiercely on the instruments and controls, forcing himself not to think about Lisha, Randy, or anything else in the past and, more problematically, the future.

What would Shakespeare—or Marc Antony—have said about taking off in a lumbering bomber, night after night, weather permitting, to trundle at a bumpy snail's pace above Germany, dropping bundles of propaganda leaflets, while gunners poured flak into the sky? It had all the glamour of driving a bus through a mine field, and the only thing that made the sheer terror of it bearable was the fact that it numbed the mind. Ten years older than most of the crew, and famous as an actor, he had felt obliged to set an example of steadiness and lack of nerves, with the result that he was awarded a Distinguished Flying Cross. The news of his decoration had finally silenced all those who had criticized him for sitting in Los Angeles while London was blitzed, and apparently had caught the attention of Mr. Churchill, who promptly gave orders to get England's more distinguished actors out of uniform and back onstage. "We can replace pilots a bloody sight more easily than we can good actors," he was reported to have told the Minister of Information, and within twenty-four hours, Vane, Toby Eden, and half a dozen other distinguished tragedians were back in civilian clothes again.

Vane had been invited to lunch at Chequers by the Prime Minister to be congratulated on his medal and given his new marching orders. "Give the people Shakespeare!" Churchill growled across the luncheon table. "It's far better propaganda than anything that bloody little dwarf Goebbels can devise!" He scowled at Vane, gesturing with the cigar that came from Marty Quick's Cuban plantation. "And pray bring Miss Lisle back from New York, if she's well enough. I should like to see the two of you together again—in *Antony and Cleopatra*, for example."

Vane had wondered then—still wondered—how much the Prime Minister knew about their problems, but the luncheon table at Chequers was hardly the place to discuss his personal difficulties, or Felicia's state of mind. Shortly thereafter, strings had been pulled and arrangements made. Felicia, who had been languishing for months at Payne Whitney Psychiatric Institute in New York, was given a stateroom on the *Queen Mary*, a privilege normally reserved for ministers of state now that the *Queen* had become a troop ship; workmen and materials were found to restore the old Prince of Wales Theatre after its bomb damage; stagehands and actors were dug out of barracks, training camps, and regimental depots all over England and swiftly demobilized; set designers who had been interned as enemy aliens were released. Nothing was to be allowed to stand in the way of a brilliant new season of Shakespeare.

Vane was alone. Some actors liked the company of their dressers, if only to keep them on schedule, but Vane's sense of timing was so acute that he didn't even need a watch. His dressing room was near the stage, and really a nice little suite, with pleasant, worn old furniture. Felicia had a more glamorous dressing room, but it was farther away, up two flights of stairs at the back of the theatre. He could hear the sound of the audience now, taking their seats, coughing, talking, a low background murmur to his thoughts.

In the old days, the great actor-managers liked to be close enough to the stage to count the house. He had no need to do that—the theatre was full—but he liked the feeling that he was separated from his public only by a few feet, that they were out there, just the other side of the wall, making themselves comfortable, the women straightening their girdles and getting their handkerchiefs ready for a good cry, the men pulling their trousers up at the knee to save the crease, unbuttoning their jackets, polishing their glasses. In his mind's eye Vane could see them, wearier and less elegant than a peacetime audience—nobody dressed for the theatre now, and many, of course, were in uniform—eager to forget about the war for a few hours, hoping, as he was, that the performance wouldn't be interrupted.

The noise of the audience began to subside. In three minutes he would be onstage. "The secret to Antony," Philip Chagrin had told him at the beginning of rehearsals, "is that the poor fellow needs to be loved. Caesar loved him. Now Caesar's dead, and Antony misses him so much that he goes and sacrifices the whole bloody world for one good fuck.''

Of course Philip *would* take that view, Vane thought. Besides, the relationship between Antony and Caesar would naturally interest him more than that between Antony and Cleopatra!

It had cost Vane innumerable hours of persuasion and flattery to get Philip Chagrin to direct an *Antony and Cleopatra* in which his arch-rival would star, but in the end it was because of Felicia, who was as close to being Chagrin's protégée as any woman could be, that Chagrin gave in—that and the fact that the assignment was presented to him as his patriotic duty.

Vane gave himself one last look in the mirror with the calm, objective concentration of a pilot performing his pre-flight instrument check. Most people, he knew, found him fairly handsome, but to him his face merely presented a number of difficult acting problems. There was a certain weakness to his nose, for example. It lacked *character*, and he therefore experimented with it constantly. For Antony, he had built it up, given it a sharper, more prominent edge, very Roman in feel. He had made it an aristocratic nose, ever so slightly bent, as if it had been broken, perhaps in some manly sport, an upper-class rugby player's nose, had Antony been an Englishman.

He was not happy about his eyes, either. For Antony, Vane had given himself thicker eyebrows and used plenty of black mascara to make his eyes stand out more, but he was still not completely satisfied.

There was more to building a character than such small details, but he always had to have someone in mind as a model before he began. He had wasted weeks trying to find the right face for his Antony, before Chagrin, with whom he was lunching at the Garrick, suddenly flicked his eyes toward a bulky, well-dressed man at the bar and hissed, "*There's* your Antony, dear boy! Ready-made for you."

Vane had instantly recognized the man—Sir Jock Campbell was one of England's most famous sportsmen, wealthy, frequently married, a World War One fighter ace who had spent the years between the wars setting speed records in airplanes, speedboats, and cars. There was no immediate physical link to Marc Antony that Vane could imagine, and yet Chagrin was right. Campbell was still a powerful, handsome man, but as Vane looked carefully he could see the first signs of age and self-doubt eating away at him, the puffiness under the eyes of the steady drinker, the hair carefully—too carefully—combed, to hide the fact that it was beginning to recede, the deep-set haunted eyes of a man who has risked his life once too often.

Of course Antony was still a fighter, a general, but the key to his character was there in Jock Campbell. Vane had seen then and there exactly how he could play Antony as the glamour-boy hero who had followed Caesar to glory, "the edge to Caesar's sword," only to become a guilty, reluctant, middle-aged voluptuary, head over heels in love with a woman who had already slept with practically everyone of importance in the Mediterranean world.

Lost in his thoughts, Vane stared at himself without seeing anything, as if the mirror had turned opaque. It was impossible to think of Cleopatra without thinking about Felicia, who "identified," as Americans were so fond of saying, with the role completely. For months her suicide attempt had haunted him, until guilt seemed like a permanent condition, but eventually the sheer terror of operational flying made it seem irrelevant. If there were any dues to be paid, he had paid them, or written them off as unpayable somewhere in the night sky over Germany, and he had reached the conclusion that he had nothing, really, to be ashamed of—Felicia had been suicidal *before* he met Randy Brooks. As for Randy, Vane put the Atlantic Ocean, not to speak of North America, between them. War made it easy to forget the past—that part of it which he *wanted* to forget—but it took no time at all to realize that Felicia hadn't forgotten a bit of it, however well she hid the fact.

Since her return to England a month ago, apparently "cured" at Payne Whitney (of what, she never specified), Lisha's passions had been fiercely aroused, and he had felt obliged to respond to them. Perhaps, like Marc Antony, his status as a decorated war hero stimulated her, or perhaps it was simply her way of making a new beginning. Whatever the reason, the nervous, fragile creature he had left in America had returned home every bit as passionate and determined to seduce as Cleopatra. And, like Antony, he had succumbed.

A year of sustained terror and celibacy—it was extraordinary how easy it was to remain celibate when you expected each night to be your last—had had a remarkable effect on what Lisha, fresh from the daily self-examination of psychotherapy, called his "libido." They had spent the first week after their long separation in bed together in the Oliver Messel suite of the Savoy Hotel, hardly even hearing the air-raid sirens. Oh, he could play Antony, all right! He understood what it was like to wallow in sensuality while the world burned. *"I am dying, Egypt,"* he had cried out in the huge, silver-gilt bed, but Lisha had stopped his mouth with a kiss and whispered, "Not yet—not until I'm through with you, darling. . . ."

He stood and glanced at his legs in the full-length mirror. In tights, they had always seemed to him too spindly (though not nearly as spindly as poor Chagrin's shanks), and for most roles he went to great trouble and expense to have Bernett's, the costume makers in Covent Garden, fashion special padding for his calves. For Antony, of course, that was no use —Antony strode barelegged, wearing only the short leather skirt and tunic of a Roman general, so Vane had set himself a rigorous schedule of exercise, had sweated away daily at a gym off Jermyn Street under the supervision of a former army PT instructor, to build up his muscles for the role. Now his thighs and calves bulged when he moved. He flexed his leg muscles and decided they were worth every painful moment of hard work.

It was the little touches that mattered in acting. Shaving your legs made tights fit better. But in a role like Antony, it paid not only to shave your legs, but your arms and your chest as well, after which Vane rubbed himself down with a mixture of olive oil and iodine to give the smooth skin a glossy, bronzed appearance. He had picked up that trick from observing women sunbathing on the beach in the South of France.

There was a knock at the door. He lifted an eyebrow. Not many people would dare to disturb a leading man about to make his entrance. He was ready to tell whoever it was to bugger off when it occurred to him, with a sinking feeling in the pit of his stomach, that Felicia might be in trouble. "Come in!" he shouted anxiously.

The door opened to reveal Toby Eden, splendidly robed as Enobarbus, Antony's long-suffering friend. Toby's face was darkened with Leichtner's #5, to suggest a Roman complexion. For reasons of his own he had elected to dress in what looked like a floor-length, multicolored velvet dressing gown, perhaps to indicate that Enobarbus, like his master, was going to pot under the African sun. The effect was striking, and only slightly spoiled by the fact that he was smoking a large meerschaum pipe. "Everything all right, old boy?" he asked cozily.

"Of *course* it is, for God's sake, Toby!"

"Ah." Eden produced a pungent fog bank of smoke. He habitually smoked a mixture of his own so strong that even hardened cigar smokers complained when he lit up in restaurants. "Bang on! As you air force chaps say."

"Toby, I'm about to go on, if you don't mind."

Eden blushed beneath the greasepaint. "Oh, dear chap, I *am* sorry. Concentration. Order. Discipline. That's the ticket, quite right! I only stopped by to give you a message from the divine Felicia, since her dressing room's next to mine. And too bloody far from the stage, if you don't mind my saying."

"Oh, Jesus! What's the matter with her, Toby?" He closed his eyes, trying to imagine how he would explain to the opening-night audience that Felicia Lisle would be replaced by her understudy. For the theatrical event of the season, with a full house, the Prime Minister and Mrs. Churchill in the management's box—and in the Royal Box the Marquess of Dumfries, whose task it was to report back to their Majesties whether they should see the play or not, since royalty, by tradition, never attended opening nights.

Eden waved the smoke away from his face. "Damned stuffy in here," he said. "Actually, Lish seemed in fine fettle to me."

"What was the bloody message?"

"Not to worry about her. Her exact words, old boy."

Vane shook his head dubiously. He felt again the full weight of Felicia's return, the endless rehearsals, and the expectations of what sometimes seemed to be half the population of the United Kingdom. Their return to the stage as a couple was headline news, all the more so since it was preceded by rumors about Felicia's health and what had led to her breakdown in America. He felt a certain foreboding. With Lisha, optimism was usually followed by a catastrophe. If she suddenly felt it necessary to send Toby Eden to his dressing room with the news that there was nothing to worry about, then it followed there surely *was*.

"Glad to have put your mind at rest," Toby said, beaming. "A full house! They sound excited, too. Always a good sign." Toby cocked his head, listening to the sound beyond the wall.

Vane heard it, too, the last stir of latecomers sitting down, the rustle of programs, a few coughs from people clearing their throats before the curtain went up. Less than a minute to go. Toby Eden's presence was oddly comforting, even with his noxious pipe and his eccentric costume. "Yes, Toby," he said, "a good sign, indeed. Does Lish *really* seem all right?"

Toby's eyes were alarmingly shrewd, even when he was playing the idiot. "My dear Robby," he said, "she may be as mad as a hatter, I couldn't say, but if what you mean is whether she's suffering from stage fright, the answer is no. God bless you, my boy."

He held up both hands in blessing, looking positively patriarchal in his robe. It occurred to Vane to wonder if Toby knew what role he was playing. He sometimes got mixed up, and had been known to appear onstage firmly playing the wrong part, as if the rest of the cast were obstinately in error.

Vane sniffed suddenly. Like most actors, he was acutely sensitive to the possibility of fire, perhaps out of some inherited, collective memory of wooden theatres, canvas tents, smoldering torches, and burning candles. "Oh, Christ!" he cried. "Fire!" Then he stared at Eden's robe, on which, at about the level of his stomach, a small patch about the size of a half crown was turning brown. As he looked, the color darkened, the edges of the patch turned bright red, and a wisp of smoke rose from an area close to Eden's private parts. "Don't look now, Toby," Vane said, "but I think your balls are on fire."

Eden looked down in horror, grabbed the pipe, which he had stuffed carelessly into his costume, and leaped into the corridor, shouting for water. Vane went back to his mirror, laughing like a madman, until his lungs ached.

"Beginners, please!" He heard the shout and put everything else out of his mind to concentrate on Antony. He had to get his walk right, or all the rest was worth nothing.

He knew exactly how to do it, he told himself, had rehearsed Antony's walk to death, in fact. It would be at once athletic and military, almost a march, perhaps a little stiff from old wounds and too many nights of sleeping on the ground wrapped in his cloak.

Vane checked to make sure his sword was free in its scabbard, the dagger secure in his belt. His weapons were always the real thing, not blunt or flimsy props. He fenced three times a week with an instructor and insisted that his stage weapons be genuine. Granted, there were occasional accidents in which blood was drawn, but he wanted stage fights that *frightened* the audience, gave them a whiff of fear, danger, death. He drew the dagger partway, tested its edge with his thumb, felt the keenness, slipped it back into its sheath, satisfied—just as Antony would doubtless have done, the old soldier, before walking out of the palace into the bright Egyptian sun. . . .

There was a knock on the door. *"Now,* sir!" his dresser said, but Vane was already moving without haste. He opened the door, passed the dresser as if he were invisible, and made his way slowly down the metal stairs, listening to the creak of the ropes and pulleys as the curtain slowly rose.

He moved at a sedate pace, looking at no one, not even

Felicia. The stagehands moved away as he approached them, giving him space as they might to a blind man, so as not to disturb his concentration. He stopped exactly on the mark, pausing to let his eyes adjust to the glare of the stage lights beyond him.

This was his moment, the moment he always dreaded. He stood alone in the shadows, sheltered behind the rough lumber and canvas of the scenery, eyes fixed on the bright edge of the stage, absolutely certain that he had forgotten his lines. Desperately, as if in a nightmare, he tried to remember them, but it was no good—they were gone, erased from his memory, unreachable. His stomach ached with an insistent cramp, his bladder felt agonizingly full. He should have peed before leaving his dressing room! He could feel sweat drenching his clothes, although it was cold backstage. His muscles were tensed for flight, like those of an animal that scents danger, but he stood rooted to the spot, too frightened to move.

He heard Philo speaking of Antony's dotage, giving the audience a subordinate officer's damning judgment of his general's unseemly behavior.

Then the flourish of trumpets sounded. He felt, rather than saw, Felicia beside him, took her arm, came to the realization that he had been standing here surrounded by the large (and expensive) retinue that was to accompany them onstage.

Ahead of them were four young women in scanty costumes ("just to shake up the old dears in the audience," Philip Chagrin had said), then several men in blackface, gold turbans, and bright Oriental costumes as Cleopatra's eunuchs ("which I believe they *are*," Philip complained, having apparently failed to persuade any of them to go to bed with him).

Vane stepped out into the glaring brightness without hearing the applause from the audience, feeling only the immense animal rush of heat that always rolled across the stage from a thousand bodies breathing and sweating in their seats.

Out of the corner of his eye he could see Lisha looking up at him, her huge, dark eyes made larger with makeup, a teasing, flirtatious smile on her face, as if she were saying to the assembled courtiers and Antony's own officers, "He's just come straight from my bed.'' She had to perfection the look that appears on a woman's face when she has slept with her lover—an expression which nobody did better than Lisha onstage, or in real life. When they had been secret lovers, he had sweated buckets whenever Lisha smiled at him in public, for it was like a clear-cut admission of guilt.

He was sweating buckets now under the oil and grease-paint, marching stiffly toward center stage in his splendid uniform and gilt laurel wreath, affecting to ignore the teasing attentions of the woman beside him—for Antony was a Roman—dignity was important to him, as well as to his followers. However much it might appeal to his vanity to have the beautiful queen beside him, he would still have wanted to keep up appearances, despite her kittenish behavior.

He made his way downstage, his lines still a blank in his mind. He felt like a man whose tumbril has been held up by a road block on his way to the guillotine. He wished the eunuchs would keep on fanning and the girls dancing—anything to delay the inevitable moment when he must open his mouth. . . .

Philo was still speaking of his commander-in-chief:

> *"Look where they come,*
> *Take but good note, and you shall see in him*
> *The triple pillar of the world transformed*
> *Into a strumpet's fool."*

Then he heard Felicia's voice ring out in the theatre, her diction as sharp and precise as Philip Chagrin's, her tone at once commanding queenlike and playfully sensual: *"If it be love indeed, tell me how much."*

Was there ever a woman who had not asked that question? Without any conscious thought, he heard himself answer, *"There's beggary in the love that can be reckoned,"* and quite suddenly his vision cleared, the sweat stopped running down his body and face, his entire part was sharply etched in his mind.

He did not look at the audience. He could hardly help

seeing them, but the real world was here onstage, where he was Antony, showing off for his demanding new conquest by dismissing Caesar's messenger rudely, while his staff officers stood around with glum faces.

He turned to face her, taking her in his arms, so that their eyes met, and he felt an instant surge of love—and with it, a moment of confusion. He was *supposed* to feel love, of course—Antony's for Cleopatra. He couldn't give a decent performance as Antony unless he genuinely felt what Antony must feel. To be really on track there could be no gap, no seam, between himself and the character. He had to *be* Antony, his everyday, ordinary self disappearing completely. . . .

But he could never achieve that feeling when he was onstage with Felicia, never had. People rhapsodized about how wonderful the two of them were together—playgoers, at any rate, if not always the more serious critics—but he had always felt that the closeness between them in real life worked against them onstage. There were lines—harmless between strangers—that were painfully hard for him to speak to Lisha, scenes that he dreaded, plays that he avoided even thinking about. Was the love he felt now Antony's for Cleopatra or his own for Felicia? Whatever it was, he was moved by such an extraordinary rush of passion that his voice almost broke as he spoke Antony's lines, his face only inches away from hers as she looked up at him in desire, his hands on her shoulders: *"There's not a minute of our lives should stretch/ without some pleasure now. . . ."*

He could see in her eyes that peculiar combination of excitement and panic that always made him uneasy. Lisha worked at the edge of herself, as daring as a swimmer whose pleasure comes from venturing so far out to sea that there is always an element of doubt about whether she can get back to the beach. Her powerful emotions were exactly what made her the superb actress she was, but they could also get her into technical difficulties, or even lead her to lose her hold on the part altogether.

How strong was she? It was the question he and Philip Chagrin had asked each other over and over again during the rehearsals. Would she "last the course," as Philip put it, slipping into the language of the racetrack, which was only natural for a man who never let a day go by without making a bet. "If you want to win, you must always save something for the finish," Chagrin was fond of saying—though in Vane's opinion, Chagrin saved too much, skimped on the beginning and the middle. Chagrin, in turn, usually complained that Vane's performances were risky, while Felicia's truly horrified him, as if he expected her to burn out at any moment like a shooting star—a fear which Vane felt now, looking at her glittering eyes. He could see something building there, but what? Was it the same panic that had stopped her dead in San Francisco? Or was she preparing some other kind of humiliation for him?

He plunged on with his lines, speeding up a little, suddenly longing for the moment when Toby Eden, hopefully not still in flames, would appear as the disapproving Enobarbus, with that stately walk of his, like that of a blind man advancing across the floor of an unfamiliar room.

The look of panic was unmistakable on Felicia's face now, and he could feel her trembling in his hands. Damn her! he thought. She had destroyed their joint reputation in one country, now she was about to do it in another. He grasped her shoulders so hard that he could see her wince in pain, warning her with his eyes not to ruin her first scene. She had only one more line to say: *"Hear the ambassadors."* Surely she could manage that! *Say* it, he prayed, for your own sake, if not for mine.

She was a beat or two late, but nothing that couldn't be retrieved. He mouthed the line, but she wasn't paying attention. Her mind was elsewhere, her eyes dilated with terror. Then he heard it—the high-pitched wail of the air-raid sirens, starting far away, on the outskirts of London, and growing louder and louder as sirens nearer to the theatre picked up the warning.

People said that if you lived with the noise long enough, you got used to it, even grew indifferent. He was used to it by now, but it still gave him a start, like an electric wire touching a raw nerve. He had watched whole rows of Regency houses fall into the street, had seen the old Savoy Theatre after it had been hit, reduced to a pile of blazing rubble that filled the Strand. A theatre was no place to be when the bombs started to fall—not that any place was safe, including the shelters, of which, like most airmen, he had a horror.

Of course, Lisha would be petrified! Since she had come back, the raids had slackened off—most of the Führer's air force was in Russia now. Lisha wasn't used to the noise of an air raid yet, nor to standing onstage waiting for a bomb to come hurtling down through the flies, the ultimate *coup de théâtre*.

Regulations called for the performance to cease while everybody sought shelter. He could feel the audience stirring, distracted—as well they might be. In the wings he could see Philip Chagrin and Toby Eden shrugging to indicate that they were helpless—the play would have to stop, for the moment.

In the distance, no louder than a cough, he heard the muffled noise of an explosion, followed by the sharper crack of antiaircraft guns. There was a faint buzzing sound, growing louder, a steady, rumbling, vibrating beat that made the chandeliers tinkle and set the teeth on edge. Vane recognized the sound of the bombers' engines. Only a month ago Germans had been listening to the same sound from *his* aircraft as he sweated his way across the sky, eyes fixed on his instruments. No doubt some poor German bugger was up there right now doing the same, though it was surely not propaganda leaflets the German was preparing to release. . . .

Chagrin was waving at him in earnest now, while Toby Eden pointed skyward majestically. Stop the play? All right, he would stop it, if only to take Lisha to safety, for she was shaking violently, pulling herself away from him. But before he could stop her, she ran, not toward the wings but toward the audience.

Oh, for God's sake, he thought, don't break down in front of the audience, not in full view, not with Winston Churchill looking on! If there was one thing the British wartime public would never forgive, it was a public display of panic in an air raid.

He gathered his cloak around him and went after her, but

before he could brush past the eunuchs and dancing girls to the footlights, Felicia was standing in their full glare, arms upraised. He could see her silhouetted, her trim figure clearly outlined, for her robe was very nearly diaphanous.

He felt a sudden peace come over him, as was often the case in a crisis. Whatever was going to happen, it was too late for him to stop it. If he was going to be humiliated, so be it. He stood behind her and placed one hand on her shoulder, reduced for the moment to a supporting player.

Now that the play had been interrupted, he saw the audience clearly for the first time. In the sea of faces before her, he could discern no sign of panic, though many people had gathered their hats and coats in their arms, as if they were ready to make a dash for the doors. At the sides of the theatre, people were beginning to stand and leave, but in an orderly fashion. To his left, looking up, he saw the Prime Minister and his party in their box, firmly seated. How many of the audience were in uniform! he thought.

The noise of the air raid was constant now, and each explosion sent small showers of plaster dust down from the ceiling, while the stage lights flickered and the chandeliers swayed back and forth alarmingly. Yet as long as Felicia Lisle stood there at the edge of the stage, arms upraised as if she were commanding them to silence, nobody in the audience was going to move. Even those who had stood up were motionless, eyes fixed on the stage.

He knew what an impressive spectacle she must be presenting from the other side of the footlights in her gleaming white pleated dress belted at the waist with gold chains. On her upraised arms she wore heavy gold bangles. The hair of her black wig was shaped in wings that emphasized her high, curving cheekbones, and on her head she wore a fantastic crown shaped like the wings of a falcon, encircled by a golden asp's head that rose above her forehead, its green eyes glittering in the stage light.

She had given herself a darker complexion, with pale white lips and fantastically exaggerated eyes. The effect was not only exotic but barbarically sensual. For Cleopatra, Felicia had let her imagination run wild—had painted on eyebrows that flared out almost to her ears, used bright green mascara on her eyelids, reveling in a role that called for a sexuality almost unique in the classical theatre.

"Ladies and gentlemen," she called out, "you have come here to see us play *Antony and Cleopatra*. Our performance has been rudely interrupted by Herr Hitler, and it may be that it is our duty to stop and take shelter. For those of you who wish to do so, we will pause, while you obey, quite properly, the law. But *I* have come here to play Cleopatra tonight, and that is what I intend to do. Mr. Vane and I will return, Mr. Hodge"—she turned and smiled at the actor who played Philo—"will repeat his speech, and we will proceed with the play. I have not come home only to let the bloody Germans interrupt my return to the stage."

There was a moment of silence. Vane waited for someone in the audience to say that clearing the theatre in an air raid was a government regulation, not a question of choice, or a patriotic gesture, but nobody did. He could see the Prime Minister nod his approval, then gradually, all over the theatre, people looked around to see if anybody was leaving, and since nobody was, settled back in their seats quietly.

He took her hand. "You're bloody mad," he whispered.

She nodded. "Yes, darling," she said, "but isn't it *marvelous* theatre?"

Of course she *was* mad, there was no doubt about it! She had taken matters into her own hands without even stopping to think that she was gambling with the lives of the cast, the stagehands, and the audience. Yet he understood exactly what was going on in her mind. Tonight she *was* Cleopatra, the queen whose courage far exceeded Antony's (he was merely rash), or Caesar's caution. Cleopatra never allowed anything to stand in the way of what she wanted, not even the fear of death. Felicia needed her own moment of heroism and had not hesitated to seize it. He bent his head and kissed her, then taking her by the hand, led her back to the wings and waited, while poor Hodge, who would perhaps have preferred to take shelter, composed himself, and while the eunuchs and dancing girls took their places again.

The noise overhead seemed to him less now, but it was

possible that Lisha had simply taken his mind off the air raid.
He had always thought of her as someone who needed to be
protected—not that he had done much of a job of it—but he
had caught in her gesture at the footlights just the kind of
reckless courage that made Cleopatra stronger than her enemies, the kind of mad, single-minded courage with which
Lady Macbeth shamed her husband into murder, and that
Juliet showed in her devotion to Romeo. He had known
Felicia for ten years, and suddenly felt that he didn't know
her at all. If she had managed to conceal her courage from
him for so long, what else had she concealed, or had he
misunderstood?

He took her arm as Philo finished his speech, noticing in
some clear, professional corner of his mind that Hodge was
making a better job of it the second time, and felt Felicia
squeeze his hand as they moved forward to repeat their entrance. "Robby, darling," she whispered to him, "I don't
suppose Randy Brooks would have had the balls to do that,
do you?"

It was the first time she had mentioned the name since her
return. He broke into a cold sweat as they advanced into the
glare of the lights and paused to accept a burst of applause
so thunderous that it drowned out the noise of the bombs and
the guns.

8

It was what she lived for, this moment, worth all the hard
work, the anxiety, the moments of fear and terror that every
actress felt from time to time onstage. Applause was an ad-
diction, like any other—the more you received, the more you
wanted—but each time she went onstage, there was always
the fear that *this* time, this once, they wouldn't applaud, and
the relief, like nothing else in the world, when they did. . . .

She sat in her dressing room, holding court, just as she

had in the old days before the war, before Hollywood, surrounded by familiar faces. Her dressing room was the center
of her world, and unlike Robby, she had lavished attention
on hers. She had insisted, even in wartime, on having the
walls repainted, the furniture recovered in bright chintzes,
even a fine Oriental carpet. There were flowers everywhere
—flowers from Guy Darling, from Binkie, from dear Willy,
from Noel (who had also sent a case of champagne), flowers
from members of the Royal Family, flowers from total
strangers. It was as if everyone who had criticized her for
being in California during the blitz, for leaving the theatre
to become a movie star, for making Robby's life miserable,
wanted to apologize now that she was back. She had thanked
them by giving them a triumph. Whatever the critics would
write, she knew a triumph when she saw one!

Ever since her return to England, she had lived in a whirl
of activity so frenzied that it seemed to frighten Robby. He
had urged her to slow down, and she knew he was right, but
what he didn't understand was that she couldn't. She had not
shared with him the details of her therapy in New York,
partly because she had no wish to discuss it, partly because
he was contented to see her "cured," and, she guessed, only
too relieved not to have to go over the reasons for her collapse
and their separation.

She had been warned that she must be careful, that she
must take things calmly, that wartime England was not the
best place to recuperate from shock and mental problems,
that she should approach her reconciliation with Robby by
slow stages—if possible, with therapeutic help. Instead, she
had won Robby back by sheer sexual energy, surprised that
anything so simple would work, and by the fact that they
were doing what appealed to him best, playing out their roles
as storybook lovers, while taking the limelight as the world's
most famous theatrical couple. Their relationship had faltered
in Hollywood, where they were obliged to work separately.
She would never let that happen again.

She sat in front of her mirror, removing her makeup with
cold cream, while well-wishers crowded into her dressing
room, bearing more flowers, more champagne, until there

was hardly room to move. Guy Darling, who had said some very unkind things about her absence from England, and had been more than a little stand-offish about offering her a part, was firmly seated in the most comfortable chair, all charm and smiles now that she had proved she could still act.

She promised herself she would make Guy sweat for her when the time came, *and* pay through the nose! Dear Noel lounged against the mantelpiece, with Binkie Beaumont, the famous impresario, at his side. Guy, Noel, and Binkie were known throughout the theatre as "the three queens." Each in his own way adored her and disliked Robby, who had never made any secret of his belief that virility was essential to good theatre. If only they knew, she thought, seeing Randy Brooks whispering in Robby's ear. But of course they must never know. . . .

There were at least a dozen people in the room, and more crowding through the door from the hallway outside, which was packed. Everybody said (or rather shouted) "Darling" and "Marvelous," and she replied to all with a wave and a smile as she cleaned her face. The Prime Minister himself had been first to appear, to growl his congratulations, but had taken his leave before the crush. The room was by now so full of tobacco smoke that she could hardly distinguish one face from another as old friends appeared. "Even Robby was bloody marvelous," she heard Guy say, in that highpitched, precisely articulated voice that had made him famous in the twenties. "Though I *do* think his Antony is more scoutmaster than general."

"Don't be catty, Guy," she called. "Robby was wonderful."

"No, darling. He was good. *You* were wonderful!"

She was torn, as always, between the welcome glow of praise—and bloody well-deserved praise, at that—and loyalty to Robby. She never doubted his genius, despised those who couldn't see it, but at the same time she yearned to be better than he was, here where it counted—on the stage.

Still, she laughed with Guy. The image of Antony as a scoutmaster was too funny not to laugh at—it was the same impression Robby had given her when she had flung herself against him in the lobby of the Savoy Hotel, after ten ghastly days at sea and a wretched train trip through the bombed-out towns of southern England. She had pressed her mouth against his and murmured, "Take me upstairs and fuck me, darling!" softly, but not so softly that the manager of the Savoy, resplendent in his striped trousers and black cutaway coat, hadn't overheard and raised an eyebrow in astonishment—or just possibly, she thought, envy.

Robby had been embarrassed, perhaps by the fact that his own greeting had been so timid by comparison, or that he hadn't been able to get away from his work to meet her at the Southampton docks. . . . Yes, she decided, Guy, shrewd old bugger that he was, would have noticed every nuance of their performance together.

"One forgets," Guy said, his singsong voice rising above the noise of conversation, "what a *sexy* play it is. Oh, not Antony, of course. He's just an ambitious general going through what the Freudians like to call a 'mid-life crisis,' but Cleopatra—*she*, my dears, is the only man in the play." Darling was used to holding court, so much so that he hardly seemed to notice whether anyone was listening or not. "That's why you're so good, Lisha, darling. I've always said that if I wanted something truly wicked done, I'd come to *you* for help before I'd go to any man I can think of."

She blew him a kiss. "Darling Guy! How you do go on! I'm sure you'd do nothing of the kind. Anyway, I couldn't hurt a fly."

"Don't you believe it for a moment, pet. If ever I wanted anybody killed, you'd be my first choice to do it."

"And mine," a deep voice said, from behind her. "It's been a long time, my dear."

It was as if, in the middle of her noisy triumph, her heart had stopped. A bomb exploding in the room would not have shocked her more, she thought. She saw her image in the mirror—eyes wide open in terror and dismay—but before she could react, she felt the lips and the familiar bristly mustache touch her cheek. She winced, as if she had received a blow rather than a kiss. She could see his face now, reflected beside hers, the predatory nose, the cruel mouth, emphasized rather than softened by the mustache, which was white and fuller than she remembered, as if he had let it grow to military proportions in keeping with the martial spirit of the times.

The kiss was something more than a peck on the cheek—he let it linger long enough to serve as a reminder that he was not just another theatrical well-wisher. She felt his hand on her shoulder and shivered involuntarily. "You're as beautiful as ever, my dear," he growled. "It's been a long time."

She leaned forward to escape the pressure of his hand. She could see it in the mirror, strong, long-fingered—he had a real horseman's hands, as he liked to boast. The hair on their backs was thick and dark, and in his youth he could bend a poker with them—perhaps still could. She was not anxious to discuss how long it had been since she was in touch with Uncle Harry or, for that matter, with the rest of her family. There had been many reasons for her decision to go to California, and Uncle Harry was certainly among them.

"And how is dear Aunt Maude?" she asked sweetly. She lit a cigarette—she had not managed as yet to accustom herself to rationing, and was still in the habit of lighting a cigarette and putting it out after one puff, whereas everyone else in England smoked theirs down to the last fraction of an inch. One of the minor casualties of the war, she had discovered, were the cigarettes named after Robby. "Vanes" had vanished from the shelves, replaced by the more martial brand of "Senior Service." She blew a cloud of smoke in the air—Uncle Harry wouldn't mind, she thought. He had taught her to smoke, after all, and much else besides.

He did not look pleased at the mention of his wife, nor had she intended him to be. "Maude's as well as can be expected," he said abruptly. Ever since Felicia had returned to England as an adolescent, Lady Lisle had lived in a state of mildly befuddled alcoholism, which her husband had ruthlessly encouraged. Early on, Felicia had made the accidental discovery that the reason Aunt Maude always had a separate teapot was that it contained gin, and that any attempt to steal a few drops of scent from her bottles of perfume and toilet water was likely to prove disappointing, since she often used them, too, as a hideaway for liquor.

Maude's drinking suited Harry very well. On the one hand, it was a good excuse for his constant womanizing; on the other, it prevented her from paying any attention to his lies and frequent absences. Harry blamed Lady Lisle's "condition," as it was tactfully known in the family, on the fact that they were childless, but Felicia knew only too well that there were other, darker reasons. "Did she come in for the play?" she asked.

"You know damned well she didn't. It's been years since Maude has been in town."

"I know. Lucky you."

Somebody in the crowd handed Lord Lisle a glass of champagne. He sniffed it suspiciously before tasting it. He had a deep distrust of the kind of champagne that was likely to be handed out to strangers in a theatre dressing room. But since it was from the case that had been sent to Felicia by Noel, it was beyond reproach.

"Perrier-Jouët," Uncle Harry said approvingly. "Glad to see I taught you *something* you haven't forgotten. Lucky me, indeed. Lucky you. There was a time . . ."

"I don't think that's a subject for discussion among all these people, do you, Harry?"

"No more is Maude."

She caught the threat instantly. Harry Lisle bullied with the precision of a good tennis player. Hit him a ball and he hit it back at you harder. He never liked to hear Maude's name mentioned when he was in London. Once, years ago, when she was hardly more than a girl, she had asked him in a moment of intimacy and, on her part, slight drunkenness, if he and Maude still made love together, a question whispered while they were seated on a banquette at Le Relais, one of his favorite little haunts in town. Without any change of expression, he had torn one of the earrings he had given her off her ear without unfastening it. She had known better than to scream, though the pain was excruciating, and spent the rest of the meal dabbing at the blood with her handkerchief. "An eye for an eye," was his motto in conversation as well as life. He believed in instant punishment and evening the score, and she still bore, faded with time, the small scars from his lessons—and, less visibly, the larger ones as well. She was no longer a terrified girl but a famous star, and she liked to think she could give as good as she got, but Harry Lisle still had the power to frighten her. No, she corrected herself, she wasn't frightened of him anymore—he simply had the power to challenge her. The game was the same, it always was with him, but she could play as an equal now, and perhaps even win. "*Dear* Uncle Harry," she murmured throatily. "It's quite like old times."

"Not quite," he said, staring over her shoulder at her cleavage, a good deal of which was exposed by her dressing gown. "But you haven't changed a bit, you know. You're looking better than ever. You were damned good tonight, by the way."

" 'Praise from Sir Hubert is praise indeed!' "

"Don't get clever with me, Lisha." He bent over close to her and whispered, "I'm not one of your pansy admirers, like Guy Darling over there."

She laughed, determined not to be intimidated, but told herself there was surely something deeply unfair about the fact that the whole world was at war, with millions of people being killed, while Uncle Harry, who certainly deserved to be bombed, was alive and well, apparently as fit as ever, his perfectly cut Savile Row suit concealing whatever weight he had put on.

To give the devil his due—and he was the devil—he had faultless taste. His dark double-breasted suit had a kind of Edwardian opulence, there was a flower in his buttonhole, his silver hair was still thick, and he wore a monocle with a gold rim on a black silk cord. Out of the corner of her eye she could see that several of the men in the room—including Guy Darling—were looking at him with a certain amount of interest, despite his age. Harry had the broad shoulders and powerful muscles of a man who spent most of his life outdoors—riding, hunting, fishing, chopping trees for exercise—but he dressed with the finicky perfectionism of an aesthete, collected antique china and silver, and loved the ballet, the theatre, and the opera. He tried the patience of his fellow peers with his interminable speeches in the House of

Lords about the evils of poaching or the importance of corporal punishment in forming the character of children—and as a result was always referred to in the more sensational newspapers as "Lord-Bring-Back-the-Lash"—but he was a man who could gently fondle a Sung vase at Spink's and who cried over Mimi's death in *La Bohème*. He was in many ways a mirror-image of her father, grasping and cunning where his brother was generous and trusting, dangerous to people while her father was dangerous only to the larger quadrupeds. He had her father's good looks, but without the vulnerability in her father's eyes that had made him so attractive to married women over the years. Uncle Harry's eyes were those of a predator, and experienced women read the danger there quickly enough, which perhaps explained, apart from his natural taste, why he preyed mostly on the very young.

"Have you heard from your father?" he asked. The relationship between Harry and his younger brother was one of poisonous dislike on both sides, starting with the fact that as the elder son, Harry had inherited the title and the fortune. She guessed there were deeper waters here, too. Harry Lisle had married Maude for her money, coldly and without passion, and doubtless had paid the price for that decision in bed, whereas her father had married a penniless beauty whose sensuality was never in doubt. Uncle Harry had never made any secret of his envy. Felicia's mother had never concealed her dislike of him, and even hinted that he had once tried to seduce her.

"A few letters," Felicia said. "You know he's not much for writing."

"Still banging away at lions?"

"No, he seems to have taken to preserving them. He's shooting at poachers now."

"I'm surprised he hasn't found a way to get back into uniform."

"I think he's a little old for that, don't you?"

"He'll never be too old to play the fool."

This was another of the rivalries that separated her father and her uncle, she suddenly remembered. Uncle Harry had spent the First World War as aide-de-camp to an important general, while her father had won what was described as a "good Military Cross" in the trenches of the Second Somme, and had been wounded in the legs.

"Father's doing what he wants to do," she said shortly.

"Oh, ay. He's always done *that*. And how is Portia?"

She felt a sharp stab of guilt. She had journeyed down to see Portia as soon as she was back in England, and had found the child sullen and resentful. It was hardly surprising. Charles had been unwilling to let Portia visit her in California, and she had been in no position to insist; then the war had made Portia's visit impossible. Felicia had done her best to keep in touch, writing regularly and sending presents whenever it was appropriate, but since the little girl had not seen her in nearly three years, and had doubtless heard her father's side of things, it was not to be expected that she would greet her mother's return with much enthusiasm. Indeed, she had made such a scene that her nanny had been obliged to carry her off to the nursery, with a forbidding glare at Felicia.

"Portia's well," Felicia said.

The dark eyes glittered malevolently. "*Is* she? She must miss her mother, poor little tyke."

She did not rise to the bait. "She's with Charles's mother, of course. For the moment. Now that Charles is in the army. She seems happy enough, what between Nanny and her pony."

"Pony? In bloody Sussex? There's no decent riding there. She ought to be at Langleit. I'd show her some real riding. Take her hunting."

"I think she's better off where she is," Felicia said firmly.

There was a sharp increase of noise as more people pushed into the dressing room, then a hush, followed by applause, which must mean that Robby was arriving.

"Your fella's on his way," Uncle Harry said. "I won't stay, if you don't mind." His dislike of Robby was well known to her—and Robby had never made any secret of the fact that he, in turn, loathed Lord Lisle. Uncle Harry's feelings she understood perfectly—he was the kind of man who remained possessive even long after he had let someone go, but Robby's antipathy toward him was harder to understand, unless it was simply an intuition that there was something more here than a family relationship. But no, she told herself, as she always had, it wasn't possible that Robby had guessed the truth. Uncle Harry always behaved toward her in public with punctilious, distant courtesy, and she in turn made no effort to hide her dislike of him. That could hardly arouse Robby's suspicions—he himself was barely on speaking terms with most of his own family to whom "his irregular style of life" was a source of bitter anger and envy.

Harry took her hand and kissed it, an act of old-fashioned courtesy which was altogether appropriate in an uncle, but which gave her an unpleasant shiver. He lingered over her hand a trifle longer than was absolutely necessary, holding it firmly while she tried to pull it away. "It's been ages," he whispered. "I'd love to chat. Lunch tomorrow? Just for old times' sake?"

"No, I can't tomorrow. And I haven't the slightest wish to chat about old times."

"Then we'll chat about Portia, shall we?" he said, in a cold, hard voice. "There are things we have to discuss. Shall we say, the day *after* tomorrow then, at The Ivy? No doubt you'll prefer to be at your favorite place rather than mine."

She nodded. The mention of Portia left her very little choice—as he knew perfectly well. "If you can book a table there," she said.

He laughed. "Oh, my dear, don't let Hollywood stardom go to your head. You're back in England now. A peer out-ranks an actress anywhere, even at The Ivy."

He turned on his heel sharply and left. Even in the packed dressing room people parted to make way for him, as they might for a bull which had broken out of its field. He had to perfection the aristocrat's easy certainty that the path would always be clear for him, that everyone would fall in with his wishes.

She saw him bow toward Robby, who had just come in— a supercilious bow with just an edge of contempt—then he was through the door and gone, leaving her to wish that she hadn't agreed to lunch.

"Robby, darling!" she called out. "Come and give me a kiss!" But even as he made his way toward her, shaking hands, accepting congratulations, putting up with the embraces of Noel and Guy and their friends (but *was* he only putting up with them? she caught herself wondering), she could see from his face that Lisle's presence had upset him. She would have to smooth it over with him tonight, she decided, however tired she might be. Well, she had learned how to do that, too. . . .

She felt, quite suddenly, tired and depressed. Three years away was not enough to erase the past.

Nothing could ever do that.

"*God*, what an evening!" Robby said, stretching, once they were home at last.

"It was sweet of Philip to give a party at his flat."

"Quite. Rather too many of *his* friends for my taste, though."

Philip Chagrin's coterie included most of London's more flamboyant "pansies" (as Uncle Harry would have called them), together with whatever young men they had brought along as their "dates," mostly young soldiers and sailors these days, giving the party a more raffish quality than Philip had probably intended.

Robby's prejudice against Philip Chagrin's "pansy" friends she found hard to understand. Robby was contemptuous of "pansies," "queers," "poufs," as if his affection for Brooks was something totally different.

Whenever she thought about it (and how hard she tried not to!), it seemed to her impossible that Robby could have the same feelings for a man as for a woman, yet she was sure he had made love to Randy Brooks. Did it give him as much pleasure as making love to her? Did it give him *more* pleasure? Was it a momentary aberration, something that was never likely to repeat itself, or was his contempt for pansies like Philip's friends just a smokescreen to hide his real feelings?

She had trained herself, in a harder school than Robby could imagine, not to look too closely at their relationship, for fear of what she might see. She had to accept him as he was or lose him, and there was no way she could let herself lose him, now that she had him back again at last.

She finished her drink—she had stopped counting her drinks, though she *had* begun to notice that after two or three the number no longer made any difference.

"Come to bed, darling," she called out now.

He slipped into bed beside her, and she cuddled up against him. Alcohol was supposed to numb the sex drive, according to Dr. Vogel, but it had quite the opposite effect on her— which perhaps explained why she drank so much at night.

But no, she was being too harsh on herself. A couple of drinks were nothing to worry about. Toby Eden drank like a fish, yet it never prevented him from giving a marvelous performance. Philip Chagrin went through a bottle of gin a day in his dressing room and could still act rings around anyone on stage except Robby. Drink did not appear to affect her father's accuracy with a rifle, and as for Uncle Harry, he never went out hunting with less than two full flasks of Rémy Martin V.S.O.P. in his coat pockets to keep him warm when hounds were working the scent.

She put her arms around Robby and pulled him close. "Tired, my love?" she asked.

"A little. Never mind, I believe it was a triumph."

"So do I. We'll see what the papers say in the morning."

"I don't give a shit what they say. We *showed* them, darling! We gave them Shakespeare with more guts than they've ever seen before. Flesh and blood!"

"The papers will say it was too sexy."

"The hell with them. Not a single person went to the shelters. I lost count of the curtain calls. You were bloody marvelous, darling, by the way."

"It *was* like the old days, wasn't it? We were *both* marvelous."

She put her arms around him and squeezed herself close. "There's nobody in the world I'd rather act with," she purred.

"Likewise, I'm sure."

She kissed the back of his neck. "My genius!" she whispered. It wasn't simply flattery, it was true—he *was* her genius. "You looked so handsome as Antony," she whispered, nibbling on his ear. "I kept saying to myself, 'I'll bet there isn't a woman in the audience who wouldn't give her eye teeth to have him, and he's *mine*!' "

He twisted around and kissed her. "Sweet!" he said. "And I felt the same about you, my darling."

Was it true? she hoped. "Do you remember the first time we did *Antony and Cleopatra*?" she asked.

"Bristol," he murmured, his lips pressed against hers.

She laughed wickedly. "You took me into your dressing room after act one, and we made love between the acts. Thank God there wasn't a costume change."

It was dangerous to remind him of the past—dangerous to think about it herself, but she couldn't help it. The past might always be construed as criticism of the present, as if she were complaining that they no longer made love between acts, but luckily he took it well and chuckled. "Oh, those were the days," he said. "But by God, we played it better tonight! Experience does count for something."

"Not just onstage, darling."

"Indeed." He drew her close to him, his arms around her, like the old days. "And how brave you were," he whispered. "I've never seen anyone braver."

"Oh, my darling. If only you knew! The moment I'd done it, I said to myself, 'God, I'm going to feel such a fool if we all get blown up.' "

"Not a chance. Hitler would never have dared!"

She felt him enter her, blanked out her mind to anything else, tried to pretend that it *was* the old days in the shabby little dressing room in Bristol, on the old leather couch, with the wind howling off the bay and the ancient steam pipes clanking, while Toby, worried by the noise, shouted out from the hallway, "I say, are you chaps all right in there?" and she almost succeeded. If nothing else, she thought, she had certainly succeeded in convincing Robby that it was like the old days, for his pleasure was real and unfeigned.

He rolled over, lit a cigarette in the dark and passed it to her, then lit one for himself.

"That was very nice," she purred. Much as she hated constantly being compared to a cat, she would never deny a certain catlike touch to her lovemaking. She rubbed herself against him softly, starting with the toes and working her way up.

"Very nice indeed," he said, turning his head to kiss her, a quick kiss on the forehead, to show his appreciation. "Talk about the old days! Wasn't it nice to see the old gang together again? Toby, Noel, Guy, Binkie with that dreadful new young man of his."

"And Gertie. And darling Rex, in uniform. How one missed them all in America!"

"Yes." He withdrew slightly from her—hardly more than a fraction of an inch, but the gesture was unmistakable. "I must say, I hadn't expected to see your Uncle Harry backstage. What on earth did the old scoundrel want?" His voice was just a touch less warm.

She stiffened. Easy does it, she warned herself.

"The old scoundrel only wanted to tell me how much he enjoyed the play." She paused, and decided she'd better tell him the truth now, while he was still in the afterglow. "I'm going to have lunch with him one day this week."

"Why on earth?"

"He *is* my uncle, Robby. I grew up at Langleit. I'm sure he'll want to tell me all the local gossip—who's sleeping with whom among the local gentry."

"Yes. Somehow that's never seemed to me the kind of thing that really interests Harry Lisle. Nor you, actually. It seems to me *you* don't really like him any better than I do. You're always telling stories about how terribly he behaved toward you when you were a girl, or toward your father, or towards poor Aunt Maude. But one look at the old reprobate in the flesh, and you're off to have lunch with him."

"Well, it's partly guilt."

"Guilt for what?"

"Not *for* anything. Uncle Harry and Aunt Maude have no children of their own, you know. I think Harry likes to pretend that I'm his grown-up daughter. When I started to live in

London, Harry used to love coming into town to take me out to lunch, the way fathers do.''

Robby raised an eyebrow eloquently. He had never discerned the slightest trace of sentiment in Lord Lisle, paternal or otherwise. Still, in principle, he could understand a family feeling, and even share it. "Yes," he said, "I can see that, actually. It must be sad to have all that money—and that beautiful house—and not have a child to leave it all to.''

She nodded, sorry that she had brought the subject up. "Let's go to sleep, darling," she said. "It's terribly late."

"I've talked to Penelope, you know," he went on. "She's long since resigned herself to the inevitable. After all these years of separation, divorce is just a formality. Surely Charles must want a life of his own by now?''

There was a time when the mere suggestion that Robby had talked to his wife without mentioning it to her would have driven Felicia into a rage, but it no longer seemed important. Once, she had thought of Penelope as a threat, the wife who had never relinquished her claim on Robby, but the past year had submerged that fear in worse ones. "Charles hasn't changed his mind, so far as I know," she said. "He's not against a divorce, but he still wants custody of Portia.''

"Darling, face facts. For all practical purposes, he's *got* custody of Portia. We'll buy a house, she'll visit, it's not as if you won't see her at all. What I'm trying to say, dear heart, is let's get all this over and done with, then we can marry, and have a family of our own. Uncle Harry isn't the only one who wants children.''

She sighed. She had never had anything against motherhood; she even thought she had been a pretty good mother, all things considered, or would have been a good mother if it hadn't been for the circumstances of Portia's birth, or the demands of her career, or the fact that she had fallen in love with Robby and abandoned her marriage, or if the war hadn't separated her from her daughter. . . . Her instincts, she felt, had always been right, even though they had led her, one step after another, in the wrong direction.

"Shall *I* talk to Charles's lawyer, then?" he suggested. "Perhaps it's easier that way?''

"Yes, of course, darling," she whispered. 'There was no stopping the inevitable; besides, she had waited nearly ten years to marry Robby. At first, his wife wouldn't let him go; then Charles, who had been reluctant to let *her* go, decided he wouldn't let Portia go; then the war had overtaken the whole tangled problem.

"We shall be very happy," he said. "I promise you."

"I know we shall," she said, in a throaty whisper. Determined to get his mind off the subject of children, she slid her hands down low under the covers and began to stroke him gently, until he again groaned with pleasure.

She slipped down into the bed, parted her lips and took him in her mouth, feeling his hands on her neck, pressing down hard, as if he meant to strangle her, but that, she knew by experience, was just a sign of his passion. And then it came to her, as it often did when her mind wasn't calmed down enough by drink or pills, that perhaps he had groaned like this for Randy Brooks.

She pictured them lying together, limbs intertwined obscenely, on the big couch in the living room of the house in Beverly Hills, the fabric of which she could remember with absolute clarity—a peach-colored velvet with a paler floral pattern woven into it—as if it were photographed in her mind, although she had already forgotten what the rest of the house looked like. All of a sudden she began to cry, sobbing and swallowing with despair, self-disgust, and rage. None of which he noticed.

They stood together in the pouring rain.

"It's *exactly* the country house I've always dreamed of," he said. The caretaker had opened the rusted wrought-iron gates for them so they could drive down the long elm-lined alley to park in the gravel courtyard in front of the house. Even on a dark, wet afternoon, the Cotswold stone had a golden glow that almost made her forget her wet feet.

Toby Eden had persuaded them to come down to the country for lunch, a journey which required considerable planning in wartime, for petrol was severely rationed. All during lunch he had raved about a nearby house which, according to him, was exactly what they wanted, whether they knew it or not. "*Made* for you!" he promised, with such determination that she wondered if he hadn't been primed by Robby, but she could see no trace of collusion on their part. "Syon Manor," he rhapsodized, "a gem of a place. Nobody living there now, needs some work, of course—all these old houses do—but just the place to sink your roots, you'll see."

As fate would have it, Syon Manor was not only just the house that Robby was always talking about, right down to the dovecote and the linenfold paneling, but exactly what she herself had always dreamed of owning. Toby, needless to say, had been too kind. The house did not need "some work"—it needed *vast* amounts of work, and even vaster amounts of money—but every detail of it appealed to her, from its original Elizabethan windows, as thick and opaque as bottle glass, to its narrow doorways and uneven stairs worn thin and polished smooth by nearly four hundred years of use. There were no bathrooms or any kitchen worthy of the name, the electric outlets were few and far between, the plumbing, by the admission of the caretaker himself, was rather doubtful, but all that could be fixed—not now, of course, but once the war was over.

She knew, without a shadow of doubt, that she would live here one day, and could already see the house in her mind's eye as it would be when it was restored.

Robby had never looked happier or more relaxed as they explored the house. Everywhere there was evidence of decay and damage, but at the same time it was impossible not to feel that history had made its mark here. Upstairs, they stood in the master bedroom together, arm in arm, looking at the ceiling, where brown-and-gold paint was peeling away to reveal a brightly painted fresco of nymphs and gods beneath. The big fireplace, blackened with the soot of ages, had a mantelpiece in which a skilled hand had carved the date 1542. "An omen," Robby said. "Four centuries. Sixty-five years before Will wrote *Antony and Cleopatra*! Would you be happy here, do you think?"

She nodded. "And you?"

"It's what I've wanted all my life. Of course it would

certainly bankrupt us. It would take *years* to restore. Still, we could do a little at a time. A decent kitchen first, then a bathroom, and of course a nursery, and a room for a nanny. . . .'' He leaned over and kissed her. "You're shivering!"

"It's the cold," she said. "And I'm wet." But of course it was nothing of the kind. The house, in Robby's mind, was inextricably mixed up with the idea of children, which was only natural.

She squeezed her arms around him and kissed him as hard as she could, just as the caretaker entered the room with a tea tray, nearly dropping it at the sight of England's most famous theatrical couple embracing.

It was just like old times, she thought.

"The child is nearly twelve," Harry Lisle said obstinately, raising his voice. "I see no good reason why she shouldn't be at Langleit. It would do her a world of good. She'd be out in the open air, riding every day—all the things she likes. Just because *you* didn't like any of it as a child, is no reason . . ."

"It has nothing to do with that," she interrupted. "It's out of the question, and that's that."

"Why? I don't suppose Charles would mind a bit. He and I have always gotten along well enough. Seen eye to eye."

She gave him a hard stare across the top of her champagne glass—there was no shortage of wine in good restaurants, though the food was strictly rationed and seemed to consist mostly of things that she hadn't thought were edible disguised to look like things that were. Meat and eggs were almost completely unavailable, and with most of the fishing trawlers now converted into minesweepers or whatever, even fish was hard to come by. She had never been much of an eater so she suffered very little, but she did miss the little things that made a meal worthwhile—real butter, white bread, fresh olives, *foie gras*, cream with her coffee. Everybody was "making do," painting on stockings (the seam down the back of the leg made with eyebrow pencil), turning back shirt cuffs and collars to hide the fact that they were frayed, mending clothes that before the war would have been thrown away ages ago. Every bathtub had a line painted around the inside, low down, beyond which you were not supposed to fill it, to save on coal—a rule which she broke every day, and over which she suffered agonies of guilt, as if an extra inch or two of hot water would lose the war.

Uncle Harry suffered from the privations of war only when he was in London. At home, his chickens and ducks gave him eggs, his cattle furnished meat, his cows milk, cream, and butter, his woods grouse, pheasant, rabbits, partridges, and enough firewood to keep every fireplace blazing. He had never looked healthier, or better fed, and despite her own memories of Langleit, she thought it would probably do Portia no harm at all to be there. She shook her head. "Charles might not mind," she said. "I *do*."

"Give me one good reason."

"Give *me* a good reason why you want her."

"Because I'm lonely there," he said. "Your aunt, as you very well know, spends most of her time drinking. If we'd had children, I might have had grandchildren by now at Langleit, but we didn't. She couldn't." He waved aside the thought of what might have been. "Well, you know all that," he said gruffly.

"I know all that, yes."

He smiled a little sadly. There was no question he'd married the wrong woman and had been punished for it by the fact that she had been unable to give him children.

But none of that justified his behavior, or what he had done to her. She wished he were old and feeble so that it would be possible to feel sorry for him, but Uncle Harry, though he must by now be pushing sixty, was as vigorous as when she had first set eyes on him, over twenty years ago, as she descended timidly from the old Rolls that had met her at the station, shivering in the cold wind of an English autumn evening, which cut her to the bone after all those years in Kenya.

"Ah, yes, you've heard it all before, haven't you? I don't suppose I kept any secrets from you, did I?"

She shrugged. "You told me too much. How much of it

was true, I don't know. Most of it, I'm glad to say, I've forgotten.''

"I don't suppose you've forgotten anything, actually. You always had an uncomfortably good memory, even when you were a child. Do you remember, I took you to see your first real play when you were—what? Twelve? Thirteen?''

She laughed. "Gilles Moncrieff in *Caesar and Cleopatra*, with Mrs. Moncrieff in the role of Cleopatra. In Birmingham, at the old Royale Theatre. It was a matinee. We had lunch first at the big railway hotel—potted shrimp and Dover sole, then coffee in the palm court, with an all-woman string ensemble playing selections from Ivor Novello. I felt so grown up. I knew the moment the curtain went up that I was going to be an actress."

Uncle Harry had taken her to museums, to auctions, to the theatre and the ballet, introduced her to antiques and art, wine and food, silver and china—given her a refined and well-educated taste for the best of everything, for which she was grateful. They had gone everywhere together like father and daughter, which most people thought they were, to Sadler's Wells and Glyndebourne, to the Royal Academy and Christie's, to Covent Garden and the Old Vic, as if Harry Lisle had found in his niece a legitimate excuse to be away from home, as well as a good reason to indulge himself in everything he liked best.

Of course, he enjoyed having the companionship of a pretty girl, as well as the opportunity to instruct her on everything from clothes to wine. The sad thing about it was that he would have made an excellent father. He liked nothing better than to share his knowledge and enthusiasms, and despite the bullying side to his nature, he was a good teacher—patient, amusing, always able to make her see *why* one painting was better than another, or why one George II silver cream pitcher was worth ten times more than another that looked very similar, or why Chanel and Molyneux were better couturiers for a girl with a slim figure (like herself) than Schiaparelli or Worth. Had she been a boy, Harry would probably have shown her the other side of his personality, for he was a

Master of Foxhounds, famous for his daredevil riding, a first-rate shot, a celebrated fly fisherman. . . .

He sipped his wine, his eyes challenging her. "Yes," he said. "I remember your telling me that you were going to be an actress. And who was it who backed you all the way? Right from the beginning? Since you've such a sharp memory, I'm sure you haven't forgotten who talked your father into it? Or who got you into RADA? Or who paid the bills?"

"I haven't forgotten, Harry, no. I believe you got something back for it, though, didn't you?"

"I would have gotten it anyway, my girl."

That was undeniably true, she thought—in actual fact, she had started sleeping with Uncle Harry long before he agreed to send her to RADA. When she looked back on it, she couldn't see that there had been any choice, really. He simply walked into her room one afternoon, a week after her sixteenth birthday, and took her, as if it was the most natural thing in the world. She had offered no resistance. She had known from the beginning that it was going to happen sooner or later, seen it in his eyes the day she arrived, and in a kind of fatalistic way she had egged him on, to see how far he would go or how long it would take him to get there.

She had flirted awkwardly with him for nearly a year, terrified all the time that her aunt would notice. At sixteen she was not at all sure of the best way to flirt, but of course she needn't have bothered: all she had to do was to look virginal and tempting at the same time, which came naturally enough.

At first, sleeping with her uncle in his own home had seemed like a grown-up game, so exciting that she had no time to feel ashamed. Later, when after he used his influence to get her a place at RADA he found a convenient little flat for her in London (convenient for him!), she began to feel like a prisoner, dreading his arrival but too frightened by then to do anything about it.

After all, whom could she have told? Her father, thousands of miles away in Kenya? Her Aunt Maude, who had turned her back on reality twenty years ago, and who sometimes spent whole days at a time upstairs in her room, hopelessly drunk? There was no one she could have turned to, Felicia always consoled herself, but part of her recognized that she hadn't *wanted* to escape, that being Harry Lisle's secret mistress had suited her very well. With hindsight, nobody was apparently to blame.

"Perhaps it would have happened," she now said. "Perhaps not."

"No 'perhaps' about it, my girl. You practically hung out the latchkey for me."

"You still didn't have the right to—do what you did."

He gave a snort of disgust, then drained his glass and snapped his fingers to signal the waiter to put another bottle of champagne on ice.

It was odd, she thought, but Harry had the kind of fingers one might have expected Robby's to be. She knew from personal experience how hard those hands could grasp—or hit—and how fiercely those fingers could dig into the flesh.

But those fingers, she remembered with guilty shame, could also be incredibly gentle. Harry Lisle's childhood ambition had been to become a concert pianist, but it had been impressed on him that one day he would succeed to the title and to Langleit, and he had given in to his parents reluctantly and had accepted his fate as a wealthy landowning peer. He envied his younger brother's freedom, and bitterly resented the fact that Felicia's father had wasted it with nothing more to show than a failed career as a gentleman jockey and trainer, ending up in Kenya, the last stop for every aristocratic failure and misfit.

"*Right?*" he asked with a sharp edge of anger in his voice. "There's no right and wrong for people like us. Talent, beauty, money, social position—what's the point of all that if you can't do just what you damn well please?"

"You used to tell me that all the time. I believed it then. I don't anymore."

"Is that so? Yet you're living with Robby, still married to Charles, and your child is being boarded with people who might as well be total bloody strangers, while you pursue your stage career. It's not what *I* would call a respectable middle-class life, if that's what you aspire to.''

"I haven't the slightest intention of being respectable or middle-class. Anyway, I didn't *plan* my life that way, Harry. That's just how it turned out. Robby will get his divorce and I will get mine, eventually. Portia will come and live with us.''

"Charles will never consent to that, and you know it. Neither will the courts, if you want my opinion. If you'd wanted custody, you shouldn't have gone off to Hollywood and stayed out of the country for so long. Three years! No judge is going to have much sympathy for that. I know a lot of the judges—see them in the House of Lords, on the rare occasions I attend. Most of them are in their eighties, dry as old sticks. I don't think your being a Hollywood star is likely to cut much ice with any of them. Then, of course, there's the question of what exactly you were doing in New York this past year. That's something that's bound to be raised.''

"Why on earth should it be?''

"Well, it's the kind of thing people wonder about, you know. Even at home, we heard rumors. That you and Robby had separated, that there'd been some kind of dreadful row between you in Hollywood . . . You're stars, my dear. It's only natural that people should gossip about you. And ask questions. Even your Aunt Maude remarked on the fact that you didn't come back to England with Robby. If *she* thought it curious, you can guess how the rest of the world speculated!''

"And what was the rest of the world saying?''

"That you were having an affair with somebody in New York. That Robby had had an affair with some woman in Hollywood, and you were paying him back in his own coin.''

She poked at her food. "None of that is true," she said. "I was ill. I was in hospital in New York. Everybody knows that. It wasn't a secret.''

"Yes, it was in all the newspapers, but the point is, nobody believes a word of it. Come to that, *I* don't believe a word of it. You look perfectly healthy to me—though you could put on a few pounds, if you want my opinion.''

"I don't. I've always been thin. I like being thin. I loathe fat people. I would rather die than be fat myself. As for the newspapers, they were right, for once."

"What was the problem, then?"

"I had a nervous breakdown, if you must know."

Uncle Harry nodded sagely. Nervous breakdowns ran in the family on the female side. Felicia's mother had been generally regarded as suffering from an extreme state of nerves, as well as nymphomania; Aunt Maude suffered from depression and migraines when she wasn't drunk; one of Uncle Harry's sisters was in a high-priced private loony bin somewhere near Oxford, from which she sent inappropriate messages, very often obscene, to each member of the family on their birthdays and at Christmastime. The Lisle men traditionally drank and womanized, while their wives and sisters went quietly—or sometimes noisily—mad. "I thought you were made of sterner stuff," he said.

"So did I."

"In my experience, Felicia, people don't just *go* mad. Something triggers it off. What the devil happened in California?"

She pushed her piece of fish around the plate, trying to hide as much as possible of it under the vegetables. It looked like sole, but the taste and texture, despite the sauce, suggested some sea creature that was less familiar. Curious things turned up on your plate these days. Robby claimed to have been served Canadian beaver at the Garrick Club, and whale steak for lunch at Quaglino's. "I forgot my lines," she said.

He gave her an exasperated look, as if to remind her that patience was not one of his virtues. "This is *me* you're talking to," he growled. "Uncle Harry. I know you like the back of my own hand. Did Vane walk out on you for another woman?" He stroked his mustache speculatively. "Or for a chap, perhaps?" he asked slyly.

She laughed. "Whatever makes you think that?" she asked, a shade too quickly.

"Just a feeling I've always had about the fellow." Harry Lisle's tawny eyes—the same color as her father's—glittered shrewdly.

"Well, you're wrong. Hollywood was bad for us, that's all. Perhaps it's bad for everyone. We were working on separate films, we never saw each other, then we decided to do *Romeo and Juliet*, and everything went wrong. We'd invested all our earnings in it from the films we made, you see, so the pressures on both of us were intolerable. And I was tired." She closed her eyes for a moment. "More tired than I'd ever been before in my life."

"Not like you to be tired, Felicia. You always had more go than anybody else I knew."

"That was a long time ago." She lit a cigarette, despite the fact that Harry Lisle didn't approve of smoking during a meal, and signaled the waiter to remove her plate, which she couldn't bear looking at a moment longer. "The truth is, I had a difficult time of it in New York," she said. "Worse than you can imagine. Worse than Robby knows."

"Difficult? What do you mean by that?"

She had been unable to tell anybody about New York. If she told Robby, he would probably think she was exaggerating, or just trying to make him feel guilty for what had happened. He thought of it as a kind of rest cure, which was fine with her. She was not about to tell him what it was like to be locked up in a place where the windows were covered with steel mesh, and where they wouldn't even let you go *near* a mirror of your own, in case you managed to break it and slit your wrists with the shards. Oh, she had learned what a "suicide watch" was like, all right, from the padded walls of her room to the canvas straitjacket the attendants put you in, just to show you what they'd do if you ever decided to make a nuisance of yourself.

She had not made a nuisance of herself—until Randy Brooks had shown up to visit her, standing in the patient's lounge with a bouquet of flowers in his hand and a look of concern etched on his face. Robby, already in England, had asked Randy to see that she was all right, and if there was anything she needed—for of course neither of them knew she had overheard them after the fiasco of the party. Brooks had tried to smile at her, as friendly as ever, but she could see the shock in his eyes at the state she was in, hair wild and disordered, fingernails cut short, wearing a hospital gown that was tied at the back.

If he had come with a joke appropriate for the occasion, she never heard it, for she flung herself at him with all her strength, howling in fury, and was dragged off by the attendants. Later on she was told that she had nearly scratched out the eyes of America's most beloved comedian, as if that were the final proof of her insanity, but she had no memory of it, and indeed found it more and more difficult to remember anything at all, once they put her on electroshock therapy. But she had no difficulty even now remembering the searing, stomach-turning pain, the taste of the sodden gag placed between her teeth to prevent her from biting her tongue off, the sudden, sharp smell of ozone in the air from the burst of electricity, the feeling that her spine was about to break as she arched her back against the leather straps at the shock.

She heard a clicking noise and suddenly realized that Harry Lisle was staring at her, snapping his fingers at her as if to test whether she was awake or not. "I asked what you meant by 'difficult,' " he said. "Then you went into a bloody trance on me."

She shivered. "I'm sorry. It was worse, far worse, than you can possibly imagine."

"You don't have to be afraid of telling *me* about it, my dear."

"I'm not afraid. Since you insist—I tried to kill myself. Poor Robby didn't know what to do, so he asked everybody's advice—oh, very quietly, you know, so there wasn't any news about it—and everybody suggested flying me to New York, even though I'm afraid of airplanes, as you know. They had to sedate me to put me on the plane. Poor Robby fussed over me all the way across the country. We made an odd little traveling party, the three of us."

"Three?"

"Robby asked Dr. Vogel, my psychiatrist in Los Angeles, to come along, just to keep an eye on me. There we sat, Robby looking his most tragic, me clutching my seat and crying, and poor dear Dr. Vogel, with his hypodermic needle at the ready in case I got a little too 'agitated.' " She seemed to be talking to herself now. "Then, when we eventually landed at New York, after I don't know how many stops, I looked out the window, and there was a big chauffeur-driven car waiting for us on the tarmac." Her voice trembled. "And standing beside it was Randy Brooks."

"The comedian chap? I've always enjoyed his films. Bloody funny fellow!"

"Isn't he, though?" she asked vaguely. "Except that it wasn't at all funny that he, of all people, was waiting with a car to pick us up. When I saw him, I had—I don't know what to call it—a relapse, perhaps. I wouldn't get off the plane, which was ironic since I'd made such a fuss about getting *on* it. I cried and shouted and clung to my seat, until eventually Dr. Vogel gave me an injection, sent for an ambulance and had me carried off the plane tied to a stretcher. That's when it was finally decided that I wasn't going back to England with Robby. He left the next day, and I stayed behind, in hospital, certified mad."

"Surely not certified?"

"Well, as a matter of fact, I think I probably signed myself into the loony bin." She laughed, as if the words were funny, though even thinking about the place still made her feel sick. "I signed so many, many things then—tax papers, contracts, letters . . . whatever was put in front of me, I signed. It seemed easier to do than arguing about it. God only knows what I signed. Anyway, I signed myself in, which was easy enough, then I discovered I couldn't sign myself *out*, but by that time Robby was back in England, training to be a pilot. . . ."

"And yet you're still with him? After all that?"

"He didn't know how bad it was. He still doesn't. And won't." She smiled. "I'm better now," she said. "I can remember my lines."

Harry Lisle stared at the cheese tray grimly. It was beautifully presented, wicker basketwork covered with a starched napkin, with biscuits on one side and fresh carrot sticks and celery on the other, the effect spoiled by the fact that the cheese consisted of a few lumps of stale Cheddar, more suitable for a mousetrap than for an expensive restaurant. He waved it away, ordered a glass of port and took out a cigar. Then he reached across the table and patted her hand. "I had no idea," he said. "It's hard to imagine you of all people going through something like that. Of course, it proves my point, you know."

"What point?"

"My point about Portia. Between your—ah—problems and the fact that Charles is off at war, it's perfectly obvious the child should be at Langleit."

She stared at him. "Harry, I won't have it, and that's that."

"I *want* her, Felicia. I mean to have her."

"Why?"

He took a moment or two to get his cigar lighted to his satisfaction. Once upon a time it had amused him to teach her how to select a cigar, roll it gently between the fingers, next to her ear, listening for the faint, moist crackle that indicated its freshness, pierce the tip with a wooden match, then place it in his mouth and light it for him. It amused him to teach her the whole elaborate Edwardian ritual, with its obvious erotic symbolism, and it had amused *her* to get it right, when she was sixteen. The memory of it gave her the chills.

"Why?" He let out a puff of smoke. "Because she's my daughter. Surely that's reason enough?"

She felt a shock as sharp and painful as any she had received during her therapy. Years ago, when she was carrying his child, she and Harry Lisle had agreed that they would never discuss it, never mention it, never even *think* about it. Charles wanted to marry her, and while Harry wasn't anxious to let her go, he was shrewd enough to see that Felicia's marriage would put an end to a potentially dangerous situation. He was, above all, a practical man, and practical men knew when to cut their losses.

In her father's absence, Uncle Harry had given her away at the altar. He had winked as she took the vow, knowing that their secret was safe—for disclosure, by now, would bring as much shame and ruin down on her as it would on him. He had bullied her into making him Portia's godfather, but until now he had never, even to her, mentioned the fact that he was Portia's father. In a strange way, she had always managed to persuade herself that if neither of them ever *said* it, it wasn't true, but now he had said it, and she felt a sharp, sudden stab of hatred for him. She did her best to control it.

"She's Charles's daughter," she said fiercely.

"He thinks so. She thinks so. But you and I, *we* know it isn't true."

There was no arguing the point. Portia not only *was* Harry Lisle's daughter, she even resembled him, with the same tawny eyes and dark hair. Charles had never noticed that Portia bore no resemblance to him, or to any member of his family. What could be more normal than for a girl to take after her mother's side of the family? He always swore the next one would be a boy and would look like a Trent, blue-eyed, with coppery hair and a brick-red complexion. "We promised each other a long time ago we'd never mention it," she reminded Harry. Her hands were shaking with anger.

"And I kept my promise, didn't I? But I'm also the child's godfather. What could be more normal than her coming to stay with me in the country?"

"Harry! After what happened between us, you can't possibly imagine that I'd allow *you* to look after my daughter?"

He looked at her coldly. "She's *my* daughter, too, Felicia. You're surely not suggesting I'd do anything improper, are you?"

"Improper? I wouldn't leave you alone with Portia for a second!"

"She's mine, Felicia, and I intend to have her."

"She's *not* yours. We settled that years ago when you didn't want her at all. And we agreed not to talk about it."

"And have *you* lived up to that? Do you mean to tell me that you haven't ever hinted at it to Robby? Or blurted it out to your god damned psychiatrist?"

"Never. I've lived with it, and I've kept it secret, just as I said I would. Robby hasn't any more idea than Charles. He's fond of Portia and always talks about how nice it will be when she can live with us. He means it, too. Did I tell you we're thinking about a house in the country? Robby wants a family of his own, you know, more than anything.''

He gave an unpleasant bark of a laugh. ''A *family*?'' he asked. ''Children, you mean?''

''That's what the word 'family' usually implies.''

''Then you haven't told him.''

She stared at him, shaking her head, eyes wide open as if she were begging for her life. ''Please,'' she whispered.

Harry smiled. ''You never fail to surprise me, Felicia. Do you mean to tell me that in—what is it, ten years?—you haven't told the poor feller that you can't have any more children?'' His expression was that of a man who has just heard about a practical joke played on somebody he disliked. ''Do you mean to say the poor sod is expecting you to produce a family for him, once the two of you have tardily tied the knot? You didn't even tell him about *that*?''

She shook her head. ''I couldn't,'' she whispered.

He clicked his fingers for the check. ''Well, well, well,'' he chuckled, genuinely amused. ''We're all prisoners of our past, aren't we?'' He gave her a wink as he paid the bill, smoothing the big white five-pound notes with his fingers— fastidious as always, even about money. At Langleit, his valet had a small machine with a handle, rather like the kind of thing that the French used to clean vegetables, in which he polished the coins from Lord Lisle's pockets every night, so they were shiny as new in the morning.

He rose and helped her to her feet courteously—he was the kind of man who, in public, behaved toward women, *all* women, with the polite ceremony of the nineteenth century. Harry Lisle could make you feel like a queen—no, like *the* Queen!—in public, but in private he took what he wanted from a woman with his fists, and when it pleased him, with a whip.

''You'll fix it with Charles,'' he said. ''About Portia's visit, I mean.'' It was not a question, it was an order, and he didn't even wait for a reply.

''God, you're a sexy woman!'' he said. He took her hand

and brought it to his lips. "I wonder, does Robby know what a lucky man he is?"

He let go of her hand and laughed. "I doubt it, poor bugger!" he whispered. Then he was out the door and gone.

For a moment Felicia was almost persuaded that she could smell fire and brimstone. The porter hailed her a cab, and she went home, her spirits as damp as the cold London rain.

The one person she wanted to talk to was Robby—but he was the person to whom she could never, ever, tell the truth.

9

Steam hissed, hot pieces of grit filled the air, floating in the thick yellow fog that rose in tendrils to the grimy roof, where a few dim distant lamps did little to relieve the dreary darkness of Paddington Station.

"Fair is foul, and foul is fair/Hover through the fog and filthy air," Toby Eden intoned, adding to the cold, damp miasma with a puff of his pipe smoke. He wore an ulster like that of Sherlock Holmes, cut from a heavy tweed so nubbly and sharply patterned that it could have been a horse blanket, and carried an old-fashioned leather portmanteau like that favored by Phileas Fogg in *Around the World in Eighty Days*.

Robby walked beside him, more sedately dressed in a Burberry with a cashmere lining and one of the hats he had done so much to popularize as a matinee idol. "This fog would do very nicely for the witches in *Macbeth*," he agreed.

"Splendidly!" Eden rolled his eyes as if the witches had just appeared. "I still think it's a mistake to begin the tour with *Macbeth*, though."

During the two-month run of *Antony and Cleopatra*, the question of what Robert Vane should do next had monopolized his thoughts, as well as those of his colleagues. That they should tour "the provinces" was clear to him. As for the play, Robby's thoughts turned again and again to *Macbeth*, despite Toby's doubts, partly because he had seldom done it, partly because it offered a superb part for Felicia. Admittedly there was an old theatrical belief that the play was jinxed, but he was not a superstitious man, and even if he had been, the casting of Felicia as Lady Macbeth was simply too good an opportunity to miss.

"It was my toss." Equals in the theatre, Vane and Eden always settled the question of who would play which role by tossing a coin—an arrangement to which Vane had never objected, since Eden's luck in such wagers was notoriously bad. They had tossed to decide who would choose the first play of the tour; Vane had called "heads" and won, choosing *Macbeth*. Then they had tossed a coin to see who would play Macbeth, and Vane had won again. Toby Eden would play Banquo—since he always enjoyed roles in which he could appear as a ghost, he wasn't all that disappointed. Besides, for the next performance the choice of the play, and his role in it, would be his. There was almost no spirit of rivalry between the two men—it was as if they had long ago settled on a truce between themselves, and had decided that rather than competing with each other, they would both compete against Philip Chagrin.

"You won, old boy, fair and square. No doubt you'll make a bonny Macbeth—why not?"

Like most Englishmen, Robert Vane loved trains, all the more so since the railway was part of an actor's life. In Hollywood you were driven to the studio at dawn in a chauffeured car, through lifeless, palm-lined streets, but to him a real actor's job was to bring theatre to the people. His youth had been spent in theatrical boardinghouses and railway hotels all over England, and trains still seemed to him in some way inseparable from his art.

Toby Eden dropped his voice to a whisper—a stage whisper which could fill the largest of theatres, and which rose easily above the sound of any number of railway locomotives. "You're not my worry, dear boy," he continued. "You'll be fine—so long as you don't make the mistake of playing Macbeth as a Scot, as if he were Sir Harry Lauder doing his

Scottish music-hall number. . . . No, no, I know you wouldn't, but it's a trap even the best of actors fall into. No, what worries *me* is whether Lisha is up to Lady Macbeth. It's a bloody awful role. No light spots, you know—murder and madness all the way.''

"She'll be fine, Toby. She wants to do it."

"Well, of course she does. I merely question the wisdom of it.''

"You saw how well she did with Cleopatra."

"But that's quite different, old boy. Cleopatra's good fun, don't you see? Determined to have a good time. Even when she decides to put an end to herself, she does it in high spirits—a basket full of figs with snakes hidden under them—I ask you! But Lady M's no fun at all. She's quite mad, and really rather gloomy. I've never known an actress who wasn't depressed by the role.''

"There's nothing to worry about, Toby. You have my word.''

"Well, I'm sure you know best. . . . I say, porter, here we are!''

In the gloom ahead of them the porters stopped and began loading the bags into a first-class compartment. From a distance, it seemed that there could not possibly be room for all of them. Felicia's suitcases alone—white leather, purchased at great expense three years ago for her ill-fated voyage to Hollywood—looked as if they would need a compartment of their own. Far behind, she was making her way up the platform, accompanied by Philip Chagrin and her maid, having sent "the menfolk," as she put it, to the slight distress of Chagrin, ahead to deal with the luggage, her progress marked by noisy whistles from servicemen leaning out the windows of the carriages.

Philip Chagrin stood on the platform, impeccably dressed, to see them off. In his own way he cut almost as splendid a figure as Felicia. An enemy had once said that Chagrin "positively *reeked* of distinction," and there was a good deal of truth to it. His profile, his slim figure, his elegant clothes, the pale ivory rose in the buttonhole of his velvet-collared overcoat, the tightly rolled umbrella that he carried in one lilac-gloved hand as if it were a fairy wand, all tended to disguise his robust common sense about acting, as well as his own genius. Although Vane had leaped ahead of him in fame, and Toby Eden was at least his equal, both were in awe of Chagrin, who had been a great Shakespearean actor while they were still playing minor roles, and who, in the opinion of many critics, would still be a great star when they were forgotten. Chagrin was looked upon by many as the heir to the tradition of Sir Henry Irving, the last actor who spoke Shakespeare's lines as if they were poetry, and it was generally agreed that he would long since have received his knighthood if it were not for the fact that he was a notorious and unapologetic homosexual.

There was a bond between the three men that went beyond their rivalry. Although each enjoyed a measure of success in films and in the modern theatre, their real passion was for Shakespeare. When Philip Chagrin had been told of Vane's Oscar nomination, he was reputed to have sniffed loudly in contempt and said, "Very nice, but of course it doesn't count."

The three were locked in a combat in which nothing counted except Shakespeare—between Shakespeare's own time and theirs, a span of more than three centuries, there had not been more than half a dozen actors who excelled in *all* the major roles of Shakespeare's tragedies. Popular newspapers wrote about them as if they were in a contest to decide which one of them was "The Actor of the Generation," but it was more complicated than this, for whole generations had often gone by in the past three centuries without a single preeminent actor, so that it could almost be said that what was at stake was to know which of the three would be "The Actor of the Century."

She leaned down and gave Chagrin a kiss. However much she loved Robby, Chagrin was the man who had picked her out at RADA, forced her to realize that she had the makings of a real actress. And she knew that Chagrin adored her with a passion that was all the stronger, in some ways, because it could never be sexual. Once, long before she had met Robby, or married Charles, she had managed to charm Philip into taking her out to dinner and had done her very best to seduce him in the candlelight of the restaurant. "You are wasting your time, my girl," he had said. "No offense, but I'm not in the least interested."

"You don't know if you haven't tried, Philip," she coaxed, giving him her most winning smile.

He had raised one eyebrow majestically—his raising an eyebrow was an art form worthy of years of study and practice—and said in a kind voice, "Oh, but I *have* tried it, darling—and it was 'cold mutton,' Lisha, as Oscar Wilde once said."

She had had the grace to laugh, and their friendship was sealed from that moment forth. Chagrin had given her her first real part, as Katherine in his *Henry V*, and had introduced her to his friends Guy Darling and Noel Coward as the ingenue find of the season. He had advised her not to marry Charles ("Dull at dinner means dull between the sheets"), not to leave Charles for Robby ("Theatrical marriages seldom work on stage and *never* in real life"), and not to go to Hollywood ("You'll only pick up bad acting habits, and a style of life you can't afford to keep up"). She had ignored all this advice, but he had taken no offense—it was only his advice about acting that he expected her to take seriously, and she did.

"I'll miss you," she said to him now.

He nodded. "I'll be there in a day or two." Chagrin, like everybody else on the English stage, was always trying to fit filming into his schedule. There was no other way to earn a decent living. He was directing Shakespeare, preparing to appear in *Uncle Vanya* and *The Cherry Orchard* (both directed by Toby Eden), and playing a dashing (some said too dashing) naval captain in a propaganda film that Guy Darling had written, all without interrupting his plans to do Shaw's *The Devil's Disciple*, with himself as Burgoyne. . . . "Just remember that Lady M is not a monster," he went on, "however she's been played before. She loves her husband, she's fiercely ambitious for the poor sod, and she supposes that if she were a man, she could make a damn sight better job of his business than he does. You shouldn't have any trouble playing that.''

"You're being bitchy, Philip.''

"No, I'm being perfectly realistic,'' he whispered. "And remember, darling: it's only a play. It's never a good idea to bring one's work home with one, but it would be a *particularly* bad idea to bring Lady Macbeth back to your hotel room every night. She has a way of making you do that, you know.''

The guard whistled, the clouds of steam grew thicker, the train gave a preliminary jerk. She waved good-bye, realizing as she did how much she had come to depend on Chagrin in the two months since her return. She refused to worry about "Lady M.''

"Sit down, Lisha,'' Toby said, patting the seat beside him.

She sat obediently, still wrapped in her fur coat against the cold.

"Like old times,'' Robby muttered, and she did her best to believe that it was true—but *then* he would have made sure that they had a compartment of their own, and by now she would already be in his arms. . . . Well, we're older now, she told herself, but it didn't help. And in wartime you couldn't get a compartment by yourselves, but that fact didn't help either.

The train banged and jolted its way out of the station and into the darkness—a darkness that was without relief now that London was blacked out. It was as if the tracks were carrying them clattering into the void. Somewhere far down the train she could hear soldiers singing, trying to keep their spirits up on the way to some godforsaken training camp or barracks. Robby dozed—or pretended to. Either he had nothing to say or his mind was on Macbeth.

Or on Randy Brooks? she wondered.

In the hospital in New York she had learned how precise her memory of Robby was. There was no part of him that she could not re-create exactly, not a single thing about him that was blurred or forgotten. Did he think about Randy Brooks that way? She felt herself tremble at the thought, knowing that this was exactly the kind of thing she mustn't dwell on.

"You're shivering," Toby said. "What you need is a drink, old girl."

"I don't suppose we'll get one."

"Ah, don't you worry! I've come prepared." He opened his satchel, removed a bottle of gin and a glass and placed it in front of him, then removed another bottle and a second glass and put it in front of her. "One bottle for you, one for me," he said jovially. "It's the only way to drink. There's another for Robby when he wakes up."

"I don't like gin, Toby."

"Don't like gin? Don't be silly. You like dry martinis, don't you?"

"Sometimes."

"Well, there you are." He pulled a bottle of dry vermouth out of the satchel, splashed a finger or so of it into her glass, and topped it up with gin.

She took a sip. Dr. Vogel had warned her about drinking until she was sick of listening to him. Her own rule was never to drink before a performance, to stick to champagne as much as possible, and never, ever, to drink with Toby Eden. But faced with a long, cold train journey, and the fact that Robby was dozing instead of chatting with her, she took a more serious swallow of her "martini."

"Good stuff, that," Toby said cheerfully. He had already drained his own glass and poured himself another, not bothering with the vermouth this time. "Chagrin likes them that way, too, you know. Splendid chap. Did I ever tell you about the time the two of us went up to Glasgow together to do *Richard the Third?*"

She shook her head. She was beginning to warm up at last—perhaps, she thought, there was heat on the train after all.

"It was bloody cold, midwinter, so we had a drink or two at the hotel, then a few more at the theatre, where it was even colder. Scottish theater managements aren't exactly lavish with coal, as you may remember. What with one thing and another, Philip is a little unsteady when he goes onstage.

He trips over his own robe, as a matter of fact, goes crashing down, and can't get up. Well, you can imagine the audience—lowland Scots, Bible-thumpers, chapelgoers, half of them teetotal, I should think. Philip just manages to pull himself to his feet by grasping the throne, when somebody shouts out, 'You're *pissed!*' With that, the whole audience starts to boo and hiss, because they're Scots, you see, angry at not getting their money's worth. Philip stands there, majestic as you please, holds his hand up for silence, and by God he looks so kinglike that in a moment or two you could hear a bloody pin drop in the balcony. 'Ladies and gentlemen,' he says, very grandly—and you know how grand he can be—'if you think *I'm* pissed . . . wait until you see Buckingham!' ''

Toby roared with laughter, and she joined in. She was home again, among actors, where she belonged, and so happy that she found it impossible to imagine that she had ever wanted to go to Hollywood. ''Cheers, Toby,'' she said, and finished her drink, warm as toast now.

He stared out the window for a moment, then turned back, suddenly glum. ''I hate the idea of doing *Macbeth*,'' he said. ''Against it from the very beginning.''

''Why? Banquo's a nice part.''

''It's not Banquo I mind, it's the whole bloody play. It's bad luck—always has been.''

''I don't believe that nonsense.''

''It's not nonsense at all. You can't deny that poor old Lillian Bailey died right before the first night of the Old Vic's *Macbeth*? And didn't Rex Pomfret get knocked unconscious during one of the battle scenes when he was doing *Macbeth* at Stratford? And wasn't it during a performance of *Macbeth* that old Gilles Moncrieff found his wife in her dressing room making love to Hughie Derwenter, who was playing Banquo, and stabbed them both?''

''He wasn't Banquo. He was playing Macduff. That's the point of the story, Toby, because Gilles cried out, '*Lay on, Macduff,/And damned be him that first cries, Hold, enough!*' just before stabbing them. Anyway, he did them no great harm, I believe. And the Moncrieffs are still married, so they must have made it up. I don't believe *Macbeth* is jinxed.''

For a moment or two they sat companionably, letting the gin do its work. She felt relaxed, happy, warm, slightly abuzz—really happier than she had been for ages.

She wished Robby would wake up and keep her company.

''I'm only saying that it's not the *best* way to start a tour, darling,'' Robby said patiently.

''If you hadn't fallen asleep on the train, as if I didn't even *exist*, it would never have happened.''

''I apologize. I apologized before. I was tired.''

''*Tired*, Robby? Or bored?''

''For God's sake, Lisha! I was *not* bored. I'm sorry I fell asleep on the bloody train, but that's not a reason to get stinking drunk with Toby and make a scene on the platform, in front of the press. . . .''

''I did *not* make a scene!''

''You called one of the women reporters a nosy old bitch. You told the chap from the *Manchester Guardian* that you were going to play Lady Macbeth as a Highland sexpot, on *my* advice. I don't suppose *that* will go down any too well with the *Guardian*'s readers, do you?''

''I can't see the harm of shaking up a pack of old biddies and their dreary husbands. We'll probably have a full house every night.''

''That's not the point.'' But whatever the point was, he didn't bother making it. He went to the window to look out into the street, knowing in advance what a cheerless sight it would be, but he couldn't move the blackout curtain without turning off the lights, so he was obliged to turn his attention back to Felicia again.

The suite was spacious by the standards of Victorian hotels, the decor, to use a favorite word of set designers, was all dark mahogany and even darker velvet, dimly lit by a few elaborate nineteenth-century gilt gas fittings that had been converted to take the feeblest of electric bulbs. A coal fire burned bricks of coal dust that left small black spots on any exposed linen. If you leaned on the mantelpiece, close to the fire, it was possible to feel a certain warmth, but if you took a single step away from the fire, you were immediately plunged into icy discomfort. The bathroom was a small tiled chamber with a ceiling so high that it was like standing in a mine shaft, and with cast-iron fixtures that had apparently been designed for a race of giants. None of this would ordinarily have given him a moment's unease, let alone claustrophobia so fierce that it was all he could do to prevent himself from running into the hallway to escape the feeling of confinement. His problem, he was quite sure, was not one of space—it was the presence of Felicia that made him feel trapped.

Felicia demanded his constant attention, and while he still suffered from the occasional pang of guilt, his mind was on other things. He had purged himself of much during his year of terror in the air force—guilt over Felicia, the failure of his marriage to Penelope, the mistakes of the past, all seemed irrelevant in the skies over Germany, where a lucky gunner, or a moment's inattention, could end his life in an instant. Somewhere in the passing of those terrible hours he had found in himself the hard kernel of what mattered—to be the preeminent actor of his time, perhaps of all time.

In the first weeks of Felicia's return, he had been happy enough to plunge into domestic bliss out of sheer relief that they had both survived their respective ordeals and were together again.

He could hardly complain about Felicia's behavior now that she was back again. Felicia was cheerful, amorous, her return to the stage had been an unqualified success, in the eyes of the world he was the luckiest of men. But her moods altered swiftly, from hour to hour, her enthusiasms gave way to sudden depressions, and she required—no, *demanded!*—his constant attention.

Even this tour was to some degree determined by Felicia's need to perform onstage in a role equal to his. He had chosen *Macbeth* chiefly because Lady Macbeth was a role that Felicia wanted to play. But he could hardly spend the rest of his professional life in plays that gave Felicia a chance to act as his partner. There was no way he could accept that kind of limitation to his ambitions, reducing them to the English equivalent of the Lunts on Broadway. He felt already the burden of having to carry Felicia's problems, and it had been this, as much as anything, that had made him close his eyes and pretend to sleep on the train. He simply had not felt like playing the eager lover for the benefit of Toby Eden, or talking about plans for the future in which they would act together for the rest of their lives.

She was standing in the middle of the dismal room, looking at once defiant and heartbreakingly pathetic, surrounded by acres of luggage. They could hardly remain in silence, he decided, like characters in a drawing-room comedy who have forgotten their lines. He went over to put his arms around her, while she stood stiff and unyielding. "Lisha," he said, "I love you. And I'm sorry."

She did not look at him. "Sorry?" she said in a low whisper. "We're all sorry. Sorry for what?"

"Sorry that you think I've been ignoring you."

"Well, and so you have."

"There's been so much to think about."

"There was a time when we'd have given anything in the world to be alone together in a hotel room. Do you remember?"

He remembered. "You'd better get some rest," he said gently.

"What you mean is that I'd better sober up. Well you needn't worry. I'm sober."

"What I *mean* is that we have work to do. We open in three days."

"I'm aware of the fact."

"And it's not an easy role."

"None of them is easy."

That, he thought, was not exactly true. Every great part was hard work, but some were much harder than others. *Macbeth* was one of the hardest, which accounted perhaps for the stories of bad luck that surrounded the play.

Vane had come to hate Macbeth over the past few weeks of thinking and planning for the role, and even in rehearsal the key to the man still somehow eluded him. He understood Macbeth's dilemma—the man makes a single mistake, commits a terrible crime, and is unable to retreat from it, while all the while, Lady Macbeth, whose contempt for her husband is only barely disguised, eggs him on to more and more evil acts. . . . He had thought long and hard about why he was uncomfortable with the role, and had come to the conclusion that the problem lay in Lady Macbeth—or, to be more exact, in Felicia's interpretation of her, even though it was partly his idea.

Felicia seemed to revel in playing a sexy and seductive Lady Macbeth, more courageous and determined than her weakling of a husband, determined to win him the crown he covets but doesn't have the guts to go after. Somehow, perhaps because of Chagrin's direction, she was running away with the play, so that his Macbeth was becoming more and more passive, a supporting figure in a tragedy of which *she* was the heroine.

"Come to bed, darling," he said, suddenly overwhelmed by fatigue.

She nodded, and he led her into the bedroom. What, he wondered, was it like for the Macbeths when they went upstairs to their room in the castle? Shakespeare left all that to your imagination. He did not show you the Macbeths getting undressed, or sitting down to breakfast, or making love—if they made love. He and Felicia had acted out *their* love affair in public for so long that they had a tendency to drop their roles as lovers the moment they were alone. They would go into the hotel lift in silence, absorbed in their own thoughts, then when the door opened, take each other's hand and walk out into the lobby, playing the star-crossed lovers for an audience of hotel porters and casual strangers.

Why was it, he wondered, that he had been able to share his innermost feelings with Randy, and could no longer share them with her? He knew the answer, of course. He had failed her in so many ways that he was obliged to hide himself away from her. He took off his clothes while she was in the bathroom, glumly lit another cigarette (he must cut down,

and besides, the bloody things were rationed now, and it was
a crime to waste them).

It was strange—sex with Randy had not been especially
exciting, beyond the predictably delicious thrill of doing
something that was forbidden. It had not been a patch on sex
with Lisha, and he had felt not the slightest desire to do it
again, not with Randy, nor with any other man. It was something else—a feeling of closeness, of shared secrets, of genuine friendship—of *fondness*, to use the exact word—that
had bound Randy and him together, a feeling which could
be sealed only by sex, because it was the ultimate sharing.
Randy had wanted it to continue, of course, but he had refused. What was it, he thought, that Voltaire had said about
homosexuality? ''Once, a philosopher; twice, a pederast.''

We'll marry, Felicia and I, he told himself. With a house
of their own and children, he and Lisha would be happy—
he was convinced of it, he would not even consider the possibility that it might not be so.

He held fast to that dream: a family of his own and fame.
If he closed his eyes (and there was certainly nothing in the
hideous hotel bedroom worth keeping them open for), he
could picture exactly the kind of life he had in mind: Syon
Manor, with its weathered, golden Cotswold stone, the grav-
eled yard, the brick stables, and beyond them the rolling
fields—*his* rolling fields—the pond, he thought, with ducks
on it, the formal garden, the maze. He imagined tea on the
lawn amidst glowing flowers, dogs at his feet, somewhere in
the background a child on a pony. . . .

He heard the clanking of the plumbing, the ancient pipes
shuddering and shaking at every turn of the tap, then he heard
the bathroom door latch click open (Lisha always locked the
bathroom door, even at home—she had a mania for privacy,
along with a fastidiousness so great that she would rather
suffer than use a public toilet). He felt her slip into bed beside
him. Even in the dark, he knew that she was lying there as
she always did, flat on her back, hands crossed over her waist,
toes straight up, like an effigy of a crusader's lady on a
tomb—she lacked only the dog at her feet to complete the

picture. Her head would be placed squarely in the center of
the uppermost of the two pillows she required, with her own
pillowcases on them, of course, her satin slippers placed
neatly on a clean towel on the floor beside her—she disliked
putting her bare feet on the carpet of a hotel room, where
countless strangers had trod before her—the blanket and sheet
(her own, of course) folded back just below the shoulders,
exactly six inches of sheet, no more, no less.

There were times when he wanted to scream, "Don't you
know there's a *war* on?" or "A speck of dirt won't kill you,
for Christ's sake!" or any number of things that would certainly have wounded her, but what was the point? There was
no changing her, and in the grand scheme of things, not much
reason to try. Would he have preferred slovenliness, after
all? Yes, by God, he told himself, a little bit of slovenliness
would do wonders: the odd hairpin on the floor, a few stray
hairs in her brush, a stain or two on her expensive lingerie. . . .

It occurred to him belatedly that in her own way Lady
Macbeth was obsessed with cleanliness as well. "*What, will
these hands ne' er be clean?*" And what was it her maid says?
"*It is an accustom'd action with her to seem thus washing
her hands. I have known her continue in this a quarter of an
hour.*"

A mania for neatness and cleanliness—surely uncommon
in ancient Scotland?—would be a useful little touch to Felicia's performance, her hands constantly straightening things,
putting them right, brushing away a spot of dirt from Macbeth's cloak. . . . He would have to talk to Philip about it.

To his astonishment, he felt her hand clutch his under the
covers. "Robby," she whispered, her voice throaty from too
many cigarettes and several hours of boozing with Toby Eden,
"I don't *disgust* you, do I?"

"Good God, no!" he said, sitting up startled, instantly
awake. He felt her run the tips of her fingers down the silk
of his pajamas. He hated the damned things, actually, and
in the RAF had slept in his shorts quite comfortably, but
Felicia always bought him pajamas of the most expensive

kind, which he felt obliged to wear. "Whatever do you mean, my love?"

"My body doesn't disgust you?"

"What on earth makes you ask that?"

"I just wondered. What do you like best about women's bodies? As opposed to men's, I mean?"

A warning bell went off in his head. "I've never found men's bodies at all interesting," he said firmly.

"I thought every man did—a little bit. Women are attracted to other women, after all, even if it's only in the mind."

"Perhaps. I couldn't say. However, I haven't the slightest interest in men's bodies. God knows I saw enough of them in the air force and at school."

"Haven't you ever wondered what it would be like to make love to another man? *I've* often wondered what it would be like to make love with another woman."

He sighed. "I have not."

"Ah." She did not sound convinced. He was sure she was counting on the fact that he was exhausted and half asleep to catch him out. It was a conversation he was eager to bring to an end. He rolled over, pulled her close to him and kissed her hard.

In the dim light from the sitting room, the last thing he saw before he entered her were her eyes, looking at him with the cold, hard stare of an interrogator, as if she had known perfectly well what he would do and knew exactly what he was trying to hide; then he lifted himself on top of her and blotted out the sight.

He did not think he had given her much pleasure—it was over fast, as if she, too, wanted to get it done with as quickly as possible.

He was half asleep before it occurred to him that it hadn't given *him* much pleasure, either. He could feel her beside him, breathing softly, her hand touching him as if to make sure he was still there.

He had never felt more alone in his life.

10

She was not happy in Manchester—not with the sets, not with her dressing room, not with the acoustics of the theatre. She was not happy with Robby's costume and makeup—about which he had not consulted her—nor with the deference the entire company showed toward Robby, which seemed to relegate her to a secondary role.

In Philip Chagrin's protracted absence in London—he had telegraphed his apologies—Robby had simply taken over everything, and while she felt a great sympathy for him, seeing how thin he was stretched and how complicated his responsibilities were, she resented both his importance and the fact that he treated her as if she were just another problem in the exhausting task of getting *Macbeth* onto the stage more or less intact. If Philip had been there to direct her—to direct *him*—she kept telling herself, everything would have been all right, but with less than a week of rehearsals to go, she felt unprepared and, worse still, uncared for.

The problems of *Macbeth* had not seemed to her worse than those of any other Shakespearean tragedy at a first reading—it was not until she was onstage, in the theatre, that she began to understand why generations of actors and actresses believed the play was jinxed. It was impossibly difficult to perform, as if for once Shakespeare had forgotten all his stagecraft.

The scene in which Banquo's ghost takes his seat at the banquet table could be played with an empty chair, or with Toby Eden, suitably ghostly and bloodstained, actually sitting there, but Robby didn't find either comfortable. He did not like acting to an empty chair, but he liked Toby's ghost even less, for try as he might, there was no disguising the "too, too solid flesh" of Toby Eden, nor the sparkle of life in his eyes. More complicated still was the dagger Macbeth sees

before him, the handle toward his hand. Both Philip and
Robby had decided that if the audience was going to see
Banquo's ghost they should also see the ghostly dagger. Endless attempts had been made to project it into the air in front
of Macbeth's eyes, using everything from a slide projector
to a specially prepared klieg light. These experiments absorbed the attention of the lighting crew to the point where
Felicia complained constantly about being plunged into total
darkness in the middle of a speech.

She cursed Shakespeare silently, as she knew everyone
who had ever played *Macbeth* did sooner or later, but she
was aware that it was Robby who was making her unhappy.
In a hundred little ways, she felt, or thought she felt, his
indifference. She wanted him to come over to her from time
to time to give her a kiss or put his hand on her shoulder, to
whisper to her, as he had during *Antony*, how much he looked
forward to being alone with her. Instead, he seemed to sur-
round himself—deliberately, she suspected—with the other
members of the company, to plunge into problems that enabled him to avoid her. She responded by pouring into her
performance her anger and her fear of losing him, with the
result, which even she could see, that she was constantly
upstaging him, so that his Macbeth seemed pallid by comparison. She could not seem to help herself—she was playing,
defiantly, to the audience, rather than to Robby, and the less
sure he was of his role, the more stubbornly she pursued hers.

She felt at the same time a vague and growing distress.
The blood and gore of *Macbeth* depressed her, its macabre
atmosphere filling her with much the same feelings she had
had when she was taken to Madame Tussaud's waxworks as
a child and been moved to tears by the sight of Mary Queen
of Scots's beheading. She slept poorly, as she always did,
but the few hours of sleep she managed to get every night
were troubled with dreams of blood, phantasmagoric daggers,
a whole grisly sequence of disturbing visions that her sleeping
mind was unable to stop. Much of it, happily, she was unable
to remember when she woke up, but one image which stayed
with her was that of her own hand, clasped around the hilt
of a silver-mounted dagger, stabbing again and again into a

human body, the blood spattering out until she was red with gore. The face of the man she was murdering shifted uneasily in her dream—sometimes the features were those of Randy Brooks, sometimes Marty Quick's, sometimes Uncle Harry's. . . . Philip Chagrin had warned her not to bring Lady Macbeth home with her, but Lady Macbeth clearly had a mind of her own.

Even thinking about the nightmares in broad daylight—or rather in the dim glow of the rehearsal lamps—made her nervous. She walked across the stage to where Robby stood, surrounded by his court, the lighting men, the stagehands, Toby smoking his loathsome pipe, his face made up alarmingly for his ghost scene, the assistant stage manager, and an enormously tall young man named Guillam Pentecost, whom she had hated at first sight, and toward whom she therefore felt obliged to be enormously polite. Pentecost was a journalist, or claimed to be, one of those young men who were mad about the theatre without having been able to find a place for themselves in it. He was enthralled by the great Robert Vane, of course.

Pentecost reminded her of Cassius—exactly the sort of lean and hungry fellow of whom to beware—though Robby had clearly taken to the young man, paying attention to his every suggestion, enjoying being worshipped. He was polite enough to her, but his politeness failed to conceal a certain contempt. Though he wrote only for the local newspaper, he was an Oxford graduate, and fancied himself as an intellectual. And she couldn't deny he was smart, with a kind of ruthless, quick, undergraduate cleverness. Pentecost had produced several experimental plays at Oxford, and had even acted in some of the University Theatre groups. Now he was supposedly writing a piece about Robby for *The New Statesman*.

"Robby, darling," she said, "I must talk to you about my lighting."

She caught, out of the corner of her eye, a brief glance between Robby and Pentecost that might have signaled "Oh, God, what now?" It reminded her of similar glances between Robby and Randy Brooks, surreptitious, knowing, impatient.

"It's being taken care of," Robby said. "I can't do everything at once." He saw the expression on her face and instantly changed his tone. "My dearest darling," he said soothingly (how she *hated* to be soothed!), "I promise you it will be all right."

She stamped her foot impatiently. "I'm in darkness half the time," she said.

"Look, until Philip arrives, I've got the whole bloody production to worry about, Lisha. We'll get you lit! Right, Rod?"

"Right, guv," the lighting man said glumly. "We'll sort it out eventually."

"I want it sorted out *now*."

"Well, it would help if you could slow down a little, darling. You're getting to your mark before the light, you see."

"I am doing no such thing! Anyway"—she pointed at Rod—"it's not *my* job to make it easy for him, is it? It's *his* job to keep the bloody light on me so I'm not speaking my lines in the dark. I don't think that's too much to ask."

"I thought it was rather effective, actually," Pentecost said in his Oxford common-room voice, which managed to convey boredom and intellectual superiority at the same time. "Komisarsky's *Macbeth* was very dark, you know—a kind of Rembrandtesque chiaroscuro, very effective, with Lady Macbeth floating in the shadows. Frankly, I don't think it's a play that *needs* a lot of bright lights."

"Interesting thought, that," Robby said, closing his eyes for a moment.

She stared at him, chilled by his unlikely reaction. She knew that when he was sure of himself, he never listened to anybody, or rather, he listened, but without the slightest intention of paying attention. He had lost his way with *Macbeth*, and now he was willing to try anything he was offered—which partly explained, she supposed, his ridiculous costume, for he had given himself thick false eyebrows, a long dark beard, with slanting mustaches that looked more Fu Manchu than Scottish, a sharp nose like Philip Chagrin's, and what seemed like endless yards of gloomy tartan.

She stared at Pentecost as rudely as she could, struck by how very much she disliked his looks. Despite his enormous height, there was something childish about his face, as if he were a wizened, half-starved companion of Oliver Twist's in Mr. Bumble's parish workhouse. Pentecost's mousy blond hair was slicked back, his big ears stuck out, his whole face had a bony, undernourished look, saved from being ordinary by extremely sharp eyes—exactly the right eyes, it occurred to her, for Iago—and by remarkably sensual lips. He could not have been more than twenty-two, but his expression was one of arrogant superiority. His clothes, like those of a schoolboy, were too short at the wrists and ankles, as if he had outgrown them in a single delayed burst, but they were worn with a kind of careless elegance despite the fact that they were neither new nor particularly clean. She was not about to be challenged or advised by this overgrown schoolboy, however entranced Robby was with him. "I don't give a shit about Komisarsky," she said. "I'm not going on in the bloody pitch-darkness. The audience is paying to *see* the play. And also to see *me*."

Lesser men, older and more powerful, would have backed away from her. Pentecost didn't flinch or blush. "Yes," he said calmly. "I daresay that's all very true. The good citizens of Manchester will want to see stars if they're paying for stars. And of course, who wouldn't want to see *you*, Miss Lisle? There's not much beauty in Manchester at the best of times. I don't think there'll be a soul in the audience able to tear his, or her, eyes away from you, not for an instant."

"That will depend on whether they can see me or not."

"Point taken. But even in the dimmest of light, you would shine out, I think."

"Please don't bother flattering me, Mr. Pentecost. I've been flattered by far more important people."

She turned on Robby. "Is it too much to ask that I be allowed to rehearse without the bloody fucking press standing onstage? That is, *when* you get around to letting me rehearse!"

There was a collective sigh from the small group around Robby. It would have been hard to find half a dozen men who more clearly wished to be elsewhere—except for Pentecost, who seemed amused and fascinated, no doubt because he was making a mental note of every word.

Of course, she knew how "loyal" people were to Robby, which only fueled her anger. Robby was adored by everyone, right down to the lowliest stagehand. He had "the common touch," just like Henry the bloody Fifth, the gift of making everybody feel they were an important part of the production, that he was as interested in their problems as he was in his own—whereas *she* was merely the temperamental star, the demanding Hollywood bitch-goddess.

She caught the look in Robby's eye—a brief flash of anger, instantly suppressed. It was followed by a long-suffering, patient smile. "Of course, darling," he said gently. "We'll be ready in a moment." He turned to Pentecost and smiled. "Guillam," he said, "you wouldn't mind . . . ?"

"Not a bit! I'll make myself scarce." Pentecost's expression was knowing—just a hairsbreadth short of a stage wink. He lit a cigarette—from a pack of Vanes, she noted, wondering where on earth he had found them—and sauntered offstage.

"Do we really need to have this pimply youth playing Boswell to your Dr. Johnson during rehearsals?"

"Actually, darling, Guillam isn't in the least pimply. And he's bright—just the kind of fellow you don't often find writing provincial theatre criticism. I think he'll do us a world of good, but if he's in the way, I'll keep him out of sight."

"Not out of sight! Out of *here* altogether!"

Robby opened his mouth to say something, but before he could get the words out, the assistant stage manager appeared, with a hasty, mumbled apology, to announce that the complicated set for the battlements of Dunsinane had been damaged in transit, that the carpenters would need to work on them all night—and before Robby had even heard him out, a small crowd of people was around him, waving blueprints, holding up costumes, waving clipboards with sheaves of papers for him to sign. Actors complained about their dressing rooms, the lighting men complained about the inadequacy of the theatre's electric system, the scene designer shrilly de-

nounced the movers who had damaged his sets, even Toby
Eden's dresser was there, requesting Robby's approval of yet
another version of the makeup for Banquo's ghost scene.
Everywhere there was chaos and people competing for Rob-
by's attention when he should have been rehearsing with *her*.
She longed for the arrival of Philip Chagrin as, to be fair,
Robby surely did.

"Five minutes, darling!" he called out to her. "Not a
moment more, I promise." She gave him a look that would
have withered a healthy tree in full bloom, stamped off the
stage, went up to her dressing room, slammed the door, and
locked it.

To hell with him, she told herself. It was not just that she
was his . . . she struggled furiously in her mind for the correct
word, for that was part of the problem. She was *not* his wife,
but on the other hand, she was hardly his mistress, nor was
she happy with the phrase "constant companion," which
American gossip columnists always used with an implied leer.

She paced the dressing room, pausing in front of the mirror
to admire herself, and to wonder how Robby, or any man,
could be indifferent to her. For Lady Macbeth she wore her
hair long and loose, framing her pale face, her dark eyes
exaggerated with makeup, her lips a pale red which she had
chosen, after much discussion with Philip, to give her an
almost carnivorous expression. She looked beautiful and terrifying, surely a woman any man would want to sleep with,
but whom all but the most daring would find a little too
frightening for comfort.

Was this the way she appeared to Robby? She tore off her
costume, put on her old robe and began to massage cold
cream into her face to remove what she had done with such
care. It had taken her a good hour to put on her makeup.

She worked on her face with a kind of fierce, driven anxiety, as if the makeup might not come off and she would be
condemned to spend the rest of her life in the role of Lady
Macbeth, washing her hands of blood. . . .

She glanced at her little enameled Cartier traveling clock
—a present from Robby in happier days. It was past four,
and she had been in the theatre since eleven, waiting for

Robby to perform with her. Even if he decided to start now, it would take her a good hour to put her face back on. Well, he would just have to wait, damn him! she thought, with considerable satisfaction.

There was a knock at the door. "Go away," she said quietly. She took a flask out of the dressing table drawer and poured herself a drink, "against doctor's orders," of course, and, more important, against her own better judgment. She never drank alone in her dressing room—she had never known an actress who did so to survive for long. You might have a drink *with* someone in your dressing room, she often did that, and you might go out after the curtain and get right royally pissed, but solitary drinking was the worst thing an actress could do. She took the drink anyway.

There was another knock, a little firmer this time. Very well, she told herself, if Robby wanted to crawl, let him crawl. She lit a cigarette, went over to the door and unbolted it. "You can come in," she said. "I'm decent."

But it was not Robby who came in, it was Pentecost. She pulled her dressing gown around her a little more snugly and faced him. "What the hell do you want?" she asked. "If Mr. Vane wants to begin rehearsing, he can come and bloody well ask me himself."

Pentecost smiled. She was pleased to see that he had awful teeth. "I daresay he can. I daresay he will. But that's not why I'm here."

She could not help admiring the young man's composure. He was a provincial journalist, only just graduated from university, but he managed to make himself seem at home in her dressing room without any effort. "Why *are* you here, then?" she asked.

Pentecost looked at her coolly. His eyes caught the drink on her dresser and sparkled with amusement, as if she had just confirmed the rumors about her behavior. "I admire Mr. Vane very much," he said. "I think he's a genius."

She nodded. All Robby's admirers thought he was a genius.

"He's been very good to me. As you know. Not many actors would let a journalist or a critic get that close to them. And of course it's fascinating to see him work."

"I suppose it must be," she said indifferently.

"It's *because* I'm grateful to him that I'm not sure how to tell him what I've heard."

She came to full attention with a start. If there was one thing guaranteed to make her sit upright, it was the assurance of a journalist, however lowly and far removed from the mainstream of gossip, that he had "heard" something. "Heard?" she asked. "What are you talking about?"

Pentecost gave a nervous shrug. "I had a telephone call from London," he said. "A friend of mine who works for one of the gamier dailies. It seems there's a reason for Mr. Chagrin's delay."

"Delay? He had some filming to do. I expect it took longer than he thought. It always does. He's probably on his way by now."

"No, that's the point. He's not on his way, and he won't be. He was arrested yesterday. It seems he propositioned a fellow in a bar—a policeman, unfortunately. You know how these things go—it's usually just a straight case of bribery. Anyway, something went wrong. Maybe Mr. Chagrin didn't offer a big enough bribe, or maybe he came up against the only honest copper in the West End, but he was arrested, charged with indecent solicitation, taken before a magistrate, and bound over for trial."

"Oh, my God! Poor Philip!"

"Well, it's not as bad as it could be. I don't think the press is likely to make too much of a fuss about it. I mean, everybody *knows* he's a homosexual, so it's not really much of a story. After all, he's not a married man with two children, or a member of the Cabinet, or a clergyman. There'll be a certain amount of fuss, but it won't last. Still, I don't think he'll be coming to Manchester, do you? Robby—Mr. Vane, I mean—is going to have to take over."

"Damn *Macbeth*!" she said. It was true. The bloody play *was* jinxed. Robby would now have to direct *and* act the leading role.

She knew all too well how difficult this would be. It had been his attempt to direct *Romeo and Juliet* and play Romeo in America that had led to her nervous breakdown. He had

been far too passive most of the time, as if he wanted above
all to avoid a confrontation with her—then, when his patience
was at an end, he would suddenly snap at her, which only
made her angry and resentful. She understood why. It was
impossible not to bring to the stage all the hurts, guilts, and
wrongs of their life together. To act with him was hard
enough; to be directed by him as well was impossible—for
both of them.

"Well, there it is," Pentecost said smugly, with the satisfaction of a man for whom bad news is more interesting
than good news. "I think Robby—Mr. Vane, that is—should
be warned, don't you? I mean, the press will descend on him
en masse, and besides, he won't want to learn about it from
the papers, will he?"

"And you don't want to be the bearer of the evil tidings,
Mr. Pentecost?"

"Just so."

"But you don't mind telling *me*?"

"If you don't mind my saying so, you seem to me to be
made of sterner stuff, Miss Lisle. Besides you're a lot closer
to him than I am, aren't you?"

She thought she detected a smirk. Distracted, she wondered
just how close to Robby the young man was? She swallowed
the rest of her drink, no longer caring what Pentecost might
think—or say. "I'll tell him," she said. Then, with a sigh,
"Poor Philip."

"Ah, yes. It *does* rather put an end to any hopes he may
have had for his knighthood, I think. I'd say he's out of the
running in the Great Actor stakes too, for the time being. It's
between Robby and Toby Eden now, and I know who I'd
put my money on, personally. Of course, a lot depends on
Macbeth, I suppose. We shall see." He gave her his knowing
smile. "I'll leave you to it, then," he said. "I imagine we'll
be seeing more of each other."

"What makes you think that?"

"Mr. Vane has suggested I might be able to help him, as
an adviser, you know, reading scripts, making suggestions,
that kind of thing . . . what the French call a *dramaturge*."
She could not help noticing that his French was awful. She

winced at his pronunciation. "Of course I'll have to get my piece done first," he went on, oblivious. "And my review. But it's an exciting opportunity, working closely with a man like him—as *you* know better than I!" He winked at the glass in her hand. "He's in his dressing room now, if you want to find him."

He gave her a quick jerky bow, ungraceful because of his height, then slipped out.

She knew without a single doubt that he would tell Robby he had found her drinking, but what was far worse was his insinuation that he knew where Robby was and she didn't.

She poured another drink defiantly, then went off, the remnants of her makeup still smeared on her face, to give Robby the bad news.

But he did not treat it as bad news. Certainly he was sorry for Chagrin, shocked at what had happened, but he seemed pleased at the opportunity to complete *his Macbeth* without Chagrin's advice or interference. She was always forgetting how ruthless his ambition was.

Chagrin's arrest had focused the interest of the press on the play. "VANE'S FINEST HOUR!" the *Daily Express* exclaimed on the front page, with two photographs, one of Philip Chagrin leaving the magistrates' court, chin up and defiant, the other of Robert Vane, brooding Hamlet-like over his increased responsibilities. In some way, "Vane's *Macbeth*" (as it was now called in the press) seemed to fascinate everyone, even people who cared nothing for Shakespeare or the theatre. Of course it had all the elements of a press drama—a sex scandal, a pair of famous unmarried lovers, a "jinxed" play, and the ever-popular relay race for the theatrical laurels, in which poor Philip had just stumbled so badly as to have virtually disqualified himself.

In two days of nonstop work, Robby had succeeded in putting his stamp on Philip Chagrin's *Macbeth*, but not in eradicating all traces of Chagrin's original conception. It was too late to eliminate the Wagnerian sets or the operatic display of smoke and colored lights that accompanied the witches,

nor was it possible to do anything about the dagger that
floated—or sometimes failed to float—in midair.

Philip had wanted Macbeth to be a cold, calculating villain,
urged on by a demanding, sexy wife. It was not an interpretation with which Robby was comfortable, so he tried to make
his Macbeth more likable, as if he wanted to communicate
to the audience somehow that he wasn't such a bad chap after
all—which had the effect of leaving Lady Macbeth high and
dry as the villainess.

Critics had accused Felicia of reverting to "kittenish
charm" whenever she was in doubt about how to play a scene,
and she could not deny the charge. "Kittenish charm" had
worked splendidly for Cleopatra, and would have worked
well enough for Juliet, but Lady Macbeth was more tigress
than kitten. She was undeniably evil, with no saving graces,
not even her love for Macbeth, which was soured by her
contempt for his irresolution.

> *"The raven himself is hoarse*
> *That croaks the fatal entrance of Duncan*
> *Under my battlements. Come, you spirits*
> *That tend on mortal thoughts, unsex me here,*
> *And fill me from the crown to the toe top full*
> *Of direst cruelty! Make thick my blood . . ."*

Nevertheless—and without much help from Robby!—Felicia had found the key to making *herself* believe in Lady M,
if not the audience. She played her with the smoldering,
dissatisfied pout of a woman unfulfilled. When in doubt, she
thought of the way Natalie Brooks often stared at Randy when
she thought nobody was looking, and everything fell into
place. She could not help noticing that she had managed to
make Robby so nervous that at one point he began to stammer.

She turned to look toward the point where Robby would
make his entrance at any moment, and caught sight of Pentecost seated in the shadows at the far end of the front row,
reading a book—and instantly forgot her next line.

"What in God's name is *he* doing here?" she shouted,
shielding her eyes against the lights.

There was a muffled sound from the shadows behind the battlements, in which she recognized a curse. Robby appeared, momentarily unrecognizable in his beard, heavy eyebrows, and ornate helmet. "For God's sake, Lisha, get on with it. '*Stop up th' access and passage to remorse. . . .*'"

"Perhaps you didn't hear me, Robby? What is that bloody young man doing there, spying on me? And how *dare* he read a book?"

"Guillam's *not* reading a book. He's following the play for me."

"Get him out of here!"

Robby moved forward onto the battlements as if he were escaping from his enemies, and came over to where she stood. "Guillam," he said gently, "be a good fellow and make yourself scarce." He glared at Lisha. "He's only trying to help."

"I don't need his help, thank you."

"Perhaps not, but I do. I can't be in two places at once."

"I will not have *my* performance judged by young Mr. Pentecost."

"He's not making any judgments. He's prompting."

"He goes or I go, Robby. That's all there is to it." She knew she was being unreasonable, and she didn't care. She realized that she was no more amenable to reason than Lady Macbeth. She had *become* Lady Macbeth, and the problem was no longer how to play her, but how to stop. Her anger with Robby was both real and in the role.

She turned on her heels, made her way back up the battlements, waited for the spotlight to catch up with her, and began again, her voice rising in triumph, a Lady Macbeth that filled the house. She swept down the battlements to where Robby was to make his entrance, saw him in the wings, and as if on instinct flung herself toward him.

Before he could even say "*My dearest love,/Duncan comes here tonight,*" she tumbled off the edge of the battlement and reached out to put her arms around him, catching him by surprise—which might not have mattered, except that the spotlight swept on past them both, plunging them into darkness, so that she missed her footing, fell to her knees, and brought Robby, on the word "*Duncan*," crashing down to the floor, with a cry of pain, followed by the noise of his helmet rolling across the stage.

For a moment she wondered if the disaster of *Romeo and Juliet* had repeated itself, but Robby rose to his feet a little stiffly and ran his hand over his extremities. "Nothing broken," he said. "That's at least one piece of good luck."

"You *might* help me up!"

He reached out his hand. For a moment she thought he was going to put his arms around her and laugh, as he would have done in the old days, but once she was on her feet, he turned, walked away and retrieved his helmet. Then he looked at her coldly from the wings and called out, "Shall we begin again?"

It was not until she was back on the battlements, cursing her luck, the lights, *him*, that it dawned on her Robby must think she was drunk.

She knew whom she had to thank for that!

Opening nights had long since lost their terror for her, if not for Robby—particularly in a place as unglamorous as wartime Manchester.

"*Is this a dagger which I see before me,/The handle toward my hand?*"

She watched from the wings as Robby stumbled in the darkness after the dagger that hovered in the air before him momentarily, only to shift suddenly toward his face so that he was blinded. She derived a certain gloomy satisfaction from the spectacle of him lurching unsteadily up the steep steps, like a man trying to catch a butterfly in his hands at dusk.

She had foretold disaster with the lighting and the special effects, and she had been right. At any moment she expected to hear that most dreaded of sounds during the performance of a tragedy—a giggle, or a muffled laugh.

Robby's strength as an actor, the sheer power of his eyes alone, was enough to keep the audience silent, for the moment. But from her vantage point she could see his look of terror as he realized he was climbing the flimsy staircase with its impossibly narrow steps in pitch-darkness, staring at the illuminated dagger as it swayed and dipped before him. At any moment he might miss his footing and go plunging to the stage in a clatter of armor and chain mail.

Serve him right! she told herself. Anybody who could act knew that nothing was more dangerous than a dark stage, unless it was a stray spotlight catching you full in the face and momentarily blinding you. Robby had managed to give himself a scene in which both were almost a certainty. He, of all people, should have known better.

She hugged herself for warmth—since California, she suffered from the cold and damp in England all the time—pulling her shawl tighter around her shoulders. Robby had reached the top of the stairs now and was poised precariously on a small platform, designed to represent the landing as seen from the audience's point of view. Here, at last, the wavering dagger flickered toward the flies and vanished, and he was able to draw his real one.

It was a good speech—not one of the great ones that older theatregoers knew by heart, so that you could sometimes hear them mumbling the lines when you were onstage—but lively enough to give Robby a good chance to win the audience over before the real fireworks of the play began. She knew how important it was to do that, and she also could tell that he wasn't succeeding. Somehow his Macbeth seemed *smaller* than life. She heard a discreet cough beside her, and turned to see Toby Eden peering over her shoulder.

"A full house," he whispered. "And every one of them awake!"

She could smell gin on his breath, though he seemed perfectly sober. Of course, you could never tell with Toby— she knew that. He had elected to play Banquo with such grave dignity that he gave the impression of being a bishop rather than a battle-hardened soldier, but he was quite capable of changing his mind at the last moment and kicking up his heels. "He's very quiet," she whispered back.

Toby rolled his eyes. "I can hear him perfectly well."

"That's not what I meant."

"He's holding something back? Yes. Good thinking!

Plenty of big scenes to come for him, what? No point letting it all out in act one, is there?''

"I don't think it's just that.''

"Steady start makes for a strong finish. Every jockey knows that, Lish.''

"There's such a thing as being left behind at the start, Toby.''

"He may be thinking about you, the dear chap. Ah, the bell! Break a leg, darling.''

She heard the bell, then the end of Robby's speech.

She moved forward for her cue, letting her shawl fall. Above her she heard a dull thud as Robby made his exit through the door to Duncan's bedchamber, closing the door behind him.

She squared her shoulders, blinked quickly (for some reason her eyes always opened wider after blinking), and walked at the slowest pace she could toward the stage, the footlights glaring up at her. She had learned never to make a quick entrance—learned it years ago, at the feet of the master, Philip Chagrin himself. Everything you do onstage, he used to tell her, seems speeded up to the audience, so always slow it down. Nothing about acting was natural, after all—the hardest work of all was to make it all *look* natural.

She reached her mark, paused a beat for the spotlight which wavered in front of her as unsteadily as it had in rehearsal.

The audience was silent—though she did not have that "you-can-hear-a-pin-drop" feeling that would have been there if Robby had pulled out all the stops for the dagger speech. There was a special quality in the silence of an audience that had just been bowled over, left numb, as they had been by Robby's Antony, but it was not here tonight.

Nevertheless, this was the moment she lived for. Nothing thrilled her more than the love of an audience. She could feel, rather than hear, the faint rustle of programs as the audience took a deep breath and craned forward in their seats for a better look at *her*, movie star, famous beauty, object of curiosity. It was like an electric current running through her body, as if the expectation of the audience was charging her with energy.

She saw the spot come to rest at last in exactly the right place, took a deep breath, and moved out into the sudden, swelling thunder of applause. She let it go on, standing there in her own brilliant pool of light, inhaling the familiar smells of dusty velvet seats, damp clothes, and perspiration that drifted across the stage along with the warmth from the audience, and waited for the sound to die down, eyes fixed on the far end of the stage, where Robby, hurrying down the ladder from the platform above, would soon make his own entrance.

It was only with the return of breathless silence that it occurred to her to wonder if what Toby was trying to tell her was that Robby was toning down his performance to make her look better. Instinctively she knew she was right, that Robby, worried by Pentecost's report of her drinking, by his fear of another *Romeo and Juliet*, on home turf this time, had deliberately set out to make her performance look good, not trusting her to do it by herself.

I'll show him! she promised herself, and with a look of rage so intense and genuine that it brought a collective gasp from the startled audience, she swept across the stage, her voice rising in a terrifying shriek as she cried out, *"That which hath made them drunk hath made me bold;/What hath quench'd them hath given me fire . . ."* so loudly that she could see Robby, eyes wide open, staring at her in horror from the wing, and heard behind her the hoarse, unmistakable, gin-sodden whisper of Toby Eden: "Crikie! What the hell's gotten into *her*?"

In his dressing room, Robby fretted. "I can't *imagine* what's gotten into her."

"You should be resting, old boy. Act five's a bugger," Toby said.

"I can't rest. I don't feel it's going well."

"It's going well enough. Felicia's splendid!"

"You don't think she's carrying things a little far, Toby? I mean, *Macbeth* is not a horror picture."

"Oh, I don't know, old boy. In its own way, that's exactly what it is."

"I'm not so sure I didn't like it better when she was 'kittenish,' to tell you the truth, Toby."

Robert Vane lay on his sofa, still dressed in his costume, smoking a cigarette and sipping at a cup of tea. On the table beside him sat his crown, his sword, and his dagger.

Toby Eden sat sprawled in the armchair beside him holding a drink, his robe fastened loosely over his costume, his face still covered with the white face paint and blood he wore as Banquo's ghost. He had the relaxed air of a man whose death and reapparition took place comparatively early in the play, leaving him two acts with nothing to do but drink and smoke his pipe. "She's got a very unhealthy gleam in her eye," he said. "Not often Shakespeare gives an actress the chance to be a real villain. Lisha takes to it like a duck to water." He puffed on his pipe. "Odd, that."

"She's playing *against* me, Toby. I blame Philip for that."

"Ah." Eden wreathed himself in clouds of smoke. "Interesting you should say that. I'm not so sure that's what Philip had in mind at all, as a matter of fact, but you can ask him yourself. He's in the audience."

"Philip? Here?"

"Fifth row, aisle. Couldn't miss him, even though he *is* wearing a false mustache. Doesn't suit him at all—looks like a clerk who's absconded with the cashbox."

Vane closed his eyes. He hated the knowledge that another actor he respected was out front, particularly Philip Chagrin. He wanted to think of the audience as an anonymous mass, not as individuals well-known to him. Those who came to see him perform made sure not to tell him in advance.

He reviewed his performance in his mind and tried to imagine what Philip would make of it. Too much noise and acting to the audience on Lisha's part, and not enough on his, he supposed. Somehow, he seemed unable to make Macbeth come alive the way he wanted him to, and he could tell the audience felt it. They were clearly awestruck by Lisha's performance, terrified by a raging, maddened and fiendish monster flinging herself at Macbeth as if she were a nymphomaniac, breasts half-exposed and heaving, clinging to him with such a show of passion that he had been uncomfortable.

He could still feel her body, flushed and hot, smelling faintly of Scandale despite the greasepaint and the powder, pressed hard against his, her hands grasping him, her nails digging into his flesh, so that when she clung to him, after the untimely appearance of Banquo's ghost at the feast, and said, *"You lack the season of all natures, sleep,"* it was a clear and open invitation to sex—which, given Macbeth's next line, *"My strange and self-abuse . . ."* had caused not a few titters in the audience, to his grave annoyance.

"I wonder what he's doing here?" he asked.

Eden shrugged. He could put more world-weary wisdom into a shrug than most men could put into a lifetime. "It's only natural. It's still his production. He'd want to see it from out front. So would you, old boy. So would I."

"Yes, of course. But what shall I do, Toby?"

"Do? Finish the play, what else? Look on the bright side—Lady Macbeth dies early in the next act."

"I mean about Philip?"

"About Philip? Ask him out for a drink, Robby. I mean to say, he's a friend, and a damned good actor." He rubbed the bowl of his pipe up against the side of his nose. "Philip may be an old bugger," he said, "but by God he's never tried to bugger *me!*"

It was the first good laugh Vane had had all night. He felt better already.

The waves of applause rolled across the stage, building to a crescendo as she and Robby joined hands. She lost count of the number of curtain calls. For the first time, she felt she was Robby's equal—more than his equal, in fact, and the clapping from the audience every time she took a bow confirmed it.

It was odd, she thought, how one could love a person and still be in competition with him. The critics tended to lump her name together with his, as if they were somehow linked, a single entity like Rolls-Royce, but there was always the suggestion, and sometimes very much more than a suggestion, that she was the junior partner, that it was only because of *him* that she was playing the female lead. "Out of her

depth'' was the phrase the critics liked to use about her performances with Robby, though often they were even more
offensive than that. Well, she said to herself, taking a final
curtsy, she had not been ''out of her depth'' tonight!

She smiled at Robby, who smiled back, despite the tension
and exhaustion that were evident on his face close up.

''Shall we celebrate tonight, darling?'' she asked, as the
curtain dropped before them for the last time.

He shook his head. ''Later,'' he said. ''There's somebody
I have to see.''

All at once it came to her—Pentecost, of course! Was it
Randy Brooks all over again? She could not believe it—not
on her night of triumph!

She turned on her heel and walked away in fury, just as
the stage manager, giving in to the continued applause, raised
the curtain again.

She did not look back. She simply continued to walk off,
her back to the audience, leaving it to Robby to bow and
smile as if what had just happened was perfectly natural.

She went upstairs, kicked off her shoes, and took her first
drink of the evening.

11

''We'll be snug in here.''

Philip Chagrin, with the genius of the great actor he was,
had managed by a single stroke to give himself a seedy, down-
at-the-heels, hangdog expression. The mustache transformed
his face, turning the noble profile into a caricature of second-
rate weakness, accentuated by the furtive eyes and the nervous
chain-smoking. Vane wondered if he could do the same—
or if he would have gone through an ordeal like Chagrin's
with as much courage.

There were limits to Chagrin's sangfroid, however. He had
been unwilling to come to the hotel or to hang around the

theatre longer than was necessary, and he had not wanted to see Felicia or Toby. "Too soon," he said. "I didn't come up here for them."

He had chosen an obscure pub only a few minutes' walk from the theatre—though a few minutes of walking in Manchester at this time of year was sufficient to produce wet feet, damp clothes, and a miserable hacking cough from coal dust, fog, and industrial fumes. Vane had been happy to get indoors and shake the water off his coat.

The bartender appeared from the public side of the bar, his face as white as a clown's. He had a mass of curly hair so improbably blond that at first Vane took it for a wig, and what looked like a trace of rouge on his cheeks. "It's almost closing time, dears," he said.

Chagrin put a couple of pound notes on the table. "I'm a traveler," he said. "I'm staying here."

"Of course you are, luv. Sign the book, then, duckie." He pushed a well-worn old ledger toward Chagrin, who scrawled a signature in it. "I always sign Binkie Beaumont's name," Chagrin whispered. "If the police ever check up, it will give him such a shock. Two whiskies, please. Doubles."

Vane took his whiskey gratefully. "I'm astonished they *have* whiskey for strangers these days," he said. "Most places won't admit they have a drop."

Chagrin touched his glass to Vane's. "Cheers. Sometimes, my dear Robby, you strike me as a total innocent. In bars like this, there *are* no strangers. Oh, that's not to say anybody knows another's real name, but the mere fact of being here means you're not a 'stranger,' do you see?"

"I had no idea there was a place like this in Manchester, frankly."

"In Manchester? My dear, there's a place like this everywhere. There's even one in Canterbury, right next to the Cathedral Close. Which tells you everything about the Church of England, as if you didn't already know."

"Is it wise for you to be here, Philip? After what happened in London?"

"Wise? Of course it's not *wise*. However, it's where I belong." There was a note of peevishness in his voice, a hint of impatience and contempt. He gave Vane a shrewd glance. "I'm where I *want* to be, Robby, which is more than most people can say."

"It was bad luck, all the same."

"Luck? It's all part of the game, isn't it? Gilles Moncrieff, who couldn't be less queer, as you know, always used to ask every attractive woman he saw if she wanted to fuck—used to come right out and ask it, just like that, to total strangers in the street. I once asked him if many of them said yes. 'No, no, Philip,' he said—you remember that wonderful plummy voice of his—'the success rate is rather low, in fact, perhaps one in a hundred. But at *my* age, if I ask a couple of hundred women a day, and get two, that's as many as I can manage.' "

He laughed. "Of course it works the other way for me. If I ask enough men, sooner or later one of them is bound to be a bobby who won't agree to forget about the whole thing for a tenner because a couple of his mates are watching. Luck of the draw, Robby. It happens to the best of us."

"It sounds a little risky, Philip."

"Well, living is a risky business, isn't it? Acting, too."

Vane sipped his whiskey uncomfortably. The surroundings did nothing to put him at ease, though there was nothing about the interior of the private bar which in any way suggested its special clientele. "It's not the surest way of making a living, I agree."

"I wasn't thinking about money, Robby, dear. You're being dense—deliberately, I suspect. I was talking about art. About *Macbeth*, in fact."

Vane looked around the tiny bar glumly, as if for relief. The bartender had vanished back into the public bar, and the only other person in sight was a stout, middle-aged, furtive-looking man with a gingery Hitler mustache and the mottled bright red nose of a heavy drinker. He might have been a commercial traveler, or a gym teacher on the prowl, or even—Vane felt a chill of apprehension—a policeman in civvies. The broad shoulders, the tweed coat, gray flannels, striped regimental tie, all had the hallmark of clothes worn by a man who usually dressed in uniform. He prayed to God the place wouldn't be raided, though nothing seemed to be going on that would tempt the police to do so. "What about *Macbeth*?" he asked.

"It's NBG—no bloody good. Well, you were onstage, you must have known that."

"We got a full house. And a damned good round of applause."

"Oh, bollocks! They were mostly applauding Lisha, not you. Even then, it was *polite* applause. 'Thank you for coming to Manchester and giving us a chance to spend an evening out of the house for a change.' It wasn't *happy*."

"It sounded loud enough to me," Vane said stubbornly, though he too had not been satisfied with it. "I'd have thought you'd be pleased they liked Lisha."

"I'm pleased for her, certainly. You know how fond I am of the dear girl. If my tastes ran to women, let me tell you, I'd give you a run for your money! But you have let her run roughshod over the play. Admittedly it's all my fault, I wasn't here, but it's been less than a week, and in that short time you've simply given the play away. You'll see! If you are trying to make Lisha happy by playing down your role to build up hers, it will backfire. Every critic will notice it, and it'll be *her* they blame, not you, mark my words. And why do it? This is art, dear boy, *theatre*, the real thing. If you've put your foot wrong with darling Lisha, make it up to her in bed, make it up to her with a diamond necklace, make it up to her any bloody way you please, but not onstage at the expense of poor old Shakespeare. There, I've said my piece on that."

"I've nothing to make up to Lisha, Philip," Vane said stiffly.

"Oh, don't be an ass, Robby. It shows a mile that you've done *something*. Never mind—fond as I am of her, I don't give a shit what you've done, or not done, so long as you don't spoil the play over it. If Lisha expects a lifetime of faithful monogamy in this day and age, she's in for a disappointment. Since I've known her far longer than you have, I can't imagine why she should feel entitled to it, but that's another story."

Vane raised an eyebrow. "It's a story I'd like to hear."

"Well, you shan't hear it from *me*. In any case, hetero-sexual behavior is *terra incognita* to me, I'm happy to say. Besides, the problem isn't Lisha, Robby, it's you."

"Because I lost control of Lisha onstage?"

"Not at all. That's bad, but easy enough to understand. Because you lost control of *yourself*! You're not *playing* Macbeth. You're showing the audience a man you don't like. You're telling them, 'You're right, this chap's a shit and a murderer, and his bonny wife leads him around like a bull with a ring in his nose, and I don't like him a damned bit more than *you* do, but it's my job to play him, so here goes!' "

Vane's good nature did not extend to being made fun of. "I wasn't that bad," he said hotly.

"You were perfectly dreadful, take my word for it. Luckily for you, the stout burghers of Manchester may not have realized quite how bad you were, and even some of the critics may have been fooled, though I wouldn't actually count on that. I mean, you're supposed to *be* Macbeth, dear boy. You can't expect the audience to like him if you don't."

"*Like* him? He's a bloody psychopath—Hitler in a kilt. You said so yourself."

Chagrin smiled triumphantly, as if Vane had said exactly what he'd wanted him to say. "If you're going to play Hitler, you have to learn to love Hitler, Robby. You can't just do the easy ones that everyone loves. Macbeth's a monster. He doesn't even pause for more than a few seconds when he hears Lady Macbeth has killed herself. '*She should have died hereafter* . . .' is the best he can say for her. He kills Macduff's wife and kiddies without giving it a thought. But if you're going to play him properly, you will have to learn to *love* him, Robby—as much as you love yourself. Until you can fall in love with the character you're playing—however wicked and beastly he may be—you won't deserve the crown, and you won't have it."

"The crown?"

Chagrin rapped him smartly on the knuckles with his cig-arette lighter. "Don't pretend you don't know what I'm talk-ing about! I'm out of the running. Everybody knows it. *I* know it. Good old Toby's a better actor than either of us—and a more decent chap, too, frankly—but he rather brushes his fences, doesn't he?''

It was easy to forget Chagrin's passion for the track until he suddenly slipped into a horsey metaphor. There were rumors that he had squandered most of his life's earnings on horses. Although the details of his private life were somewhat mysterious, he was said to have lived for years with a well-known jockey. Vane had been at Chagrin's mews flat often for drinks but had never seen any trace of the jockey, though the decor was that of a racetrack clubhouse. Even Lisha, who was as close to Chagrin as it was possible for a woman to get, had never met him, though she did claim to have once glimpsed a pair of tiny slippers, like those of a visiting Munchkin, under the bed. It occurred to Vane that although he had known Chagrin for nearly fifteen years, had made his debut on the serious stage in one of Chagrin's productions, he had no idea what made Chagrin tick.

"Toby's a fine actor," he said loyally. "Very strong."

"What you mean is that he's a very *masculine* actor. And you're right, of course. But that's his limitation. At heart Toby's a character actor, raised to the sublime. He's so good at playing dotty Englishmen—after all, he *is* a dotty Englishman—that he simply turns every character he plays into one, Lear as a dotty Englishman, Mercutio as a dotty Englishman, Brutus as a dotty Englishman—it's all one-dimensional.''

He smiled sadly at Vane. "I think Toby's perfectly happy to be himself—quite content to be Toby Eden. But you and I, we'd rather be someone else, wouldn't we? And since we *can't*, we've settled for becoming Romeo, or Hamlet, or Richard-the-bloody-Third.''

It occurred to Vane that Chagrin was probably—no, surely—drunk. From time to time he had tapped his glass with his cigarette lighter, and the bartender had emerged to refill it—and Vane's as well. It occurred to Vane, in fact, that he might be drunk as well. Felicia, he had no doubt, would wonder what had become of him. But that didn't seem to matter at all. In the dim light he could see there were other people in the bar now, but his attention was fixed on Chagrin, whose eyes had taken on a messianic quality.

"No," Chagrin said, lighting a cigarette with graceful, if unsteady, hands, "the crown is yours, I'm afraid. Or ought to be. By default, if for no other reason."

"I'm not interested in the bloody crown, Philip. It doesn't exist."

"Balls! It's all you care about. Well, and why not? I'd have given you a damned good run for your money, Robby, but I've come a cropper. Face it: you've got the energy for it, the body for it. . . ." He gave Vane a look of feline bitchery. "With some hard work and training, my dear fellow, you might even have the *voice* for it one day. But none of it will add up to a thing if you don't love the person you're playing more than you love yourself. Or anyone else."

"Anyone else?"

"Surely. That's the tragedy of being a great actor, Robby. It's easy enough to love a character more than oneself—who wouldn't prefer being Antony to being you or me?—but hard to accept that one will never love any flesh-and-blood person as one loves Antony. It can make for a lonely life, you know."

"I don't see why it should."

"Then you haven't tried it yet. You're still skating on the surface of the bloody part, saying 'See what a clever boy I am.' You weren't Macbeth tonight. You went through the motions, that's all. Take somebody in Shakespeare you loathe. Take somebody *everybody* loathes. Learn to love him as if you were he. Then play him!"

"Somebody more loathsome than Macbeth?"

"Somebody *everybody* hates."

Vane closed his eyes. "There's only Richard the Third," he said.

Chagrin's smile was beatific. "Precisely. The hunchback. Could you learn to love *him*, do you think? Could you learn to enjoy every wicked, evil thing he does?"

"I don't know," Vane replied testily. "I *had* thought of doing it. There's not really a part in it for Lisha, though."

Chagrin bared his teeth and gave a howl of laughter.

"Would Richard care about a thing like that? To be good as Richard the Third you've got to *think* like Richard the Third. If you're going to spend the rest of your life doing only those plays that offer Lisha an equal role, forget about the crown. You'll be the English Lunts—nice work if you can get it, but not serious theatre."

Vane closed his eyes, trying to think about *Richard III*. The play had been out of favor for years, perhaps because it was considered too blatantly theatrical, perhaps, too, because Richard of Gloucester was a villain with no redeeming features. He was evil incarnate, not even humanized by marriage, like Macbeth, or by passion, like Othello. It was impossible to imagine loving him, let alone making the audience love him.

He tried to imagine what Richard should look like, and suddenly he saw the long, broken, thrusting nose, the gleaming dark eyes reveling in their cynicism and wickedness, the heavy black eyebrows joined at the center in the manner that caused Italian men to touch themselves at the crotch to ward off the Evil Eye, the jutting jaw covered with the shiny blue-black traces of a beard that started to grow back fiercely the moment it was shaved, the cruel, sensual lips curled in a mocking laugh. It was the face of Marty Quick.

In the morning, his head still aching from drinking with Philip Chagrin, Vane was awakened by Felicia, angry and white-faced, waving a newspaper at him.

For a terrible moment, he imagined it was Lady Macbeth rousing him from uneasy sleep—given her white nightgown, her face pale with rage, hair disheveled from one of her usual sleepless nights, the sight of a bloody dagger in Lisha's hand would not have surprised him a bit. "Bastard!" she said, in a low, throaty moan.

Vane pulled himself upright in bed while noticing with one part of his mind how beautiful she was. At a time of the morning when most women, even those who passed for great beauties, would have looked puffy-eyed and unappealing, Lisha looked as fresh and clear-eyed as if she had been on her feet and made up for hours. Her nightgown revealed two small but perfect breasts, heaving now with emotion. She was leaning over him, half on, half off the bed, one leg exposed to a thigh which was firm, muscular, unblemished, so smooth that he had a momentary desire to reach out and touch it.

He tried to take the paper out of her hand, but she rolled it up, apparently intent on clubbing him with it or prodding him in the chest. "I can't read it if you don't let me have it," he said in a reasonable tone of voice.

"Take the bloody thing, then," she said. She was still leaning over, one breast fully exposed. He wondered for a moment what she would say if he slipped down in the bed a foot or so and kissed it. The expression on her face made it clear that it would be the wrong move. He should have come back to the hotel with her last night; at any rate, he should not have stayed out drinking with Philip Chagrin for so long that she was asleep when he got back to the hotel, or pretending to be. He knew he had made a mistake, but he did not feel guilty. Was that a step forward? he wondered.

Sitting in bed with Felicia hovering over him made him feel vulnerable. He rose, put on his bathrobe, went over to the window and pulled back the curtain. Through the partly open window he could hear the sound of traffic. There was a smell of kippers and burned toast rising from the hotel kitchen that made him realize how hungry he was. It was raining again, a steady, light rain, which gave the impression that it could go on forever.

He unfolded the newspaper and searched for whatever it was that had set her off. He found it without difficulty.

"MACBETH K.O.'D," the headline read. Below it was a byline: *"From our Dramatic Critic and Special Correspondent Guillam Pentecost."*

"Mr. Robert Vane's genius as an actor is a well-established fact, as is his close relationship over the years with the tempestuous and beautiful Miss Felicia Lisle, whose success on the Silver Screen in Hollywood for a time quite unjustly eclipsed Mr. Vane's own fame. Watching his Macbeth is at once an exhilarating and a

distressing experience, like seeing Leviathan hobbled by a silken thread. Mr. Vane's Macbeth is devious, crafty, deep, perhaps too quiet and subtle for the average theatregoer to appreciate, but it is hard to appreciate the delights of this finely crafted performance, since Mr. Vane seems to feel himself obliged, for who knows what domestic reasons, to mute his own genius in order, one presumes, not to overwhelm Miss Lisle's more fragile talents. Unfortunately, Miss Lisle has chosen to respond to this affectionate (and misplaced) courtesy with a performance apparently designed to blow Mr. Vane out of the water (or off the stage), her big guns drowning out the carefully thought out subtlety of his Macbeth. She vamps, she rages, she simpers, she flirts.

"But Lady Macbeth is not Lysistrata, nor does the shrill anger in Miss Lisle's voice sound like the kind of enticement that would spur most men to commit murder on her behalf. What we have here, alas, is an eagle, in the shape of Mr. Vane, held in check by a sexy sparrow, and the result is that what might have been one of the most memorable Shakespearean performances in recent times, wholly naturalistic and 'modern'—with Macbeth played not as a monster, but as a doubting, guilt-ridden man, sickened by his own ambition and overanxious to please his wife, the quintessential upstart bourgeois, in other words, driven by his own insecurities to 'get ahead' at any cost—dribbles down to a sex farce with tragic overtones, in which Miss Lisle takes on Macbeth, Shakespeare and the play, and wins by a knockout in five rounds—sorry, acts!"

Vane read the review slowly. There was more, much more (it seemed to go on for pages), and it gave him a curious feeling of guilt and fear combined with pleasure and admiration. Pentecost had understood *exactly* what he was trying to do with his Macbeth, and had put his finger, most unfortunately, on exactly what had gone wrong. There was hardly a word in the review with which he did not agree, hardly a thought which had not already occurred to him, however secretly.

Pentecost was bloody clever, and completely correct—but there was no way he could share that opinion with Lisha, who was lying on the bed herself now, her eyes filled with tears, kneading a wet lace-edged handkerchief in her hands as if she wanted to tear it to pieces. "He's *your* bloody protégé," she said, spitting out the word with icy precision. "*You* bloody well put him up to this."

He put down the paper with a sigh. "It's Pentecost's opinion," he said judiciously. "I don't share it, my sweet, and I'm not responsible for it."

"Oh? You're the one who 'discovered' the bloody little twerp and brought him to the theatre. He wouldn't have to be a genius to notice the way you were treating me. And I'm sure the two of you had plenty of nice long *chats* together. . . . About *me*?"

"Pentecost is a student of the theatre. An 'intellectual,' much as I hate the word. We talked about plays—ancient and modern. We did not discuss you."

"I'll *bet* you didn't!" She turned over on the bed and plunged her face into the pillow. Vane could hear the rumble of traffic, building to a crescendo now—it must be close to nine. He knew they should both be up and dressed, but he felt unable to move.

One thing he was sure of—he was not about to give up Guillam Pentecost merely because Lisha disliked him. The boy was brilliant, devoted, a walking encyclopedia of the theatre. For the future, it might be helpful if Pentecost could be persuaded to say something nice about Felicia; nevertheless he had the kind of quick mind and original point of view that Vane hadn't encountered for ages, not since—it suddenly occurred to him—the long talks he used to have with Randy Brooks in L.A. The thought appalled him, and he was glad that Lisha, still sobbing into the pillows, could not see his face.

"And where the hell were you last night?" she moaned, her voice muffled by the bedclothes.

"Out drinking with Philip Chagrin. I didn't feel I could say no."

"*Philip?* Don't be silly. If he'd been here, he'd have come to my dressing room to see me."

"Well, he didn't. I'm sorry. Probably he was ashamed to, after what happened."

"You're lying. You were out with Pentecost. It's Randy Brooks all over again, isn't it?" she wailed.

He felt as if he had been kicked in the groin. They had never discussed Randy openly. It was somehow understood that his was a name neither of them could ever bring up. "Randy Brooks?" he asked, affecting surprise. "I don't know what you're talking about."

"You know, damn you. You know what was going on between the two of you in California, and so do I."

"I know no such thing. Randy and I were—*are*—friends."

She swung herself off the bed, stepped out of her nightgown and stood in front of him, a naked, living tableau of accusation. "Look at me!" she cried. "What's *wrong* with me?" She gave a harsh, bitter laugh, loud enough to make him nervous that at any moment the floor waiter or the chambermaid might appear to ask what the problem was. "No," she corrected herself. "What's wrong with *you*? How could you possibly have preferred Randy Brooks to me?"

She stood motionless, tears pouring down her cheeks, bosom heaving. For some women, standing naked might have meant nothing, but Felicia had an acute sense of modesty, even in moments of passion. Stark nakedness for her, he knew, was either an act of aggression or the warning sign of a breakdown.

He gave her his iciest stare, as if her nakedness was of no interest to him at all. "Control yourself," he snapped. "Whatever you may think, I have no interest at all in boys or men. Randy Brooks was and is a friend, whose talent I admire. Guillam Pentecost is a young man whose gifts, despite this deplorable review, interest me. I did *not* put him up to this review, and I will severely chastise him for it. However, he is entitled to his opinion, and to be quite frank, both you and I have had far worse things said about us onstage, and by far more distinguished critics. Now put your robe back on, this instant.''

But she still did not move. ''Robby,'' she said, in a calm voice which spelled trouble, ''when I came back, after all that treatment in New York, we made love the way we used to in the old days, in our suite in the Savoy, do you remember?''

''I remember.''

''I thought everything was going to be all right between us, then.''

''Everything *is* all right between us, Lisha.''

She shook her head.

It was strange, he thought—she was thirty-three years old, and yet she could have passed for seventeen. Unhappiness made her seem younger, more fragile. When she moved her head, her black hair settled in tumbled curls around her face, like a young girl's. Without makeup her lips were the color of coral, her skin an almost translucent ivory, unblemished, unlined, perfect.

''You'd better get bathed and dressed,'' he said as gently as possible. ''Whatever we think of Pentecost's damned review, the play needs work. He's right about that. We're going to rehearse until we've got it.''

''Robby,'' she said quietly, ''to hell with the play. Make love to me. Now.''

How simple it would be to buy a day's peace, he thought, but he wasn't going to give in to her that easily. He was tired of living up to what she expected of him—tired, he supposed, of playing the part of the great lover with her. He wanted a change in the plot, marriage and children. . . .

''Get your clothes on and let's have breakfast,'' he said. ''We have work to do.''

For a moment, he thought she was going to obey him quietly. Then she rushed across the room, tore the paper out of his hand and began to tear it into strips, throwing them out the open window like confetti.

He reached out to grab her. He couldn't have half the God-fearing working folk of Manchester look up and see Felicia Lisle, stark naked at the window of her hotel room, throwing a torn-up copy of the *Manchester Guardian* into the street at rush hour. Perhaps even more, he feared the possibility of her shouting God knows what accusations against him to the crowds below—though there was little possibility she would be heard over the growl and rumble of traffic. Whatever his concerns—and he was vague about what they were even as he acted on them—he took hold of her arm and pulled her away from the window.

To his surprise, she flew at him with the speed of an enraged cat. He felt her nails claw across his face before he saw her move, and for a moment, as he felt the sting on his eyelids, he thought she had blinded him. Blood was trickling down his face, mixing with tears from the sudden pain and shock. Through the mist that clouded his vision he could see her face, which was now almost without expression. He expected to see rage there, her features contorted, her eyes blazing— certainly that is how it would have been played onstage— but Felicia's face reflected only calm composure, as if tearing his eyes out were all in a day's work. He loosened his grip and saw her hand strike out at him again. Without a moment's thought, he took a step back and hit her, so hard that he felt the pain shoot from his hand right through his elbow and up to the shoulder joint.

He had never hit her before. He had never, in fact, hit any woman. Come to that, he had never hit anyone in anger since his schoolyard days. He was used to enacting violence on-stage, but nothing that he could imagine in normal life would have led him to strike a blow—and yet he had just hit Felicia hard enough to have broken something in his hand. He felt a bottomless depression at the sheer tawdriness of it all, the dreary depths to which his life had suddenly descended. If they had both been drinking, then it might perhaps be supportable, but in the cold, gray morning light the act seemed incongruous, inexplicable. He had hit her with his fist, and he had knocked her across the room. He might have killed her.

She lay slumped beside the bed, sobbing.

"I never thought you'd do that," she whispered.

"Neither did I."

She pulled herself up a little—he felt no impulse to help her, or touch her.

There was a bruise beginning to spread across her right cheek and a gash on her forehead, which she had presumably hit against some piece of furniture in her fall.

"You might have killed me," she said, dabbing at the blood on her forehead with her handkerchief.

He went to the bathroom, came back with a towel, and gave it to her. "Yes," he said calmly. "I might have. I don't think it's a good idea, all this violence. I don't think we should let it happen again, do you?"

"No." She giggled. "Some people find it sexy, you know."

He helped her back up onto the bed. The cut was beginning to bleed in earnest now. A doctor would have to be called, stitches would have to be sewn, explanations demanded and given. He felt incapable of making a decision. "Sexy?" he said. "I suppose so. I've had no personal experience, have you?" It seemed easier to carry on a polite conversation, however incongruous in the circumstances, than to accept a doctor's bustling intrusion into their lives.

"Some," she said.

"And was it—enjoyable?"

"It depends. Sometimes. Not if it produces a bloody war wound, it isn't. Am I going to have a scar?"

"I shouldn't imagine so. But I do think you'll need stitches. We'll have to get you a doctor." He took her hand. It was ice-cold. "This violence that you found so—sexy," he said, "was it recent, or a long time ago?"

"A long, *long* time ago, darling. Never fear."

"Surely not with Charles?"

She closed her eyes and sighed. "Poor Charles! You're right, of course."

"He always seemed the most forgiving of husbands to me."

"How one longed *not* to be forgiven. . . . Give me a ciggie, please, while you call the doctor."

He lit a cigarette and passed it to her. "I don't think I'd want to make a habit of hitting women," he said. "I don't like myself for having done it."

"*Like* yourself? My darling Robby! What a luxury! I haven't liked myself in years. It's something you'll have to get used to, like the rest of us. Now you'd better hurry up and call the doctor before I bleed to death."

He picked up the telephone and banged on the hook until he finally caught the attention of the operator, then spent a few moments convincing her to call a doctor for an "accident."

He felt calmer than he had for ages, as if violence had finally cleared his mind, stripped him of illusions. He felt guilt for what he had done, anger at her for what *she* had put him through. But he also knew he still wanted to marry her.

He sat down on the end of the bed. "I'm not having an affair with Guillam," he said quietly. "You're quite wrong about that."

"Then you wish you could. Which is just as bad. Or worse. Because not doing it makes you hate me, whereas the other way you might like me more. He's bright, witty, full of good ideas—and of course he thinks you're a genius, which is true, and tells you so all the time, which is clever. I suppose I'm lucky that he's not some scheming stagestruck little drama student with long blond hair and good legs, aren't I? Though perhaps that isn't quite true, either. . . . No, don't frown like that, Robby, please. We may as well speak the truth just this once, even if we never do again. Your problem *there*, darling, is that you're not really attracted to men at all. Not physically, I mean. Oh, I've had all the time in the world to think about it since Hollywood, and I know I'm right. In a way it's rather a pity."

"Of course I'm not 'attracted' to men, for God's sake! And nothing happened in Hollywood to start you on *that* chain of thought."

"We both know better, and don't give me the Othello stare, please. You've already bashed in my forehead this morning. You may get away with that, but I don't think you'll be able to explain away strangling me with a scarf or suffocating me with a pillow.''

She breathed out a cloud of smoke. The cut was beginning to congeal now. It looked worse—a long, ragged tear that seemed almost obscene on such a beautiful face. The bruise was swelling, too, turning from dark yellow to angry purple, like a piece of fruit going bad. Vane's arm throbbed. He had marred the face of his co-star so badly that her understudy would surely have to go on as Lady Macbeth, and he had perhaps damaged his arm so badly that he would be unable to perform the swordplay that the end of *Macbeth* demanded. He might just as well go down to the theatre and nail up the closing notices himself. It was San Francisco all over again —professional disgrace and bankruptcy, except that this time it was *his* fault.

"Poor Robby," she went on, hardly even looking at him. "It's a bloody shame you don't have any fun. I mean, if you'd *enjoyed* hitting me, it might have been worth it. For you, at any rate."

"Let's drop the subject, please. I'd like to get on with our lives, Lisha. If I could go back to the way things were between us, I would. But we can't, either of us, so we may as well go forward instead."

"Like 'Onward, Christian soldiers'? Where to?"

"To London, for a start. We'll spend some time together without working, for a change. Or working quietly. Toby can take over the bloody tour. He's done *Macbeth* before. Done them all."

"It's *you* they want, Robby. And me."

"Yes, but they'll take Toby. Oh, we'll sell a few less tickets, Binkie Beaumont will make a bit less money, but that's not the end of the world, is it? We'll move out of the Savoy and into a flat, first off. We can't spend the rest of our lives like transients. We need roots, a place of our own to live in, like real people. You'll see. Things will be better."

Despite her wound and her bruise, Felicia seemed perfectly reasonable now, even content. He reached out and held her hand, as much to comfort himself as her.

"I won't give up the tour," she said. "That's out."

"I think you should."

"No. We'll say I slipped in the blackout."

"Nobody will believe that."

"I don't care. We'll need to rehearse. Loathsome as your friend Pentecost is, he's not stupid. You're playing down."

He nodded. In many ways, he thought, she had more courage than he did, or perhaps just a stronger sense of self-preservation, for she knew exactly when to stop, how far she could go, and what to say to put things, however temporarily, right between them again.

His instinct, too, was to continue the tour, to put a good face on things, "to carry on regardless" as the wartime phrase went, but he worried whether Felicia could see it through. Dr. Vogel, all those months ago in California, had cautioned against trusting her own estimate of her strength. But if she was determined to go on, there was no way of stopping her without precipitating a new crisis. Besides, it was what he himself wanted to do.

"Guillam pointed out something I hadn't thought of, you know. Most actors fail at Macbeth because he doesn't *grow*. After he kills Duncan, he gets smaller and smaller, as if his crimes were nibbling away at him, do you see? It's as if Macbeth is *shrinking* for three acts, until he finally vanishes quietly from the play. So one's tendency is to put it all into acts one and two, because that's where the good scenes are. I think I could reverse that—give the audience a Macbeth that *builds*. . . . Well, we'll give it a go, shall we?"

"If you like, darling."

Felicia was not interested in theory, he knew that. The stage for her was like life, something you plunged into and *did*. But it dawned on Vane that by putting his energy into just those scenes in acts three, four and five that most Shakespearean actors let go, the play's center would come later, *after* Lady Macbeth had more or less vanished from the stage in madness.

He might not be able to find a way to love Macbeth, as Philip Chagrin had said he must learn to do, but he could easily reclaim the play and make it his.

There was a knock on the door. "Coming," he said in an easy, self-confident voice, and fixing his face in an expression of concern, he got up to let the doctor in, his mind already working on Macbeth.

He felt better already, as if the whole terrible scene had already receded.

12

"It was *madly* brave of her," Guy Darling said to Philip Chagrin. "Going on with the tour after such a ghastly accident. Stitches on that beautiful face! One shudders to think! Of course, I don't believe a word of their story. Tripped and fell, my foot!"

"You don't think that Robby *hit* her, surely?"

"I do. He hurt his arm somehow, didn't he? I hear he had to do the last act without his sword. Fond as I am of Lisha, I hope he *did* hit her, frankly. Quite apart from whatever was going on—or not going on—in their personal lives, she was ruining *Macbeth* for him."

"I still can't imagine Robby striking her, frankly. He's devoted to her."

"That's not devotion, Guy, that's *guilt*. The truth is, Robby had no business leaving Penelope for a woman as difficult and complicated as Lisha. Robby was in over his head and didn't even know it. The curious thing is that he's a late starter—oh, as an actor, too, by the way. . . ."

"Sour grapes don't become you, Philip."

"I am not without sins, Guy, but envy is not among them. An old queen I may be, but not, I trust, a *jealous* old queen. What I tell you is simply the truth. What I'm trying to say is that every time Robby reaches some kind of plateau of achievement, instead of resting there, the way the rest of us would, he takes off and leaps one step higher. Once he put Lisha back in her place, however he did it, his Macbeth got better and deeper, until in the end it was *his* play. I saw it in Birmingham, and I couldn't believe my eyes. Oh, you *clever* fellow! I told myself. The audience may go into the theatre to see the famous Miss Lisle, star of stage and screen, but they'll *leave* thinking only of Robert Vane. Poor Lisha! He didn't just hit her. He stole the play away from her.''

''Are they going to get married?''

''Oh, I should think so. They've made every other mistake.''

The two men sat in the back of a taxi on their way to the new home of Robert Vane and Felicia Lisle, for what had been described as a ''housewarming'' party, an Americanism that Guy Darling, who had spent far longer in the States than Philip, was obliged to explain to him.

Getting a taxi had called for transatlantic guile. Taxi drivers in the West End stopped only for ''Yanks'' these days, since they were big tippers. Luckily for Darling, his flat in Eaton Place drew visiting Americans like a magnet—half the Broadway theatre world was in uniform these days—and there was always a house guest in American uniform happy to go down and hail a taxi for him.

To the miseries and deprivations of war, so familiar by 1943, was added the presence of hundreds of thousands of Americans, ''overpaid, oversexed, and over here,'' as the newspapers complained. Hollywood movie producers dressed up as colonels filled Claridge's, the Connaught, the Dorchester and the Savoy. Americans outnumbered the natives at the theatre and in the more expensive restaurants; everywhere their exuberance and wealth emphasized the dreary poverty in which, by now, the English lived.

Robby Vane and Lisha Lisle were a port of call for every London-bound American movie or stage personality, who in much the same spirit that they had once brought flowers, now brought steaks, scotch, canned hams, nylon stockings, and cartons of cigarettes. Lisha's return to England after such a huge and unexpected triumph in Hollywood had made her something of a heroine at home too. The notion of her sacrificing a successful screen career for love or patriotism was taken in the movie industry as evidence of something approaching sainthood, and made every studio and major producer all the more determined to get her under contract as soon as possible. Even her agent, Aaron Diamond, had turned up in London, dressed in the uniform of an Air Corps colonel.

Chagrin stared out into the rainy street. American flags flew from half the buildings in the West End, and the pavements were full of American soldiers looking for women. "It's as if we were living in Rome after the barbarians had taken the city," he said with a sigh.

"Oh, do stop, Philip. You've never liked Americans, ever since you flopped on Broadway in *A Midsummer Night's Dream*. Just think of the alternative—the streets full of Germans in their ghastly gray uniforms."

"Could it be worse?"

"Don't be *silly*. The Germans put people like us in camps, Philip. Ah, here we are."

They clambered out of the taxi, Chagrin dressed with his usual elegance, while Darling still affected the more flamboyant fashions of the twenties, when he had made his reputation, first as an actor, then as a playwright. His black hair was slicked back as if it had been painted on his head; he carried a cigarette in a long ivory holder; he wore a dove-gray suit of such perfect cut that it was a wonder he was able to sit down in it, patent leather shoes, a black overcoat with a fur collar flung over his shoulders, a long white silk scarf wound loosely around his neck. He wore, as he always did in the evenings, a pale lavender hothouse orchid in his lapel. "Thank you, my good man," he said to the driver, taking his change and handing the man back sixpence.

The driver, wrapped in layers of old overcoats in the open driver's seat of the cab, examined it critically in one string-gloved hand. "What's this, guv?" he asked.

"A tip."

"Is it now?" He gave Darling a hostile glare from under the peak of his cloth cap and spat into the street. "That Yank who hailed me would have given me two bob, or half a crown, at least."

"Well, I'm not a Yank, and sixpence is quite enough."

"No, you're not a Yank, I can see that. You're a bleeding

pouf is what you are, and you can take your fucking sixpence and shove it.''

The driver hurled the coin at Darling, who ducked, then stood up grandly and shouted, ''Sod off!'' at the cabbie in a voice that could be heard to the end of the street, and with a diction so perfect it was like a hard-edged crystal.

There was a moment's silence as the driver took in the perfect pronunciation and saw, in the dim light, the two men on the pavement staring haughtily at him, shoulders squared, as if they were a pair of Guards officers on parade. He took in their faultless tailoring, their noble profiles, the anger that flashed in their eyes, and with the Pavlovian reflex that was built into anyone who had come of age in the British class system, he gave ground. ''Sorry, guv,'' he mumbled, and with a clash of gears he made his exit down the street, hunched behind the wheel, not looking back.

''I don't know what the world's coming to,'' Darling said sadly. ''There's no respect left for anything. I'm old enough to be his mother.''

''If you don't like *this*, wait until peace comes. It's sure to be worse. Look there, down the street. Isn't that Guillam Pentecost?''

Darling took a gold-rimmed monocle out of his breast pocket, screwed it in one eye and peered into the distance. ''It looks like him,'' he said. ''*Such* a bright boy. And so eager to please. He sent me a nice piece he wrote about me for one of the papers. Surely *he* can't be invited? Not after what he wrote about Felicia. What was it I read? 'What a shame Mr. Vane is so gallant that he's prepared to sacrifice a noble career to keep a minor actress, however beautiful, in parts she lacks the talent to play.' I'm surprised Robby didn't hit *him*.''

''Oh, my dear, they've made their peace, Lisha and Guillam. I believe *she* gets Robby's body, while Guillam gets his mind. Whether that's the way Robby wants it is quite another question, of course. . . . Good evening, Pentecost. Going to the Vanes'?''

Pentecost towered above the two distinguished men of the theatre, though neither of them was short. His work with

Robby Vane had brought him, at last, out of the provinces and into the capital, where his quick wit and his awesome knowledge of the theatre had won him instant recognition and the foretaste of fame. He nodded politely. "Not 'the Vanes' yet," he said. "One always thinks of them as married, doesn't one? But they're not. You've heard the news?"

"What news would that be?" Chagrin asked. "If it's Sicily, I'm already bored with it. I can't imagine how Hitler can seize most of Russia while we can't even get to Palermo, apparently. . . ." He led the way up the steps and pressed the buzzer.

"No, not Sicily. The theatre. Robby has taken a lease on the old Duke of York Theatre. He's going to put on his own plays there."

Chagrin stared at the younger man. It was well known that he had wanted his own theatre for years, and had intended to form a company of players that could do everything from Shakespeare to experimental theatre. Any chance he had of getting it was gone now, since his arrest, but somehow he had not expected that Vane would manage it so quickly. Vane, Vane, Vane, he thought, he was all one heard about, as if there were no other actors. And yet he could not feel jealousy, would not *let* himself feel it.

A maid opened the door and let him in. Chagrin had a brief impression of warmth and light, unusual in wartime London. Wherever she was, Felicia somehow managed to create an atmosphere of luxury and comfort—it was one of her gifts. She had performed miracles, by any standards, in putting the new house together, haunting auction houses, art galleries, old Crowther's storehouse of antiques, finding workmen when half the adult male population of England was in uniform, dealing with a whole new class of shady entrepreneurs who sold what had once been ordinary goods —paint, plaster, wiring—on the black market. She could, Chagrin thought, have made a fortune as a decorator, and very likely been much happier doing it. Of course, she was extravagant, impulsive, romantic, everything he would like to have been himself, had he been born a woman—and most of it wasted on Robby. . . .

He looked across the crowded drawing room and saw, over by the fireplace, a familiar painting—David Garrick, eyes glittering, standing in half-armor on a sparsely wooded heath, sword in hand, his expression at once defiant and doomed. It had been painted in the mid-eighteenth century to celebrate Garrick's triumph as Richard III, and the instant Chagrin saw it, he knew that Vane had followed his advice.

At the far end of the room he saw Vane, who caught him glancing at the picture. Vane gave a grin—sardonic, devilish, triumphant, his dark blue eyes darting toward the painting, and Chagrin caught his breath, for in that one brief moment, he *was* Richard III. Then the moment was gone and he was himself again, a good-looking, successful English gentleman, surrounded by his friends, and the next thing Chagrin knew, Felicia's arms were around his neck as she kissed him. "Darling, I've never been so happy in my life!" she shouted.

Chagrin's spirits sank. Things were even worse than he had thought.

"So Robby still hates Hollywood? So what? Listen, it's okay for *him* to be over here doing Shakespeare on the stage, but you had a real chance there."

"I hated every moment of it."

"Bullshit! You loved winning an Oscar, being a star. Well, what's not to love about that? You just pretended to hate it because Robby wasn't happy. Don't argue. I *know*! All I'm saying is, don't close your mind. Si Krieger would have you back like a shot, you name your price. No, forget that. I'll name it!"

"I'm doing what I want to do, Aaron."

"You'll change your mind. Speaking of Si Krieger, there's something I meant to ask you. He heard a rumor around town that you signed up to do some movie."

"Well, of course I didn't, Aaron. Why on earth would anybody think that?"

"Beats me, *bubbi*, but that was the word. I told Si he was full of shit. He asked me to give you his best, by the way, for what *that's* worth. . . . Hell, everybody in L.A. misses you. You wouldn't recognize the place. Everybody's in uniform, not just me.''

Aaron Diamond brushed an imaginary speck of lint off his custom-tailored olive-drab tunic. If you didn't look at the tough, lined face, the shaved head that gleamed as if it had been waxed, the predatory little eyes flashing restlessly behind the thick lenses of his gold-rimmed aviator's glasses, you might have thought he was a child dressed up in the costume of an Air Corps colonel, his uniform a perfect miniature replica of a grownup's. Diamond not only wore what was surely the only full-dress uniform in the United States Army made for a man under five feet tall, but seemed also to have added several touches of his own to it so that it had a certain Ruritanian swagger. He seemed to have awarded himself an improbable number of ribbons as well. ''Your old pal Mark Strong's a lieutenant commander in the Navy, making training movies, believe it or not. They should use *him* for the ones that warn you about V.D. Randy Brooks turned down a commission and went in as a private, to entertain the troops.''

It was amazing to Felicia that the name was still capable of causing her pain. She tried to imagine Randy Brooks in a private's uniform, but failed. It occurred to her in an unkindly way that at least he'd be happy in a barracks, surrounded by men. ''I'm surprised Natalie and her father didn't get Randy made a general,'' she said.

''Well, they would have, probably, but he dug his heels in, for once. He didn't think a comedian should be an officer. And you know something? He's right. Army humor is mostly *against* officers, see? There's no way an audience of privates is going to love a comedian who's got bars on his shoulders, let alone eagles, and Randy *has* to make them love him. . . . Say, this is a great party, doll!''

It *was* a great party. She could feel it herself. She was light-headed and happy, despite the fact that she had been careful to keep her drinking down to the bare minimum, nursing a single glass of champagne for ages. In the aftermath of *Macbeth*, she was being discussed, at last, as an accomplished classical actress in her own right, even though there were still many critics who dismissed her as a glamorous movie star or, like Pentecost, argued that she remained in Robby's shadow.

"What are you doing next, honey?" Diamond asked—the standard Hollywood question.

"I don't know. *Othello*, perhaps. After Robby has done *Richard the Third*."

"You're not in it?"

"There's no part for me."

"That a fact?" Diamond's knowledge of Shakespeare was minimal. He bobbed his head as if it all made sense to him, but from his point of view as an agent, it was clearly crazy. If you had two stars, you needed a script with two major roles—anybody knew that, even Shakespeare. His expression indicated that if this were Hollywood, he would have insisted the studio write in a suitable part.

In truth, though she was not about to discuss it with Diamond, she herself had been more than a little disappointed by Robby's insistence on doing *Richard III* next.

She glanced around the room, content for now with her role as hostess. There were people she would just as soon not have present—Pentecost, for one—but Robby was insistent on inviting his new "discovery," and was relying on Pentecost to cut the text of *Richard III* down to manageable length; however, everybody she wanted to see had come: Philip Chagrin, Guy Darling, dear Noel, Toby, old Gilles Moncrieff and his latest wife, Binkie Beaumont and his new boyfriend, most of the film producers, a leavening of reviewers, critics, and writers, enough famous people to establish firmly that Felicia Lisle and Robert Vane were still together, "at home" and as much in love with each other as ever.

"How the hell *is* Robby?" Diamond asked. "He looks kind of thin, you ask me."

"He's been trying to lose weight to play Richard. Not hard to do, on our rations. But he's well enough. Very absorbed in the play." She laughed—he was always absorbed in a play. "His divorce is final, you know."

"No shit! And yours? Is he going to make an honest woman of you at last?"

"It's too late for that, I'm afraid. But I think we're getting close. Charles—my husband—has given in, more or less. As a matter of fact, Portia is staying with us at the moment. A trial run."

She smiled brightly, though the relationship was anything but comfortable or easy. Even with her nanny in tow, Portia had not been overjoyed at the prospect of visiting her mother's new home, much as she liked Robby. She made it clear in a hundred small childish ways that she had not forgiven her mother for abandoning her or for being away so long.

Felicia had gone to America leaving behind a frightened six-year-old, and returned to confront an angry and unforgiving girl of nearly ten. She no longer knew what to say to Portia and too often talked to her as if she was still the baby she remembered. Besides, if she was to be candid with herself—and how hard she tried to avoid doing just that!—Portia was not only hostile, but gawky, plain, and mulish in temperament, and showed as much contempt as a child could for her mother's concern with glamour and beauty.

Nor, now that she was close to it, did the prospect of marriage give Felicia the kind of pleasure it ought to have given. It was not that she didn't *want* to marry Robby; it was simply a certain resentment at the fact that he, and everybody else, it seemed, regarded it as inevitable.

If Diamond noticed her hesitation, he did not show it. "That's just *great*!" he said forcefully, following the Hollywood tradition of firmly avoiding other people's personal troubles. He edged closer, his eyes flickering behind the thick tinted glass of his spectacles as if he were about to impart a major secret. "Listen," he said, lowering his voice to a gravelly whisper, "you're *sure* you're not holding out on me, honey?"

"Holding out on you?"

"Hiding something," he snapped impatiently. "What's the matter? I'm talking English, right? This contract you're supposed to have signed for a movie is what I'm talking about."

"Honestly, Aaron, I don't know *anything* about a film contract. Robby hasn't mentioned it, and we do talk about these things, whatever people may think."

"Okay, okay, maybe I heard the story wrong. I got a lot on my mind lately. I've got four groups touring for the troops here, singers, dancers, you name it. You wouldn't believe the problems the girls give me. . . ." Diamond rolled his eyes. One of his favorite stories about himself was that early in his career he had taken an all-girl string orchestra on tour through the backwoods mining and logging towns of Alaska, and so there was nothing about dealing with young women surrounded by sex-starved men that Diamond didn't know. "Hi there, Robby," he shouted, reaching over to shake his host by the hand as he passed by on the way to the bar. Despite his size, Diamond had a grip like a steel vise. "I was just telling Lisha I could get the two of you a movie deal, right now, no sweat, name your price," he said, in his fastest machine-gun delivery.

"I don't think we're interested, Aaron," Robby said smoothly—but there was an uncertain quality in his polite smile, a nervous edge to his voice that Felicia recognized instantly.

It was one of the curiosities of Robby's character that great as he was an actor, he was a poor liar in real life, with hardly any natural gift for concealment. She wondered what he had to hide this time. So, apparently, did Diamond, whose suspicion was as sharply honed as a divorce detective's. "Not *interested*?" he asked. "Not interested in half a million dollars?"

"I thought you were in the army, Aaron."

"I *am* in the army. That doesn't mean I can't do business. Listen, I represented you guys in L.A., in case you've forgotten. You can't do a deal behind my back and cut me out."

"We wouldn't do that, Aaron," Felicia said. "And we're *not*, are we, Robby?"

"Of course not," Vane said, with a broad smile that would hardly have convinced a ten-year-old child. "Not a chance." His eyes were pools of desperation despite the smile.

"I made your Hollywood deals and I did a pretty god-damned good job, too. Who warned you not to do *Romeo and Juliet*? Who told you not to put any of your own dough into it? Who begged you not to make a deal with Marty Quick? What I'm saying, is, what you do here, that's your business, I don't have anything to do with it. You got agents here, *mazel tov*, but you can't cut me out on a Hollywood movie, see?" Diamond's face took on an expression of moral outrage and extreme pain. "It wouldn't be *fair*," he said, as if fairness were the major concern of his life. "It wouldn't be *right*." He paused, not certain he had made his point. He tried again. "It would be a shitty thing to do."

"But we haven't done it, Aaron darling," Felicia said.

"Okay, then," Diamond said grudgingly.

What, she wondered, was the matter with Robby? His smile was fixed in place as if his life depended on it. She knew he hadn't the slightest intention of making a film, certainly not another Hollywood film. And although Robby had his own agent in London, the elegant Piers Mainwaring, the last of the old-school theatrical agents, perhaps the most elegant man in London, and she, too, had her own, good old Joe Collins, with his flashy suits, his big cigars, his East End Cockney accent, and his dark-eyed stunning daughters, neither of them would have made a movie deal without involving Diamond. "Everybody who matters has two agents," Mainwaring had once announced, his speech more elegant than a duke's, "his own—and Aaron Diamond!" There was no piece of paper, no contract, binding them to Diamond, but it didn't matter. Leaving him out was at once unthinkable and dangerous, for he never forgot an insult.

She gave Robby a look that was meant to say, "What's going on here?" and edged her way closer to him, but before she could drag him out of Aaron's earshot there was a hush, and everybody looked up toward the landing, as if something unusual was going on there.

Felicia raised her eyes in time to hear a clear, piping child's voice, rising clearly above the muted expressions of interest. "I want to go home."

She turned and ran up the stairs, as fast as she could, silently cursing Nanny, but at the sight of her, Portia burst into tears and backed away.

"It's all right, darling," Felicia said, smiling, but Portia was not about to be charmed by her mother. Her face was red, tears were running down her cheeks, and she seemed poised for a tantrum in full view of almost everybody who mattered to Felicia.

"Darling," Felicia cooed—where the *hell* was Nanny?— "do let's go back to bed like a good girl. We'll talk about it tomorrow."

"I want to go home to Daddy."

"And so you shall, my pet," Felicia said, through clenched teeth. "But not tonight."

"I want Uncle Robby to take me home."

"I'm sure he will, if he's not working."

"I want to go to Langleit and stay with Grandpa Harry."

"He isn't your grandpa, darling."

"I don't care. I don't want to be here. I want to go there. I hate you."

Portia was huddled resentfully in full view of the guests beneath the painting Laszlo had done of Felicia as Cleopatra—a gift, ironically enough, from Uncle Harry, to celebrate her return to the English stage.

Not knowing quite what else to do, Felicia whispered, "You *shall* visit Uncle Harry, darling, I promise," then lunged forward to put her arms around the little girl and bundle her off to her room—but no sooner had she got the child in her arms than Portia gave way to complete hysteria, sobbing and screaming in a voice that filled the house. Felicia stood there for what seemed like an eternity, struggling with the child, before Nanny appeared and carried her off. Portia's sobs ended at the very sight of Nanny.

From below, Aaron looked up and shook his head. "Funny," he said to Robby, "like mother, like daughter. Remember what happened at your party in L.A.? Maybe these things run in the family."

Vane smiled brightly, as if he were summoning back the

party spirit. "A spot of nerves," he said. "Nothing to worry about. Lisha will be back in a moment." But his own spirits had plummeted at the sight of Felicia's face when the child mentioned Harry Lisle. For years he had tried to put Harry Lisle out of his mind, always resentful of the influence he seemed to have over Felicia, and yet Harry was the only person, it seemed, who could control Felicia.

Why she was afraid of him—if it *was* fear—was one of those things she never discussed. She had never mentioned the Laszlo painting, even though she must have had several sittings for it, so it could hardly have come to her as the surprise she pretended it was. And why should she care so much that Portia referred to Harry as Grandpa?

He felt, as he so often did when the subject of Felicia's past and family came up, a kind of horrible fear, like a traveler stepping into quicksand. They had been so absorbed in each other, and in their careers, that they had never paused to learn the secrets of each other's families. In any case, he had a secret of his own to confess to her, thanks to Aaron Diamond.

For the first time in months he wished he were back in the air force.

"You *might* have told me you made a deal with Marty Quick!"

"I quite forgot."

"I don't believe that for a moment."

"All right, it wasn't a question of forgetting. I simply didn't want to upset you. Look, there wasn't a choice. You were in no position to make a decision. Marty paid our debts. . . ."

"So you could rush back to England, leaving me behind?"

"Be sensible, Lisha. I couldn't spend the rest of the war in California, could I? And you were in no shape to come back with me. You know that! So I signed us up to make a film with Marty, took the money, and ran. I thought to myself, well, why not? I might have been killed in the RAF. England might have lost the war. The whole thing might never happen. . . . Damn it, it *still* might never happen. I haven't heard boo from him in over a year, and no doubt he's got other things in mind by now. When the war is over, if it ever bloody ends, we can worry about it. If we have to, we'll pay him back, a little at a time. I haven't any intention of doing *Don Quixote*, and the odds are he's never going to do it anyway. It was the expedient way out of a terrible situation.''

"If you think Marty is simply going to walk away and forget about it, you're wrong. Anyway, that's not the point. You had no right to make an agreement in my name.''

"I had your power of attorney. I didn't see any alternative. I did it. You have to understand how bad things were, darling. We owed people their salaries, we owed the government taxes, we had to pay off performance bonds and pay for scenery and costumes. Marty's deal was the only way out. Look on the bright side. Here we are, home again, our debts from *Romeo and Juliet* paid off, with every chance of a new life. I have a theatre of my own. . . .''

She had never understood how bad things had been, and now felt a terrible guilt. Still, she doubted the wisdom of it all. "How much chance do you think you'll have of keeping it if Marty comes looking for his four hundred thousand dollars, Robby,'' she asked. "And he *will*.''

"We'll face that when the time comes.''

He poured himself a drink and stood in front of the fire, below the portrait of Garrick as Richard. For an instant she found the resemblance to Robby startling—the thick, dark eyebrows that joined above his nose, the dark, impenetrable eyes, the sardonic turn to the lips, the impatient energy.

"It was a wonderful party,'' he said, closing the subject.

"Yes.'' She was more than willing to close it and call a truce.

"Everybody thought the house looked beautiful. I'm only sorry Portia isn't as happy here as I'd hoped she'd be.''

"She'll get used to it. In time.''

"Why do you mind her going to visit Harry? After all, you did grow up there, and he *is* your uncle—as close as the girl's going to get to a grandfather, so long as your own father stays in Kenya.''

"I don't think he's a good influence for a child of her age, that's all.''

"You've always seemed fond enough of him. Extraordinary thing, him giving you that painting."

"It's just the kind of grand gesture Harry loves."

"I suppose he'd spoil Portia outrageously, given the opportunity. As I'm sure he did you. Still, I can't see any great harm in that, not at her age."

"She's *my* daughter, Robby. And I don't want her there, so that's that."

"Well, then you shouldn't have promised her that she could go, even to shut her up. She won't forget, you know."

"She's a child, Robby. She'll do as I say."

"I realize it's none of my business, but you can't break a promise to a child—particularly to a child, in fact."

"You're right. It's *not* your business."

"She's fond of me. And I shall be the child's stepfather —unless you've changed your mind."

"Changed my mind? About what?"

"About our getting married."

" 'Our getting married'? I don't know that I like that way of putting it at all! What I'd *like* to hear is that *you* want to marry *me*. I mean—I haven't been *asked* yet, have I? A girl does like to be asked."

"Of course you have been asked."

"I haven't been asked properly. Or recently. Aren't you supposed to get down on one knee and ask for my hand?"

"Consider yourself asked, then."

"I'm not going to consider myself anything. I want to be properly asked, then engaged."

"*Engaged?* We've been living together for ten years!"

"Living together is not at all the same thing as being engaged, Robby."

"Do we put an announcement in the *Times*? Buy an engagement ring? Do people do any of that now, in wartime? Surely they just go down to Caxton Hall, and do it in front of the Registrar? I'm not even sure, strictly speaking, that divorced people can *be* engaged, can they?"

"*We* are going to be, and that's that! My last engagement was to Charles, and looking back on it, it wasn't any fun at all—though I must say he sprang for a very nice ring . . .

well, you've seen it. But otherwise it was awfully dull—lots of tea parties to meet his relatives, and dinner parties to meet his chums. No fun at all, and not made a bit better by the fact that I was pregnant and felt sick as a dog most of the time.''

"Pregnant? I didn't know that. It's funny, but Charles wouldn't have seemed to me the kind of man to go to bed with his fiancée until they were married. I always thought him frightfully *pukka*. As I was, then, another proper young Englishman, living by the rules—*believing* them, too. I didn't go to bed with Penelope until we were married, you know. Oh, not that I didn't want to—I thought about nothing else, I remember. And not that she wasn't game for it—I believe she'd have said yes like a shot if only I'd asked her. But we believed we should wait—*I* did, anyway.''

"So did Charles. I had a hell of a job changing his mind.''

She smiled at the thought—though, in fact, her situation had not been all that funny. Charles's resistance to premarital sex had come to her as a severe shock—one that placed her in a very risky position indeed.

The hours she had spent overcoming his scruples were among the most trying of her life—whatever feelings she had for him were mortally wounded by those many hours on the big tufted leather sofa of his bachelor flat at the Albany, and in his beloved British Racing Green Lagonda, endlessly trying to seduce him into doing the one thing her whole future depended on. She could still remember the sensation of leather against her bare thighs and buttocks, for between the car and his sofa, they always seemed to be embracing and half-undressing on shiny, polished leather, and the touch of it against her skin, at once cold and sticky, no doubt from earnest polishing by housemaids or the chauffeur; she could still remember the desperation she had felt as she worked so tirelessly at the buttons of Charles's waistcoat or his trousers.

In her own house she made sure there was no leather upholstery—she had come to hate the feel of sitting on it, even in cars.

Robby saw her smile, and he smiled himself, relieved no doubt that she was in good humor and had not pressed him hard on the subject of the film contract. "Come darling," she said, giggling, "say your piece."

He fell into the role immediately, dropping to one knee so quickly that he took her by surprise. He seized her hand, kissed it, drew the signet ring off his own finger, the only legacy his father had left his eldest son, and slipped it on hers. *"Marry,"* he called, *"so I mean, sweet Katherine, in thy bed./And therefore, setting all this chat aside,/Thus in plain terms: your father hath consented/That you shall be my wife; your dowry 'greed on;/And will you, nill you, I will marry you. . . ."*

It had been almost a decade since they had played *The Taming of the Shrew* together, but Robby's Petruchio was as witty and full of charm as ever. Still, she had a moment's uneasy pause, for how could she know whether the smile was his or Petruchio's, the gleam in his eye part of his performance or genuine? Did he know the difference himself, for that matter?

She brushed the thought away. *"I'll see thee hanged on Sunday first,"* she said, glancing at the ring, which hung loosely on her finger, and laughed. "No I won't. No hanging. Whatever Kate might say, Felicia accepts."

"Thank God! My knee is giving me hell." He raised his head, put his arms around her, and kissed her. "My darling Lisha," he said. "We'll make a go of it, won't we?"

"We'll *'ave* a go, anyway, ducky," she cried, in broad Cockney—the Cockney that had won such praise for her Eliza Doolittle in Shaw's *Pygmalion*, with Philip as Henry Higgins, before the war. She always used it when she was happy—it was a kind of code between them.

"God knows we've *rehearsed* enough!" she said.

13

"I still say you don't need all that."

"And I, my dear Guillam, say you're wrong! The ancient Greeks, as you must surely know, played naked, but wore masks on their faces. Why, you may ask? Because an actor's *face* is his weakness, his shame, *not* his private parts. Our ordinary faces aren't good enough for great theatre, don't you see? Look at mine, for God's sake! As plain and lumpy as a hot cross bun! That was the first thing Si Krieger said when I went to Hollywood: 'He's ugly! What son of a bitch sent me such a goddamned ugly actor?' And the ignorant old bastard was right! I *am* ugly. We're all ugly—and ordinary—and that won't do."

"Not Felicia, surely?"

"Well of course not, dear boy—hand me that bottle of spirit gum, there's a good fellow. Lisha's beautiful, but that's just as bad. Worse perhaps. The audience sees all that beauty, but that's *all* they see. In the theatre, beauty ought to be hidden behind a mask as well. The real face is always the actor's enemy, Guillam, to be overcome at all costs. If I'm going to *be* Richard of Gloucester, I need a new face to do it. Oh, yes, I know, I have to get inside his mind, inside his heart, I've read all those books you lent me by that Russian chap—"

"Stanislavsky."

"Stanislavsky, then." He laughed. "Randy Brooks used to do a wonderful skit about Russian names: '*Tchaikovsky, Mussorgsky, Stravinsky . . .*' He'd go on and on, rattling them off faster and faster, an amazing performance. The man's a genius."

"Stanislavsky? Of course he is."

"No, you fool! Randy Brooks. Though I *agree* with most of what I read in Stanislavsky. I'm all for understanding the character's motives, going deeper into him, but I also need to invent a face for him, a mask for me to hide behind. The sharp, jutting chin—determination, you see. The rattrap mouth, set in a mocking, lopsided smile—sinister charm, eh? The nose—pure Marty Quick, take my word for it! The swarthy complexion, by the way, is the stroke of genius. The Plantagenets are all blond, tall, fair-skinned, handsome—Norman stock, you know—but here's Richard, with his lank black hair, his dark complexion, his great beak of a nose, completely different from the rest, not just because he's a hunchback with a withered arm and a crippled leg, but because his *face* is different. The nose, you see, dear Guillam, is far more important than the hump.''

He turned for a moment to face Pentecost, who blinked as if he had seen the devil, though Vane's makeup for Richard was already familiar enough to him. Vane stared at himself in the mirror with satisfaction. One of his eyelids was taped, to make Richard's eyes uneven, one larger than the other.

''All the same, Robby—three hours to make up for a part! It must be some kind of record.''

''I have no idea. I hardly find it tedious at all, Guillam, to tell you the truth. I *enjoy* the feeling that I'm becoming Richard. I suppose it's rather similar to Dr. Jekyll's experience every time he turned himself into Mr. Hyde—the freedom not to be obliged to be nice, or polite, or honest, or any of the things we're taught to be. For an Englishman, what an enviable state!''

''Can one really enjoy being evil, I wonder? Without regrets or guilt?''

''Oh, my dear boy, you simply haven't been to Hollywood yet!''

''I've never heard you sound so happy and confident.''

''I *am* confident, at least of what I'm going to do. Whether or not the audience will accept it is quite another question. I can make them laugh, but can I scare the shit out of them at the same time? That's the challenge.''

''You scared the shit out of *me* at the last dress rehearsal.''

''Perhaps you're easily scared, who knows? It's nothing to be ashamed of. There's always someone in the audience who screams when Hamlet stabs Polonius hiding behind the arras, even though everybody knows what's coming. One has to find new ways of surprising people.''

"Speaking of surprises—what's Felicia going to think of your Richard? I notice she hasn't come to any of the rehearsals.''

"I asked her not to. I wanted her to see Richard in finished form, with an audience.''

"That can't have been an easy conversation. Think she'll like it?''

"My dear Guillam, why ever not?'' He wasn't about to tell Pentecost how much Felicia hated the idea of his doing a play without her.

He peered into the mirror to admire his handiwork. Most actors had Richard's hump sewn into the costumes, but he wouldn't hear of it. The moment he arrived in the theatre, he stripped down to his shorts while his dresser fixed the padding to his back, layer after layer, held on with sticky tape. The hump must be part of the man, something he, Vane, could feel in place between his shoulder blades, solid and permanent.

Some actors limped only when they remembered to (John Barrymore, playing Richard, had refused to limp in the love scenes, and Toby Eden frequently forgot to limp at all), but Vane had gone to the trouble of having an orthopedic craftsman alter his shoes and design a special knee brace of Swedish steel, with leather straps, that *obliged* him to limp all the time. These he put on as soon as his hump was secure; he had two hours to walk about in them, getting used to the limp so that it felt natural to him before the curtain rose.

The brace was agonizingly painful, no matter how much cotton padding his dresser used to relieve the pressure of the tightly buckled straps, but Vane didn't mind. Pain, he thought, was surely part of Richard's life from infancy, his crippled bones and joints gnawing away cruelly at his nerves night and day. His upper arm was bound to his body so tightly that the circulation was often cut off, leaving it numb, and giving him agonies when the blood started to flow again. Who would know more about pain than a hunchbacked cripple with a withered arm? Who would have fewer scruples about inflicting it on other people?

Vane had the two middle fingers and the thumb of his left hand taped to his palm, to produce a stunted, maimed, distorted appendage, useless but somehow terrifying. It was as if the two remaining fingers, curled over stiffly, were symbolic of the devil's horns, so that when he reached out to touch the lovely Anne with them, the entire audience would shudder at the thought of those ugly stumps of flesh on Anne's fair, blushing cheek.

He spent two hours every morning at the gymnasium, building up his shoulders and chest—he wanted his Richard to convey a kind of top-heavy muscularity, as though the powerful trunk and the short, thick neck were almost more than the crippled legs could bear. For the scene in which Richard descends from the balcony to greet Buckingham, he arranged to swing out into the air on a rope, then drop fifteen feet to the ground. For the end of the play, he had constructed one of his beloved walls, this one designed to look like the bank of a fairly steep ditch, and at the famous cry *"A horse! A horse! My kingdom for a horse!"* (surely the most familiar line in the English theatre), he had trained himself to fall down the bank, rolling to the very edge of the footlights, so that his body was almost off the stage, his head and shoulders hanging down, as he was hacked to death by Richmond and his men.

Both these tricks had cost him scrapes, bruises, rope burns on his palm, and a twisted ankle, but he was determined to give his Richard every sign of physical strength and daring.

Chagrin's lesson in Manchester had hit home. Vane loved Richard as he had never loved any role, loved him, in fact, as he had perhaps never loved *anyone* before. It amazed him, and he was beginning to realize that it alarmed Lisha.

He picked up a stick of mascara, gave himself a large mole at one corner of his mouth, then decided it looked too much like a beauty spot, wiped it off, and covered the smudge with another layer of greasepaint.

There was a knock on the door. "Good luck, old boy!" he heard Toby Eden say. "Thanks," he shouted back. Toby had stepped into Buckingham's part as effortlessly as he stepped into every role, without fuss or drama. Shakespeare's lines were enough for him. Like a sleepwalker, he made his way through the play in a straight line, sublimely indifferent to obstacles that would have tripped up a more thoughtful actor.

The door opened without a knock, and Felicia came in. He recognized her perfume before he saw her in the mirror, and he turned to greet her. To his surprise, she backed away, an expression of horror on her face.

"You gave me a start," she said. "You look quite horrible, darling."

"That's the idea."

"You don't think you've carried it a bit too far? You're not playing the Hunchback of Notre Dame, you know."

"No, no, the Hunchback of Notre Dame only *looked* horrible, Lisha. Richard *is* horrible, through and through." He gave her a leering smile. He had thought of wearing a set of false teeth for the role to give Richard a snaggle-toothed look, but had decided against it, not so much because of the difficulty of speaking the lines, but because it somehow seemed more in character for Richard to have small, perfect teeth. He wanted to show that in many small ways Richard was fastidious, elegant, a prince, after all, born to the manor, however crippled and distorted. There was a tendency to play him as a slovenly thug, perhaps because he himself complains so much about his appearance throughout the play, but Vane found it more sinister to give him an eerie foppishness, a constant, fussy attention to detail, a slightly effeminate streak that made him at once more loathsome and more human.

"It will feel strange to be in the audience, watching you, instead of onstage," she said, sounding a little forlorn.

He nodded. He knew he ought to say that it would feel odd to be on stage without *her*, but he felt no such thing—on the contrary, he felt a certain relief, a sharp pleasure at the prospect of being out there on his own without having to worry about Lisha's nerves, Lisha's lines, Lisha's notices. For once, he would have the stage to himself for almost the entire play—which was, as Guillam Pentecost had pointed out, one of the attractions of *Richard III* for an actor. There was hardly a scene in which he would be offstage—indeed it was one of Shakespeare's longest roles, nearly three blessed hours. Vane would not have wished it to be a moment shorter.

Felicia gave him a quick kiss, careful not to smudge his makeup. "Good luck, darling," she said. "I love you."

"I love you, too," he said, but his mind was already onstage, and his voice was already Richard's, not his own.

He waited for the shock of stage fright to spread through his mind and body like a swift-acting poison paralyzing him. But to his surprise, he felt completely calm, as if something of Richard's ruthless spirit had entered his. He saw Felicia looking at him in astonishment, waiting for the inevitable moment when his lines escaped him and he felt nothing but despair. He could see suspicion in her eyes as he stubbed out his last cigarette before the curtain—a gesture that usually reminded him of the condemned man going before the firing squad, but this evening seemed to have no drama to it at all—and he stood up as a voice cried out in the hallway, "Beginners, please!"

He hardly even noticed Felicia's departure—or the presence of Pentecost, who was clearly reduced to silence by Vane's obvious self-confidence, or perhaps overcome by the presence of Richard. For there was already a ghastly smile on his face, the thin, pale lips curled, almost white against his swarthy complexion, the eyes, by some trick of light—or perhaps art—sometimes flat and dead, then suddenly glinting with malicious glee. He was at once alarmingly alive and completely dead.

It was like nothing Vane had ever experienced before: a light-headed feeling, the kind of thing people who took drugs, opium, or hashish wrote about.

He limped his way down the hall, his right hand clutching the hilt of his sword, and shuffled clumsily down the iron stairs toward the stage.

14

The wind sent the dark gray clouds scudding across the flat horizon. The rain seemed to fill the air like one of those showers in the locker room at the Hillside Country Club where the water was sprayed at you from every direction.

Marty Quick shivered and wrapped himself tighter in his non-issue Burberry raincoat with the camel's hair lining and more buckles, D-rings, and straps than he knew what to do with. That was the first thing you did when you got to the U. K., Papa Hemingway had told him—buy the Burberry and get yourself a pair of handmade cordovan jodhpur boots from Foster's on Jermyn Street. Well, not exactly the first thing, Quick reminded himself—the first thing to do was to make sure you had a nice quiet suite at Claridge's, on the right side of the hotel, and a good-looking Brit driver. He had done both. His suite was high up, overlooking Brook Street, just below Sir Alexander Korda's penthouse, the one that Sam Goldwyn always took before the war, and his driver, whom he had chosen out of the ATS drivers' pool, was Lance Corporal Sylvia Hanbury-Tennyson, a raven-haired, supercilious, upper-class beauty, with aristocratic manners, the sexual appetites of a born slut, and an apparently insatiable desire for American cigarettes, steaks, nylon stockings, and whiskey.

Even if he lost every other talent, Quick told himself, he could still make a living somehow, just picking the right girls. He could look at a dozen long-stemmed beauties (he always compared them to roses in advertising his shows), and tell in an instant which ones would put out without a lot of persuading. The main thing was never to marry one, of course, but you also had to have a fine nose for that moment when you were taking more shit than the fucking was worth.

If he prided himself on anything, it was knowing exactly when that point had been reached. He hadn't reached it yet with Sylvia, though it was getting close, he could tell—in fact, the next time she gave him the ice-cold, stuck-up Brit superiority number, he planned to loosen a couple of her front teeth for her and send the bitch back to the motor pool!

In the meantime, he congratulated himself, he had it made—the right suite, with the art deco mirrors, the marble tub, the heated towel racks, and the big double bed with Sylvia curled up beside him, managing to look superior even when she was bending over to suck his cock. Which made it even more irritating that he was obliged to tear himself away from Claridge's and drive through the grim, gray English countryside just for a talk with Randy Brooks.

Rain lashed at the windows of the army Packard, formed great pools and puddles on the secondary roads, and made even the thought of leaving the snug warmth of the car intolerable.

Quick lit a cigar, filling the car with smoke. "Where the fuck are we?" he growled.

"Almost there, sir."

"Cut out that 'sir' crap when we're alone, Sylvia. It's not my fault it's raining. It's your fucking country, not mine."

"It *used* to be my country. Look at that!" An endless line of U.S. Army trucks filled the road, lumbering slowly in the other direction. Men waved, cheered, shouted insults, gave Sylvia wolf whistles, as they sped by.

"They're just kids, Sylvia. They don't wanna be here any more than you wanna have them. Fuck it."

"Thank you, Colonel. I'll keep that piece of wisdom in mind. Another witty Broadway bon mot. I must write them down so I don't forget them."

Quick stared at the back of her head, her hair pulled up tightly in a bun so she could wear her khaki peaked cap.

Why, he wondered, did he always pick the ones who despised and humiliated him? But he already knew the answer—it was more fun teaching the hard ones that they couldn't fuck around with Marty Quick than taking on the broads who were submissive. He had learned a long time ago there was no pleasure in hurting women who wanted to be hurt, or didn't really mind being hurt.

"Don't get smart with me," he snapped. "I can send you back to your own people, since you're so fucking fond of them. You can drive Brit officers around, live on rations, wear those nice thick cotton stockings, the ones that scratch your skin. . . . I mean, what the fuck, so you'll be living in a barracks again with twenty other girls, instead of at Claridge's. I guess you won't mind, so long as you're with your own."

"You bastard!"

"That's my girl. I think we're almost there. Christ, it's bleak!"

"We're actually rather proud of Essex. The marshes are considered quite a tourist attraction, in fact."

"Spare me the travelogue, Sylvia. These boys are going to be so eager to leave here they'll be *happy* to get on the invasion barges!"

"Surely Randy Brooks isn't going with them? He doesn't look as if he can tell one end of a rifle from the other."

"Are you outta your mind? Randy's a star. He's not going on any goddamn invasion craft. You think Ike's gonna let a movie star get killed?"

"Then what's he doing here?"

"Living with the troops. Proving he's one of the boys."

"Isn't that a little cynical?"

"It's not cynical, it's smart. But let me tell you something, Randy wouldn't want to be an officer, live at Claridge's, have a driver. He turned all that down to be an ordinary soldier. The guy is practically a saint." He paused. "Or an asshole, depending on how you look at it."

Quick did not add that Brooks's decision to serve in the ranks was a major source of annoyance and inconvenience to everyone involved. The army didn't want a famous thirty-five-year-old comedian in the ranks. Officers were reluctant to give him orders, his fellow soldiers treated him as if he were more important than a five-star general, and since his work consisted of entertaining the troops, he was never obliged to appear on parade, eat in the mess, or look after his own kit. Randy Brooks had a room to himself, a sergeant to see to his travel arrangements and keep him on schedule, and several thousand young men to keep him company.

Ahead of the car two military policemen in white helmets and ponchos huddled in a shed beside a red-white-and-blue-striped pole barring the road. Sylvia straightened her hat and pulled to a halt. "Colonel Quick to see Colonel Fruchter," she said crisply, lowering the window just a few inches. You couldn't beat the Brits for that, Quick thought—they had a natural gift for giving orders and bossing people around, the legacy of a rigid class system and an empire to run. He wondered what it would be like to live here when they woke up to the fact that they'd lost their empire and had nobody to boss but one another.

The two MPs straightened up, snapped a quick salute and raised the pole. Sylvia could have made a German general jump by just looking at him.

She drove through the pouring rain, past rows of dreary, sodden Nissen huts. There was not a tree in sight, nor any building that looked as if it had existed longer than a few months ago. The whole vast, ghastly encampment looked as if it had been dropped, prefabricated, onto the Essex marsh-land, like an urban slum-clearance project. As soon as the invasion began—if it ever *did* begin!—the huts would be empty, the place a ghost town. That's why we're going to win the war, Quick told himself. The Germans are better trained, better equipped, better led, but we can afford to build a whole fucking town out here in the middle of nowhere, then abandon it like an old movie set.

"Here we are, Colonel," Sylvia said crisply, as she stopped in front of a weather-beaten tar-paper shack marked "Headquarters." "Shall I wait for you?"

"Nah, you come with me." Quick buttoned up his tunic, put on his cap, stubbed out his cigar, and waited for Sylvia to get out of the car, come round to his side, and open the rear door for him with a salute. He rather enjoyed showing her off to other American officers. Sylvia was living proof of his importance, his virility, his ability to get things done.

There was no way he would waste all that by having her sit outside in the car unseen.

He returned her salute and stomped into the headquarters building on his spit-polished jodhpur boots, with Sylvia following behind, her nonregulation high heels clicking on the linoleum. Quick shoved open a flimsy plywood door, puffed out his chest, and strode right past a top sergeant and a middle-aged bespectacled captain, working at their desks.

"Hey, you can't go in there!" the captain shouted, but he was too late, for Quick had already shoved aside the low wooden gate barring the entrance to Colonel Fruchter's office and had his hand on the colonel's doorknob.

He did not knock. Years of Hollywood experience had taught him that you never got anywhere unless you took people by surprise. If you tried to make an appointment to see anybody who mattered, you could forget it. People like Harry Cohn or Louie Mayer would keep you waiting for days, if they saw you at all, so Quick learned to barge into people's offices unannounced.

Fruchter was lying back in his desk chair snoring, his feet resting on the shiny bare top of his desk, his uniform cap pulled low over his eyes to block out the light. There was a stove in the corner glowing red, with a pot of coffee simmering on top of it. In the opposite corner was a ceiling-high pile of cartons—cigarettes, canned hams, nylons, whiskey, chocolate. "What the hell!" he cried, swinging his feet off the desk and removing the cap from his eyes. "Who the hell are you?"

Quick snapped his fingers at Sylvia, who produced from her tight-fitting tunic a crocodile cigar case, selected a Partegas #3, took out a gold cigar cutter, and carefully trimmed off the end. Smiling suggestively, she licked the end of the cigar, lit a wooden match against the sole of her shoe, exposing a good deal of thigh as she bent over. She puffed at the cigar until it was burning nicely, then handed it to Marty Quick.

Quick prided himself on training his girls well. There were husbands all over the world who had cause to be grateful to him for their wives' skills. All Quick's girls learned—fast!

—how to light his cigar, how to mix his martini the way he liked it, how to warm his brandy, how to go down on him —no detail was too small to ignore when it came to his comfort. It was as if his girls were graduates of some elite finishing school, which in a way they were. Quick took off his cap and his gold-rimmed aviator's sunglasses and put them on the desk, grinning. He blew cigar smoke in Fruchter's direction.

"Jesus!" Fruchter said, with evident relief. "Marty Quick and his Flying Circus. I was afraid it was an inspector general."

"I *bet* you were, *bubbi*. What are you running here? A trading post?"

Fruchter glanced at Sylvia admiringly. "You know how it is, Marty," he said. "We all want to make friends with the natives. Plenty squaw in the villages around this fort, not too many warriors."

"Zane Fruchter," Quick said to Sylvia, by way of introduction. "Used to write scripts for cowboy-and-Indian pictures, then he went bad injun, became a producer."

"Now I'm just a simple dog soldier. Care for a drink?"

Fruchter's appearance was remarkably unmilitary, even for the U.S. Army. He was a big, burly man with a grizzled gray beard, long hair, bushy eyebrows, and the dark, soulful eyes of one of the larger and more friendly breeds of dog, a Labrador or a Newfoundland, perhaps. His shirt was unbuttoned, revealing an astonishing amount of chest hair, and the backs of his hands were covered with a thick simian pelt, which contrasted oddly with his perfectly manicured nails. There was a piratical swagger to him—with a gold earring and a parrot on his shoulder he could have played Long John Silver. He opened his desk drawer, took out three glasses and a bottle of scotch and poured drinks. "Welcome to Fort Laramie. We live rough, but as they say in these parts, '*Mia casa, sua casa.*' What can I do for you?"

"I have to see Randy Brooks."

Fruchter knocked back his drink. "Why ask me?"

"You're his commanding officer."

"I'm in charge of entertainment personnel, yes." Fruchter

opened another drawer in his desk, took out a package of Camels, and lit one. The drawer seemed to be filled with garter belts, brassieres, and stockings in various colors and styles—more trade items for the local squaws. He blew a smoke ring. "Randy's a pain in the ass," he said.

"Tell me about it. What's the fucking problem, anyway? I used to be able to call him on the phone, send a car for him, whatever. Now I can't get ahold of him at all, for crissakes. Not even Aaron Diamond, his own agent, can reach him. It's like he was the man in the iron mask or something."

"So far as I'm concerned, he can go anywhere he wants, and the further, the better. You wanna know why Randy can't come to the phone? It's because he went to some big base down south to do a show, and he made fun of General Patton! The troops loved it, but Patton was so pissed off he had Randy put under close arrest. As for Aaron, it's news to me that privates in the U. S. Army need an agent."

"Everybody needs an agent. And most people who matter have two—"

"I know, I know, their own and Aaron Diamond," Fruchter cut in, finishing the old Hollywood line. "War is hell," he said with a sigh. "Randy's lucky he's not facing a firing squad or being dropped on Krautland without a 'chute. What do you want him for?"

"I just need to talk to him."

"He's not supposed to talk to anyone. That's what 'close arrest' means. I had him booked all over the fucking place, two shows a day, and I had to cancel everything. He's sitting in his room with an MP outside the door. That's no way to win a war."

Quick gave Fruchter a look of disgust. "I want Randy in London whenever I need him, okay? I get him out of close arrest, I get first call on him, okay?"

"Patton's fighting mad, Marty. Even *you* can't get around that. Anyway, what are you going to do with Randy in London?"

"None of your goddamned business, Zane. I get the order lifted, you get to play your bookings, I can have the son of a bitch whenever I need him. Deal?"

"Deal. But you're wasting your time."

Quick scribbled a number on a piece of paper and handed it to Sylvia, who went outside, sat down on the captain's desk, exposing a good deal of creamy thigh and a glimpse of a very unmilitary black garter strap clipped to her stocking top, and began the normally tedious business of placing a priority call. She was put through in an instant. "Captain Butcher at SHAEF on line one for you, Colonel Quick," she said crisply, swinging one leg back and forth.

Quick picked up the telephone. "Harry!" he barked. "You're about to go up shit creek. So is your boss. I just talked to Winchell in New York, and Walter's heard Ike put Randy Brooks under arrest for telling a joke about Pat ton. . . . Uh-huh, uh-huh. . . ."

Quick rolled his eyes, blew a smoke ring, winked at Sylvia, made a face to show how boring Butcher's side of the conversation was. "Well, sure," he said, "I *know* Ike's a fan of Randy's—hell, who isn't?—but Winchell's going to write a lot of crap about how Ike's locked up America's most beloved comedian. I mean, Winchell's mad as hell, Harry, I just talked to him. You'll love his lead! *'Why doesn't Ike pick on Hitler instead of Randy Brooks?'* Yeah, I agree it's unfair. . . . Well, of course you didn't know, but so what? Well, I *could* ask Winchell to kill the story. . . . Yeah, he *might* do it as a favor to me. . . . But I'd have to tell Winchell Randy's a free man—a free soldier, anyway." There was a pause. He held his hand over the mouthpiece. "He says to let him go."

Fruchter shook his head. "I got orders from Patton. I can't let Randy go on the say-so of a captain."

"He's a *navy* captain. Four stripes. Same thing as a full colonel."

"Fuck that. Patton's a four-star general."

Quick nodded. If Fruchter needed his ass covered, he would cover it. "Harry," he said, "no dice. Colonel Zane Fruchter here—who is, by the way, not only a *close* personal friend of Gary Cooper and Jimmy Stewart, but a major Hollywood producer who gave up his career to serve overseas —doesn't want to be sent to the Aleutians by George Patton to freeze his balls off for the rest of the war. Uh-huh. I'm sure that will cover it, Harry. I'll fix things with Winchell. And give my best to Ike.''

He hung up. "You'll get a message from SHAEF on your teletype right away, lifting Randy's arrest—a direct order from Ike. Solved your problem, *kimosabe*?''

Fruchter lifted his glass in a mocking toast. "The Great White Father wins again! Where do you want Randy delivered?''

"To the car.''

"I need him back ASAP, Marty. Since he stuck it to Patton, everybody wants the son of a bitch. If I could charge money for him,'' he said wistfully, "I'd be a rich man.''

"Hey,'' Quick said, with a leer, sending Sylvia on her way back to the car with a pat on the bottom. "Money isn't everything.''

Fruchter stood up. On his feet, he towered over Quick, his arms dangling down like those of one of the larger orders of apes. "I never thought I'd hear *you* say that, Marty. But I guess you're right. Money *isn't* everything.''

He lowered his voice and bent down until his mouth was close to Quick's ear. "There's nooky, for example. I don't suppose you'd want to let me have your driver, would you?''

"Why would I want to do that? She's in mint condition, not a nick or a dent on her. What am I offered? Besides Randy Brooks, which I got.'' His eyes glittered darkly, as they always did when there was a deal on the horizon.

"Trading goods?''

"Fuck that. I got all I need.''

Fruchter shrugged. "Tell me, Marty,'' he said, "what do you think people are gonna want when we get to France and Germany?''

Quick studied the tip of his cigar thoughtfully. He was always willing to learn something new. "Food?'' he suggested.

"Well, sure, but the guys in Supply are going to have all the food, right? You and I aren't going to be standing in the mud selling off powdered eggs by the truckload. No, what they're gonna want is to see all the movies they've missed.

Gone With the Wind, Marty. *Rebecca. Casablanca. The Wizard of Oz. Jungle Book.* Gable and Lombard. Robby Vane and Felicia Lisle. I've got prints, Marty——dozens of pictures. What I need is somebody who knows the European distributors.''

Quick nodded. He knew a good idea when he heard it. ''I could find a guy,'' he said. ''You'd have to move fast. A week after we've taken Paris, the majors will have guys there. It'll be business as usual.''

''I got that taped, Marty. My prints are going in right behind the tanks.''

Quick put his cap and his dark glasses back on again. ''Fifty/fifty, and we got a deal.''

''I was thinking more like seventy/thirty, Marty. Fifty is high for just a name.''

''Sixty/forty, and I'll throw in Sylvia as well, Zane. I'll have her orders cut the moment I'm back in London.'' They shook hands. Quick walked out, strutting, then paused on the threshold. ''Oh, Zane,'' he said, in a low whisper, ''no kid gloves with Sylvia, you know what I mean? She likes it rough and tough.''

Fruchter waved. ''You're an officer and a gentleman, Marty.''

Outside, Sylvia waited next to the car, standing at attention.

He dropped his cigar butt into the nearest puddle. Six months or so up here in the boonies would do her a world of good, he decided. ''When I get back to London,'' he said, ''remind me to call a guy I know about getting film prints, a Hungarian guy named Szabothy, there's a good girl.'' Why settle for 40 percent, when he could have the whole thing? Stockpile the prints from the army's supply that was used to entertain the troops, get them into Europe ahead of Fruchter's, then make a deal with the studios to get the prints back again, once they discovered there were bootleg copies of their biggest movies being shown everywhere. A nice deal all around, Quick told himself. But there was no point in getting a reputation as a welsher, even with a guy like Fruchter. He would let Sylvia go.

He opened the door and sat down next to Randy Brooks.

"You never know when to stop, do you?" he growled. "Lay off generals."

He extracted a silver pocket flask from his Burberry, took a swig, then selected a cigar and leaned forward to crank up the window that divided the driver's seat from the passenger compartment. He glanced at Randy and shook his head. "You look really terrible, kiddo. Sit back and relax. We gotta talk."

They sat, wreathed in Quick's pungent Havana smoke, in the warmth of the private bar in the roadside pub, waiting for their meal. The smell of fresh bacon and eggs frying in real butter was rising from the kitchen, while Quick sipped his Johnnie Walker Black Label and Brooks a cup of English tea with a double shot of rum and three spoonfuls of sugar —an unheard-of luxury.

This was as good as it was going to get, Randy thought to himself. He would have liked a hot bath, scented soap, plenty of warm towels, and someone to rub his back dry. He let his mind drift to one of the MPs who had been guarding him, and tried to think what it would be like to see him naked in the steam, sweat running down his chest and shoulders as he rubbed the big towels hard against Randy's skin.

He shook his head. There was no point in fantasizing here, with Marty Quick, of all people! Life in the army had nearly made Randy a nervous wreck—it was a real problem to spend every day and night surrounded by young men, never quite sure which ones might be interested in getting a little closer to a famous star. He had had his share of young soldiers, he guessed, starting on the troopship on the way over, but it was a dangerous, risky game. So what else is new? he asked himself. Why should the army be different?

Danger was part of the excitement, always had been, even in the old days when he had worked the Catskill bars, telling jokes between strippers to audiences of garment center hot-shots in their brand-new golf clothes, escaping from their wives and children at Grossinger's or the Concord every afternoon. From time to time you guessed wrong, and paid the price. He remembered getting beaten half to death in the men's room of the Stag Lounge, a roadhouse near Ellenville, by an

enraged jazz musician whose attentions Randy had miscon-
strued. Marty had smoothed that one over, as he had before,
and as he would again.

That was the thing that nobody really understood, Randy
thought, or ever would, he hoped—Marty had cast himself
as the big brother right at the beginning, way back when they
were hardly more than kids, when Randy was just a scrawny
young Jewish comedian, desperately trying to work a laugh
out of guys who were only waiting around for another drink,
or for the next stripper to come on, or for the hooker they
wanted to come back and perch on a stool at the bar. Marty
was a stocky, muscular guy who never needed a bouncer to
help him run a bar, and Marty had saved his life many times.

He closed his eyes. He could still see Marty as he was
then—not so very different, except for the sports coats in
gambler's checks, and the shirts with the rolled collars and
Windsor knot ties. Marty had learned how to run a bar the
hard way, getting his chance to rise from floor waiter to
bartender in a mob-owned joint in Coney Island by waylaying
the bartender one night in the parking lot and breaking his
hands, then boldly taking the man's place.

In any joint Marty ran, there was always a resident bookie
and a crap game in the storeroom behind the bar. Once, when
a couple of armed hoods tried to rip off the game in Marty's
place out at Sheepshead Bay, he knocked the guns out of
their hands, then beat them to a pulp with the baseball bat
he kept next to the cash register. Nobody ever tried it again,
and the rumor spread that he was not only "protected," but
crazy.

It was curious, Randy thought—one of those things that
made you glad to be a comedian, because you could only
deal with it by laughing—but it was actually possible that he
loved Marty Quick, that in fact he might be the only person
who ever had, except for Marty's mother, and even that
wasn't sure, since Marty never mentioned her. Stranger and
funnier still was the possibility that Marty might love *him*.
He poured some more rum into his tea from the bottle on the
table.

"When did you start drinking?" Quick asked.

"Coming over, on the troopship. The ship in front of us was torpedoed at night. I was standing on the deck, and I could hear people screaming in the water, calling out to be rescued. . . . And we didn't stop. I was praying we wouldn't, Marty. I didn't want to hang around, waiting to be torpedoed, too."

He paused. Sometimes, late at night, when he was alone, he could still hear the screams. He had despised himself for his own fear, for the cowardice that made him pray the ship wouldn't slow down or stop, for the fact that he was still alive, telling jokes, when the people in the water were dead.

It was one thing to be funny when you were feeling low and rotten—Christ, he told himself, all comedians felt shitty a lot of the time, and some of them with good reason, because they were real shits!—but it required very special guts to be funny when the rest of the world was dying. However shitty life had been, he had never taken to drink, having seen what it had done to his father, who had slipped from being the proud cantor of a Lower East Side temple to a clerk in an East Harlem pawnshop, a Jew buying cheap stolen goods from the *shvartzers* to enrich a bunch of dago mobsters, and had brought his whole family down with him.

He stirred the rum into his tea and sipped it gratefully, telling himself that maybe his father—whom he had despised—had the right idea after all. You needed something to keep you from crying, or breaking down at the sight of so much pain and waste.

He had toured the hospitals to tell jokes to the wounded, the young men with their hands and faces burned off, or their genitals shot away, or their legs gone, forcing himself to make them laugh, astonished at how easy it was to do, and at the awe with which they greeted *him*, the big star. But afterward, on the long drive back, he needed the whiskey to put the smells, the bloody stumps, the ruined faces, out of his mind.

Only once had he broken down, when his performance in the open air at a bomber base had been interrupted by the emergency landing of a damaged B-17 from some other group, and he had volunteered to help remove the wounded from the plane. When they got the hatch open with an ax and a crowbar, the inside of the crew compartment was bright red, so red that for a moment he supposed it was painted that color for some reason. Then as his eyes adjusted to the dim light, he realized he was looking at a slaughterhouse. The top gunner had been hit by cannon fire—his head and shoulders were still strapped into his turret, and his hands were still fixed on the handles of his twin Brownings, but the rest of him had been spattered all over the cockpit, shredded into bits and pieces of gristle and bone, his blood covering everything as if it had been applied with a carelessly operated spray gun.

Randy had turned his back on the carnage, had sat down on the damp grass, and begun to cry, as if a few tears could matter, or change things. The men were nice about it, but he could see they were also a little impatient. They didn't need his tears or his sympathy, they didn't want to know about his grief and horror, they only wanted him to be funny, and there was nothing funny about a middle-aged Hollywood comedian hunkered down on the runway beneath the shattered nose of a B-17, sobbing his heart out, his hands sticky with someone else's blood.

Since then, he drank, without pleasure, hating the taste of the stuff, indifferent to what he was drinking. Drink erased the pictures that haunted his mind, liberated his comic spirit, made it possible for him to laugh again. Maybe his performances weren't as sharp as they had once been, maybe his famous timing was off a bit, but the troops didn't seem to notice it, and he didn't much care. It was a reasonable trade-off. You gave up a little sharpness and polish for the larger gain of being able to do it at all.

He did not feel like explaining any of that to Marty Quick. "It's the only way to keep warm in this fucking country," he said.

"I'll drink to that. How are you doing otherwise?"

"Great. No complaints."

Quick leaned across the table angrily, like some kind of sleek, aggressive small animal—a wolverine, perhaps, though Randy had never seen one. Quick's black hair was slicked back, his clenched teeth were sharp, white, and even, the dark little eyes, half-hooded by the drooping lids, glittered with anger.

Once upon a time, Randy had lived in fear of Quick, friends though they were, but the war had taught him that there were things a lot more scary than Marty Quick's eyes. "Cut that crap out!" Quick snapped. "This is Marty you're talking to, not some dumb Brit reporter. When *I* ask a question, I wanna answer. 'No complaints,' my ass! You look like shit."

"Most of the time I'm cold, tired, lonely, and scared, but so is practically everybody else except you, Marty, so I'm not complaining, okay?"

Marty gave a calculated smile, as if to show there were no hard feelings, but his expression was puzzled. He wasn't used to Randy fighting back. "In Hollywood they're saying you're a fucking hero," he said. "Even the people who don't like you. That story about how you helped pull the crew out of a bomber that crashed, then went on with your show . . . great, stuff, kiddo! Si Krieger's lobbying the President to get you a medal."

"I don't want a medal. And that isn't the way it was."

Quick nodded, his expression dark. "I didn't figure it was, kid," he said sadly. "It never is. Back when I used to fight, before I met you, I went ten rounds as a welterweight in St. Nick's Arena, with Benny DeFeo—"

Randy stifled a yawn. He had heard it all before.

"I didn't have a chance against him—shouldn't have been in the same ring. Fight was supposed to be fixed, but when I got in the ring, Benny whispers to me, 'Fuck it, I'm not gonna throw this one, Marty!' He was going out with this blond shiksa, see, and he didn't want her to watch him lose."

Randy nodded. It was a familiar story—a central part of the Marty Quick myth. Quick went ten rounds with DeFeo, a boxer who outclassed him ten to one, and finally won by a decision, after taking a broken nose and a fractured jaw without telling his handlers or the referee. "I know the story, Marty," he said. "I heard it before, remember?"

"So you heard it before. So what? What you *didn't* hear before, Randy, is this—I was shit-scared. Oh, over the years

I've turned it into an upbeat story, sure. Every time some journalist prints it, I come out sounding like some kind of hero. '*You had to be there, Chollie!*' '' He shook his head. ''You had to fucking *be* there. I was scared, see, *really* scared. I figured, if I let Benny beat me, they'll probably kill me. And I knew Benny could smash me to a pulp, right there in the ring, if I tried to win—I mean, he was so much better than I was, it wasn't even close. . . . So there I was, this scared kid, overmatched, figuring whatever I did I was either gonna get a bullet in my head or my fucking bones broken, and all I wanted to do was to get outta that ring and run for my life. That's the part nobody tells—not me, not nobody else. I never told nobody how it feels to go a couple of rounds with a fractured jaw and a broken nose, or a cut on the forehead so bad that half the time I couldn't even see Benny because there was blood in my eyes. Nobody wants to hear about how I sat in the shower afterwards, crying and throwing up. You want my advice? Keep the truth to yourself, and if they offer you the fucking medal, take it.''

''I don't deserve it.''

''I didn't deserve to win over Benny DeFeo, dummy. That's the point of the story.''

Randy nodded. Marty was right: there was probably nothing he could do about the medal except grin, accept it, and keep the truth to himself. Truth was the one thing nobody ever wanted to hear, particularly from a man who was supposed to be funny.

The public didn't want to know the truth about the war any more than Robby Vane wanted to know the truth about himself, he thought bitterly. ''Okay, Marty,'' he said. ''I'll *take* the medal. What else do I have to do?'' With Marty there was always something he wanted—he was the living embodiment of the old adage that there was no such thing as a free lunch, or even a free cup of tea with rum.

Quick leaned closer. ''Robby Vane,'' he whispered. ''How is he?''

Despite the rum, Randy was suddenly alert.

''Christ, Marty,'' he said, aware that his speech was slightly slurred, ''how would I know?''

"I figured you'd keep in touch."

"You think we're pen pals? You figured wrong."

Quick gave one of his famous smiles, a sharklike flash of white teeth unaccompanied by any discernible change in the mirthless little dark eyes. "I think maybe I liked you better when you didn't drink," Marty said, still smiling. "I didn't have to take this kind of shit from you, of all people."

"There's a war on, Marty. There are people out there a lot scarier than you are, believe it or not. Hitler, for instance."

"Hitler scares you? It isn't Hitler you should be scared of, *bubbi*. You wanna know what *your* trouble is? You're taking this goddamn war too seriously. It's gonna be over, one of these days, pal, then real life begins again."

Randy shrugged. He no longer thought about when the war would be over. It seemed to him it would probably go on until everybody involved had been killed and there were no young people left.

Quick relit his cigar and pointed the burning tip at Randy's face. "Why are we in uniform?" he asked dramatically.

Randy closed his eyes. He had no idea why he was in uniform, let alone Quick. He could not believe that either one of them was contributing anything worthwhile toward winning the war.

Quick waited a few moments, then answered his own question. "When the war's over, pal, it's the guys who were in uniform who are going to be runnin' things. You'll see. It's gonna be the best thing you ever did for your career."

"My career is down the toilet, Marty. So long as I'm here in uniform, nobody's gonna notice, but it's a fact. I'm not funny anymore."

"Bullshit! You're just depressed, that's all. Take it from a friend."

"A friend? Why do I have a feeling that my friend is gonna ask me to do something I don't want to do?"

"I want what's best for you, Randy," Quick said with his most sincere expression. "Christ, we've been friends for what? Twenty years?"

"Twenty years a queen," Randy said, in a clipped, upper-class English voice. Folding his napkin, he placed it on his head, crossed his hands in his lap, stuck out his lower lip, and gave his imitation of Queen Victoria.

"Cut that *out!*" Marty was always made nervous by the slightest hint of homosexuality on Randy's part. A limp wrist, a lisp, a doubtful *double-entendre*, even in jest, never failed to enrage him. Once, to raise money for the Los Angeles Foundling Hospital, Randy, Cary Grant, and Randolph Scott had agreed to appear dressed as infants, in old-fashioned baby clothes, blond wigs, and lace sunbonnets. The idea was for Scott and Grant to push Randy around the stage in a pram, while the three of them sang "Baby Face." Marty, who had volunteered to produce the program as his contribution, fought against the number bitterly, and lost only because Cary Grant was too big a star for him to bully successfully. Everybody else in Hollywood thought it was uproarious fun (though Randy had to admit there *were* a few sly winks at the sight of the industry's three most famous closet queens camping it up on stage in lace dresses and fright wigs), but Marty had been so angry about it that they didn't speak for almost six months.

"Look," Randy said, removing the napkin, "I just want to know what's going on. You didn't drive all the way up here in the rain just to buy me a black-market lunch."

Quick stared out the window at the rain-lashed countryside. He looked hurt. "What's the most important thing in life?" he asked.

"If you try to tell me 'friendship,' I'll throw up."

"Paying up when you owe somebody, right? *That's* the most important thing there is!"

"Marty! That from you? You've been welshing on people all your life."

"Yeah, but nobody welshes on *me*."

Quick's view of life was essentially a one-way street in which all the traffic moved in the direction he wanted it to go. From time to time, Randy asked himself why he put up with him, but he knew the answer: years ago, Quick had been his only friend, the one man who had given him a chance—more than that, the only person who not only knew his secret but had saved his ass a dozen times. When there was trouble, *real* trouble, the kind Randy wouldn't have wanted Natalie or her father to know about, he would always go to Marty first. After all, there was one thing to be said in favor of Marty—he wasn't easy to shock. Besides, thanks to Marty, Randy had poured his earnings, bit by bit, into real estate, orange groves, dry cleaning establishments, parking lots, all over greater Los Angeles—businesses that were short on glamour, but long on cash. "Who welshed on you, Marty?" he asked.

"Your pal Robby."

"How so?"

"What'sa matter with you? I gave him four hundred thousand dollars, for God's sake. For *Don Quixote*, remember? I offered to pay his debts and I did. You were there."

"The night of the party." Randy closed his eyes. It had been the happiest moment of his life, the night he and Robby had sat together in the darkened living room—even though it had been spoiled by Felicia's suicide attempt. . . . "I warned him not to get involved," he said.

"Well, he did anyway."

"What the hell, Marty. It's never gonna happen. Forget it. Robby will pay it back one day. Leave him be."

"It's gonna happen. You can bet on it. I'm gonna make the picture, Randy, and you're gonna be in it. So's Robby. So's Lisha." He grinned. "It's gonna be the first big postwar picture, Randy, and I'm gonna use it to take over a studio, just the way I always planned. Then I'm gonna eat those fuckin' zombies in Hollywood *alive*! They're not gonna know what hit 'em. It's all coming, Randy—television is the future. The old guys, Mayer, Goldwyn, Cohn, they're gonna fight TV all the way, and they're gonna lose. The difference between me and them, see, is *I'm* a showman! I put on a show, I don't give a fuck *how* the public sees it, so long as they pay, right? There's no law says people always gotta sit in a movie theatre—they can stay home and watch in their own living rooms, am I right or am I wrong?"

Randy poured himself a little more rum in his tea. "Right," he said. Nobody who cared for his own peace of mind ever said Marty was wrong.

"Marty," he said, "if you're going to take over television, then a studio, what do you want to make a big movie for? Go home, round up the gang from Lindy's, tie them up with contracts, *bubkes* down, and start *hondling* with Sarnoff and Paley. Forget about the movie."

Quick's enthusiasm evaporated. "I can't," he said quietly. "Between what I loaned Robby and what I've already paid for scripts, I'm out about a million one. I gotta show I can do something with the million, understand? It's a question"—he sought the right word—"of credibility."

"Whose million was it?"

Quick shrugged. "Some from here, some from there . . . you know how it is."

Randy knew how it was. "Would some of them be guys who like spaghetti carbonara and build casinos? Old friends from the nightclub days?"

"They might be," Quick said uncomfortably.

"And they want to see something happen for their money, right?"

Quick nodded glumly.

"Something big, something flashy, something with major stars?"

"It could be, yeah."

"And I guess, in Chicago and New York, no news is not good news, right? They're used to getting their money back in a hurry—the jockey pulls the horse the way he was supposed to or you break his hands afterwards so he can't ride again, right?"

"Maybe."

"You had to be out of your mind to go to your friends in the mob for money."

"You think I could go to a fuckin' bank? And say what? Loan me a million bucks so I can pay off Robby Vane's debts from his Shakespeare tour, then tie him and his crazy, suicidal wife up to make a big movie that's gonna cost maybe ten, twelve million more? . . . There are times when you gotta take a risk, Randy, you know that."

"You sure took one, my friend. You've had their money for almost two years? They must have a standing order for

fresh concrete to stick your feet in before they dump you in
Lake Michigan.''

"That isn't funny.''

Randy knew it took a lot to scare Marty Quick, but he
could see fear in Quick's eyes. "I got news for you,'' Randy
said. "I didn't *mean* it to be funny. So what do you want
from me, Marty? Break it to me gently. I've got shows to
do all over England now that you got Patton off my ass.''

"I want a big favor and a small one.''

"What's the big one?''

"I'm not going to tell you about the big one yet. The small
one is, You finish your tea, put on your hat, and come with
me.''

"Where? I'm due back in an hour. Fruchter is waiting for
me so he can lock me back up in my cell.''

"Forget Fruchter. I got you sprung for the night, my
friend,'' Marty said, his spirits returning.

He lit a new cigar, dropped a crisp one-pound note down
on the table, and gave a piercing whistle to alert Sylvia that
he was ready to go: "You and me, pal—we're going to the
theatre!''

15

He plunged into the dark. Normally he would have paused
to wait for his entrance, but instead he simply walked straight
onto the unlit stage, his sword clanking slightly in its scabbard
as he stopped and took up his position behind the throne,
staring at the fireproof backing on the curtain, behind which
he could hear the buzz of the audience as the house lights
dimmed.

This was the way Vane had wanted it, the way he had
planned it for Richard from the beginning, alone on the stage
in the dark, alone with his thoughts. He had never felt more
powerful, more in control.

He heard the curtain begin to rise, focused his eyes beyond it, and waited a moment or two, patiently. A small spotlight went on, and suddenly the audience realized he was there, had been there for a few moments, a shadow in the dark, observing them from his hidden vantage point. He had made *himself* the Peeping Tom and caught them unawares, adjusting their clothes, fanning themselves with their programs, clearing their throats. He heard a subdued murmur, a few gasps of shock, then the big spot flashed on, creating a pool of light in front of him, and, lowering his shoulder, he limped slowly out from behind the shadow of the throne, ran his crippled hand over the carved wood as a man might caress a woman, or stroke a beloved horse, and smiled obscenely, wickedly, as if he were letting the audience share some private moment of pleasure. He brought his finger up to his lips, asking them to keep his secret, then edged forward into the full, bright light, smiling malevolently at them.

As a rule, he tried not to look at the faces in front of him. As mountain climbers fear to look down, so he feared to recognize a particular face in the audience, but such was his power tonight that he searched the front rows until he saw Felicia, and gave her a bold wink. It went with the role—Richard was, after all, a politician, as skilled at wooing his listeners as he was at killing his enemies. He would not have hesitated to give a pretty girl in the crowd a wink, not for a moment.

The audience expected him to speak. Instead he simply stared back at them silently.

Then he heard the flourish of trumpets and drums offstage that was his cue to begin, and lurching one uneven step farther toward the footlights, his hand still touching the throne, as if unwilling to let go, he began to speak.

"Now is the winter of our discontent," he hissed, conscious that he had found at last a way of getting past Philip's superior voice—by delivering the line in the precise, slightly high-pitched, fussy tone of a schoolmaster lecturing his pupils, the voice, as it happened, of his own father, and uncannily appropriate to Richard, a bully on a broader and more savage scale, but with the same pedant's

weakness for explaining everything and teaching everyone a lesson.

"*. . . But I, that am not shaped for sportive tricks,*" he went on with a smirk, tossing his head as if he were already relishing his love scene with the mourning Princess Anne. He looked again at the audience. And just as he took a deep breath before plunging on to the next line, he saw, seated three rows behind Felicia, on the aisle, two familiar figures in uniform, and for the first time that evening he broke out into a cold sweat of fear.

Felicia drew her breath in sharply. For a single heart-stopping moment it seemed to her that Robby, not even half-way through his opening speech, was about to lose control of himself. He stood there "sweating blood," as he would have said, eyes staring into the audience as if he had gone mad, the pallor showing through his makeup.

His terror was so intense that he stopped limping, and for an instant she wondered if he had suddenly been taken ill. Surely, she thought wildly, he was too young to suffer a heart attack or a stroke? Yet that was exactly the appearance he gave, as if with his next breath, he would fall unconscious to the floor. She felt a wave of anxiety run through her body, felt it physically, a kind of shock wave with the speed of an explosion.

I love him, she told herself. Please don't let him die, she prayed silently, though she was no believer in prayer. As if it were a scene in a film, she imagined Robby falling, saw herself leap from her seat, run to the footlights, scramble up onto the stage to kneel beside him, cradling his head in her arms. . . . She had these moments of fantasy, often so sharp and detailed that they seemed more real than real life to her. This one—like all of them—seemed to go on for an eternity, but in fact it was over in the brief moment it took for Robby to take a quick breath, and plunge forward with his speech.

"*Nor made to court an amorous looking-glass,*" he said, faltering momentarily on the "amorous," then, as if nothing at all had happened, he resumed his role completely: his limp returned, his cheeks and lips darkened again, his eyes projected that peculiar combination of manic high spirits and deadly menace that was his concept of Richard.

The whole episode, she thought, could not have taken longer than a second, if that, and nobody else in the audience, not even Guy or Philip beside her, seemed to have noticed anything out of the ordinary. She let out her breath, relieved that there had been no catastrophe, and settled back in her seat to observe his performance.

There was a quality to it that she found even more disturbing than Robby's moment of hesitation. He was taking the art of acting further than anybody she had ever seen before, anywhere. She could feel the excitement building in the audience. Chagrin's expression was that of a man witnessing a miracle, while Darling, usually a fidgeter, sat as if he were frozen, visibly overcome.

This was not a performance to be compared to one of Philip's or Toby's, or even rated against what people remembered of "The Old Man." Nobody, not Sir Henry Irving, not even Garrick, she felt sure, had ever dominated the stage as Robby was doing tonight. His wicked, gloating Richard, slyly sharing his secrets with the audience as if they were coconspirators, owed nothing to anyone—it was *his* creation, a Richard at once completely repellent and obscenely fascinating.

It was a bravura performance, and it occurred to her for the first time that Robby had managed to find in himself some of the qualities—or defects—that made Richard so formidable. What was best about his Richard were just those things which existed, in a different and less lethal form, in Robby himself. Had he been born with the strength to be a villain, this was what he would have been! But there was more to it than that, she decided, as she watched him gleefully speed his brother Clarence on his way to the tower and death. Those who did not know Robby as well as she did might conclude that he was merely having a good time, but she understood what the critics surely would not: from somewhere deep within himself, Robby had managed to breathe life into Richard, a man who was only an abstraction, words on paper. However patched and improvised Shakespeare's Richard was, Robby was one with him, in a way that no actor had ever been before.

She felt a sense of envy—she had always believed they were partners, but there was no question that he had at last taken one giant step ahead of anything she could do, and had taken it without her help, excluding her from it, in fact, as if to prove to himself that he didn't need her.

She watched him carefully as he played his love scene with Anne—a role, she realized, too late, that she should never have agreed to turn down on the grounds that it was too small! Jane Rutland, one of Rex Pomfret's little "protégées," a pert-faced charmer who managed to expose most of her plump little breasts every time she bent to pray, was doing her best to attract the audience's attention, and no doubt Robby's.

Now that she thought about it, despite his fatigue (not to speak of *hers*), their sex life had become far more active—though Robby had somehow seemed different, more aggressive, more appreciative of her beauty, sometimes even a little cruel in his lovemaking. It was almost as if he wanted to extract from her a response, to force her into arousal. He tore off the bedclothes, pulled her into positions they had not assumed since the first, heady days of their romance, kept his lovemaking going until she was involuntarily caught up in it herself, astonished as much by her own reaction as by the strength of his passion.

She had always preferred to make love with a little light —seeing the face of her lover was part of her pleasure, and Robby, always the actor, had never objected—but now he insisted on darkness; and at the sight of his face, with the glittering eyes, the lips set in a cruel smile, and the curiously distant expression he had, even in their most intimate moments, she had been happy enough to switch off every light herself.

Somehow, she had guessed that it wasn't a case of Robby's not wanting to see *her*, but some deeper need of his not to *be* seen, as if he were deformed, ugly. Now she realized that his was the behavior of Richard of Gloucester, who would surely have hid himself in the dark as much as possible. . . .

Philip had told Robby to fall in love with his character.

He seemed to have succeeded all too well, and with one of the more detestable characters in the English theatre at that!

She realized now—months, years, too late—that in Hollywood he had begun to sound like Randy Brooks, that at some point he had begun to drive with one hand on the wheel, to move with the comedian's crouch, shoulders hunched, arms swinging, as if he might have to defend himself against the audience at any moment. Randy Brooks owed his broken nose to an irate patron in a Catskills bar who thought Randy was making fun of his wife, and forever after he had approached the microphone onstage, and most people in ordinary life, as if he expected them to take a punch at him.

She should have seen! And what she was seeing now was a man in love with Richard, besotted with him, reveling in his duplicity and self-mockery, as much in thrall to him as he had ever been to her. He had never found it easy to love, but now he had discovered the ability in himself, and turned it on the hunchback king with such intensity that the audience was breathless.

She felt Philip's hand grasp hers, his long, "artistic" fingers, so unlike Robby's, gripping hers as if he were in terror. He, too, knew what he was seeing, was aware that he was watching any chance to be acclaimed the greatest actor of his time evaporate before his eyes. She could feel the tears running down her cheeks, tears of happiness for Robby, tears of misery for herself. Robby was onstage, slouched in a corner, half hidden in the shadows, his posture and sly smile, she realized, not unlike Randy Brooks's, though his face was that of Marty Quick, evil, menacing, yet somehow seductive, as he gave his orders for the murder of his brother Clarence. *"Your eyes drop millstones when fools' eyes fall tears,"* he whispered, smiling wolfishly. *"I like you, lads; about your business straight./Go, go, dispatch."*

He dismissed them with a foppish wave of his gloved hand, gave the audience a knowing grin and another wink, limped slowly across the stage, then turned just before he slipped away and stared out as if he were looking for someone in the audience. She waited for his eyes to find her, but instead they seemed to lock on somebody seated behind her, with a look of such intensity that she could not help wondering who had caught his attention.

He paused, gave a little grin, as if to say, "I told you so," an expression that was at once furtive and triumphant.

The audience burst into applause as if it had been a curtain call, even though the murderers still had to dispatch poor Clarence before the act was over. Robby's hold over them was so great that the rest of the players might as well have been removed from the stage. The clapping went on and on, echoing inside her head until it seemed to give her a physical pain, while the two murderers stood there helplessly, waiting for it to die down so they could go about their business.

She turned in her seat and gave a gasp of horror. Three rows behind, seated on the aisle, were two men in United States Army uniforms, one of them with officer's insignia on his epaulets, the other wearing the battle-dress tunic of an American soldier, both of them applauding as hard as they could.

Even in the dark, it was impossible to mistake the fact that the officer's face bore an alarming resemblance to Robby's portrayal of Richard.

But it was not Marty Quick who made her catch her breath. Beside him, a look of awe on his face, his red hair as curly and unruly as ever, was Randy Brooks.

Without even thinking, she pushed her way to the aisle, and ran from the theatre, in the cover of darkness, leaving Philip and Guy behind.

"I've never seen anything like it," Brooks said hoarsely, still trembling from Robby Vane's death scene. He had never watched anything so terrifying onstage in his life, nor in the movies. From somewhere Robby had mastered the old magician's trick sword routine by which you saw the sword plunged into the victim, and the point, covered in blood, emerge from the other side. Like most good tricks it was dangerous, and magicians didn't have to do it in the full heat of a stage battle. Randy had seen it done a thousand times before from the wings of vaudeville theatres, but even so, he had given an involuntary cry of fear, muffled with the knuckles of his hand, when he saw the sword plunge into Robby's chest, its point thrusting through a joint in the armor of his back, spattering blood across the stage.

Robby's eyes rolled until only the whites showed, his mouth opened wide, his gloved right hand grasped the sharp blade of the sword as if his life depended on drawing it from his body, then he let out a cry, not of fear or horror, but of anguished disappointment at his own fate, a cry of pure, sweet, startling sadness.

Transfigured, like a martyr, he fell to his knees, feebly jerking at the sword, while blood gushed from the cuts on his fingers, then he stared sightlessly at the audience, a ghastly grin on his face, as if to say, "Richard would kill you all if he could!" and falling forward, he slid down the steep incline of the stage, armor rattling, and came to a bone-shaking stop against the footlights, his torso and head hanging over the edge, his fallen crown, rolling beside him, flying off the stage and into the orchestra with a crash.

Randy had bitten his knuckles so sharply that they were covered with blood. Even Marty looked awestruck.

His normally swarthy face was so pale that Randy thought he might be about to faint. "You okay?" he asked, raising his voice over the roar of applause. Marty nodded. "Yeah," he said, but he didn't look it.

His silence lasted all the way backstage and up the grimy metal stairs to Vane's dressing room, which was blocked by a large crowd. The mood was festive, but subdued, as if everyone had felt the touch of greatness, the sense that this was a moment in theatrical history that would be remembered forever.

Marty stood for a moment on the fringes of the crowd that filled the hallway, as if he were catching his breath. He leaned on the wrought-iron banister, looking down toward the darkness of the stage, as if what he had seen there was still haunting him. "I've never seen anything like that," he said quietly.

"Nor me."

"He's gotta be the world's greatest actor."

"It's possible."

"Don't give me 'possible.' It's a fact. No doubt about it. And I own him."

"How do you figure that, Marty?"

"He owes me four hundred thousand dollars, right? He's gonna have to do what I tell him to or pay up, right?"

"Robby may not see it that way. He's not the same guy that played Romeo. He may not be as easy to push around as you think," he said. "Not anymore."

Quick still seemed a little dazed, almost reluctant to enter the dressing room. "I've never seen anybody stabbed like that on stage before," he said. "It scared the shit out of me, you wanna know the truth."

"It's a trick, Marty. You've seen magicians do it."

"It's the way his face was, not the trick. It's funny—everybody has a nightmare, you know, about death. It's really strange, but I've always had this fear of being stabbed."

"I guess not too many people have a good feeling about getting stabbed, Marty."

"I saw a guy stabbed once, in the chest, inna gang fight in Coney Island, when I was maybe fourteen. I remember thinking, Christ, I'd hate to go that way! I've never forgotten it."

"The odds against you going that way are about a thousand to one, Marty."

"I have to go, I wanna go on top of a broad." He shook his head, like a fighter trying to recover from a punch. "Jesus, I don't know what's the matter with me tonight." He took out a cigar, bit off the end, and lit it. "Let's go see Robby."

He pushed his way unapologetically through the crowd, using his elbows and treading on people's toes until he had carved a way for himself into the dressing room, followed by Randy. Vane was seated at his dressing table, a glass of champagne in his hand, a look of concern showing through what remained of his stage makeup. From time to time he glanced up toward the door as if he were expecting someone.

Randy and Marty Quick were standing just behind the last row of well-wishers, and as Robby glanced at him, Randy saw that whoever Robby was waiting for with such obvious anxiety, it wasn't he.

He wondered if it might be Lisha. He hadn't seen her in the audience—he had looked carefully during the intermissions—and she didn't seem to be in the dressing room. Was it Felicia, or somebody else, whose absence was apparently giving Robby such pain? Randy still wished he were the person, wished it the way he had a lifetime ago in Beverly Hills.

He cursed himself for having allowed Marty to drag him here. Painful as it was to have been separated from Robby, hard as it was to be in the same country at last, where they were never far apart in terms of distance, Randy had steeled himself to keep away from Vane, not even to write. He followed Robby's doings from afar with an interest that struck even him as unhealthy, but which he seemed unable to control. It was an obsession, carried to such extremes as seeking out Robby's tailor and having an identical suit made, or buying one of Robby's trademark hats at Herbert Johnson's. When he went to London on leave, Randy often dressed exactly the way Robby did—the rakish hat, the double-breasted suit, the suede shoes, the coat thrown over his shoulders—and the resemblance was all the more uncanny since they were roughly the same height and build. He had mastered Robby's walk, his habit of jamming both hands into the pockets of his jacket, with just the thumbs showing, his erect, straight-back posture, almost military, the product, no doubt, of a harshly disciplined childhood followed by years of training in acting school to play heroes and generals. Randy did such a good imitation of Robby that from time to time —in the dark, at any rate—people actually *mistook* him for Robby, but he was still troubled by his need to do it, as if the only way he could get close to the one person he loved was to dress as him. Their lives had brushed for only a brief moment, but the cost of that moment had been dreadful.

In the two years since he had met Robby, he had made no movies—he was unable to make up his mind about a script or an idea—and had the war not given him the chance to do something different, people would have started talking about him as a has-been.

He gave a cocky smile, aware that people were staring at

him now, whispering to each other, "Isn't that Randy Brooks?" Even Guy Darling and Toby Eden and Philip Chagrin were looking at him with curiosity, and a trace of envy. He was a Hollywood star, after all, famous as none of them, not even Robby, could ever hope to be. "I'm gonna have to watch out, Robby," he said. "You really know how to make the audience laugh."

Robby sat there for a moment, the expression of anxiety still fixed on his face—then he threw his head back and started to laugh. "It's been a long time," he said, recovering. "I saw you in the audience. Damn near forgot my lines, I was so surprised."

Randy walked over close to the dressing table, and leaned one shoulder against the wall. Even with the remnants of his makeup still clinging to his face, Robby looked as boyishly charming as ever, with the roguish gleam in his eyes, the firm cleft chin, balanced out by the girlish curl of his lips. His eyebrows were dark and thick, meeting above the bridge of his nose, a difference that Randy couldn't help noticing, for in Hollywood they had insisted on plucking and shaving them. The real change lay elsewhere. Robby didn't seem older, not by a day, but his face seemed to have acquired more solidity. There was a hardness to it which could only have come from having lived through Felicia's illness, an air of authority that must have come from having finally found a way to put all his genius to work for him.

Robby had succeeded gloriously, while Randy was sullenly traveling around the U. K. doing the same comedy routines he had performed three or four times a night twenty years ago, for soldiers who were young enough to be his sons.

"You were terrific," he said in a low voice. "All that time ago I told you you were a genius, and I was right."

Robby looked directly into Randy's eyes, his expression solemn, unsmiling, a little frightening, and nodded. "Did you like Richard?" he asked, in a commanding voice.

Randy felt a shiver run down his back at the voice. He wondered what Felicia thought of Robby's triumph—and where she was. "How's Lisha?" he asked.

Robby gave a nervous glance toward the door. "She's in splendid form," he said, managing to sound both devious and unconvincing at the same time. "Couldn't be better."

"I'm glad. But she's not here?"

"She—ah—wasn't feeling well. Touch of the flu, she thought. Went home early."

Randy instantly perceived a problem that went far beyond the natural embarrassment Robby might feel at their meeting like this after almost two years. He felt his spirits plummet —again he wished he had never come here. "There's a lot I'd like to talk to you about, Robby," he said gently. "One of these days, perhaps?"

Robby's expression was guarded, cautious. "One of these days, certainly," he said unwillingly, almost in a whisper.

It's all right, Robby! Randy wanted to say. *All I want is to talk to you, about the past, about what's become of me, about you*—but there was no way he could say it in this crowded room, and before he could even try, Marty Quick shouldered his way through until he was directly in front of Robby.

"Robby, *bubbi*, you were great!" he shouted, as if Robby were dying to hear his opinion. From somewhere he had acquired a bottle of champagne and a glass. With a dramatic flourish, he refilled Robby's glass, then his own. "To our future," he said, clicking his glass against Robby's.

Robby's expression was frosty, a little imperious, rather like Richard's when Buckingham asks him for the earldom he was promised.

"To *the* future, indeed," Robby said, with a chilly smile. "Yours, mine, Randy's. May we all be happy and successful. Each in our different, separate ways, of course."

Marty sipped his champagne thoughtfully. "I don't have a separate future in mind for us."

Robby gave a small shrug. "I think you should, old boy."

"We're going to make a movie together. Or have you forgotten?"

Robby laughed. "That was a lifetime ago."

"So what? A deal is a deal."

"Don't worry. You'll get your money back, Marty. It may take some time, but I'll repay you—even though a good deal of it you took from us in the first place, I expect."

"I don't want the money back."

"You want your pound of flesh?" Robby's face was stony. "This is not the place to have this discussion, Marty. I may not want to make a film for some years. If and when I do, I think it will be one of Shakespeare's plays, not some big Hollywood production, with cameo performances from every star you can sign up, and dancing girls doing the hoochy-koochy in authentic native dress. . . . No, no, my dear fellow, I'm not trying to insult you, I'm simply anxious to make it clear that I won't go back to what I was doing in Hollywood, not for you, and not for anybody else. Now if you don't mind, I must change. Felicia is waiting for me at home."

Marty's eyes glittered shrewdly. "Funny place for her to be on an opening night like this. She okay?"

"She's fine."

"Give her my love. I'll be in touch."

"Whenever you like."

"Soon," Marty said. "Very soon."

Randy stared at Robby for a moment. He mouthed the words "Be very careful" but he could see in Robby's eyes that he already knew that.

"What was all *that* about?" Randy asked, stretching out in the back of the car and loosening his tie. He scratched his neck, gently at first, then fiercely—he doubted whether his skin would ever get used to army-issue shirts.

"Just a look-see. Let the great Robby Vane know we're here." He leaned forward. "Sylvia, honey, we got things to talk about," he said, and wound up the glass partition. "What she don't know, she can't tell. Look, I didn't *expect* Robby to ask when we're gonna begin shooting. I did him a favor, so I'm on his shit-list—that's natural. After all, he's an actor. I just want him to know I haven't forgotten our deal, even if he has. The rest is just a question of time."

"Time? A year from Shevuess, I'd say."

"You're wrong. I've done my homework. I always do my homework, Randy—don't ever forget it. Robby's in hock nearly a hundred thousand pounds for the lease on the theatre, he's about to marry Lisha, of all the dumb things to do, and there's talk he's gonna get a knighthood. So you tell me— does he want any trouble, financial or otherwise?"

Randy looked at him suspiciously. "What's 'otherwise,' Marty?"

Marty waved his cigar nonchalantly. "You know," he said, with a wink.

Randy's eyes opened wide in horror. "You must be kidding!" he cried.

"Look, it's no big deal. You know what happened. He knows what happened. I know what happened."

"You don't know a fucking thing!"

"Randy, you and I have known each other, what, twenty years, maybe more? You don't have any secrets from *me*, my friend. You never did."

"Marty! You're talking about *blackmailing* Robby for something that never even happened, believe me. You're talking about blackmailing *me*! What *are* you? Crazy? You got no proof to begin with, and even if you did, what's in it for you, destroying two careers? His and mine? Hell, forget the careers. Two *lives*!"

Quick waved Randy's indignation away in a cloud of cigar smoke. "Grow up," he said. "I'm not gonna *do* anything, for crissake. Just a gentle nudge in the right direction, okay? That's all. All Robby has to know is I can put him into bankruptcy if I wanna—"

"You don't even know what the bankruptcy laws *are* over here."

"Who gives a shit? What's to know? You sue a guy and he can't pay, that's bankruptcy, here, any-fuckin'-where. If that doesn't persuade him, then I'll just hint there's stuff about himself he wouldn't wanna see in the newspapers. *He* wouldn't wanna see it, the king wouldn't wanna see it, not about somebody who's being considered for a knighthood— and most of all, Randy, old pal, *Felicia* wouldn't wanna see

it. And I think Robby would do anything in the whole goddamn world not to have Lisha go off the deep end again,
don't you? I can't say I blame the poor bastard, either. I'd
feel the same way.''

"I'm not going to play, Marty. Count me out."

Quick reached across and pinched his cheek. The pinch
was supposed to hurt, and it did. "Don't be dumb," he said.
"You did what you had to do. You called on him backstage
with me. With a little help, he'll figure the rest out for himself.
He's no dummy."

"And you think I'll just go along?"

Quick considered the question carefully, eyes narrowed.
"Not easily, no. But you will, eventually. I'm not worried."
He pointed out the window. "I couldn't get you a room at
Claridge's," he said. "Too many generals in town. So I got
you a nice little suite at the Ritz. Sylvia will take you back
to camp in the morning. It's all been cleared with Fruchter,
so you don't have to worry about a thing."

Outside in the rain, Randy could see the rough stone co-
lonnade that sheltered the Ritz Hotel's entrance on Piccadilly,
shiny with moisture. Huddled under it in the semidarkness
were a dozen shadowy figures. He did not need to look closely
to guess who they were, or what they were doing there. He
had an eye for that sort of thing—though it did occur to him
for one moment that Marty might have had just that in mind
when he booked him into the Ritz.

"I won't go along with it, Marty," he said. "He was my
friend."

"Hey, you and *I* are friends, too, Randy. Don't you forget
it." He managed to make friendship sound like a threat. He
rapped on the glass and signaled Sylvia to pull over for a
moment, just short of the door. "Who kept you outta jail?
Who's been there, right beside you, ready to help whenever
there's a problem? Remember the kid from Santa Monica?
What was his name? About three years ago, right? Gilbert
something-or-other? Said you'd invited him home to use your
pool on a hot day, he figured it was okay because he knew
you were a famous star, then you helped him off with his

clothes in the poolhouse, and asked if you could kiss his cock? He was—what—fourteen, fifteen?''

"The little creep told me he was seventeen,'' Randy said indignantly. "How was I to know?''

"Hey! *I* understand. Who talked to the cops, who made a deal with the parents, who set Gilbert up with a nice little college-tuition fund? Who hushed up the papers? Who made sure Natalie never heard a thing? *I* did, that's who. And you fuckin' know it.''

Randy nodded. There was no point in denying it. He could have pointed out that the kid had seduced *him*, that Gilbert whatever-his-name-was had been doing this for years, probably since he was twelve, making a good living out of hustling rich movie stars, then threatening to go to the police—but it would have been a waste of time painting himself as the victim to Marty, of all people, who didn't give a shit. "I know,'' he said, in a tired, neutral voice. "And I'm grateful. You know that.''

"You *better* be grateful! I got a good memory, Randy. There was the kid from Sherman Oaks, the one whose father wanted to kill you, remember? I had to set the old man up in his own business for you—plumbing fixtures, I think. If it weren't for me, you'd be as dead as Kelso's nuts in show business.'' He puffed on his cigar. "What I'm saying, Randy, is, don't push me, okay? Don't get in my way. I'm not asking you to carry the ball on this one, but don't go off for a little talk with Robby to clue him in, or warn him, or anything like that. You owe me, friend, so don't even *think* of crossing me.''

"I think I'm gonna throw up.''

"Nah, you'll get used to it. It's time to act like a *mensch*, that's all. If it makes you feel sick, that's okay. Anyway, look atta bright side, Randy. What am I asking Robby to do? Kill Felicia? Stand up in the theatre and say something nice about Hitler? No. All I'm asking is he stars in a movie for me, for which I've already paid him nearly half a million bucks and which will probably make him more money than a lifetime of Shakespeare. Am I asking him to play with some no-talent hooker with big tits like Virginia Glad? No. A specific part of the deal is that he co-stars with Felicia, which oughta make both of them happy. And who else is gonna be in the picture? Robby's old friend Randy Brooks, America's most beloved and talented comedian! If he's smart, he'll jump at the chance.''

Randy needed a drink, needed a hot bath, above all, needed to get away from Marty. His eyes strayed to the young men under the arches. He needed that, too, if he was going to make it through the rest of the night. ''Yeah,'' he said, with a low sigh, ''but the problem is, it isn't what he wants to do, Marty.''

Quick rapped on the glass partition, and the big car drew slowly up to the entrance, where the porter, resplendent in his gold-braided frock coat and black top hat, ran forward with an umbrella to open the door. ''That's a pity,'' Quick said, reaching over to shake Randy's hand. Quick was smiling, his teeth glistening white, the dark eyes gleaming as if he'd just heard a terrific joke, his tanned face creased in what would have indicated, in anyone else, high good humor. ''But tell me, who gets to do what they *want* to do in this world? Sleep well, kiddo. Your money's no good here. The room's comped on me, so have yourself a good time.''

Randy got out stiffly, while Sylvia removed his canvas kit bag from the trunk. He never came down to London without his civilian clothes—his ''Robby outfit,'' as he thought of it, despite the regulations against servicemen's wearing civilian clothes. Still, who would stop a Hollywood star from doing whatever he wanted to? Certainly not your average MP, he thought, who would have been astonished to see a private get out of a staff car and shake hands with a colonel, while a British ATS driver handed his luggage to the top-hatted hotel porter.

He entered the familiar palatial lobby, signed the register, and stood there for a moment under the glittering chandeliers, a strangely contradictory figure—a soldier in a shabby, travel-creased uniform, and at the same time a famous star, the center of attention, treated by the staff as if he were royalty. The contrast no longer struck him as odd.

He ordered tea and a bottle of rum sent to his room, then turned back to the front door to take a little late-night stroll in the fresh air. He felt in his pocket for a brand-new five-pound note. He was pretty sure that for five the porter could find a way of getting "a friend" up to Mr. Brooks's suite quietly, by the back entrance, if he was asked to. . . .

One look at the man's face as he went out the door told Randy he was overpaying, but he didn't care.

16

"You *might* have sent word."

"I didn't want to spoil your triumph."

"To *hell* with my 'triumph,' as you call it! It was just the usual booze-up in the dressing room. I didn't stay long. Philip told me that he thought you'd been taken ill. He ran after you, but you'd gone. Worried the hell out of him. Worried the hell out of me, when I heard about it. How did you get home?"

"I walked."

"*Walked?* On a night like this? In the blackout?"

"I know the way."

She did not feel it necessary to add that it had been like a descent into hell. She had not wanted to walk, but the car would not appear until after the curtain, and there were no taxis to be found—besides, she had no money. She had run down the Haymarket in a cold, light rain, her shoes instantly sodden, her dress clinging to her, the tears running down her streaked cheeks the only warmth she could feel.

Soldiers whistled at her or reached out to grab her, offering cigarettes, nylons, money. In the side streets leading to Piccadilly, the prostitutes, huddled in the doorways, some of them actually performing their trade in the dark, shouted at her angrily. One painted woman, her skirt hiked up around her waist, pressed into a doorway by a soldier busy getting his money's worth, threw an empty bottle at her, screaming, "Off my beat, you filthy bitch!"

Women taunted and jeered at her, all the way down Piccadilly, until she reached St. James's Street, where the male prostitutes, luckier, sheltered under the covered archway of the Ritz Hotel, taking advantage of the fact that its brilliant prewar lights were now replaced by dim blue bulbs. In the misty darkness of the archways, cigarettes glowed in the faces of hardened boys. Here there were fewer Americans but lots of British sailors, and furtive elderly gentlemen in civilian clothes, their hats pulled low down over their eyes, the collars of their coats turned up higher than even the damp, cold air required. She had paused for breath there, leaning against a stone pillar, but the commissionaire of the Ritz appeared suddenly from the snug warmth of the porter's lodge, a burly man with the bearing and manner of a regimental sergeant major, resplendent in a silk top hat with a gold cockade and braiding and a dark green coat laced with gold, medals clanking on his chest. He brushed a drop of moisture off his waxed mustache and gave her a hard stare, his eyes small and mean, like those of the boars she remembered in the pigsties at the farm in Langleit. "Buzz off!" he growled. "You've got no business 'ere, my girl."

Curiously, she remembered the man from years ago, bowing obsequiously as he opened the door of the Bentley with his white-gloved hand. It had been "Good evening, Miss Lisle," then, and he had hardly dared raise his eyes to look at her. She stared back at him boldly now, enraged. "I'm Felicia Lisle," she said sharply in her most commanding voice. "I need a taxi."

He winked, his face set in a smile that managed to convey no trace of good humor at all. "Yes," he said, "and I'm Robby bloody Vane." He gave her a push, hard enough almost to unbalance her on the slippery pavement. "Now fuck off," he said. "It's bad enough chasing away the nancy boys, but I'm not 'avin the likes of you selling your wares at my front door." He gave her a close look, like a man inspecting a horse for sale. "Clean you up a bit and you'd do, skinny as you are. . . ."

The door behind him opened, and a couple emerged, the woman in a long evening gown and furs, the man in uniform. "Get on with it," he snarled. "Off my patch, on the double." He gave her another push, harder this time, and she turned on him in blind anger. Eyes blazing, she slapped him, hard. She saw his face turn red, and braced herself for his attack, but with the couple standing behind him, he was unwilling to hit a woman. "Next time I see you, I'll break your bleeding neck for you," he whispered fiercely, and the expression on his face, indeed his whole posture, was like that of a Cape buffalo about to charge.

She could see the couple staring at her curiously as they huddled under the canopy, while the commissionaire went off to find them a taxi.

She felt drained, as if the slap had used up all her reserves. What worried her was not that she had slapped the brute—she would have been happy to have *killed* him!—but the way it had happened. There had been no thought on her part, no decision that she could remember, nothing.

Her father had been a great believer in instinct in the bush. She had been with him once in the Mara, on one of those calm, still days in the early afternoon, when the heat is like that of a furnace, the only noise the maddening, metallic buzz of the fever birds, burning their way into your brain. Her father had been lounging comfortably on a black volcanic boulder, smoking his pipe, about to pour a cup of tea from his thermos, when suddenly, without a moment's hesitation or warning, he picked up his rifle and fired one shot, hardly seeming even to aim, killing a big male leopard in mid-leap. She had not seen the animal charge, had no idea it was even there until it fell at her feet, its teeth still fixed in a snarl, savaging the earth with its paws. Her father could not explain how he knew the leopard was near, or about to attack them, nor did he show any interest in trying. "If you think too much about that kind of thing," was all he would say, "you can't do it anymore." He skinned the big cat, and later had its claws made into cuff links, which he wore on festive occasions.

She felt a hand touch her softly on the shoulder and saw one of the young men in the arcade, furtive and ghostly in the half-light, offering her a lit cigarette. " 'Ere you go, love," he said in a soft voice, " 'ave a fag." She took the cigarette gratefully, a Wills Woodbine from the harsh taste of it, the kind that poor people bought one or two at a time at cheap tobacconists. "You lost?"

She shook her head. "I know my way home."

"Ah. That's all right then. But you're wet. That coat is ever so thin—lovely stuff, but not for wearing outdoors on a night like this. You'll catch your death."

"I'll be fine."

"I've got an umbrella. I'll walk you home."

She shrugged and gave in, more out of the need for company than the fear of getting any wetter.

"I've been wanting to 'it that bloody bastard for years. Never 'ad the nerve. Walkin' you 'ome is the least I could do."

"I accept. Gratefully."

"Where do you live?"

"Wilton Place."

He raised an eyebrow. Shabby, thin, pale, it was hard to imagine him as a sex object for anyone. He might have been—perhaps was—a bank clerk down on his luck, in his frayed blue suit and his cracked, down-at-the-heels shoes.

"That's where you live?" he asked.

"I'm staying with a friend," she explained quickly.

"Ah, I see. Lucky you. We'd all like a friend with a nice flat. You know, I laughed when you told the commissionaire you were Felicia Lisle—it was bloody cheeky!—but you do look a lot like her. Has anybody ever told you that before?"

She laughed. "All the time."

"No, I'm serious, luv. Felicia Lisle is one of my favorites."

"Mine, too."

"I love the theatre. I've got a friend—" he hesitated for

a moment—"who's a famous actor. It must be lovely to be a star like Felicia Lisle, don't you think?"

"Perhaps. I suppose she has her troubles, too."

"Don't you believe it, duckie! Warm as toast every night, rolling in money, married to Robby Vane . . ."

"They're not married yet."

"Oh? I thought they were. . . . Is this it?"

"It's just around the corner."

"Ah," he said, shifting from one foot to another. It occurred to her that he probably expected to be invited in for a cup of tea or a drink, but there was no way she could do that, not without giving herself away. She would have offered him a couple of pounds, but she suspected his feelings might be hurt—besides, she had no money on her. "You've been very kind," she said. "I'd like to thank you one day, properly."

"I'll tell you what. When you're in the money, we'll 'ave a drink, shall we? Ask for Billy Dove at the Fox and Grapes, Darlington Street. They all know Billy there. Or outside the Ritz, any night."

"I will." She touched his hand, moved by the genuine kindness of the young man.

"I'm talking to you, darling," she heard Robby say impatiently, and she came out of her reverie with a start. "What made you run away?"

"You know."

"Marty? Randy? I was surprised to see them myself, but one or both of them was bound to turn up in England sooner or later, and what of it? They came round to my dressing room after the curtain for a drink, by the way, and were perfectly charming. Both send you their love."

She stared into the fire. Sent her their *love*? Randy Brooks who had defiled—there was no other word—her relationship to Robby? Marty Quick who had jeopardized their careers and had treated her as if she were a hysterical tramp? She knew, without a shadow of doubt, that their return would lead to trouble, and Robby was naive if he didn't think so himself. Still, it was not an argument she was prepared to have with him at this time of night.

"But the performance," he said. "You missed most of it. Why? Did you dislike it that much?"

How to tell him that he had been so good he frightened her, so good she was no longer sure there was a place for her alongside him? "You were wonderful," she said, feeling the tears in her eyes and hoping he would think they were tears of joy. "It was the best thing you've ever done in your life." She was telling him the truth, and her voice told him so. She watched the flames rise, reminding herself that coal was rationed and that it was a crime to waste it, but beginning to feel the warmth at last. She was silent for a few moments, then, as if the question had just come to her out of the blue, she asked, "Have you ever heard of a pub called the Fox and Grapes, darling?"

Robby looked startled. "The Fox and Grapes? Why on earth do you ask that?" He gave a nervous laugh.

"I was just wondering. Somebody mentioned it tonight."

"It's a bloody strange thing to be wondering about, Lisha. As it happens, I *do* know about it, yes, if you mean the one in Darlington Street. It's a pub for the, ah—pansy crowd. It's where Philip got himself arrested, if you must know. A well-known 'knocking shop,' as I believe they're called."

"Are they?"

"They *used* to be. I wouldn't know what they're called now."

Did she believe him? Whatever his feelings might be for Randy, she could not imagine Robby seeking out somebody like Billy Dove in the dark London night, or sidling up to him in the public bar of the Fox and Grapes, either. But did he *want* to?

There was a knock on the door downstairs. Robby looked at his watch. "It's nearly one in the morning," he said. "I can't imagine who that can be."

Robby returned in a moment, holding a long white florist's box bound in green ribbon.

"What a strange time of night to be delivering flowers," she said.

"It wasn't a florist's delivery boy. Actually it was a rather nicely dressed old fellow with a bowler hat and a velvet collar. A retired gentleman's gentleman, perhaps. He handed me the box, then vanished into the night, without waiting for a word of thanks or a tip. Let's see what we've got." He opened the box, carefully saving the ribbon, as those who have grown up poor do by instinct, and unwrapped the tissue paper. Nestled inside were a dozen white roses, a magnificent gift at this time of year. Among the flowers was a bright, shining object about eighteen inches long, which Robby removed gingerly from the box as if it were a booby trap. An expression of awe settled on his face.

He put it down on the coffee table—a battered dagger, clearly old. The scabbard was silver, heavily worked, the blade of mottled blue Damascene steel, the ivory hilt wrapped with braided silver wire. As such objects go, it was simple, deadly, and sinister, with none of the flash of a stage prop.

"What on earth is that?" she asked.

He opened the card that had accompanied it, his expression reverential. "Burbage's dagger," he said, brushing it with his fingertips. "It was a gift to him from Shakespeare. Burbage wore it the first time he played Hamlet. The first time *anyone* played it, as a matter of fact. It's the famous 'bare bodkin' that Hamlet holds up during the soliloquy. '*When he himself might his quietus make, with a bare bodkin.*' "

He slipped the blade out of the scabbard and ran his thumb along it, drawing a fine line of blood. "Burbage probably wore it every day, hanging from his belt, and used it onstage as well. Why not? Pointless to have two. Can't have been a cheap gift. Will must have been fond of his favorite actor."

"Doesn't it belong in a museum?"

"Oh, of course it does. But by tradition it's been passed on from actor to actor. Here. Read Philip's note."

Chagrin's handwriting was precise, fussy, spidery, his notepaper pale mauve. " 'Robby,' " she read, " 'This is The Dagger which Shakespeare gave Burbage, and which has passed, over the centuries and through many adventures, from Garrick to Kean, from Kean to Irving, and eventually to me. Irving's daughter—an old lady by then—gave it to me after seeing my Hamlet. Tonight, as Richard III, *you* have earned it. May it bring you the greatness you deserve, and—dare I add?—more happiness than it has given me.' ''

She picked up the dagger, halfway expecting to feel an electric current run through her fingers—she was holding an object that Shakespeare himself had touched and that had been owned by the greatest actors of the past three centuries. But there was nothing. It might have been a carving knife, except that the fluted blade was sharper and more pointed than that of any kitchen utensil she had ever seen. The silver pommel was engraved with a shallow pattern of intertwined roses—the roses of Lancaster and York?—against which it was still just possible to make out the archaic, faded gilt lettering: ''RB frome his friende WS.''

As she held it, it seemed to grow warm in her hand. She assured herself that the metal was simply picking up her own warmth or taking on the temperature of the room, but it still seemed to her that the dagger was taking on a life of its own—that it had some special meaning for *her*. The blade seemed to shimmer in the light, the silver braid handle became uncomfortably warm in her hand—burning hot now, in fact. She winced in pain as if she had grasped the handle of a frying pan without realizing that it hadn't yet cooled.

Clenching her teeth to hold back a cry, she dropped the dagger onto the table, grasping her right hand in a tight fist and holding it against her lips. To her surprise, the pain stopped instantly. When she uncurled her hand it was unmarked, though she had expected to see blisters and charred flesh on her palm. She shivered in shock.

Robby looked at her with alarm. ''Be *careful*, Lisha! Did you cut yourself?''

She shook her head. ''No, no, it just slipped out of my fingers.''

''Yes, it's heavy. That knob on the end of the handle, that's not just for decoration, you know.''

He picked up the dagger and thrust it fiercely into the air in front of him, then raised it above his head, the point toward the ceiling, and brought the handle down sharply, as if he were smashing the knob into an enemy's skull. ''One! Two!

Three!'' he shouted. "First, a stab in the guts, then a bash on the head.'' He lunged again in a quick extension of the movement. "Another stab, and—the other fellow's—dead!''

He drew a deep breath and laughed. "That's how it was used, you see. One, two, and three! Just like that, quick as a flash.'' He slipped it back in the scabbard. "Nasty little thing. Probably just as deadly as a pistol at close range in the hand of someone who knows how to use it.''

"It doesn't feel strange to you, the dagger?''

"Strange? You mean to hold so much history in one's hand? Yes, of course. The odd thing is, I've heard about it for years from Philip, and now that I have it, I feel it belongs to me. I know one's supposed to say, 'Oh, I don't deserve it,' and all that modest rot, and of course in public I'd say just that—and shall. But between the two of us, darling, I felt tonight I *did* deserve it, that it was *meant* to be mine. Does that sound awful?''

"No, not really. I think you deserve it, too. And more.''

"I don't know that there *is* more. People talk about the crown of acting, but this is as close as you can come to it, this dagger. Burbage carried it in 1600, at the Globe, to play Hamlet for the first time! It's the nearest thing our profession offers to the Victoria Cross, or the Order of the Garter, or the Nobel Prize. Better, really, because it passes from actor to actor. No committee, no judges, none of the pomp and ceremony of a knighthood, say.''

"That's next, isn't it?''

He looked a little sheepish. "Too soon, too soon,'' he said. "Sir Robert and Lady Vane?'' He laughed. "It has a nice ring to it, though, doesn't it?''

It had no attraction for her. Her Uncle Harry was a peer, after all, and her father, as second son, was entitled to call himself Captain The Honorable Edward Travers Langleit Lisle, M. C., had he chosen to do so. She had always thought the custom of knighting successful actors—or, for that matter, successful stock-market speculators, merchants, and politicians—was vulgar. There were no circumstances in which she would be prepared to give up her own fame as Felicia Lisle for the "honor" of being called Lady Vane.

"Well," he said, "we'll see. I hear it's been mentioned."

"I'm sure it has. Would you accept it?"

He shrugged, aware of her lack of enthusiasm. "If the Prime Minister were to put my name on the Honors list, it would be bloody hard to turn it down, don't you think? It would be a splendid thing for the theatre." He gave a jaunty smile. "Besides," he said more firmly, "if I *can* have the bloody thing, I want it."

"That's more like it."

"And why the hell not? Philip ought to have the honor, but he did himself out of it. Toby, deserves it as much as I do, but if I get mine, he will soon follow. Besides, the honor is *ours*—we went on playing during the air raids, toured the factories, gave up Hollywood to come home and do our bit. If it happens—and please note the 'if'—it's for *both* of us. Whatever it's going to be, up to and including a dukedom, it won't mean as much to me as the Shakespeare dagger. I must call Philip, however late it is."

She looked at it, sitting on the table. Had Philip actually worn the thing onstage? She had seen him a hundred times, and thought not. Presumably he had kept it locked away somewhere, as a relic, where it belonged. In a world where doubtful first folios of Shakespeare's plays—which Shakespeare had neither seen nor touched—were snapped up by American collectors for millions of dollars, it was surely strange that a precious object which he had not only touched, but actually *bought*, ordered to be engraved, presented to his best friend and partner, was almost an unknown artifact. Was there a reason why generation after generation of actors had kept so quiet about an object which in its own way was as valuable as the crown jewels? She was not more superstitious than most theatre people, but it crossed her mind that there might be a "curse" of some kind on it. Was this what Chagrin meant, she wondered, by suggesting in his note that it had brought him bad luck—or made him unhappy?

She looked at the dagger and shivered. So many things could come between Robby and what he wanted—a scandal, the bankruptcy of his theatre, the wrong choice of film, or play, or friends—any of these things might plunge him from first place into the darkness, like Philip Chagrin's arrest.

She closed her eyes, as if from fatigue—for it had been a long night, and she had still not recovered from being cold and wet. She saw, in her mind's eye, a swirl of dangers: Marty Quick's wolfish grin, the dagger, Uncle Harry clutching Portia, the Duke of York Theatre, Robby's dream, in flames, the curtain blazing like dry wood in a fireplace, the gilt decorations melting in the blaze. . . .

She opened her eyes, wondering exactly when real life had become more bearable than her dreams, being awake less frightening than sleeping.

Robby was staring at the dagger, as absorbed in his own way as she was in hers. "Put it away, darling," she said quietly. "You can call Philip to thank him tomorrow. Let's go to bed."

He nodded, stood up, yawned. It was nearly two in the morning and he had been on his feet since dawn, preparing himself for the performance that would finally make it clear that he had no rivals. He took the dagger, wrapped it in what was left of the tissue paper, and placed it in the drawer of the desk.

She hoped she would never see it again.

ACT THREE

All the World's

a Stage. . . .

17

The discreet little story in the legal column of the *Times* noting that a decree nisi had been handed down in the divorce case of Chenevix-Trent vs. Chenevix-Trent had been followed within days by an even smaller announcement in the social column of the engagement of Robert Gilles Vane and Felicia Lisle, and now the marriage was almost upon them.

The more sensational dailies had a field day. The *Daily Express* had tracked down the Bond Street jeweler which sold Robby Felicia's engagement ring, while the *Daily Mail*, more daringly, stationed a photographer with a telephoto lens on the roof of the houses opposite theirs and got a picture of them having breakfast in bed—Robby in his pajamas reading the *Times*, she, partly hidden by the teapot and the flowers on her breakfast tray, opening her mail.

Since Portia had been visiting, there was also a photograph of the little girl and her nanny walking down the steps of the house. The headlines above the pictures read, ENGAGED—AND ALREADY LIVING TOGETHER! to Robby's fury and embarrassment.

Felicia had not taken the matter seriously and accused Robby of being stuffy and humorless—but his concern turned out to be justified. The other dailies took up the cry instantly, the *Express* leading the pack with a story that asked, *"Is this a fit home for a child?"* while the *Evening Standard* ran a full page of photographs of Felicia in various flirtatious poses from her films, under the question, *"What kind of a mother is this?"*

Jenny Lee, the firebrand Labor MP, actually raised the question in the House of Commons, asking why it was that while millions of people were fighting and suffering for their country, two famous actors were living in open adultery with a child in the house. What kind of example did this set for ordinary people?

In the House of Lords, Uncle Harry made one of his rare speeches in their defense, on the theme of "Let him who is without sin cast the first stone," pointing out as the child's godfather, great-uncle, and moral guardian, that she could surely come to no harm.

Eventually, the storm, like all storms, blew over, but not before a discreet messenger from Buckingham Palace had appeared in Robby's dressing room to emphasize how very much their Majesties were looking forward to offering their congratulations on the marriage of two of their favorite performers. The message was clear enough, and coincided, as it happened, with Robby's own impatience to put an end to what Guy Darling called "the longest-running adulterous relationship in theatrical history."

The news that they were actually getting married at last made them seem in the eyes of the world, even in the eyes of critical clergymen and scandal-mongering reporters of the big Fleet Street dailies, once again "romantic"—perhaps the only breath of romance in a country now in the fifth year of war, and waiting breathlessly for D day, while overhead the German buzz bombs stuttered their way across the sky like malignant toys, bringing back the horrors of the 1940 blitz. The country was tired, tired of heroism, tired of fear, tired of death. The English were beginning to grumble again, the old class hatreds apparent; they were ruder toward each other, less patient, quicker to take offense.

People wanted to be reminded of prewar glamour and romance, to experience it even vicariously, most of all wanted to think about something that wasn't about the war. Or perhaps it was just that it was spring, and anything was better than waiting for a buzz bomb to fall on your head, or for Britain's last army to cross the Channel to be annihilated on the beach.

Any hope Felicia and Robby might have cherished of keeping the wedding quiet and private vanished under the onslaught of publicity. The women's pages of the newspapers wanted to have photographs of her wedding dress, but it was only at the last minute that Robby realized somebody would be bound to ask how she had managed to save up enough clothing coupons for a new dress, so she was obliged to dig out a prewar Molyneux dress, in dove gray, with a lot of frothy gray lace—old, but not too old, formal, but not too formal. The only Church of England clergymen who were willing to marry two people who had been divorced were those publicity-seeking iconoclasts whom Robby most wanted to avoid, like the Bishop of Breedon, a notoriously dotty rebel who had preached a much quoted sermon on their relationship with the unwelcome title "Free Love in a Free Land," or the "Red" Dean of Canterbury, who seemed to believe that the two of them were victims of class warfare and bourgeois-capitalist hypocrisy.

Robby happily settled on the registry office at Caxton Hall, where the divorced usually got married without the benefit of clergy. Except for the fact that Caxton Hall had none of the beauty of London's more fashionable churches, Felicia was not upset by the choice. From Cairo, where he was making quite a name for himself on the staff of the Commander-in-Chief, Charles sent his somewhat guarded congratulations, together with his consent for Portia to attend; while Felicia's father, from somewhere deep in the bush, managed to cable a badly garbled message of good wishes, some of it in Swahili, the opening of which read, "Thought you two were married already, but sure you know best." Uncle Harry contrived—deliberately, she was sure—to annoy Robby by sending her a beautiful little Turner watercolor sketch, one of her favorite small paintings from his personal collection at Langleit, dramatically upstaging the antique ruby-and-diamond necklace Robby had bought, with Philip

Chagrin's expert help and advice, on auction at Spink's. Toby
Eden, who had agreed to act as best man, sent a small chow
puppy as a wedding present, which promptly destroyed two
carpets, bit the housemaid, and was banished to the country.
Philip, with his usual good taste, sent a beautiful antique
silver tea service; Marty, a beautifully bound early copy of
Cervantes's *Don Quixote*, an obvious hint; Randy, a Degas
bronze of a ballet dancer.

As the day approached, Felicia found herself growing more
and more blue—"depressed," as Dr. Vogel would have said.
It was not a feeling she could share with anyone, nor could
she justify it to herself. The world, it seemed, was ready to
throw rose petals and confetti at her, while she glumly dealt
with the details of getting married.

It was easy enough, she thought resentfully, for Robby,
who was still appearing triumphantly as Richard III. Every
evening at seven-thirty (curtain time had been moved forward
because of the wartime difficulty in getting home after the
theatre), he stepped onto the stage to the applause of nearly
fifteen hundred people, knowing that he was going to give
them a performance they would never forget.

That was a pleasure against which it was hard to compete,
and if the ordinary details of life—or his impending
wedding—failed to hold his attention, or, as was sometimes
the case, irritated him, that too was easy enough to understand. She felt the same way herself when she was
working—but, alas, right now she was merely rehearsing
with Robby every morning, for he had decided, this time, to
direct *Othello* himself, with the help of Guillam Pentecost.

On the whole, she supported his decision. Garrick, Kean,
Sir Henry Irving, Philip Chagrin, all had staged their plays
themselves, without the benefit of a director, and Robby had
long chafed from the fact that for most of his career he had
not. *Could* he direct a play with several important roles *and*
play the leading one, the critics asked? Could he successfully
direct a leading lady? More to the point, could he direct Felicia
Lisle?

More to the point still, she wondered, could she play Desdemona? The more she studied the part, the less she liked it. Desdemona seemed to her spineless and credulous, suffering the moods and suspicions of her pompous, self-deceiving husband long past the point at which any sensible woman would have walked out on him. Felicia found herself beginning to despise her, as well as feeling that she herself was at least five years too old to play a giddy virgin infatuated with an older man, whatever his color.

Worst of all, the whole notion of her death in the play disturbed her more than she was willing to admit. She had always had a mild fear of suffocation, and for that reason slept on hard pillows, with the windows open. Dr. Vogel had diagnosed it as a mild case of claustrophobia. She knew it was hardly unusual—her father elected to live on the African plains, pitching his tent in places where the view stretched for hundreds of miles; her mother had feared the darkness and had kept the lights on in her bedroom all night.

Her terror of being suffocated at the end of the play was real and intense—so much so that it made her jumpy, forgetful of her lines, and unable to concentrate during rehearsal. It was like having an appointment with the dentist at the end of the day—no matter what else the day offered, it was spoiled by the knowledge of the pain to come. As the hours of rehearsal went by, all she could think about was the awful moment to come when Othello—Robby—placed the pillow on her face and pushed her down on the bed.

Robby complained that she was fighting against the part, fighting against *him*. She knew what he wanted, of course— a Desdemona doomed by the strength of her own love, swept away by the sexual passion Othello has unleashed in her, for *Othello* was in many ways Shakespeare's sexiest play—but she couldn't give that Desdemona to him, partly because of the way in which he himself was determined to play Othello.

He had set out to create what he called "a real *Negro* Othello." It took him three hours or more to paint his body from head to toe, for he felt he needed to *be* black in order to act black. Previous Othellos had been content to make themselves a shade or two darker; Robby not only dyed himself jet-black but rubbed black shoe polish onto his skin, then buffed it with a damp rag in order to produce the glossy sheen of a full-blooded African Negro. He painted his palms pink, wore a set of gleamingly white false teeth, thickened his lips, wore a single gold earring, gave himself a curly gray wig, transformed himself somehow into an Othello at once exotic and barbarous. Felicia could not help feeling that she was being upstaged at every turn.

She felt overwhelmed by this new and remarkable manifestation of Robby's ability to transform himself, but where did it all leave her? How on earth was she to make the audience pay attention to her as Desdemona, when he was dominating the stage, ebony-black, teeth gleaming, ebony chest exposed, moving and sounding like an African chief?

Of course, she understood that he was exhausted, rehearsing one play while appearing in another, and he had also fatally underestimated the pressures of running his own theatre. He found himself being called away from rehearsal to deal with leaks in the roof, bomb damage, plumbing problems, in a building that dated from the early eighteenth century, and was probably jerry-built then.

Still, fatigue was only part of the story, she suspected. Just as they were stepping into the public eye again as romantic lovers, they were living a life almost entirely without romance.

It did not seem to bother Robby, who was perhaps too busy to notice or care, but it rankled her all the more since she had to put up daily with his dissatisfaction at rehearsals. She could see he was unsatisfied; she could read in his face his anger and unhappiness when she ran through a scene, but she couldn't get a straight answer out of him. "Splendid," he would say without enthusiasm, through clenched teeth. "It's coming nicely." But she knew it wasn't.

It was in a spirit of simmering irritation that she prepared for her marriage, with its inevitable problems, most of which seemed to be beyond her control.

She glanced at the familiar photographs on her dressing table. Portia, of course, would be dressed as a tiny bridesmaid—Felicia hoped that giving the child a pretty muslin dress, a bouquet of wildflowers to carry, would make her at least a *little* enthusiastic about the occasion.

Uncle Harry had offered to give Felicia away in her father's place—"insisted," she supposed, might be a better word, for he bullied his way into the role, largely by threatening to keep Portia away if he was excluded. Step by step he had manipulated himself into the position of being the child's *de facto* guardian, winning Charles's consent by long distance, which was easy enough, since Charles had always been delighted to have a peer as an uncle-in-law, and thought Langleit and all it represented the ideal place for his daughter to grow up.

Of course she was in no position to tell Charles the real reason for her fear. "It's so often the way in families," Charles wrote, in the spidery, precise copperplate that was apparently taught to every Etonian, "that those *in* the family see each other less clearly than an outsider does. You have always been suspicious of your Uncle Harry, but I have never observed him to respond with anything less than generosity and concern to any problem, and in my absence, he has done untold favors, large and small, for me, even though I am merely, at this point, your *ex*-husband. Dear little Portia is fond of him, as you know—and always has been—and I can frankly see no sensible reason why his affection for the girl, who adores him, should be discouraged. Her happiness is what should be on our minds, not any desire on your part to settle 'old scores,' whatever they may be."

That was Charles, she thought savagely—always giving her moral lectures without the slightest clue about what was really going on!

She couldn't help herself—whenever she looked at her daughter, she felt that fate had somehow played a mean trick on her. She told herself that she would surely have loved Portia just the way she ought if the girl were graceful, pretty, charming, full of winning ways, but Portia stubbornly refused to charm her, or be charmed by her. Unsmiling, she fidgeted restlessly through the fittings for her dress, her square-jawed little face set in an angry pout.

When *she* had been a little girl, Felicia remembered, she

had loved dressing up, or watching her mother dress, in the days before they went to Africa. She would have given anything to be a flower girl or to carry the bride's train at a big wedding. Her favorite moment of the day was watching her mother get ready to go out to dinner or the theatre. Felicia had yearned to be just as beautiful one day, prayed every night that she, too, would be perfect, graceful, infinitely desirable, with a handsome man—as handsome as her father—waiting impatiently for her downstairs, pacing the carpet in his gleaming patent-leather evening pumps, glancing at his gold evening watch, his face lighting up suddenly as she finally came down the staircase in a fragrant cloud of scent. . . .

She closed her eyes, and let her mind drift to the past. Schiaparelli's Scandale in its elaborate, lace-and-flower-entwined bottle—how she loved it! Her mother had always used the perfume. She had leaned over often to rub a drop of it behind Felicia's ear, the smell of it blending with the fresh flowers that were always on her dressing table and the pot-pourri, which was sent to her from Crabtree & Evelyn, in London, all the way to Nairobi, at regular intervals. Packages arrived for her mother often, sent and paid for by her brother-in-law, Harry Lisle, who even from a distance of ten thousand miles seemed determined to look after her comforts.

Even as a child, Felicia could hardly fail to notice that Uncle Harry went out of the way to take care of her mother, for her father hated his older brother and made clear his resentment of the gifts, the letters, and the bundles of magazines, with the juicy bits of news and gossip marked out for her in Harry's own hand.

When her father and mother argued about Uncle Harry, they might have been talking about two different people, so much so that as a child she did sometimes imagine there were two Harry Lisles. Over the years, the mere mention of Uncle Harry had been like the opening shot of a battle in her family; often, when the subject of Uncle Harry came up, she would run into the garden and hide under the scarlet-flowered frangipani—which made it all the more remarkable that after her mother's death her father had sent her home to Langleit.

"You'll be better off at Langleit," he had told her sadly, the edge of defeat clear in his voice, despite the beginning of the slight drunken slur that crept into it every night long before the boys were ready to serve dinner. "It's where you bloody belong."

Well, she had not belonged there, in the end—unlike Portia, who clearly *did*. Sometimes, in her "blue" moods, Felicia found herself wondering if there was a pattern there. The thought never failed to terrify her. Her mother had been "close" to Harry Lisle, as if perhaps she felt she had married the wrong brother. Felicia herself had been Harry Lisle's mistress (no other word would do, if she was to be honest with herself) for over six years; and now *her* daughter—the very child that Harry Lisle had given her and wanted her to "get rid of"—was living at Langleit, and all too clearly devoted to him.

Felicia shuddered. Thinking about her past always led her back to the moment when Harry Lisle had learned that she was pregnant. Efficient as always, he had made an appointment for her at a discreet private clinic off Park Lane, but for the first time in her life she had stood up to him, refusing to go.

Her mind echoed still, years later, with the violence of that quarrel, with his fury, with the pain of his big, strong hands grasping her wrists so tightly that he cut off her circulation, while he shook her as a terrier might shake a rat, pausing to slap her again and again, so hard that each time he did she could feel her neck snap with the shock. Then, exasperated by her refusal to see "reason"—*his* reason—he threw her onto the bed, picked up a pillow and pushed it roughly down on her face, holding it there while she began to suffocate, gasping for breath, ice-cold with fear, trembling from the lack of oxygen, unable even to plead for mercy, until finally he removed the pillow.

Afterward he swore that he had only meant to frighten her, but she had not believed him then, nor did she now. She had seen the look in his eyes just before he forced the pillow over her face. He had meant to kill her, and it was, she suspected, only the dawning realization of the consequences that made him lift the pillow at the last moment and walk stiffly from the room, defeated for once.

She owed her life to that moment of fear. So did Portia, for Harry had had two lives in his hands that afternoon in the peaceful room overlooking the rolling hills of Langleit, to which she had returned, with such ambivalent feelings, for the weekend—while Aunt Maude no doubt dozed drunkenly, or sat in her armchair, spectacles perched crookedly on her nose, trying to knit with fingers made clumsy by drink, in the red sitting room on the floor below, not twenty feet away.

"Felicia! Come *on*, darling. We're going to be late."

"Coming, darling," she shouted back, without making the slightest attempt to hurry.

She was absorbed in her own reflection in the mirror, trying to decide if her lipstick was exactly the right color. This was her sixth try so far. She decided it was the kind of red that was suitable only for a vampire in a Hollywood Technicolor horror movie. She wiped it off and started again.

"For God's sake, Lish! You're going to be late for your own bloody wedding!" he shouted.

"Only half a mo more." She could picture him pacing the hall downstairs, handsome in his new dark blue suit, white shirt, pale gray checked tie, pulling the wafer-thin gold watch she had given him out of his waistcoat pocket every couple of minutes to glance at the time, wondering how long it would take them to get to Caxton Hall. It was a shame he *couldn't* wear a black cutaway coat and striped trousers, but somehow that didn't seem right in wartime. . . .

Dear Robby! she thought, so impatient to get the wedding they had waited nearly ten years for over and done with as quickly as possible—presumably so he could go back to thinking about *Othello*. Let him bloody well wait! she told herself.

She had begun dressing, as she always did, with every intention of being on time, but then she changed her mind about the dove-gray Molyneux at the last moment and started trying on alternatives. No matter how many she tried on, none of them seemed right. By the time she had dressed and undressed half a dozen times, changed her stockings twice, smudged her makeup so that she had to start all over again, and reduced Alice, her long-suffering maid, to tears, she was hopelessly late and back to her first choice, the Molyneux. She finished putting the lipstick on, licked her lips carefully, examined the results. "How do I look then, Alice?" she asked.

Alice was putting the rejected clothes back onto hangers slowly to show her resentment, with an occasional damp snuffle, a sound which always got on Felicia's nerves, as she very well knew.

"Smashing, miss," she said glumly.

Felicia nodded. She knew perfectly well she looked smashing, and didn't need Alice to tell her so, but the easiest way of apologizing for having raised her voice at Alice earlier on was to ask her opinion.

She lit a cigarette, ran the tip of her tongue lightly over her lips again, to remove the slight smear which would have been invisible to anyone but her. "I just don't know," she said at last. "You don't think it's *too* dark, do you?"

A look of horror crossed Alice's face at the possibility that Felicia might be about to start all over again. "Oh, *no*, miss!" she cried. She hesitated for a moment. "I beg pardon, but Mr. Vane sounds a little anxious, if you don't mind me saying . . ."

"He'll wait," Felicia said. "He can't very well get married *without* me, can he?"

Another snuffle. "I suppose not, miss."

Alice was a comparatively recent find, a peace offering, as it happened, from Harry Lisle. Half the maids in England were making good money working in war factories, but landowners like Harry still had access to country girls for whom servanthood was a step up the ladder.

In innumerable small ways lately, Harry had slipped back into her life, gradually beginning to fill a place as the family provider. It was not just servants that he produced, but hams, eggs, chickens, wine from his cellar, paintings loaned from his collection to put on her walls, antique furniture—all the luxuries that made life easy, attractive, convenient, and which remained, for most people, unobtainable, however much money they had. She knew it was in part his way of saying "Thank you" for the fact that Portia was at Langleit, but it went deeper than that, really, to his need to control everything and everyone in sight, whatever it cost him.

"I'm ready," she said, then reminded herself that Alice could never keep designers straight. "The gray one."

Alice sniffed resentfully. "That was the first one."

"I shall put it on again. Perhaps I'll feel better about it this time."

She rose, and stood for a moment, arms raised above her head like a diver about to plunge from the board, while Alice put her slip on for her, then she slid into the dress as Alice held it for her. Over the years, Felicia had grown used to being dressed by other people—in film work it was not only usual, but necessary, given the complexity of so many costumes. She stood still while Alice smoothed the dove-gray silk.

She had bought the dress in 1937 during a visit to Paris. Robby had gone to Molyneux with her, perched on a spindly gilt-and-velvet chair, the kind that seemed to be made in France only for couturiers and hotel lobbies, and intended to discourage anybody who weighed more than a hundred pounds from sitting at all, while she tried on dress after dress. Nevertheless, Robby had sat there for a whole afternoon, keeping up a flow of chatter, laughing, occasionally leaning over to give her a discreet kiss or to whisper in her ear.

He had been such good company that afternoon, the perfect lover, happy to be with her while she bought clothes, eager to go back to the hotel—the Ritz, wasn't it?—and go to bed with her. . . .

She felt tears welling in her eyes at the thought that the same man was downstairs, stamping about impatiently, already upset at the thought that marrying her might take more than two hours out of his day! He had no little jokes to tell her now, didn't seem to want to be alone with her. Even today, of all days, he had risen hours before her, read the *Times*, dealt with his post; he made calls to Cecil Beaton about the costumes for *Othello*, to Bobby Longhi about the backdrops of Venice and Rhodes, to Billy Sofkin, the choreographer, about a dance he wanted to include. . . . If he had been performing the role of a bridegroom onstage, how much better he would have played it!

There was a brief wail of sirens outside, then, high overhead, the noisy putter of a V-1 "doodlebug" making its way across the sky. Alice began to snuffle even harder, kneading a damp handkerchief with her hands.

The noise reminded Felicia of expensive motorboats idling at the dock at Eden Roc, a slow, deep-throated rumble that she associated with long luncheons under an awning surrounded by flowers. . . .

There was a rapid volley of sharp explosions as the antiaircraft guns opened up, the windows rattled—then, quite suddenly, there was an ominous silence.

"Oh, God!" Alice wailed. This was the moment everybody feared. When the V-1's jet engine stopped, it fell, gliding hesitantly at first, on its stubby, ugly little wings, then plunging down to explode where it landed. One bomb was enough to destroy a whole row of houses, and in the fifteen or twenty seconds between the time the engine cut out and the explosion, there was no time to run or hide or seek shelter—at best, you might say a few words of prayer if you were so inclined. Felicia wasn't. "Oh, *do* shut up, Alice," she said crisply. "It's miles away."

"Yes, miss." Alice's eyes rolled in her head, like a frightened horse's, but she was more scared of displeasing Felicia than of being blown to bits by a German buzz bomb, so she went back to straightening the shoulders of the dress, her lips moving in noiseless prayer. There was an explosion of such violence that it took the breath away, apparently just around the corner. The curtains flapped, the whole house seemed to rise off its foundations and fall back again, dishes and glass fell and shattered. Outside, the air was black with smoke and flying debris; in the distance, ambulance bells and police whistles could be heard, then the first high-pitched wails of the injured and wounded. "What did I tell you?" Felicia said impatiently.

She was fed up with the war, as everybody in England

was, and the buzz bombs seemed like the last straw, as if death were by now so mechanical that it no longer required a living enemy to drop the bomb that killed you. In the year 1944, you sat, she thought, in your bath with four inches of lukewarm water and a tiny sliver of soap, shivering with cold, waiting for a flying bomb to fall out of the sky and blow you to pieces.

Robby, perhaps unconsciously, perhaps simply because he shared it, understood the public's change of mood. They no longer wanted to be inspired. The thirst for the "patriotic" plays was over—people no longer wanted to see *Henry V*, or hear about "*this England . . . this sceptered isle . . . this precious stone set in the silver sea*"—they wanted instead, love, passion, romance, anything that did not involve warfare and the patriotic spirit.

His choice of *Othello* was a stroke of genius, for there was no way to relate it at all to present circumstances, or to read into it parallels with Hitler or the war situation. In an age when millions of people were being murdered in cold blood, the headlines and the public interest were turned, once again, on those who killed for love—and no doubt the same would prove true of Othello. . . .

Hands still trembling, Alice put Felicia's hat on her carefully arranged hair, and pinned it in place. Bobby Longhi's boyfriend had designed it especially for the wedding, for wartime fashion mostly revolved around hats, which required no more than a few scraps of cloth or fabric, and for which no clothing coupons were needed. Before the war, nobody wanted to wear a hat; now they were the rage, and the more outrageous and elaborate, the better, which was just as well, for this one was puckish, saucy, extravagant and—to be perfectly frank—silly, a kind of silver-gray toque, swathed in lace and velvet, sporting a plume of egret feathers pinned on the side with a diamond brooch, the one Charles had given her as a first anniversary present.

Robby, she knew, must be approaching the boiling point by now. No doubt he had calculated the exact amount of time it would take to reach Caxton Hall and had added five or ten minutes for safety's sake. Still, even allowing for his caution, she knew there was no putting it off a moment longer. "It will have to do," she muttered, as much to herself as Alice.

Alice looked crestfallen. "Oh, miss, you've never looked prettier," she said, with a sniff that came, this time, along with real tears. "It ought to be such an 'appy day, mum, only you don't seem pleased at all."

The annoying thing, Felicia thought, was that the bloody woman, for all her snuffling, was right. She *wasn't* pleased. She had no intention of letting anyone call her "Mrs. Vane," or even "Lady Vane," if it ever came to that, as she suspected it would, and before long. She suspected, in fact, that the marriage was hardly more than a kind of entrance fee for Robby's knighthood, that despite his denials, someone had made the whole thing crystal clear to him: no marriage, no knighthood.

She shook her head. This was not an appropriate thought for her wedding day, nor was it really fair. For years, *she* had wanted to be married as much as he did, but she had grown used to the idea that it would always be in the future. She knew what Robby wanted most—children of his own, a family like the one he had grown up in, but without the poverty and bitterness, and she had never dared tell him that it wasn't possible, consoling herself always with the fact that since they weren't able to marry, there was no need to face it.

If Robby was going to be told the truth, then the time to have told him was ages ago, at best, or yesterday, at worst. In a few minutes, after they had exchanged rings, it would be too late to tell him without destroying their marriage. Of course, there was no reason for him to know, no reason for him to suppose that anything more was involved than an accident of fate or biology. After all, who *knew*?

But one person, of course, *did* know, she reminded herself, and knew a good deal more besides. Just at that moment, there was a knock at the door—not a tame, respectful knock, but a full-bore banging. "Get a bloody move on," Uncle Harry said through the door. "Everybody's waiting."

"I'll be down in a moment."

"I should bloody well hope so."

"What are you doing up here, anyway?"

"Doing? I came upstairs to use the loo. Robby is wearing out the living-room carpet waiting for you, my girl, and Portia is working herself up into a state—for which there is no one to blame but you. Everybody's fed up with it. If I were Robby, I'd walk out and leave you at the altar, but I don't suppose he has the guts. Are you decent?"

"Of course I'm 'decent.' "

"One never knows." He opened the door and stepped in, impressively solid, like a large, glossy, well-fed animal. He wore a flower in his buttonhole, but his expression was more suitable for a funeral than a wedding. He frowned at Alice. "Buzz off," he ordered, in the tone of a man who expected to be obeyed. She gave a quick curtsy and ran from the room, much to Felicia's annoyance.

"What the hell is the problem?" Harry asked.

She stared him down. "There's no problem," she said. "I'm getting dressed."

"Balls. I know you, my girl, and don't you ever forget it. If you wanted to be ready, you'd be ready. You're putting it off, aren't you? Keeping everybody dithering around downstairs because you don't have the guts to say you don't want to tie the knot?"

"Don't be silly! Of course I want to tie the knot, Harry. I've waited ten years."

"And you'd probably go on waiting another ten if he'd let you, the poor sod. Do you know what he told me downstairs?"

"No, and I don't care."

"Care or not, you'll hear what I have to say. We're standing there in the drawing room, chap hasn't even offered me a glass of sherry, and he tells me how nice it will be for Portia to have brothers and sisters!"

"Brothers *and* sisters?"

"He thinks big. He was one of four or five children himself, I forget which. He loves big families. I think it's a rather middle-class idea, myself."

"Oh, nonsense! You'd have loved having a lot of children, and you know it."

He brushed his mustache with his forefinger and gave her a roguish wink. "I'd have loved the *making* of them, perhaps, if you'd been the mother. Can't see myself surrounded by brats. Always wanted to be the center of attention myself. . . . Never mind. Point is, you're still leading the bloody fellow on shamelessly, and there's bound to be trouble, I don't care how clever you think you are."

"What's it to you?"

"Oh, no skin off my teeth, admittedly. Vane's problem altogether, not mine. But it's going to backfire on you one day, my girl, and I don't want Portia caught up in it."

"Harry, thanks to Charles, you've won. You've already got her at Langleit, more or less over my dead body. What more do you want?"

"If something should happen to you or to Charles, I want her."

"I am not going to give you my daughter, Harry."

"She's mine, too." The threat was clear.

She slapped him as hard as she could with the gloves in her hand—not much of a weapon, to be sure, but she was hardly even conscious of the gesture. The instant the gloves touched his face, he reached up one big hand, as quickly as her father had fired at the leopard that had almost killed her, and seized her wrist. He held her the way he might have the halter of a recalcitrant horse, and with as little show of anger.

She struggled to free her wrist, but it was useless, as she should have guessed. How many times had she struggled to free herself from Harry Lisle's grip before? "Let go," she said.

He did not. With his free hand, he screwed his gold-rimmed monocle into his eye and examined her closely, as if she were an interesting specimen from his collection. "You still have your temper, I see. Mind, I *like* that in a woman. Always have. As you know. Many's the time I've had to rack my brains to explain the scratches on my face, eh?"

"I had to explain bruises. And worse."

He nodded. "Oh, ay," he said with satisfaction. "I've no doubt I gave as good as I got. Nothing wrong with that."

"*I* was the one who got the beatings. *And* a dislocated

shoulder once, in case you've forgotten. I didn't like it then, and I don't now.''

He looked at her skeptically, then laughed. "You liked it well enough then, and you'd like it now, I daresay." He tightened his grip a bit, the long, elegant fingers like clamps of steel. "Not that Vane's the man for that sort of thing. Still, you picked him, so you'd better get on with it. But you'll keep in mind what I said? About Portia?''

"I'll think about it, Harry."

"You do that, lassie. Think about it bloody hard, or perhaps I'll find a way of letting Vane know he hasn't a hope in hell of fatherhood with *you*.''

She gave him a look of such malevolent hatred that it would have brought an audience to the edge of its seats, but it had no visible effect on Harry Lisle, who merely smiled.

"I don't believe you'd do that," she said. "I can hardly imagine you sitting down over a glass of port to tell Robby the truth—about *us*.''

"No more can I. But there *are* ways to turn his mind in that direction, you know, so don't get cocky with me.''

"You do anything like that, you bastard, and I'll kill you," she said, smiling sweetly as he continued to hold her close to him.

He nodded. "I believe you mean that, my dear. It's one of the things I've always liked best about you. However, I frankly don't think you'd do it. To some other sod, yes, but not to *me*.''

"You flatter yourself. Why not?''

"We're too much alike, that's why." He winked. "Besides, dear girl, I'm your own flesh and blood. I'd see it coming a mile away, and get you first." He let go of her wrist. "Let's go," he ordered crisply. "It'll be the *second* time I've given you away." He threw back his head and laughed. "Third time lucky, eh?''

She took his arm and started downstairs with him.

The registrar's office smelled of linoleum polish and damp paper, a schoolroom smell which she found distinctly depressing. Nobody should go to her wedding with schooldays on her mind, she thought. She had hated every moment of boarding school. It had been Uncle Harry's solemn promise to bring her home from school and have her privately tutored at Langleit that had won her over with such little fuss.

She shook her mind loose from the memories and back to the business at hand. She retained only the dimmest recollection of her first marriage, which had been performed at a fashionable London church, with Charles's family and friends sitting on one side, many of them showing their disapproval of his marrying an actress, niece of a peer or not, while her own theatrical friends tittered and giggled through the ceremony on the other side.

She looked around her—Robby, hardly mollified, was standing next to Toby Eden, whose flushed face suggested that he had been getting an early start on celebrating; Portia, looking more sullen and resentful than ever in the pretty little flowered muslin dress, clung to Uncle Harry's side, as if she wanted to have him all to herself; the registrar glanced nervously toward the door, for the corridor outside was jammed with journalists and photographers, making a frightful racket. The world was waiting for the news of D day, which was rumored to be "imminent," whatever that might mean, but in the meantime, the marriage of Felicia Lisle and Robert Vane was going to be on the front pages of every newspaper in the English-speaking world except the *Times* and *The New York Times*.

The biggest scene in the picture for which she had won her Oscar was her marriage to Yancey Farrell, played by Mark Strong, America's muscular heartthrob. Millions of women had cried their way through that famous wedding scene. The billowing dress she had worn in it, even though it was modeled authentically after the fashions of the 1860s, became the wedding gown that every girl in America wanted to be married in, and garment manufacturers made fortunes with replicas of it. Her reply after the clergyman asks her The Question—"I do—I *really* do!"—was still being used by brides from one end of America to another, not to speak of those in England and the Commonwealth.

All over the world there were people for whom *that* wedding, *that* kiss, *that* line had been the high point of their lives, as if there were no other weddings, including their own. There were people in America who believed that she really was married to Mark Strong, and even in England people found it difficult to separate her from the role that made her famous. So it was hardly surprising that her wedding was news, or that the streets around Caxton Hall were crowded with fans waiting patiently just for a glimpse of her. No doubt they would be disappointed, she thought, that she wasn't wearing the gown from the film, and probably even more disappointed to see Robby in his dark suit instead of Mark Strong in the uniform of a cavalry officer. . . . To hell with them, she told herself. She put her arm through Robby's, raised herself up on her toes, and kissed him on the cheek. "I love you," she whispered.

He smiled and squeezed her hand as they walked forward to where the registrar stood holding a dog-eared book—not a Bible, judging from the look of it, but some sort of collection of official regulations, his script, no doubt, for the ceremony he was about to perform. "I know you do," Robby said, his voice low, serious.

"And I always will."

He nodded. "I know that, too." He might almost have been forgiving her.

"I *enjoyed* that!" Toby Eden said rapturously, as if her wedding had been a play. He was standing in front of the drawing-room fireplace, monopolizing the fire.

He had been drunk—"tipsy" might have been a more accurate word—even before they arrived at Caxton Hall, his cheeks glowing bright red, like a milkmaid's, his pale blue eyes glazed and unfocused. He dropped the ring twice—the second time, it rolled out of sight, and the entire ceremony had to be interrupted while he and Robby got down on their hands and knees to look for it.

They had made a quaint little tableau: Robby, looking more nervous than he ever had onstage; Toby beside him, swaying to and fro; Uncle Harry, giving away the bride with obvious reluctance, while Portia, sullen and unmoved by her mother's moment of happiness, clung to his side, revealing a resemblance that would have raised eyebrows had anyone been paying attention. Guillam Pentecost, in fact, had glanced at the small Lisle contingent with scarcely concealed curiosity.

Felicia looked at Robby now, greeting people in the drawing room as they arrived for the reception, so handsome in his dark blue suit, a single white carnation in his lapel (which she had placed there herself this morning), and thought how much she loved him, and how little faith she had in her ability to make him happy.

The drawing room was full of well-wishers. If a buzz bomb had dropped on the house, most of the English theatre world would have gone with a bang, Felicia thought sourly—so many loud voices calling out "Darling!" to each other and to her, so many faces reddened by years of greasepaint and gin. All the guests seemed to be more in the spirit of the thing than she was. Champagne corks popped, more people crowded in, the temperature rose. It was a hot, breathless summer's evening, with occasional bursts of warm rain and wind, weather in which the invasion everyone had been waiting for surely would not take place—no weather apparently being good enough for General Eisenhower.

She had been conscientiously drinking soda water, as she did on important occasions, a last vestige of obedience to Dr. Vogel's advice, but she decided her gloom was the result of avoiding champagne at her own wedding. Surely, if there was any event at which it was in order, even *necessary*, to drink champagne, it was at your own wedding.

She grabbed a glass as a waitress passed with a tray, downed it, and took another. She felt better instantly—after all, it was ludicrous to mope at your own wedding reception before the cake was even cut. Though what a sad cake it was! Even by pooling their coupons, borrowing from family and friends, and relying on Uncle Harry to make up the difference, it was still impossible to find the ingredients for a decent-sized wedding cake.

At her first wedding, the cake had been enormous, and Charles had cut the first slice with a saber, as befitting an officer in some City of London territorial cavalry regiment of stockbrokers and merchant bankers; his fellow officers had formed up outside the church in Ruritanian dress uniforms so she and Charles could leave under a glittering arch of drawn swords.

There was a bustle at the door. A couple of GIs appeared, carrying an object about five feet high, covered with a sheet. Behind them, in uniform, marched Marty Quick.

The men rested their burden on the table in silence. Quick basked in the silence as the master of the staged surprise.

The GIs pulled back the sheet, revealing a monster of a cake, tier upon tier of sculptured white sugar, sprinkled with icing birds and flowers, rising to a kind of spun sugar terrace on top of which, in lively color, was a small grouping of a man on horseback, a man on a donkey, and a beautiful young woman on foot. There was a moment of puzzled silence while everybody tried to work out the significance of this small tableau in which ordinarily the bride and groom would be portrayed. "Joseph and Mary?" Toby Eden suggested, in a stage whisper, as if Quick had presented them with a party game—and certainly Felicia could see a certain faint resemblance to the Biblical scene, except that Mary, surely, should have been riding the donkey, with Joseph walking behind her, and there was no place for a man on a horse. . . . Then she realized that the figurine of a woman was *she*, wearing a Spanish dress, with a shawl over her shoulders, and a mantilla on her head, while the one on horseback was Robby, dressed in tarnished, rusty armor. She did not need to look more closely to guess whom the figure on the donkey represented.

She looked up and to her surprise saw Randy lurking shyly in the doorway, as if unsure of his reception. Randy was out of uniform this time, dressed in a fashionable double-breasted suit, very much like one of Robby's. He even wore the same suede shoes, and a shirt and tie that might have come straight from Robby's wardrobe. Now that Randy was in London, he had apparently gone shopping, and the result was that if one didn't look at the face, he might actually have *been* Robby —a fact which she found deeply irritating. Still, this was her wedding day, and this was her house. She gave him a quick little smile, the barest of welcomes, but enough to satisfy her social obligations, and determined to avoid him as best she could for the rest of the evening.

"Don Quixote!" Quick shouted triumphantly, though his pronunciation left many people in the dark. Not that it made any difference. There were only three people in the room— no, *four*, she corrected herself, for Aaron Diamond was glowering at her—who knew the significance of the figures. Most people were simply too awed by the size of the cake—more importantly, by the amount of butter, sugar, and eggs that must have gone into it—to bother with the figurines on top.

Quick seized a glass of champagne. "It's gonna be the biggest movie ever," he said, a little desperately. "Starring my friends, the newlyweds." He drained his glass. "And Randy Brooks, America's greatest comedian."

Robby stared at him with frank—and unfriendly—amazement. "You're dreaming, Marty," he said.

"No way. It's a sure thing."

"I wouldn't bet on it, Marty."

He shrugged. "I already did." For a moment his high spirits seemed to have deserted him.

He left Robby standing where he was, went over to Felicia and gave her a big hug. "How's my girl?" he asked.

"I'm *not* your girl, Marty."

"You oughta be. Congratulations, anyway. I never thought you two would actually do it. How long's it been?"

"Ten years."

"Ten years! Jesus, if you can still get married after living together for ten years, things have *got* to be okay between the two of you. At least there aren't gonna be any surprises on your honeymoon, I guess."

She laughed. "Well, there *might* be a few," she said. "We're rehearsing *Othello*."

"I didn't mean that kind. As you know."

She shook her finger at him. "The cake was a waste of rations," she said. "He'll never do your *Quixote*."

"What makes you so sure he won't?"

She could hear the anxiety in his voice. "He doesn't want

to. It's as simple as that. It's never going to happen, Caliban, darling.''

''You know me better than that. I'm gonna *make* it happen. It has to, Lisha.'' He hesitated a moment. ''Talk to him.''

She was startled. Marty pleading? Why? she wondered. ''I can't,'' she said. ''He won't do it. And I won't do it if he doesn't. And I also won't do it with Randy. So there you are, darling. I'm sorry.''

Quick nodded, but she could tell he wouldn't accept the answer. ''You're awful hard on Randy, Lish-baby,'' he said. ''If looks could kill, he'd be dead, with the smile you gave him when he came in. Loosen up. You guys used to be pals.''

She shook her head. She didn't exactly blame Randy for whatever had happened between him and Robby, but she wasn't going to forgive him either, and the less she saw of him—more important, the less Robby saw of him—the happier she would be. ''How do you propose we cut this cake?'' she asked.

He slapped his hand against his forehead. ''Jesus! I knew I forgot something. Can't you just use a bread knife?''

''Never mind. I know just the thing.''

She went to the desk, opened the drawer, unwrapped the dagger, and held it up, its point glittering in the light. Marty backed away in a sudden, involuntary motion of terror, genuine fear in his eyes—the first time she had ever seen it there—while Philip Chagrin stared at her with a very different kind of shock on his face, his pain evident to her even from a distance.

She stood for a moment, as if she were striking a pose, puzzled. She had not even noticed that she had slipped the blade from its scabbard. The act had been so automatic that the light gleaming along the double edges of the blade caught her by surprise. She felt the same curious burning sensation, as if she had picked up a hot poker.

It occurred to her suddenly that Philip's embarrassment was as genuine as Marty's fear. She wished she had never thought of the damn thing in the first place, but it was too late now. ''Robby, darling!'' she called out, and he turned, smiling. Then his smile was replaced by a black pinpoint in his eyes, a clear signal of anger. There were certain things he took seriously, and the Shakespeare dagger, as she knew well, was foremost among them.

"*What* a clever idea, darling!" he said, and placing his hand firmly over hers, he took the dagger from her, ran his thumb down the blade as if to make sure she hadn't damaged the edge, and held it up. There were not more than a couple of dozen people in the room who knew what it was, all of them theatre people, but to them the sight of it in Robert Vane's hand was bigger news than his marriage. It was obvious to Felicia, too late, that Robby might well have preferred to keep the whole thing a secret between himself and Philip.

Marty Quick hissed in her ear, "Let's get this show on the road!"

Robby, still smiling, though a little rigidly, said, "This dagger, once given by William Shakespeare to his friend and leading man, Richard Burbage, passed from hand to hand across the centuries—" he gave Philip a shrug, as if to make it clear that none of this was *his* fault—"has never been put to better use!"

He took her hand, placed it over his, and jabbed the dagger into Marty Quick's cake so hard that it seemed likely the point would go through the platter, then slipped the edge down through the cake, making a ragged mess of it, then speared a piece clumsily onto a plate. He let go of the dagger, put his arms around her—stiffly—and gave her a kiss on the cheek, while a couple of photographers took pictures.

"Philip will never forgive me," he whispered.

"I didn't mean to . . ." But her apology could not be finished because people were crowding all around them to shake Robby's hand and kiss her, some of them actually crying—including Randy, to her annoyance. Philip kissed her gently on one cheek; Guillam Pentecost, towering over her, swayed back and forth while he tried to make up his mind whether he was entitled to kiss her or not, and eventually decided on a flabby, damp handshake; and the last person to kiss her grabbed her so tightly that she was breathless, one hand holding her neck so that she couldn't back away, the other running down her back several inches lower than was proper. She closed her eyes, but there was no mistaking the aroma of expensive cologne and cigars.

"Kissing other people's brides is always a lot more fun than kissing your own," Marty Quick growled. "Cheaper, too. Okay to buy the bride lunch one day this week? Claridge's?"

"If it's on your coupons."

"Deal." He leaned over, his mouth next to her ear. "You're more woman than Robby deserves, you want my opinion. He's a lucky guy." He gave her a wink. "I hope he knows it."

"The dagger apart—poor Philip!—I thought everyone had a good time. And I've no doubt Philip will recover. Don't you think so, darling?"

She didn't care. It might have been nice if Robby were worried about whether *she'd* had a good time, but of course he was too busy still thinking about Philip Chagrin's feelings. After all, nothing had happened to the damned dagger! she told herself. And she had apologized to Philip, who had been as gracious as ever.

Robby was standing in front of the dresser, removing his cuff links, with the self-satisfied air of a man who has been through a long and difficult evening and looks forward to getting to bed at last.

She was sitting at her own dressing table, fetchingly bent forward, her breasts half-exposed, her slip raised so that the tops of her stockings were plainly visible. One black high-heeled Dalmain pump dangled from her foot. If all that didn't constitute an alluring picture, she couldn't imagine what did, and yet, there was Robby, apparently more concerned with the crease in his trousers.

She drained her glass of champagne and refilled it from the bottle she had brought upstairs. She was light-headed, but not by any standard that she could think of, not even Dr. Vogel's, was she drunk, having merely reached that stage at which her inhibitions were gently lowered. She finished wiping off her makeup except for the eye shadow, which made her look, she thought, waiflike and appealing, at least a decade younger than she was—but then, the lighting was flattering here.

"*Do* forget about Philip, darling," she said. "I'm sorry. Really sorry! I know I shouldn't have touched it. But I had no idea the dagger was a secret between the two of you, like a pair of Masons. He'll get over it, I promise you."

His expression was doubtful. Really, she thought, she was not going to have her wedding night spoiled by Philip Chagrin, however fond she was of him. "To hell with the dagger!" she said. "To hell with Philip! This is *my* night."

A guilty look crossed his face—or was it just the look of a man who felt he'd played the scene wrong? He shuffled from one foot to another briefly, put out his cigarette, picked up his drink, and came over to her. He leaned down and kissed her on the cheek. "Of course it is, darling," he said softly. "Congratulations! It's been ten years—but worth waiting for."

"I should hope I'm *always* worth waiting for, however long."

"Oh, absolutely." He held up his glass in a toast. "I've been thinking. Let's buy Syon Manor, darling. It's going cheap. It's only a couple of hours from London. Wonderful place for kids to grow up."

"I wouldn't want to be pregnant for *Othello*," she replied, laughing, without even thinking about what she was saying. "We'd have to think carefully about the timing."

"Certainly there *are* some things that matter more than the theatre."

It was on the tip of her tongue to point out that that was easy for *him* to say—he wasn't the one who was going to be pregnant—but of course neither was she. Still, she could not help thinking that all his life Robby had put the theatre first, before her, before everything, and now he expected her to put it aside to give *him* a child. . . . "Of course there are other things that matter, darling," she said. "Would you unfasten my necklace?"

She bent forward, exposing her neck, like Anne Boleyn to the headman's ax (a role she had once tested for and lost to a girl called Queenie, who had gone on to become Dawn Avalon). Give a man something to do that involved touching your skin when you were half-naked and the rest was assured, she told herself. But Robby just stood there holding his glass, his mind clearly on something else. "We've got plenty of space here, upstairs, for a nursery. Just a question of getting it decorated. Of course, buying the Manor, rebuilding the top floor here, keeping up the theatre, it's all going to cost a packet. I was thinking—if *Othello* works, what would you say to making a film of it? Sex, glamour, Shakespeare—done the right way, I think it would go."

She gave a small, impatient sigh. "It all sounds wonderful, darling, but what about Marty?"

He shrugged. "I'll pay him back, Lisha. Bit by bit, by installments. I can't think why he wouldn't agree."

"I can."

"Oh?"

"He wants to get his own way. Always."

"Well, don't we all?"

"Not the way Marty does."

Robby stared into his glass. "I'd better have another word with him. I've been putting it off, frankly. The moment I saw his bloody cake I knew it was a mistake to have delayed."

"I loved the cake, myself. People wolfed it down. I tell you what, though, darling, why don't you let *me* talk to Marty first? He might listen to reason more easily from me than from you."

"Yes? Perhaps you're right. You don't mind?"

"Not a bit."

"That might be a good idea. He's got a soft spot for you—if he has a soft spot for anyone, that is."

"Robby," she said firmly, "it's my wedding night. Take off your clothes and come to bed."

He smiled, the same smile he always had in the posters of the two of them together, before the war, the dashing, romantic, sexy smile she loved, then kissed her just the way he used to then, when they were first in love.

She finished her champagne, stripped off her clothes, got into bed, and turned out the lights. She could hear him undressing in the dark, then she felt him slip in beside her. She turned and put her arms around him, and it was not until they were making love that she realized she had, for the first time in years, forgotten to insert her diaphragm.

For a moment, she had a wholly irrational fear: What if I get pregnant? Then, as always, reality reasserted itself—it had always been a sham, and now that they were married it was an unnecessary one.

Robby might have noticed, too, for when they were through, he kissed her gently on the lips, and in a soft voice whispered, "Thank you, darling, for the best of wedding presents."

She held onto him tightly all through the night.

The theatre was damp, cold and dusty in the early morning. Much as she loved being in it—in *any* theatre, for that matter—she found it depressing. In the mornings, in the harsh rehearsal light onstage, the theatre seemed shabby and run-down, stripped of all its glamour and excitement. Her wedding had been only two days ago, but it seemed a lifetime away.

She sat on a hard little wooden chair to one side of the stage, the single bar of an electric fire glowing dully at her feet, wrapped in the mink coat that Charles had given her when Portia was born—a luxury then, and a necessity now, for she was always so cold that she had grown used to hearing her teeth chatter. Other actresses wore woolen underwear onstage, but Felicia refused to consider that. She lit a cigarette, as much from the need for warmth as from any desire to smoke. Guillam Pentecost loomed glumly over her, staring out at the stage like a mariner searching for a ship on the horizon, one massive hand shading his eyes. "He's bloody marvelous!" he said. "Isn't he?"

"Mm." She didn't bother to fake agreement. "You don't think it's just a touch exaggerated?"

Pentecost gave her a pitying look from beneath his bushy brows. "Exaggerated? Not at all. He doesn't know it, but he's bringing the English theatre into the twentieth century, and about time, too. You have to exaggerate to make the

point, don't you see? Othello isn't Toby with dark greasepaint
on his face. Othello is *black*. That's the point of the play.''

Time had not reconciled her to Pentecost, who filled certain
of the less intimate functions of a mistress for Robby. He
was always available for company, having no private life of
his own; and, most important of all, was (or appeared to be,
for Felicia was never completely convinced) an absolutely
sincere admirer, never at a loss for words of praise and flattery.

She looked up at Pentecost, whose face was fixed in an
expression of adoration as he watched Robby. ''I thought
Othello was about jealousy, Guillam,'' she said. ''It's a love
story.''

He shrugged insolently. ''A love story? Perhaps. Iago is
jealous of Othello. The *real* love interest is between Iago and
Othello, of course.''

''Oh, balls!'' she snapped, delighted to see that she had
shocked Pentecost—or perhaps merely made him cautious,
since he was presumably under strict orders not to provoke
her.

From center stage, Robby waved to her. She put out her
cigarette and let her coat fall from her shoulders, determined
to show him what acting was! She took one step onto the
stage and felt the transformation come over her, the silencing
of the fears and problems of her own life. Other people
dreamed of being someone different, but for her it was something she could achieve at will when she was working. It did
not happen to her when she made a film—the work was too
repetitive and fragmented for that—but in the theatre she felt
liberated every time she made her entrance, even for a rehearsal. The mere prospect of performing cheered her up—
like some kind of wonderful explosion of light inside her,
not so very different from an orgasm, in fact.

It was here, amidst last night's scenery for the final act of
Richard III—the gnarled trees and blackened gorse of Bosworth Heath—that she could still experience those feelings
that had once drawn her to see every film and play he appeared
in, over and over again, to eat lunch day after day in the
same restaurant just to catch a glimpse of him, to smoke his

brand of cigarettes, to wear a replica of his fedora, cocked as he wore it, praying that one day, sooner or later, he would notice her.

She paused on the threshold of the stage, her eyes devouring him as they had so long ago in the past. Desdemona was usually played with a kind of soppy innocence, but she would have none of it. She intended to make it instantly clear to the audience that *her* Desdemona's relationship with Othello was passionate and deeply sensual.

Oh, she knew the score, did Desdemona, Felicia told herself, and as her eyes caught Robby's she managed to convey it all, the new-born lust, the fierce passion, the fear of a woman who senses that her husband is pulling away from her, drawing back into his busy, well-ordered life, where there is no place for her, getting his pleasure from the admiration of his troops and officers, the terror of his enemies, the respect of Venice's rulers, conveying, too, that she is afraid his withdrawal might be her fault, that perhaps he does not find her as appealing as he once did, that some flaw of *hers*, some hesitation or vestige of girlish prudery, may have angered or disappointed him.

All this she poured into her eyes. Oh, there were tricks you could do with your eyes. When she was still a student at RADA, Philip had taught her to look directly into a floodlight before making an entrance, so as to contract the black spot in the center of the pupil to a narrow pinpoint, emphasizing the color of the eyes. And Toby—whose eyes were a major theatrical asset—had showed her years ago a series of exercises that enabled her to open her eyes so wide that they dominated her face, forcing the audience to read into them all the emotions of the part. She had learned most of this as part of her craft, but nevertheless there was a spark, a depth, in her eyes that went beyond technique. The look in them was at once predatory and vulnerable, demanding and submissive, proud yet begging to be abased, used, humiliated, if that was what the man she loved wanted—and all this she focused on Robby, who hesitated for a split second, then reacted to it with the precision and perfect timing of the great actor he was.

His forehead furrowed, his expression was that of a man delighted and suspicious at the same time. Even without the makeup, even in an old double-breasted gray flannel suit, he somehow managed to project the solidity of a much older man. All his eccentric preparation for the role seemed to have paid off. He moved with a stealthy grace that was not at all English, suggesting by the way he hunched his shoulders and carried his neck that he was an old soldier who bore on his person the scars of many wounds.

She raced across the stage toward him, then stopped a couple of feet away from him, demurely bent her neck and gave a slight curtsy, hardly more than the graceful suggestion of one, as if she had remembered at the last minute that she was a wife, and owed her husband a certain respect. He reached out, an expression of sudden joy on his face, took her outstretched hand and drew her close to him.

> "The heavens forbid
> But that our loves and comforts should increase,
> Even as our days do grow!"

His dark blue eyes, which so often had the cold hardness of lapis lazuli, seemed as warm as the Mediterranean on a calm summer day. He took her weight in his arms and swung them both gracefully around so that they faced the audience. She leaned back as he bent to kiss her, almost as if they were dancing a tango.

The electricity between them was so powerful that she heard a low whistle from the wings, then the highpitched voice of Pentecost saying, "Gosh!" followed by noisy applause from Toby.

She felt as if she were back onstage as Ophelia to his Hamlet, their first appearance together, when they had been passionate lovers onstage and off. And she waited for him to say, as then, "I love you," before they moved upstage to place themselves for the following scene.

But instead, he merely let go of her as if nothing had happened between them. Did he resent and fear her brilliance? Did he want the stage to himself? Had he been merely acting what she had *felt*? The frightening thing, if that was true, was that he had fooled her so completely!

"Very nice," was all he said, dryly, the way he might praise a few lines from a minor player.

She played the next scene woodenly, the edge of her enthusiasm gone.

By one, she was happy to break off for lunch.

18

Felicia always thought of Claridge's as "smart." Even now, she felt a tingle of excitement as the porter escorted her from her taxi to the front door on Brook Street under his umbrella.

Walking down the long marble hall never failed to raise her spirits because it was associated in her mind with growing up. It was here, in the lounge, in front of the fireplace, that her father sometimes took her for tea when she was a little girl, here that Uncle Harry brought her for lunch, when they came "down to town" for the theatre or to visit the art galleries, here that she used to meet Charles for cocktails during their brief courtship. Besides, it was one of those places, like the Veranda Grill on the *Queen Mary*, or the Polo Lounge at the Beverly Hills Hotel, where the entire staff lit up at the mere sight of someone glamorous, famous, or wealthy.

Felicia enjoyed her fame, and was not ashamed of the fact. As a child she had walked down this same art deco hall wishing that one day people would look at her and whisper to each other: "But how thrilling! Isn't that Felicia Lisle? She's so beautiful." It had not been clear to her then what form her fame would take, but she had an image of herself grown, beautiful, wearing a fur coat, a frivolous hat, lizard pumps with tiny straps and delicate high heels, an expensive diamond bracelet, while all around her women stared enviously and men devoured her with their eyes, and the staff bowed as she passed by, murmuring, "How *nice* to see you, Miss Lisle." Although that dream had long since come true, she still felt a glow of pleasure at the experience, undiminished by familiarity.

She swept into the Causerie, the dimly lit little "American" bar, where Marty Quick waited for her at a small table in the corner, outranked by a dozen generals and admirals, several of them accompanied by very much younger women in uniform. Their faces were strained, as if they were waiting for news—but in the fifth year of the war, most people looked strained.

Marty waved his cigar, got to his feet, and kissed her on the cheek. He was grinning with pleasure, but she guessed that most of it came from being envied by men with two or three stars on their shoulders and many rows of medal ribbons.

"Siddown," he growled. "You're looking great."

"I feel like the dove arriving back on the Ark."

He raised a heavy eyebrow. "I don't get it."

"The symbol of peace. A sign that the flood is receding, dry land is appearing. Apart from the barman I'm the only civilian in the room."

"You could be right. You heard the rumor?"

"Which one?"

"The invasion is on. We landed in Normandy this morning."

After all the waiting, she could hardly believe it. She knew it might mean nothing—the war could still drag on for years while the Germans fought from ditch to ditch, their V-bombs descending on London all the while, or the invasion might fail, in which case there was no imagining how long the war could last—but she felt, quite suddenly, a sensation of lightness, a breath of hope that the fear and the drabness were about to recede.

"Is it a success?" she asked.

Marty shrugged. "They're saying it's successful, yeah. Heavy fighting, big losses, but it looks like maybe we're there to stay, at last. The Second Front is open for business, baby! I'll bet you we're in Paris by July fourteenth. How about you and me, we celebrate Bastille Day in Paris this year, Lish? Stay at the Ritz, watch the fireworks from the Tour d'Argent, dance in the streets?''

She laughed. It *was* a lovely idea, just the kind of thing she adored. "We'll see," she said. "I think Robby and I will be working, alas.''

"Hey, I didn't invite *Robby*. To hell with him! I invited *you*! Listen, we might as well get an early start, celebrate the invasion.'' He snapped his fingers, and the barman appeared with a bottle of 1933 Dom Pérignon. She liked all good champagne without being discriminating about the brand or the vintage, but she knew enough to guess that this was probably the most expensive bottle in the hotel. A waiter brought a silver-and-crystal bowl full of caviar, resting on a bed of ice, while the barman opened the champagne with a discreet pop, not the bang that is the sign of careless handling or inferior wine.

Quick surveyed the table without any sign of satisfaction. "I want some toasted *black* bread, as well as the white,'' he snapped. "And you can take away the goddamn chopped onions. Just because I'm American don't mean I'm fucking ignorant.''

"But of *course*, Colonel Quick." The barman barked an order to the waiter, there was a quick flurry of activity behind the bar, she could hear voices whispering, *"Vite, vite!"* and within no time at all Marty's toasted black bread was on the table, the champagne poured in chilled glasses, and the of-fending accompaniments to the caviar removed.

Quick shared with Uncle Harry the gift of absolute com-mand over waiters, though with him it was not the aristocrat's natural tone of authority, but sheer ferocious determination to get his own way, reinforced by lavish tipping. Quick was known throughout show business as "The Prince of Schmeer"—he greased every palm he saw, and his arrival at a restaurant or hotel was like that of a hero returning home from the wars.

"A gift from the commies," he said, spooning caviar onto a piece of toast and handing it to her. "Stalin wanted a whole bunch of Hollywood movies, and I got him prints. You like vodka? I'll send a case over to the house. Diplomatic stuff, the real McCoy, not your usual eighty proof export shit.''

"I *love* vodka, but only a teeny bit, served really cold. It goes straight to my head.''

"Yeah. Now that I think of it, I remember that from San Francisco. Let's forget the vodka.'' He held up his glass, and she clicked hers against it. "Cheers, as you guys say over here. Here's to victory, peace—then let the good times roll again.''

"I'll drink to that.''

"Here's to you, too, Lisha.'' He leaned forward, frowning, as if he'd been asked to put on a serious expression by a drama coach. Quick's face seldom reflected what was going on in his mind, and at the moment, he was projecting sincerity. "Listen,'' he said, his gravelly voice reduced to a hoarse whisper, "do you mind if I tell you something?''

She nodded.

"I *admire* you,'' he said slowly and gravely. He put one hand gently on her knee—just a quick, brief touch. "You've won your victory, too, Lish, I mean it. You were down and out there in L.A. A lot of people thought you were out for the count, but you came back! Here you are, more beautiful than ever, married, playing Shakespeare, for chrissake— and do you know what that took?''

She shook her head. She felt Quick's hand on her knee again. This time he left it there, either for emphasis or because he was getting to the point of his argument. She had the impression that the hand was a little higher than it was the first time, more on her thigh, just below the stocking top, but she didn't give it much thought, for Marty's face was close to hers, his eyes staring straight into hers, damp with emotion, but hard behind the tears.

"It took *guts*!'' he said. "That's what I wanted to say. You are a very gutsy lady, as well as a sexy and beautiful one.''

"You left out 'talented' ''

He laughed. "I *said* 'talented,' didn't I? I must have. If I didn't, it's because I'm embarrassed talking to you like this.

You've got class. You've got all the talent in the world. And the main thing—guts. In my book, you're a very special person.'' He paused as if he had just given a testimonial.

"Thank you, Marty,'' she said, genuinely touched, if a little wary.

"You don't have to thank me, for chrissake. I'm only telling you the truth. More champagne?''

She held out her glass as the barman and the waiter both rushed to refill it. Perhaps it was unwise to be drinking champagne on what was virtually an empty stomach, except for a couple of spoonfuls of Marshal Stalin's caviar, but the morning rehearsal had been so full of frustrations that she felt the need. "Eat up," he said.

He himself spooned caviar onto his toast as if he hadn't eaten for weeks. He ate greedily, without any attempt at delicacy, piling the caviar on in mounds and occasionally licking the spoon. "Good stuff," he said. "I know a lot about caviar. I used to be inna restaurant business, you know? Ran nightclubs, restaurants. Never could unnerstan' why people ordered caviar, then crapped it up with chopped onions, sour cream, chopped eggs. . . . When something is really good, the simpler you keep it, the better, right?''

"Right. I had no idea you were interested in food, Marty.''

"The restaurants I ran, we made our money in the bar or with the floor show, not with the food. But if you wanna make money, you gotta give people better quality than they know they want, you get what I'm saying? I always had good chefs, good maître d's, real pros, and I *listened* to them— no point hiring good people, you don't learn something from them—so I learned to eat good. It's not the most important thing in my life, but what the hell, why eat crap when you don't have to?''

"Why indeed? It sounds like a perfectly good approach to life to me.'' She held up her glass for a refill. One of the nice things about being with Marty Quick was that you didn't have to pay a lot of attention to what he said. As long as you gave the appearance of agreeing with him from time to time, he was happy.

"Class,'' he said reverently. "That's what matters. I used

to tell my people, I don't mind hookers in the bar, it's part of the business, but if they *look* like hookers, throw 'em out. Nice, good-looking girls, well-dressed, lotta class—that's good for a joint.''

"I'm not so sure I've ever seen a hooker with class."

"Honey, then you never met my second wife. Or my fourth. Anyway, my point is, you got class, the real thing, in spades, and that's something I like. I want us to be friends."

"I thought we *were* friends, Marty."

"Well, yeah. I mean *friends*. Say, you're not eating any of this.''

"I've had plenty, thank you, Marty. A little bit of caviar goes a long way. I wouldn't care to make a lunch of it."

"Who says we're gonna make a lunch of it, baby? How would you feel about baby lamb chops? New potatoes? A salad with blue cheese dressing, just like home? A good Camembert? Fresh peaches in cream?''

She stared at him. She and Robby received all sorts of off-ration goods from American friends and admirers, not to speak of Uncle Harry's occasional largesse, but baby lamb chops were an unheard-of luxury, and Camembert unthinkable. "How on earth did you manage that, Caliban?" she asked.

He gave a reckless smile. He had remarkable teeth, gleaming white despite the constant cigar, the kind of teeth you saw only on American men. They made his smile strangely appealing, like a wicked child's grin. "The lamb chops were easy. I remembered you liked them—you had them at the Pump Room in Chicago, the night before we opened with *Romeo and Juliet*, you should forgive the expression. I had somebody bring them from 21. The Camembert, *that* took some doing! I did a couple of favors for some Frog general at deGaulle's headquarters, and he told one of his people who goes over there to see the Resistance leaders to bring the cheese back for me. It was bought at Fauchon, in Paris, last week.''

"You're making that up, Caliban."

"On my mother's grave! No, better than that, fuck her,

I'll show you the wrapping paper. I never lie about anything unless it's really important. On the small things you can trust me almost a hundred percent.''

"It has been rumored that you've not always been known to pay up money you owe.''

He looked hurt. "That's not *lying*, honey! That's cheating and stealing. Cheating and stealing I do, sure. So, what say we eat? Are you hungry?''

"Indeed I am. I've had a long morning rehearsing.''

"I wish I'd seen it.''

"No, you don't, Caliban. You were bored stiff when we rehearsed *Romeo and Juliet*. Your idea of a rehearsal is a lot of pretty girls kicking up their heels.''

"Nothing wrong with that.'' He sipped his champagne, looking at her reflectively over the rim of his glass. "I'd have been interested, anyway. I had other things on my mind, back there in New York, and Robby was being a real pain in the ass. I always like watching a pro work out, you know? When I was a kid, I used to go out to the track, early mornings, watch them breeze the horses. You wanna know which horse to put your money on, you gotta watch them train, not race. You watch the races to rate the fucking jockeys, is all.''

"That's not a very flattering comparison, Caliban.''

"It wasn't a comparison, Lish. Just a thought. You learn more watching workouts than the real thing, every time. I'd like to have seen you working with Robby again, too. How is he? Still pissed off with me about the fucking cake?''

"He's angrier with me than he is with you, as a matter of fact. He didn't like the cake a bit, but he liked my using Philip Chagrin's dagger to cut it even less.''

Quick sipped his champagne, his face set in a smile. He played the tough guy so well that it was hard sometimes to remember how young he was. He had packed such a lot of wheeling and dealing into his thirty-two years.

He held his cigar loosely between his index finger and his forefinger, the tip gently glowing. The cigar was Churchillian in size, and it was rumored that Quick had succeeded in winning over Churchill by taking direct charge of the Prime Minister's supply line of cigars. Like most of the more unbelievable stories told by or about Quick, it was true. He had found a job in Hollywood for a nephew of President Roosevelt's, he provided prints of Westerns for General Eisenhower to screen in the evenings at SHAEF, he had arranged for the publication in America of General deGaulle's book on war, and had persuaded Aaron Diamond to act as the general's agent—there were simply no limits to Quick's energetic generosity when it came to doing things for the great and powerful, nor did he press them for favors in exchange. The fact that he was known to have access to the White House or 10 Downing Street was enough of a reward for him. He would find a way of cashing in on it later.

His fingers were remarkably slender for such a burly, rough-hewn little man, the nails exquisitely manicured, his skin deeply tanned, even here in England, where the sun never seemed to shine for more than an hour at a time. Although he was never seen to walk a step farther than he had to, Quick still had an athlete's body, flat-waisted and broad-shouldered, and he gave the impression that he could probably still hold his own in the ring.

He had a formidable reputation as an arm wrestler, and had once beaten Hemingway four out of five, at a hundred dollars a time, in a much publicized grudge match, late one night at La Coupole in Paris, with Marlene Dietrich as umpire. It was a story Felicia had always assumed was apocryphal until she saw a photograph of it in Marlene's house in Coldwater Canyon.

"Chagrin's dagger?" he asked. "It looked like a stage prop to me."

"It's the acting equivalent of King Arthur's sword, Marty. It once belonged to Shakespeare."

"No shit!" He gave her a steely smile. "That's the dagger Shakespeare gave to Richard Burbage, am I right? And that got passed, one way and another, from Garrick to Keane to Sir Henry Irving? I guess it *is* kind of like Arthur's sword, isn't it? 'Excalibur,' right?" He grinned triumphantly.

She laughed. "You're always full of surprises, Caliban. How do you do it?"

He shrugged modestly. "I read, baby. I'm an insomniac.

You can't sleep, you've already gotten laid, what are you gonna do, lying there in bed, middle of the fucking night? It's read or stare at the fucking wall."

"Don't I know it."

"I figured. But why did that *putz* Chagrin give it up?"

"Robby says it was a noble gesture."

"My ass! Philip just wants people to think he's got more class than Robby. He can't beat Robby as an actor because he doesn't have the *cojones*, so he does the next best thing, which is to surrender gracefully, so everybody will say he's so fucking noble. Smart move, when you think of it. And think of this, too, honey baby: Philip *gave* Robby the fucking thing, right? In a way, that makes him senior to Robby, see? It's *Chagrin* who decides who gets the prize, like Robby was a bright boy in school and he was the principal."

"Headmaster. But, yes, I do see what you mean." As usual, Quick's Machiavellian view of life was persuasive.

"Headmaster, principal, whatever. Somebody does something for you, you always gotta ask what he's gonna get out of it. Robby should have done that when I paid off his debts in L. A."

"*Our* debts."

"*His*, Lisha. If they were just yours, believe me, I'd a paid them and torn up your marker." His eyes flickered to the doorway, where the headwaiter was standing, holding up a menu to attract his attention. "Lunch," Marty said, getting up. "No point letting those lamb chops get overcooked. We'd better go up to my suite."

She raised an eyebrow, surprised, despite the euphoria of the champagne. "Your suite? Caliban! I'm a respectably married woman."

"So what? It's comfortable up there, and we can talk. This is a strictly professional lunch. I plan to deduct it. I mean, what's the problem? I wanted to jump you, I'm not gonna do it with a couple of waiters in the room, am I?"

"Stranger things have happened, I'm told. Still, I expect you're right."

Quick's suite, as promised, seemed a safe enough place to be. A waiter stood beside the table, holding a chair out for her, while the wine waiter stood by with a decanter of red wine and the headwaiter hovered in the background, fussing over the details.

A fire blazed in the fireplace, there were flowers all over the room, and on a delicate antique folding easel by the window stood a small Renoir still life of flowers, so brilliant that the colors seemed to glow brighter than the fire. She had a sudden vision of herself as a child, wearing a white dress and a big sunbonnet decorated with wildflowers, running through a garden full of flowers to where her father and mother waited, her father incredibly handsome in his pale gray suit, her mother dressed in pastel chiffon that fluttered in the breeze.

"Richebourg 'Twenty-seven," she heard Quick say, his pronunciation surprisingly good. "I remember you liked it the day we all had lunch together in New York at Le Pavillon, when we went to see the World's Fair." He turned to the wine waiter. "I hope you gave it enough time to fucking breathe?"

"Of course, Colonel," the wine waiter replied deferentially, with a low bow. "I decanted it myself at eleven this morning. I think you'll be more than satisfied."

"I better be."

They sat while the lamb was served, the aroma filling the room like some reminder of happier, easier days. She tasted the wine and nodded. The wine waiter had done Quick proud. "That's a nice little Renoir," she said, pointing at the painting.

He tasted his wine and nodded at the wine waiter. "It's okay," he said. "You can stop grinning. I picked the fucking wine, not you." He turned back to her, cutting into his lamb and inspecting it carefully to make sure it was exactly the right shade of pink. "You Brits! It isn't a 'nice little' anything. It's a *great* painting."

"Possibly. I didn't know you were a collector."

"I been collecting important works for years. Hemingway took me to see Picasso, oh, I don't know, in 'Thirty-five, 'Thirty-six, I guess, when I was in Paris, and I bought a couple of paintings from Pablo, things he didn't even want to sell, they were so good. . . . Nelson Rockefeller practically went down on his knees to get me to donate them to the Museum of Modern Art, but I like them right where they are, in my bedroom in New York. Then I picked up a few Chagalls, a Braque, and pretty soon I had me a real collection. I've got a sculpture garden out at my place on Long Island, better than Billy Rose's—Moore, Brancusi, Rodin, you name it. When Aldous Huxley saw it, he said it was the finest thing he'd seen in America, except for the Pacific Ocean. You take my word, that's a very important Renoir, with an impeccable provenance. There are a couple of museum directors who are gonna wanna slit their throats, they hear I bought this one." He chuckled. "Lamb okay?"

"Delicious. What are you going to do with the painting, Marty? Send it back to the States?"

"It ain't my painting, Lish."

"I thought you said that you'd bought it?"

"I did. But it ain't mine." He chewed and swallowed, took a sip of his Richebourg, and shook his head with wonderment, as if he was thinking of the long journey that had taken him from rolling drunks under the boardwalk and running errands for bootleggers on Coney Island to a suite at Claridge's and a thirty-thousand-pound painting. He winked at her. "It's *yours*."

She put down her glass. The rich wine, on top of the champagne, had made her slightly dizzy. "Mine, Caliban? What do you mean?"

"I bought it for you. The moment I saw it, I thought of you. I don't know, it was something about the flowers, the colors—what the fuck, I just *knew*, that's all. It's funny, there's nothing in it but flowers, but it's a very sexy painting, you look at it long enough. Anyway, it's yours. Enjoy it in good health." He lifted his glass in a toast. "*L'chayim*, as the Jewish people say," he announced, as if he weren't one of them.

"Marty, I can't take it."

"Why the fuck not?"

"Well, in the first place, what on earth would Robby think?"

He continued eating, calmly. "Let Robby think whatever the fuck he wants to. It's my gift to you, that's all."

"But why? *why*?"

"Why not? Maybe just because I feel like it. Maybe because the first time I met you, back there in New York when you and Robby and I were talking about taking *Romeo and Juliet* on tour, I thought you were the most beautiful, classy, and talented woman I'd ever met, and nothing that's happened since has changed my mind."

He gave her a rueful, boyish smile. "What the hell," he said gruffly, his eyes tearing over, "the truth is I fell in love with you at first sight, you wanna know, and I've loved you ever since then. I guess I always will, who knows? And never once in all these years—four, right?—have I ever put the make on you, or tried to take you away from Robby."

He shook his head in wonder. "That's not my style, honey, you know me. I see someone I like, I go for her right away, whether she's married or not. With me the chick says yes or no, and that's that. I'm not the type to hang around begging, or feeling sorry for myself. This is the first time I've ever been lovesick in my life." He laughed bitterly. "Marty Quick lovesick? Christ, that's gotta be one for the books!

"That's the story," he said briskly, snapping his fingernails on the rim of his glass to bring the waiter running from the next room. "We'll have some more of this with the cheese, and bring the paper it was wrapped in to show the lady."

"Very good, sir."

She stared at her plate until the waiter removed it. There was something moving—or naive, depending on how you looked at it—about his feeling that he was owed something for his self-restraint over the years. "Marty," she said softly. "I'm flattered by all this. I mean, I'm touched." She reached over and brushed his hand.

He pushed hers away. "*Touched?* Don't talk crap to me! I love you. You don't love me. That's the bottom line. Just do me a favor and take the goddamn painting. And get him to make the movie. That's all I'm asking.''

The cheese was served, along with its wrapping paper, presented separately on a silver platter for her inspection; then the waiter withdrew. "I can't do either, Marty. You know that," she said.

"What *is* it with you people? Robby takes four hundred thousand dollars of my money, signs a contract, then won't make the movie. . . ."

"He'll pay you back, Marty. Bit by bit, but he'll do it."

"I don't want his money bit by bit! I need *him*. And as for *you*, I offer you a beautiful painting out of the goodness of my heart, with real feeling, and you turn me down cold. *I'm* supposed to be the tough guy, the shitheel, the man everybody loves to hate—but you two guys make me look like a patsy."

"Marty, Robby's grateful for what you did, he's determined to pay you back, however long it takes, but he doesn't want to spend a whole year on *Don Quixote*, and besides, there isn't a chance in hell you could put it together until the war is over, *if* then, and you know it. So does he."

He cut himself a piece of cheese, tasted it, smiled. "There are things only the French know how to do," he said. "Cheese is one of them. . . . Listen to me carefully, honey," he said, holding up a hand in a warning gesture. "First of all, I'm gonna *get* financing and I'm gonna make this movie—so don't tell me my own business. But there's something else you have to know. When I raised the money to give Robby, I had to get it from some very tough people. I made them promises, understand? They're the kind of promises that have to be kept."

"I'd help you if I could, Marty, but I can't persuade Robby to change his mind. Not about this."

"Come on, Lisha. You got the guy wrapped around your little finger."

"Not anymore."

"I don't believe that. Christ, Lish, this is gonna be a big, big movie—an *event*, unnerstan' what I'm saying? It's gonna be the first big international postwar production, maybe the first movie ever to be sold to television. Robby should be *happy* to be in it, baby. He'll thank me, you'll see.''

"He's not the same actor anymore. Or the same person."

"I know all about that. Chrissake, Lish, I'm not a dummy. He's at the top! Great. I'm glad for you both. I even hear, from *very* high sources, he's gonna get a knighthood offered to him very soon. You're gonna be Lady Vane, if that matters to you."

"I don't think it's been decided yet."

"It's been decided, believe me," he snapped. He lit a fresh cigar, taking a deep breath. "Listen," he whispered, "take the painting, *please*. Just to show you're not mad at me. And talk to him. Try. How often do I say 'Please'?"

"I can't."

He shrugged, then rose from the table, took the painting off the easel and walked over to the fireplace with it. He held it up, glanced at it, then moved the fire gate away.

"Marty!" she cried. "You can't do that!"

"Who says? I paid for it, I can burn it."

He pushed the painting into the fireplace, cigar clenched between his teeth, stirring the flames with the poker in his other hand.

She leaped to her feet, rushed across the room, and pulled it out of his hand. The gilding on the frame was slightly singed, but otherwise there seemed to be no damage. She clutched it to her. "You're mad," she said breathlessly.

"No. But I always mean business, Lish. Don't ever forget that."

She was standing close to him, trembling slightly from the sudden shock of seeing him about to destroy an irreplaceable work of art just to make a point. She took his hand and squeezed it, thinking how strangely lost and helpless he looked—as helpless as she had once been when he slapped her back to her senses. He said nothing. Then he took her in his arms and hugged her hard, squeezing her against him, and kissed her.

She broke loose, still clutching the painting. "I think I'd better go," she said.

"Stay. We still got things to talk about."

She shook her head.

She ran out while she still could run.

She briefly contemplated telling Robby about the lunch, but decided against it. Telling him how badly Marty wanted him in *Don Quixote*—*needed* him, perhaps—would be a waste of breath. Telling him about the painting, she decided, would be even more foolish. She wrapped it in a towel and placed it in her closet, with the vague idea of having the frame regilded at the earliest opportunity. One of these days there would be an occasion to tell Robby. Until then, she consoled herself with the thought that the Renoir was safer in her hands than in Marty's.

That night, when Robby crept into bed beside her and fell asleep without touching her, exhausted from a day of rehearsals and aggravation at the theatre, she lay awake with her eyes closed, seeing the Renoir on the wall, facing the bed, its colors glowing as if it were spotlighted.

She turned on her face, burying her head in the pillow, but she could still see the painting through closed eyes.

She knew perfectly well that Marty's declaration of love was largely motivated by the hope that he could use her to put pressure on Robby—she didn't have to be a genius to guess that—yet she believed he loved her. There had always been a strong mutual attraction between them, even during the debacle of *Romeo and Juliet*, much as she despised herself for feeling it.

She got up, went downstairs, poured herself a drink, and lit a cigarette. She sat in the dark, remembered Marty's kiss, the feel of his embrace, the knife-edged *hardness* of him. She knew very well that the best thing she could do—the only sensible, intelligent thing—was to avoid seeing him again. He was a dangerous man—she had heard it said too many times to doubt it, and to see him again would be playing with fire—and at just the moment when Robby's knighthood was in the balance.

She decided she would send the painting back with a note. Alice could take it to Claridge's, and the sooner the better.

She went back upstairs, feeling better already, hoping for an hour or two of sleep at last.

"Mr. Quick, please."

"Yes, madam."

She carried the painting, wrapped up like a clumsy parcel, under one arm. She had taken it to the theatre and left it in her dressing room during rehearsal, then had come here, hardly knowing why she had decided to return it herself.

Keeping the painting at home would have seemed like a terrible betrayal. She didn't have to worry that Robby would find it—if only he *had* the kind of curiosity that would make him search through her drawers or look into her closets!

"Mr. Quick will be down in a few minutes, madam, if that's all right."

"Tell Mr. Quick that I'll come up, instead." A fleeting concern for her reputation made her suddenly aware that there was a clear risk to being seen standing here at the hall porter's desk at Claridge's in the late afternoon, with half of fashionable London either finishing tea or ordering cocktails. She did not dare look around to see how many people she knew, since that would only make her look more conspicuous—and guilty.

"Very good, madam," the hall porter said. "Shall I have the package brought upstairs?"

She shook her head. She was here to give the painting back to Quick.

She would hand it to him, and go.

The door was open. She walked into the sitting room, but it was empty. She heard the sound of water running in the bathroom. "Be with you right away!" Quick shouted. "Sid-down, have a drink."

There was a fire burning, and a large silver tray laid out with bottles, ice, glasses, as well as a bowl of lemons and limes, extraordinary luxuries here in wartime England. She walked over to the desk to look at the newspaper, even though, like almost everyone else in England, she listened to the BBC news three times a day, desperate for every scrap of news about the invasion front.

Quick's correspondence was scattered over his desk—out-of-date copies of *Variety* and *The Hollywood Reporter*, piles of clippings sent from his office in New York, bills from the best tailors, bootmakers, and shirtmakers in England. She felt a combination of guilt and curiosity, but it was the latter that was stronger—she had never been able to resist looking through other people's desks. Quick certainly had made no effort to hide anything, which was usually a sign that there was nothing of interest to be found. There was a pale blue piece of notepaper that caught her attention, simply and elegantly engraved with the legend *"10 Downing Street, London, W1,"* bearing a few neat handwritten lines from Winston Churchill, thanking Colonel Quick for some unspecified favor—no doubt it had been left out deliberately. She smiled. Marty's fabled talent for self-promotion had clearly not deserted him. Sticking out from under it at an angle was a letter in what was clearly a woman's handwriting.

She pushed it with her finger until she could read part of it. ". . . you're an unspeakable fucking bastard to kick me back into the driver's pool and get me assigned to this hairy ape Fruchter, with his big paws. . . . I didn't deserve it, and you know it! Wishing you nothing but the worst—Sylvia."

Propped against the leather blotter was a card engraved with the crest of the Ritz Hotel on which Marty had scribbled in his forceful writing, all heavy lines and ink blots, as if he were trying to drive the pen through the paper, *"Billy Dove, Fox and Grapes,"* with a scribbled telephone number beneath it. All around the writing was a complicated pattern of intertwined dollar and pound signs, as if Marty had been doodling while he talked to someone, Dove perhaps. It occurred to her that "Billy Dove" was a familiar name, but she couldn't place it. There was a famous English music-hall artiste named Billy Dove, of course, but Felicia thought she was of her mother's generation. It seemed to her unlikely that Marty might be thinking of putting an ancient Billy Dove in a Broadway show, but before she could give the matter any further thought, the bedroom door opened and he appeared in a silk bathrobe, smoking a cigar, freshly shaved.

"You got yourself a drink?" he asked. He had a jaunty smile and seemed not at all surprised to see her.

"Not yet. I mean, I don't really want one. I just stopped by for an instant."

He looked at the parcel. "To give me back the fucking painting?"

"Yes."

He shrugged. "Well, fuck it. What's a Renoir between friends?" Yesterday he had been adamant about her taking it. Today he didn't seem to care. Even for someone as mercurial as Quick, it seemed a rapid change. He went over to the drink tray, took a bottle of Dom Pérignon out of the ice bucket and popped the cork expertly. She wondered if he kept a bottle on hand all the time or if he had simply assumed she'd be back.

He poured out two glasses and they drank. "Robby tell you to send it back?"

"I didn't tell him about it."

"Well, at least *that* was a smart move. You coulda sent it over, though. You didn't have to deliver it yourself."

"It was on my way."

"That a fact? I guess I just don't know London as good as I thought I did. How'd the rehearsal go today?"

"It was ghastly, thank you."

"You ever considered you're making a mistake? You're a good actress—a real one. Maybe you and Robby don't need to be joined at the hip. Look what happened when the two of you did *Romeo and Juliet* together."

"We did well enough in *Macbeth*, in case you failed to notice."

"You got mixed reviews, honey—be realistic. What I meant was, how did you and Robby get along?"

She closed her eyes for a moment and sighed. "Terribly," she said. "We had awful scenes and fights. I was miserable. So was he."

"Well, there you are. So you're *not* the goddamn Lunts, so what? There's no law that says you two gotta act together.

Look at Robby. *Richard the Third* is the biggest thing he's ever done, and you weren't in it. Maybe he ain't any happier about *Othello* than you are, Lish. I mean, face it—it's hard enough to live together without working together on top of it. I found that out when I married Kassie Blake.''

"Which one was she?"

"She was the one won the Olympic gold medal twice as a swimmer. I hired her for my first aquacade, made her a big star, then married her. . . . Talk about mistakes! We had a lousy marriage and she gave up swimming, so I lost both ways.''

"How long did it last?"

"The marriage with Kassie? I don't know. Six months, maybe.'' He looked wistful. "She had a great body.'' He smiled at her. "So do you, you know.''

"Thank you. I'm afraid I'm not the Olympic gold medalist type, though, Marty.''

"You got nothing to be ashamed of in the figure department, Lish, take my word for it.''

It had been a long time since anyone had admired her figure as well as her face. Before the war, the popular press used to call her "The Girl with the Million Pound Eyes,'' all because a film producer had insured them with Lloyd's of London as a publicity stunt, but the fact was that her first moment of fame had come when she appeared in *Vogue* at the age of twenty wearing a diabolically sexy black silk Molyneux evening gown that clung so tightly to her body that it seemed to have been painted on. With her tiny waist, long, slim legs, perfect bosom, and swan neck, the photograph was the talk of London, and it was that, as much as Philip's recommendation, that got her her first West End part.

That had been a long time ago—longer than she cared to think about—but the years had not spoiled her figure a bit, even if *she* was the only person who noticed it. "I'll take your word for it, Caliban. I don't think I've got anything to be ashamed of, either.''

"I'll tell you what you need, Lish, honey. The first thing is a play of your own. You gotta prove to yourself that you can act *without* Robby.''

"Of course I can!" she snapped angrily. "Everybody knows that."

"That so? It's been a long time since you tried. 1939, right? And you won an Oscar, which is more than he did. But that was a movie, Lish. You need a *play*, and if you leave it to me, I'll find you one. I got people reading scripts all the time."

"Perhaps."

"No perhaps. You can count on it. Don't sell yourself short. You got your own reputation to think about."

It was a thought that had occurred to her often. *Why* did she need to tie herself to Robby, and to the limited number of plays in which they could act as lovers together with equal billing? And why persist, even when it was apparent that Robby was getting bored and irritated with having to link his career to hers? "I'll think about it, Marty," she promised. "What's the next thing I need?"

He put his cigar down carefully in an ashtray, came over and stood close to her, put his arm around her. "Me."

It was the moment to go, and she knew it, just as she had known what was almost certainly going to happen if she came here with the painting. Somehow she had managed not to make a conscious decision—she had simply allowed each step to happen without thinking about the next one, pretending all the time what she was doing was perfectly innocent. She tried to pull away from him now, but he held her effortlessly, with one arm, pressed tight against him. With his other hand, he took her jaw and pulled her face to his. He kissed her, hard, holding her so tightly that she could hardly breathe.

She began to struggle, kicking at him as hard as she could, but he didn't loosen his grip. She couldn't open her mouth because he was trying to force his tongue through her clenched lips. "I'll bite it off!" she threatened.

He chuckled. "I'll bet you would, too! Listen—relax, Lish! You want this as much as I do."

She shook her head fiercely. She managed to wriggle one arm free from his grasp and gave him a stinging, raking slap at close range that opened two or three trickles of blood on his cheek.

This time he didn't laugh. "You cunt," he said calmly, without apparent anger. Holding her as tightly as ever with one arm, he let go of her jaw, brought his right hand back and slapped her so hard that she gave a sudden shriek. The pain was as sharp as if she had been cut by a whip. She actually felt her teeth rattle against each other, and her eyes filled with tears. "Bastard!" she moaned.

"You bet," he said, and raising his hand, he slapped her again, even harder this time. Her head snapped back so violently that for a moment she thought he had broken her neck. Before she could move it to find out, he picked her up, carried her over to the sofa, ignoring the blows and kicks she was raining on him, threw her down and flung himself on top of her.

She struggled for breath, eyes closed, feeling his weight crush her down against the cushions. His body was hard-edged, muscular, ungiving. Somewhere on the way to the sofa she had lost her shoes, so her kicks were unlikely to do him much harm. She stopped, feeling herself growing warm from the exertion. Then, quite suddenly, as she opened her eyes and saw his face close to hers, she felt a warmth of a very different kind. Her cheeks still burned and stung, her palm throbbed, there was pain in her back and in her toes, but she recognized the excitement she had felt, so long ago, with Harry Lisle. Now, as then, the pain and the physical struggle had released her from guilt. Whatever happened was not her fault; he had forced her. "You're ruining my clothes," she said calmly. "And I do think you might take your own off."

Quick rose to his feet cautiously in case she decided to hit out again, then decided he had won. "In there," he said, pointing to the bedroom.

She walked in and pulled her dress off carefully, brushed out the wrinkles, and hung it neatly over a chair. She glanced around her and realized at once that the bedroom seemed familiar. She had once spent the night in this hotel with Harry Lisle, after seeing *Le Nozze di Figaro* at Covent Garden, either in the same suite or one that was identical—or were all the bedrooms at Claridge's similar? She took off her earrings and her bracelet and placed them on the bedside table, along with her slim gold Cartier watch, a present from Robby. . . . If Robby had paid more attention to her, she would not be here in the first place, she told herself firmly.

"Christ, you're beautiful!" she heard Marty say from the doorway.

"Draw the curtains," she said.

He shook his head. "I want to see you."

She walked over to the windows and pulled the cords that closed the curtains, then the heavy drapes. "I'm the wrong age for bright light, Marty," she said. "You want your Olympic swimming gold medalists for that."

"You're more beautiful, believe me. And I know." He was carrying, with some dexterity, the bottle of champagne and two glasses, one of which he handed her.

She took a sip of champagne, sat down on the bed, and started to unfasten her stockings. "That's reassuring and very sweet of you to say. But over thirty I think there are some secrets a woman should preserve."

"Keep 'em on," Marty said hoarsely.

"Why?"

"That's the way I like it."

"Well, it's not the way you're going to get it. I hate going to bed in my underthings. It's uncomfortable, and they get ruined. Besides, I have to go home in them. One day, perhaps, but I'm afraid today you'll simply have to take me as I am." She took off her things, one by one, folded them neatly, then slipped into bed. "Do take off that ridiculous robe and come to bed," she told him. "I hope you don't have cold feet. I can't stand men with cold feet."

"Nobody's complained so far."

"Poor things, I expect they were afraid to, that's all. Or perhaps they didn't mind cold feet."

Quick glanced down at his feet as if he were wondering how to warm them up.

She laughed, delighted at his discomfiture. In the space of only a few minutes, she had turned the tables on him. It was a game, of course, one at which she excelled. Teasing and ridicule were the only weapons she had had at her disposal against Harry Lisle, and they were as effective as his fists. Sometimes, of course, she had used them too sharply, or misjudged his mood. Then, they had the same effect on him as the *banderillas* on a bull; if she had not drawn the curtains, Marty Quick could still have seen the results of those encounters.

She could tell by his smile that he was torn between his dislike (and fear) of being made fun of and the novelty of the experience, and that, for now at least, he was prepared to find the novelty charming.

He slipped out of his dressing gown—an elaborate creation of paisley silk, with a black moiré shawl collar, the kind of thing that Noel Coward might have worn onstage.

It had been so long since she had seen any man's body but Robby's that she felt a certain amount of curiosity at the sight of Marty's. He was undeniably hairy—but she had expected that, after all, from the backs of his hands and the fact that despite his shaving, he had a blue-black sheen to his face. But there was no denying that he had a powerful and muscular body, very broad in the shoulders, with the flat stomach and well-defined ribs of a much younger man. She caught only a fleeting glimpse of him before he was in the bed beside her, gripping her tightly in his arms, his lips pressed so hard against hers that she couldn't have teased him even if she'd wanted to try.

She let herself relax, content in the knowledge that it had been a long time since anybody had wanted her as much as this—a long time, too, since she herself had felt so pleasurably wicked and free. . . .

His feet were as warm as toast.

They lay in the dim half-light finishing the champagne, while she smoked a cigarette. "I'll have to be going," she said.

"Sure."

She was comforted by the fact that Marty did not appear to think it necessary to beg her to stay. Besides which, she suspected, he would probably be happy to see her go and get on with whatever he was doing. "Who is Sylvia?" she asked.

"You've been reading my mail." He didn't sound surprised.

"If you don't want women to read your mail, you know, you ought to put it away before leaving them to cool their heels in your sitting room."

"I guess I'm out of practice. That's what comes of being a bachelor. Sylvia was my driver, if you must know."

"She has a remarkable way with words for a chauffeur."

"I guess you could say she's a girl of many talents."

"She seems to feel you dismissed her unfairly."

"Look, I'm a colonel and she's a corporal. How are we gonna win the war if an officer can't transfer enlisted personnel without a lot of hysterical complaining from them?"

"I see. Was she—ah—*failing* in her duties?"

"No. She was just becoming a pain in the ass, is all."

"And are there many Sylvias?"

"I'm only entitled to one driver, Lish."

"Poor you. But I meant—are there a *lot* of girls? Am I at the tail end of a long list, or just a medium-sized one?"

"Average. This is war. We all gotta make sacrifices."

"How true. What's 'average'? Ten? Twenty? It's not really any of my business, I admit."

"It varies. I guess I'm seeing a few girls. Maybe a half-dozen."

"That seems modest enough, Caliban, darling, for a man like you. What would you tell me if I asked you to give them up for me?"

"Off the cuff, I'd tell you to fuck off. But on second thought, we could probably carve out some kinda deal."

"I don't suppose you'd tell me the truth anyway. You'd *say* you'd given them up, but you'd still be sleeping with them when I wasn't around, wouldn't you?"

Quick gargled with his champagne, then swallowed it. "Probably," he said in a good-natured tone. "Most of my wives asked the same question. Look, you don't owe me anything, I don't owe *you*. You're married, for God's sake, you're still sleeping with Robby. I'm not asking you to stop."

"I should hope not. He *is* my husband, after all."

"Yeah. To tell you the truth, I used to wonder if there

really was anything going on between the two of you, back there about the time you froze doing Juliet.''

''It was a difficult period.''

''Is Robby really *interested* in women? I mean, I never got the impression he was all that hot for you, back then. Or now, you wanna know the truth. Of course, he's a Brit, and it's sometimes hard to figure the Brits out, when it comes to sex. The men, I mean. Women are the same everywhere.''

''Robby's libido is perfectly normal, thank you. And could we please stop talking about him?''

Quick had been lying next to her on his back, one arm around her shoulders, spread out in the relaxed way of a man who has given his all to sex. He could afford to feel satisfied with himself, she thought. What he lacked in finesse—and he lacked a good deal—he made up for in sheer vitality. He had treated her like a whore, telling her what to do, forcing her to assume whatever position he wanted by sheer physical strength, grabbing her so hard that she was pretty sure her thighs and buttocks must be livid with bruises. Every joint and muscle in her body ached, but pleasantly, and she, who never even perspired, was still covered in a fine sheen of sweat.

She tried hard to feel guilt, self-contempt, disgust at what she had just done—had allowed him to do, even encouraged him—but she could feel none. For a while, all her demons had been calmed, her mind emptied of *Othello*, of her problems with Robby. For the first time since Robby had started to drift away from her, she had experienced that total blankness of mind that had once seemed to her the greatest, the *only*, peace she knew. She could not deny that she would rather have found that peace again with Robby than with Marty Quick, but Robby could no longer give it to her, or perhaps could no longer be bothered to try.

Marty was already in motion, sitting up, glancing at his watch, casting an impatient look at the bedside telephone, giving every indication of a man whose ability to lie in bed was strictly limited. She recognized, without difficulty, on the bedside table, the marks of a fellow insomniac: the stacks of magazines and papers, the bottles of pills, many of them the same as the ones she took—and, she supposed, just as useless—the notepads and pencils, the crossword puzzles. With Quick, she suspected, it was not so much a question of being unable to sleep as regarding sleep as a waste of time.

"Talking about Robby," he said, "it's fucking weird, isn't it? We're always talking about him, all of us. You, me, your friend Chagrin, Toby Eden—whenever any of us get together, the first thing we talk about is Robby Vane. What's he going to do next? How's he getting along with Felicia? Is he gonna get his knighthood? It's the same with you. You talk about him all the time, you think about him all the time, but does he think about you? No. *His* mind is on his work, right? I noticed a long time ago, Robby's got this funny little smile when he talks to anyone, as if he really liked that person and cared about what he had to say, but then you look closer, and his eyes are as blank as Little Orphan Annie's. He just ain't *there*, you know? Is he the same with you?"

"I know what you mean," she said, resentful at being brought back to the real world, "but not really."

"Don't hand me that shit," he said. "I've seen him with you. It's an act. A good one, sure, but I bet it doesn't work in bed, does it?"

"I don't want to talk about it."

"Look, if it weren't true, you wouldn't be here. I know that, and so do you, so let's not bullshit each other."

"Robby can be distant sometimes, yes. It's something you learn to live with."

"*Have* you learned to live with it, Lish? It's funny, but Natalie Brooks told me that the first time she met the two of you, back in L.A., you reminded her so much of herself and Randy that she almost cried."

The mention of Randy Brooks's name was always enough to catch her full attention. "Natalie said that? To you?"

"Right. I've known her for years—I'm the one who introduced her to Randy, you know. She was looking for a husband, and let me tell you it wasn't easy. Leo Stone's daughter! Well, I guess there were plenty of guys in the industry who wanted to become Leo's son-in-law, but mostly not the kind of guys a girl like Natalie'd want to marry—

momzers, yes-men, creeps. Guys she *might* have married, guys who were already successful, like Milton Aura, the producer, or Abel Grief, the director, they had to figure if they ever made Natalie unhappy, they'd have Leo coming down on them like a ton of bricks, trying to ruin their careers. Who needs? So for Natalie, Randy was a perfect choice— he was a big star, he didn't need Leo, and if Leo needed him, all he had to do was call Aaron Diamond and make a one-picture deal. As for Randy, he needed to be married, the sooner, the better."

"Is that so?"

"You bet, but that's a whole other story—which maybe the less said about, the better. What I was getting at was that Natalie could see Robby treated you the same way Randy treated her. He *acted* the part of the loving husband, did it pretty good, too, but he didn't *feel* it. Natalie once told me, I remember, 'It isn't easy living with a man who can pretend to be anything he wants, including a loving husband—and make you *believe* it!' I guess it's one of the things Randy and Robby have in common, now that I think of it. . . ."

She was on edge now. "What are the others, Marty?" she asked.

"Christ," he said, changing the subject rapidly, "have you any idea of the fucking time? If you don't get home pretty soon, Robby's gonna be sending the Seventh Cavalry out to scout for you. I gotta go, too."

"Another corporal to discipline?" She was relieved, in a way, not to know more than she did.

"Gotta keep up discipline, honey. We start lettin' some twenty-year-old broad in uniform talk back to a colonel, no tellin' where it's gonna end. The new one's name is Amelia, by the way, and she's waiting downstairs so she can drive you home, since your chance of gettin' a taxi is zero, star or not."

She swung out of bed, conscious that he was watching her, and pleased by the fact. How long, after all, had it been since somebody had taken pleasure in looking at her naked? She gathered up her things and went to the bathroom, leaving Marty to light up his cigar at last.

She looked at herself in the mirrors and sighed. There were bruise marks all down her buttocks and thighs, just as she had expected, as well as several bite marks on her breasts and stomach. Given the state of Robby's ardor, she might easily conceal these until they were healed, but it was her face that was the problem, not so much because of the smudged makeup and disheveled hair, which she could more or less repair, but because she saw in her eyes, her skin, even the set of her lips, the unmistakable glow of a woman who has just made love. But then, she asked herself, would Robby even notice *that*?

Marty Quick's bathroom looked like a well-stocked drugstore in L.A. For a man in ostensibly good health, he was prepared for every possible illness or affliction, not to speak of soaps, powders, creams, ointments, pre-shaves, aftershaves, colognes of every description. Clearly he spent a good deal of his time in the bathroom, which was one of the good things about American men. Across the bath was a chrome stand with an ashtray, several scripts, a notepad, and a jar full of pencils.

Here, presumably, Marty lay in his scented bubble bath (there were half a dozen different varieties of colored bath salts in jars around the edge of the big marble tub) and read his mail—or dictated it, for there was a chair next to the toilet and the bidet, on which some woman had left a steno pad and an army-issue gas mask, a haversack containing cosmetics, a spare pair of unmilitary nylon stockings, a clean pair of even less military silk panties with lace edges, and a diaphragm case. One look at her watch told her that if she didn't hurry, even Robby might begin to wonder why she had left the theatre at four and arrived home at half-past seven, and she had no ready-made explanation to offer.

She finished her face, working as fast as possible. Could she have stopped off to see a film? No, it was out of character, and Robby would never believe it. An air raid or a buzz-bomb attack would have been useful, since she could have stopped to take shelter somewhere, but the Germans, still desperately fighting in Normandy, presumably had other things on their minds.

She tried to think of people she might have met by accident. Most of her friends were theatre people, and there was always the danger that Robby might have spoken to them, or seen them himself, so she plumped for Uncle Harry, safely ensconced at Langleit, who would certainly have dragged her off for a drink or tea had they met in the street.

She glanced at the edge of the mirror, where Quick had stuck cards, reminders, miscellaneous notes. There were membership cards to strange clubs she had never heard of in Mayfair and Soho, several photographs of young women, some with telephone numbers scrawled on them, a note from George Bernard Shaw thanking Quick for taking care of some unspecified problem with his U.S. royalties and politely declining the offer to write a film script of *Don Quixote*, a similar note from H. G. Wells, pasteboard invitations for drinks or dinner from an extraordinary range of people, including the Duke and Duchess of Westminster, Sir Alexander Korda, Binkie Beaumont, and Sir Meyer Meyerman. At the very bottom of the mirror was a note in Quick's handwriting that read, "Billy Dove, £100," and below that, in letters that might have been formed by a backward child, "Received," then a signature that might have been anyone's.

There was a puff of cigar smoke; she looked up to see Marty, standing in the door, wearing his dressing gown, his hair plastered back, neat and shiny as the paint on a Rolls-Royce. She hated men who put grease on their hair, but for some reason she didn't mind it in Quick, whom it suited so well that it was difficult to imagine him wearing it any other way. "Amelia's waiting for you downstairs, honey. You can't miss her. She's a Robin, or whatever the hell they call them."

"A *Wren*, darling! Navy, as opposed to army or air force."

"Robin, Wren, what's the diff? Blue uniform, gold buttons, weird cap. She's got blond hair."

"I'll bet she does! Marty—who is Billy Dove? It's driving me mad. It's a familiar name, but I can't place it. A music-hall star? A comedienne?"

A furtive look crossed Marty's face, the grim, blank expression of a man who has been caught out. His smile was as brilliant as ever, but his eyes were half-closed, as if he were thinking up an answer as quickly as he could; the deep, dark pouches under them were blue-black, as if he were suddenly exhausted. "No," he said cautiously. "He's just a guy I met, did something for me. No way you could ever have met him."

"It *is* strange. The name sticks in my mind."

Quick flipped his cigar into the toilet, put his arms around her and gave her a kiss, gently, on the cheek, so as not to smear her makeup—the mark, she thought, of a man who knew how to deal with women when he put his mind to it. "You are some sexy broad, Lish," he said. "We should have done this a long time ago, way back in L.A., when we had the chance."

"It wouldn't have been a good idea then, darling. I'm not so sure it's a good idea now, for that matter."

"You only live once, Lish, honey. I've never regretted anything I ever did that gave me pleasure."

She squared her shoulders and walked to the door. "You're a lucky man, Marty," she said, with just a touch of sadness in her voice. "I wish I could say the same."

Amelia was easy enough to find—a tall, slim, blond young woman in a well-tailored navy uniform, standing to attention beside a black Bentley with an American flag on the front fender—apparently Quick had upgraded his transport as well as his driver.

There was an unmistakable gleam of curiosity and hostility in the young woman's eyes, however polite her manners were on the surface.

"Colonel Quick gave me the address, Miss Lisle," she said crisply, in the clear, clipped tone of the upper class. "I'll have you home in a jiffy," she added breezily.

"Thank you." Felicia sat back in the car, all too conscious that she was at least fifteen years older than the girl driving it, whose skin had the look of a baby's, and who swung the big car around the corners with the careless abandon of youth. She closed her eyes, feeling suddenly tired, feeling, she supposed, "her age."

She rang the bell. The maid let her in so quickly that she must have been waiting behind the front door, with an expression that made it clear Robby had been asking where the hell she was for hours. Before she could get inside, she felt a tug on her sleeve, and turned to find Amelia standing beside her. "Mr. Quick asked me to make sure you got this," she said, and pushed into Felicia's arms the same carelessly wrapped parcel she had brought to Claridge's.

Before Felicia could say anything, the younger woman had turned on her heels. Felicia could not help noticing that the heels were higher and slimmer than they would have been on any footwear issued by the Royal Navy, and that Amelia's sheer black seamed stockings did not have the look of navy clothing either. She wondered if the blond naval rating was the one who took dictation while Marty was in the bath, and whose haversack was hung from the back of the chair. She had slept with Marty only once, and already she was feeling possessive, which was ridiculous, since he was clearly not a man any one woman could hope to possess.

"Where *have* you been, darling?" she heard Robby say, holding his anger in check in the presence of the maid.

"I quite forgot the time," she said. "I'm so sorry."

"Did you also forget that we're due for dinner at the Tarpons at eight?"

"Oh, *God!*"

"Well, it's all very well to say 'Oh, God!' as if they were the greatest bores on earth . . ."

"But they are, or as near as matters."

"Sir Herbert *does* just happen to be the one man who can get the Arts Council to put up money for rebuilding the theatre."

"Is Lady Tarpon the one with the blue-rinsed hair who looks like a not very convincing transvestite wearing an Edwardian evening gown?"

". . . And Lady Tarpon is one of your great admirers."

"I don't believe that for a moment."

"She told me so herself."

"She was lying. Or *you're* lying to make me feel better about going. I suppose I'd better change."

"We're going to be terribly late."

"Well, I can't go dressed like this, can I?"

"I shall have to telephone and say we'll be late. It's damn rude."

"Tell them it's my fault. If she's such a bloody fan of mine, she won't mind. You know perfectly well they'll have invited a lot of boring political people to show me off to."

"I know no such thing," he said sharply, his lips thin with anger and his jaw jutting forward, though a certain shifty narrowing of his eyes made it clear to her that he knew perfectly well that this was exactly what the Tarpons would do. He probably even knew who their fellow guests would be. "You still haven't said where you've been."

"Of course I did."

He looked baffled. "You did no such thing."

"Oh, Robby, darling, don't be tiresome. You've been so busy shouting at me about the ghastly Tarpons and their bloody dinner party that you didn't listen to a word I said. I saw Uncle Harry looking for a taxi outside White's, so I gave him a lift to the Connaught and he asked me to have tea with him. We were talking about Langleit, and time simply flew."

"I thought you hated talking about your childhood."

"Oh, don't exaggerate. Parts of it, perhaps, but not all of it. He looked rather well, I thought. The wicked flourish like the green bay tree, I suppose."

"And has Harry joined the navy? I noticed you came home with a Wren driver."

"I couldn't get a taxi, darling. You *know* what it's like at the Connaught, this time of day. A darling old admiral offered me his car, and knowing how madly late I was, I jumped at it. Now be a dear, make me a quick drink, and I promise I'll be bathed, changed, and ready to go in half an hour."

"Twenty minutes."

"Make it a double and you're on."

He was not exactly appeased, but the edge of his anger was blunted. The truth was that he disliked winning over people like the Tarpons as much as she did and enjoyed being "showed off" as if he were a circus freak no more than she.

She started up the stairs, already thinking about what she was going to wear. Just because it was certain to be a boring evening with people she despised was no reason not to dazzle them. She knew just the dress to do it, too, if she was going to sing for her supper—one of the last things Molyneux had made for her, a glorious ivory silk informal evening gown, so clinging and light that it might almost have been an exquisite short nightdress, with a lace neckline that was at once elegant and startling. There was not much she could do with her hair, but that was perhaps just as well, since wearing it simply made her look younger.

"Lisha, darling," she heard Robby call from the hall, "what's in the package?"

"Just a present from Harry," she said on the spur of the moment. "A painting he wanted me to have." Even as the words were out of her mouth it occurred to her that he would surely jump on the absurdity of what she'd said. If she had met Harry by chance, standing outside his club, why would he have with him a painting to give her? A child could see through it, she thought angrily. So much for improvisation!

But Robby didn't question it—nodded, in fact, as if it made perfect sense. "What is it?" he asked, instead.

This time she felt her heart flutter, like a fish that has just been landed. Sooner or later, Robby would see the painting, now that she had brought it into the house openly—she could hardly hide it away forever, or refuse to show it to him.

In for a penny, in for a pound, she thought, in sudden panic. "A Renoir," she said.

"A *Renoir*?"

"It's just a little one, from Harry's collection. I've had my eye on it for years. He gave me my lovely Laszlo portrait, remember?"

"That's quite different. Besides, I don't remember ever seeing a Renoir at Langleit."

"It used to be in Aunt Maude's sitting room, upstairs. Apparently, she's taken a dislike to it. You know how she is. You wouldn't have seen it. I'll never be ready if you keep asking me questions, Robby.''

"But why in God's name would Harry give you a painting as valuable as that on the spur of the moment?"

"It isn't 'the spur of the moment,' darling. I've been pestering him about it for years. Besides, it's not *that* valuable. There's always been some doubt that it's genuine. Not that it matters to me. Real or not, it's just as pretty.''

"A rose by any other name . . .'' she heard Robby say, as she closed her bedroom door—but of course, it wasn't true. Part of the Renoir's beauty lay in its authenticity.

She would just have to hang it and hope for the best, she decided, as she slipped out of her clothes while Alice poured her bath. She glanced at her watch—she was cutting things very fine. Then, as she lowered herself into the water, longing for the day when it would be lawful again to fill the tub to the top, she realized, with a deep, sinking feeling, that she had gotten herself into a deeper mess than ever.

She would have to talk to Harry Lisle and persuade him to back up her story.

When Robby brought her drink, she leaned back in the foam of her bathwater—no point taking the risk that he might notice her bruises—and drained it in one gulp, feeling the impact as the alcohol hit her stomach like a falling brick.

It didn't make her feel any better, at first. If there was anybody more bloody-minded than Harry Lisle when he wanted to be, she had yet to meet him—unless he was tickled by the situation, or was offered something he wanted in return. Well, she would have to tickle the old dragon in his lair. . . .

Suddenly, unexpectedly, she felt light-headed and optimistic. She was downstairs, fully dressed, made up, and ready to go, in twenty-two minutes flat. She hoped they'd arrive at the wretched Tarpons in time for another drink before dinner.

She had no doubt she was going to need it.

19

"You can't imagine how dull the Tarpons were."

"Yes I can. I've met 'em. He's a capon, she's a vulture who feeds on 'culture,' as she likes to call the arts and artists. Why on earth would Robby drag you there?"

"To impress them. Tarpon is supposed to be the man who decides on government grants to the arts."

"Oh, I daresay he is. One of 'em, anyway. So your husband—funny, I can't get used to calling Robby that— has bitten off more than he can chew with his theatre, eh? He should have listened to my advice."

"I don't think you offered any."

"Years ago. Warned him then. Every actor/manager in theatrical history has gone bankrupt trying to run his own theatre—Garrick, Kean, Irving, they all died paupers, or as good as. . . . Of course, the modern solution is to get the government to foot the bill, but mark my words, in the end that'll mean you'll have a Tarpon telling you what plays to put on. If Robby can't see that, he's an even greater fool than I thought he was. Why didn't he just go to the City and raise the money, like any other businessman? Because he doesn't have the guts, that's why."

"Harry," she said quietly, "shut up."

She had begun to notice that Harry Lisle's opinions were more extreme than they used to be, and that once he was started on a favorite subject, he was unable to stop. She wondered if it was simply that she was old enough now to have firm opinions not always in accord with his, or if he was showing the first signs of senility.

"Robby's my husband, Harry," she said. "I won't have you say that kind of thing about him to me."

"Oh, very well. Your loyalty does you credit. What brings you up to Langleit in such a rush, may I ask?"

"Well, I wanted to see Portia."

"I'm sure that's what you told Robby, and he may even believe it. But since you've managed to go for years without seeing her, I'm a little skeptical about this sudden onslaught of maternal feeling. Try again."

They were sitting in the garden in the late afternoon on one of those rare days when the English summer delivers warmth and a cloudless sky. Across the Channel, no doubt, the Allied troops in Normandy were at last receiving the air support they had been praying for, but here, looking out at the broad lawns trimmed and rolled every day by a small army of gardeners, it was impossible to imagine that war was so near. Behind them was a long terrace, hewn out of golden, warm Cotswold stone; on either side of them topiary bushes towered in extravagant profusion. A butler and two maids stood by in formation, ready to appear on call, but far enough away so as not to be able to overhear their conversation.

"Robby knows what he's doing when it comes to the theatre, Harry."

"Maybe. We'll see. I hope you haven't come looking for money to bail him out of his troubles. If he thinks the theatre is expensive, he should try thinking about what it costs to run *this* place! The gardens alone are enough to bankrupt a rajah. I don't know how much longer I can carry on, to tell you the truth."

This was a familiar, sad refrain. As the elder brother, Harry had received the Lisle family fortune intact. He owned coal mines in Wales, huge holdings of agricultural land in Canada, Australia, and Argentina, potteries in Derbyshire, a glass-works in Ireland, even a brewery. He was rich by any standards, and his only obligation was to maintain Langleit and pass it on intact and in good condition to the next heir. He lavished attention on Langleit for his own pleasure and kept it up to standards that were the envy of dukes. Why not? Having no children, he had money to spare. Like most of his fellow aristocrats, he pleaded poverty when it suited him— he had refused to let her come out as a debutante because of the expense, though perhaps it was just as well, since she had gone to RADA instead—but unlike some, he made no effort to hide his wealth behind a facade of shabbiness.

"I don't think he'd take money from you, Uncle Harry."

Lisle stared into his teacup as if he were going to read her fortune and chuckled. "Oh, I daresay he would, push come to shove. Most people do." He took the crocodile cigar case from his pocket and lit a cigar, preparing it with his usual delicacy. Lisle puffed contentedly, eyes half-closed as he watched the birds swoop and quarrel for the crumbs. "Havana," he said. "I was running short—never imagined the war would go on as long as it has—then, very luckily, I met a friend of yours, an American named Quick, and he managed to get me a new supply." He gave her a piercing look. "Remarkable fellow."

She lit a cigarette and looked into the far distance. "Yes?" she said, in a bored tone. "I suppose he is. Where did you meet him?"

"Sotheby's. He was bidding on a pair of Maillol bronzes. Nice little pieces. He overpaid for 'em, in my opinion, but I suppose he can afford to."

"I should think so."

"We fell into conversation, so I took him to lunch at my club. Thought it would be a treat for him, you know, lunch at White's for an American, bit of history, but it turned out he has lunch there all the time, had been there the day before with Hughie Percival—bloody servants all knew Quick as well as they knew me."

She laughed. "That *does* sound like Marty."

"He seemed to know a lot about me."

"Marty 'does his homework,' as he would say."

"Does he, indeed? But I think it went deeper than that. You must have told him a great deal about me. He knew all about your childhood at Langleit. Well, not all, perhaps, but a surprising amount. Knew things even I had forgotten. The name of your dog, believe it or not. You must have spent a lot of time chatting with him."

"There's always time to kill in the theatre. Let alone films. Hours of waiting."

"Oh, quite." He clearly didn't believe her. "Speaking of films, he tells me you and Robby are going to be doing *Don Quixote* for him. That should solve Robby's money problems, I'd imagine."

"I don't think so. Robby's dead set against doing it, as a matter of fact. If he makes any film, it will be Shakespeare. And he'll want to produce and direct it himself. He's had enough of Hollywood film-making."

"I don't get the impression that Quick is an easy fellow to say no to."

"Robby's quite good at saying no. To him. To anyone."

"So I've noticed. His attitude about Portia is bloody awkward, particularly when you consider that he's not the girl's father. I mean, he's been her stepfather for only a few weeks, and he's already asking that she come 'home.' It's damned impertinent."

"He wants a family."

"Does he now? Well, he can't expect to get one ready-made and off the shelf." He gave her a knowing look.

Across the lawn, in the far distance, there was a hint of purple haze as the afternoon drew to a close. She felt a warning trace of chill and dampness and pulled her shawl around her shoulders. "Harry," she said, "I need a favor."

He nodded. He had undoubtedly assumed that from the moment she called. Looking at him, she knew she ought to feel revulsion for the man, even hatred, but at the moment, she felt nothing of the kind. It was not so much that she trusted him as that there was nobody she trusted more. After all, for all practical purposes, he was the only family she had, however much he may have abused his position. It would have been ridiculous to say that Harry Lisle treated her like a daughter, in view of what had happened between them, but there was a certain truth to it. She turned her eyes on him. "It's important to me."

His eyes were hooded, almost as if he were asleep. "Go on," he said.

"There's a painting I received—as a present. I told Robby—well, I know this will seem silly—that it came from you. That it was part of the Langleit collection, something I'd admired for a long time.''

''A painting? What kind of painting?''

''A Renoir.''

He said nothing.

''It was a foolish thing to tell him, I realize that, but it was one of those things one blurts out, on the spur of the moment. . . .''

He knocked the cigar ash onto the lawn. ''It never fails to amaze me how a woman who is such a gifted actress can be such a bloody bad liar.''

''I'm not lying.''

''Not to me you're not, no. You simply haven't gotten around to telling me any of the truth yet. I meant to Robby. Why on earth would he believe such a farrago of nonsense?''

''Well, why wouldn't he? But the problem is that it isn't true. I need you to back me up.''

''What? Call Robby and say, 'Yes indeed, old boy, just in case you're wondering, it *was* me who gave Lisha the Renoir'? Don't be daft, girl.''

''If he should ask, I meant. If the subject should ever come up.''

''I don't even know what the bloody thing *looks* like, do I? What am I supposed to say if I see it? 'Oh, is *that* the painting I gave Lisha? Funny, but I didn't recognize it at first.' ''

''It's a small still life of flowers, very bright and colorful. I can describe it.''

He grinned. ''No need. I was at Christie's when it was sold. It was in Billy Ponsonby's collection, and he had to let it go, along with some other quite pretty things, now that Moira's asked him for a divorce. She should have known to begin with, the silly bitch, that if ever she found Billy in bed with someone, it wouldn't turn out to be another woman. . . . Still, to give him his due, he does have good taste, like a lot of pansies. It's a nice painting. Quite fancied it myself, but the price went beyond me. That's the trouble with the impressionists nowadays. They're pretty and they're fashionable—

and they look good on the walls, so decorators love 'em. Once that's happened, my dear, when the rich Americans, the rich Jews, and the rich queers start buying up a painter, or a period, or a school, it's all over for the rest of us. Your friend Quick paid a packet for that painting, but it's going to be worth a lot more to anyone who has the patience to wait. You're a lucky girl.''

''Well, he's very keen to have me in this film of his . . .''

''Keen enough to spend thirty thousand pounds on a painting, then give it away? And if that's all that's involved, why bother to cook up a cock-and-bull story about me, for Robby's sake? Why not just tell him, 'Look, darling, Marty's so keen to have us in his film that he gave us this lovely painting.' Of course, you're a grown-up woman, and you can do as you please, but if you were going to begin an affair with someone not three weeks after your marriage, Mr. Quick, much as I appreciate his help over the cigars, may not be your wisest choice.''

One look at Harry Lisle's face was enough to tell her that denials would merely irritate him. ''What makes you say that?'' she asked instead.

''For one thing, he's not discreet. When we had lunch together, he never stopped talking about you for a moment. It was Lisha this and Lisha that, the whole luncheon, and of course the chap's got a voice that carries, doesn't he? So I expect half the membership of White's overheard him. Mind you, I rather liked him, myself. Not sure at all you wouldn't be better off with him than with Robby, who's always struck me as a bit of a cold fish offstage, as you know.''

''I won't hear a word against him, Harry.''

''My dear! I'm not the one who's carrying on behind his back before the wedding presents have even been used. Just out of curiosity, how do you justify all this to yourself?''

''I don't. I can't. I love Robby. It's just that we used to be the most romantic couple in the world, for us, for everybody, and now we can't live up to our billing anymore, like a pair of old troupers who are too stiff in the knees to dance, but don't know anything else to do. . . .''

"You shouldn't have married him, you know. You left it until it was too late. No marriage succeeds without illusions."

"Perhaps. But it's done."

"And now you're in the process of undoing it?"

"I don't think so."

"Are you falling in love with Quick?"

"Does it matter?"

"Surely not to me. But to *you*? I think it ought to. If Quick is just a little healthy fun on the side, all very well and good, *if* you can get away with it—no harm done, really, or not much. After all, Robby's lost interest in you. Maybe he's found someone else, maybe he's wrapped up in his work, maybe he still can't cope with whatever happened in America between you. Whatever the reason, he's not giving you what you want, and he probably hasn't for a long time, and marriage is no substitute for it, no more than a knighthood or appearing onstage every night as the world's most glamorous theatrical couple is. So if Quick is the antidote, and it works, by all means take it. On the other hand, if you're falling in love with Quick"—he pronounced the word "love" with acute distaste, as if it were a middle-class notion, like not running up debts with one's tailor or eating "dinner" at lunchtime—"that's quite another matter."

"What if I am?"

"If you are, you're making a serious mistake. Quick's probably quite a decent bloke in his own rough-hewn way, but I suspect he's absolute hell on women who fall in love with him, and a real terror if he thinks he might be falling in love himself. I've seen it before—a thousand times. To a chap like Quick, love's a chink in the armor, if *he* feels it, and a weakness in you, if *you* feel it. He's like a shark that scents blood in the water. He has to bite—even if he tears open his own belly." He puffed contentedly. "Sad, really."

It occurred to her that he was talking about himself as much as about Quick. Harry Lisle was the master pragmatist. Once upon a time the slightest hint of sentiment had been enough to make him snarl. "I wouldn't call Marty 'sad,' frankly," she answered him. "I've never seen him looking sad for an instant. To begin with, he has no capacity for reflection that I've ever noticed. That's part of his charm. Robby's always acting, or thinking about acting, locked up somewhere inside himself where I can't reach him, but Marty's all there, right on the surface: 'What you see is what you get,' as he's so fond of saying."

"You may get more than you bargained for, that's all I'm saying. Poke your fingers too far in the cage and the animal will bite. So you mustn't blame anyone but yourself when you lose your fingers. You can push Robby hard and the worst he'll do is to sulk and play rough, but you push a chap like Quick just a little bit and he'll go for you. I recognize the type."

"Do you now?"

"Don't be smart with me, my girl. I suspect he carries things a lot farther than I ever did. Doesn't have the breeding, you see—doesn't have our English passion for putting up a respectable front." He gave her an appraising stare, like a man admiring a horse. "Lucky fellow, I must say. Maturity suits you. If Robby's too bloody dense or self-absorbed to take advantage of it, it's a good thing *someone* does. Shame to let it go to waste."

He stood up, not as steady on his feet as he used to be. Until recently, he had carried a cane for show, but now he leaned his weight on it for real, the knuckles of his right hand white with pressure. "Getting chilly," he grumbled. "We'll go inside, have a drink, then perhaps you can pop up to the nursery to see Portia."

He waved toward the servants, signaling them to remove the tea things, and put his arm in hers, not, as she was instantly aware, from affection, but so that she could help him climb the stone steps.

Even when they reached the smooth, flat surface of the terrace itself, he walked with the precise, careful steps of the old, as if at any moment something unseen might trip him up. He made his way through the open French windows into what was always known as the "small drawing room," to distinguish it from the much larger and more ornate room which had been the province of Lady Lisle until she turned herself into a recluse.

He seldom entered the bigger one, in which it would have been possible for a dozen people to sit without any of them being close enough for easy conversation. His drawing room was beautifully paneled, hung with some of his favorite paintings, brilliant with flowers that were grown year-round in his own hothouses, and the haunt of his most favored dogs. It was a room that reflected his personality, a curious combination of country squire and aesthete. She shivered slightly as she entered it. It held ambiguous memories for her.

In front of the fire was the big leather sofa on which, as a girl, she had spent so many hours of humiliation and shame. Above the fireplace hung a Romney portrait of an early Lady Lisle, in whom Felicia had always seen a startling resemblance to herself. The other paintings in the room were less conventional—a Klimt nude, so overblown and decadent that it seemed not only foreign but subversive in the English countryside, an Utrillo, a Pre-Raphaelite painting that she had always loved, a Modigliani nude, and one of Turner's sunsets, glowing in brilliant red and gold against the burnished wood grain of the Grinling Gibbons paneling. A chrome Brancusi sculpture, perhaps a bird, perhaps a stylized phallus, rose spotlighted from a marble base on which Harry Lisle had—almost certainly not by chance—draped several dog leashes and hunting whips. The carpet was a priceless Bokhara, one she had sought for years to find the equal of, but it was covered with grimy old pillows on which the older and more favored of Lisle's many dogs lay wheezing and growling in their sleep.

Lisle made his way through them to a table laden with bottles and made them both a drink. The silver ice tongs with their little claws had always fascinated her as a girl. There was something sinister about them, the suggestion of an instrument of torture, which had made her shudder every time Harry Lisle picked them up. From time to time she had had nightmares about them, seeing those beautifully sculptured sterling silver claws red with blood. She shuddered now as he used them to pick up an ice cube and drop it into her glass.

He lowered himself heavily into his favorite armchair, sighed, and put one foot up on an upholstered gout stool. The room had the unmistakable odor that remained forever associated in her mind with maleness, a blend of old leather, dogs, and cigar smoke—for Lisle was old-fashioned enough not to smoke indoors except here and in the dining room, after the ladies had withdrawn, when he gave a formal dinner party. Behind him on the wall was an old linenfold corner cupboard, the key to which he carried on his watch chain. She wondered if it still contained his collection of what he liked to call his "erotica"—the braided dog whips, the cunningly wrought little chains, purchased in some sinister backstreet shop in Paris, the rows of leather straps and masks, the carefully selected library, bound in the finest leather, the photograph albums that had once appalled and fascinated her. . . . She told herself she wasn't afraid of him anymore, and almost believed it for a moment. "You haven't answered my question," she said.

"Which question would that be?"

"I need you to back up my story."

"Ah, yes. The Renoir. It's a bloody silly story. Not up to your standard at all."

"Admittedly, but it will have to do." She watched as he sipped a drink, something of his old energy coming back to him. "I'm asking for a very small favor, Harry," she said. "After all that's happened between us over the years, it's not much to ask."

"Oh, ay? It's not the first time I've pulled your chestnuts out of the fire for you, is it? And precious little I've had in return."

"Are you going to make me beg, Harry?"

"The thought *had* crossed my mind. You used to be good at it, but I suppose we all learn new tricks. Or forget the old ones." He gave her an acidulous smile. "We had some good times, right here in this room, on that sofa, didn't we, lass?"

"*You* did, yes. I don't want to think about it."

"Do I detect the voice of conscience making itself heard after all these years? You were a very willing pupil, my dear. A willing victim, too. But of course that's part of your attraction, isn't it, even now? The illusion of vulnerability—it's the most potent of aphrodisiacs.''

''For some men.''

He shrugged. ''For the kind of men you seem to like, my dear, to be quite fair. Alas, Robby isn't one of them.'' He stared at her over the rim of his glass, cheerful now that he was in control of the situation. ''What if I were to tell you that I'll back your story up if you strip off your clothes and get down on your knees in front of me?''

She felt the sudden warmth of anger on her cheeks. ''I'd tell you to fuck off, Harry,'' she said, trying to keep her voice as level and unemotional as possible.

''You're blushing. A very pretty—and unexpected—effect. Modesty becomes you, I must say, even if you have discovered it rather late in life.'' He laughed, showing his strong white teeth. Just like her father, he was not only devilishly handsome, but had grown more so with age, the way a certain kind of Englishman always does. It annoyed her that she still found him attractive. ''It's all right,'' he said. ''I've never been tempted to repeat the past, even when I could. It's invariably disappointing. I was just curious to see what you'd say.''

''Harry, Marty Quick has a delightfully vulgar phrase he uses all the time: 'Stop jerking me off.' If you don't understand, I can explain it, but in the meantime, *Stop jerking me off*! If you won't help me, *don't*! I'm not getting down on my knees to you.''

He nodded, obviously pleased with himself. ''A brave little speech. I should applaud. But you and I both know it's all sham, dear heart, don't we? In the end, you'd do *anything* to prevent Robby from knowing the truth—anything at all. I suppose that's a form of love, if you like, a way of protecting him—or his illusions. I've done the same for Maude for years.''

''I've never seen the slightest sign that you love her.''

''Then you don't know a bloody thing about love,'' he snapped, his good humor evaporating instantly. This was the Harry Lisle she remembered and feared. In her childhood these changes of mood had usually been accompanied by physical violence, and even now she found herself wincing involuntarily, preparing for the blow. But nothing happened, except for a brief flash of triumph in Harry's eyes as he noticed her fear. She raged at herself—twenty years of acting, and she had not managed to hide her emotions from him.

"I'll tell you what I want," he said. "I want the girl."

"Portia? What do you mean?"

"Have you ever thought what's going to happen to all this?" He waved his hand at the paintings, like a magician about to perform a trick.

"Not really. I don't care a damn."

"Yes? That's part of the problem, you see. I have no children. When I die, Langleit will pass to your dear father, together with the fortune and the title, but there's a catch. In his youth, your father could never forgive me for having been born before him. He would have sold his soul, had he been religious, to be the heir to Langleit. Now, paradoxically, he doesn't *want* it, just to be bloody-minded, I suppose. In the event that he should outlive me, he will not accept the title, the money, or the estate. What am I to do? If he wishes to end his days living in a tent, in the company of lions and savages, it is hardly for me to persuade him otherwise. *You* have not shown the slightest interest in having Langleit over the years, and though Charles could probably do a perfectly good job of running it, you are no longer married to him. *Do* you want Langleit? Not that I'm promising it to you."

"Absolutely not."

"Just so. Your father refuses, and you don't care. I propose to see that Portia gets it, in trust. It will mean that the title dies out, but that can't be helped. Langleit has always mattered to me more than the title. I want somebody with my blood to have it, and keep it together—paintings, swans, and all. I'd rather it were a boy, but since there isn't one, it's going to have to be my daughter. . . ."

"I will *not* have you saying that she's your daughter!"

"Whatever you will or won't, we both know she is." It was getting colder in the room. He leaned over and stirred the fire with the poker. The effort seemed to tire him, and it occurred to her that his concern for the future of Langleit was not altogether abstract. "I wish to be her guardian *in loco parentis*. In return she shall be my heir."

"You can't imagine that I'm simply going to give you my own daughter?"

"I can't imagine that you'll refuse. Charles has already agreed. And why not? The child will be heir to a fortune and one of the great houses of England. Besides, I'm not proposing to send Portia to Australia, or to cut her off from her parents. She will continue to live here—where, by the way, she is perfectly happy. She thinks of Langleit as her 'home,' and it will become so in fact, legally, that is all. She can visit you, you can visit her, just as you do now, but her home will be here, with me."

"Harry, here, in this room, of all places, I don't see how you can even *suggest* this. . . ."

"Be sensible. I can't change the past. Neither can you. She's a little girl, and she loves it here."

"With you?"

"With me, of course, as long as I live. She loves me, you know. In my old age, I'm discovering paternal qualities I never knew I had—or *grand*paternal ones."

"Robby will be furious."

"He has no possible right to be. The fact that he gets along with the child—or that he thinks he likes children—is no reason for him to expect to have Portia as if she were his. Besides, how much time would Robby have to give a child? He's an ambitious, busy man, who by your own admission is very seldom home. If you agree to this, you have my word I will back up your story about the Renoir. It's not a bad bargain, when you think about it."

"I want to see her."

"So you shall."

He rose to his feet stiffly and shuffled toward the door, holding out his left arm for her to take. Together they made their way out into the enormous Palladian hall, with its marble floors and painted ceiling, the folly of the second Lord Lisle, who returned from a grand tour of Italy determined to emulate the glories of Rome at home, and went bankrupt in the process. Lisle's progress on the marble floors was painfully slow, as if he were terrified of slipping, and several servants appeared as soon as he entered the hall to station themselves at strategic intervals in case he did. His progress up the broad marble stairs was slower still, and she noticed that his face had turned an unhealthy white, his lips an unpleasant shade of violet. He paused for breath halfway up to the first landing, legs shaking. One of his eyes seemed unable to open fully, the other was filmed with tears—of anger, she guessed, at his own impotence. "Shouldn't you have a lift put in?" she asked. "These stairs can't be good for you."

He looked at her blankly with the one eye that was open, his breath coming in ragged gasps. "Lift?" he asked thickly. "What do you mean? Who the bloody hell are you?"

She thought he was joking, but then, quite suddenly, she realized that for a moment Harry Lisle hadn't had the faintest idea who she was. Had he had a stroke recently?

His breathing evened out; as his lungs filled, his color returned a little, his eyes became more animated. "I'm sorry," he said, in a more normal voice. "What did you say?"

"I said you ought to put in a lift."

"Don't need one. Couldn't have it done in wartime, anyway, Lisha, you know that, for God's sake. I'm just a little tired. Had a bout of the flu a few weeks back. Haven't recovered yet."

He seemed to pull himself together, and he made it up the rest of the stairs rather more briskly—but clearly he had been absolutely unable to recognize her for at least thirty seconds and, just as clearly, didn't even know it had happened. She could not help wondering just how good his word was—in a bout of sudden senility he might blurt out anything, or forget what he had promised. Considering the secrets he had so far kept to himself all these years, it was a frightening prospect. She had always thought of him as evil, with the devil's own strength, but a weak Harry Lisle frightened her more.

Harry opened the nursery door, to reveal Nanny, arms crossed in front of her bosom, standing guard implacably, her rimless pince-nez glistening. "Good evening, madam," she said in a tone that suggested she would be just as happy never to see Felicia again—but that was always the way with nannies when they were allowed to take over a child. They might forgive an absent father, but never an absent mother.

"Good evening, Nanny," she said. "How is Portia?"

"All this excitement isn't good for her. She won't sleep tonight, you mark my words. I shall be up at all hours making her warm milk. Perhaps it would be better to see her at breakfast. . . ."

"I have to leave tonight, Nanny, dear. I could *only* come down for the afternoon, you see, Mr. Vane and I are in rehearsal." She hated herself for sweet-talking Nanny, particularly since it never did any good.

Nanny sniffed, disapproval evident in every line of her face. "I daresay. Portia, dear! Your mother is here."

A door opened, and Portia peeked out, her face set in a sulky adolescent's frown as she looked at her mother. Felicia felt the familiar combination of intense love and deep resentment at her daughter's determination not to charm. She smiled and threw her arms open, as Portia dashed into the room, bigger and stronger than ever, and ran to put her arms around Harry. "Kiss your mother like a good girl," he said gruffly. Portia obeyed with a wooden reluctance that made Felicia want to cry.

She looked up at Harry Lisle, expecting to see a triumphant smile on his face—but what she saw instead was an expression of love so deep as to be unmistakable, transforming the evil seducer of her childhood into an altogether softer person.

Harry had always told her that what he had wanted most out of life was a child. He had taken her as a woman, instead—and the irony of it was that in the end she had given him the child he wanted.

She nodded her agreement.

All the way home in the Bentley, she cried.

"You're blue."

"Why 'blue,' I wonder? People are always saying they're blue in American songs. Why not green, or yellow? But I suppose I *am* blue, yes."

"How come?"

"I went to Langleit yesterday to see my daughter. It was an upsetting day."

"Kids are a pain in the ass."

"I'll treasure those words of wisdom."

"Don't get snotty with me, Lish. I'm sorry you had a bad day, but it wasn't my fault."

She rolled over in bed, glanced at the clock, concluded that she didn't have to get dressed just yet. She wasn't dying to see Robby again, not after six straight hours of rehearsing *Othello*, most of them spent arguing with him. It was as if his only concern was how *he* would be received in blackface, with no thought at all about *her* performance. What was worse was that whenever she touched him, he drew away, as if she were contaminated. Of course, she recognized that it was a clever touch, a way of showing the audience how repelled Othello is by the slightest physical contact with Desdemona when he no longer trusts her, how disgusted even the faintest reminder of his sexual passion for her makes him feel, once Iago has succeeded in poisoning his mind—but it seemed to her that Robby's reaction was unstudied, even spontaneous. It made her realize, too, that in fact he drew away whenever she reached out to him. Before long she was beginning to cling to him desperately, which wasn't in character for Desdemona at all, and the rehearsal soon degenerated into an angry scene between them, played out in public, with Toby Eden, beet-red from embarrassment, and Guillam Pentecost, radiating malevolent *Schadenfreude*, as peacemakers. She could not imagine how they could be ready for the opening in three days.

She turned over and put her arms around Marty, feeling the comforting hardness of his muscles, the still unfamiliar shape of his body. Lying in bed with him was like being a tourist in a strange country with a landscape still to be learned. She touched him constantly, not so much in passion as out of curiosity, as if she were looking for part of herself. "Marty," she said, "just shut up and fuck me, please."

It was strange, she thought, but Marty Quick brought out the bitch in her, as well as the slut, as nobody ever had before. Odder still, he was unable to hide the fact that he didn't like it. Classy women didn't talk in bed like whores.

In his own way, she thought, he was a romantic, who genuinely believed in the fundamental purity and innocence of women, which, of course, he wanted to despoil—and this, despite having been married to what he himself described as "some of the toughest broads this side of a prison matron," and a lifetime of seamy experiences with women.

She found herself talking to him with just the kind of upper-class contempt that he rightly described as "snotty," and which wasn't her usual style at all. To some degree, of course, he asked for it—he *wanted* her to be a bitchy, aristocratic Englishwoman who despised him and didn't bother to hide it, but who couldn't stay away from his bed or his cock. She recognized, too, that she was flirting with danger, which was part of the excitement of an affair with Marty Quick in the first place. She had no doubt that if she provoked him hard enough he would strike back with real violence, but she didn't know how far she could go before that happened, so she tested him constantly. It was like poking a bear in the ribs, but she was unable to stop herself.

"You wanna be fucked, I'll fuck you," Quick said, in the tone of a man who was hoping to be left alone for a catnap. One thing she had to admit—if what you wanted was sex, Marty could certainly give it to you. He was not an inspired or an imaginative lover, but in his matter-of-fact way he was always ready for more. Which was just as well, for sex was the only thing that made it possible, these days, for her to forget about the rest of her problems.

"Turn over," he ordered.

"I'm quite comfortable as I am," she snapped back. She had drunk two glasses of champagne on an empty stomach, after a whole day of rehearsals, which, far from calming her down, made her nervous and edgy. Certainly she was not about to be told what to do in bed by Marty Quick after a day of being told what to do onstage by Robby.

"I said, 'Turn over!'" Quick slapped her sharply, not hard by his standards, but hard enough to sting. Instinctively she raised her hand to claw his face, but he caught her wrist, twisted her arm behind her back and used it to flip her over. Once she was facedown he straddled her, despite her struggles and moans, which, she had no doubt, were exactly what he wanted to hear. She gave in, willing enough to submit for the moment.

She waited until he was finished, then snuggled up close to him, letting him kiss her. But just as their lips touched, she ran her nails hard down his back, drawing blood, and laughed.

"Shit!" he shouted, more out of surprise than pain, and hit her hard with the flat of his hand.

Well, you got what you wanted, girl, she told herself, her head still ringing from the blow. You got fucked, and you got hit, good luck to you! But she felt a burst of nausea and pain, combined with sudden self-disgust. She wondered whether it was the affair or the drinking that was the problem, or whether it might be a good idea to give up one of them.

Quick was out of bed, standing naked at the foot of the bed, running his hand down his back. He looked at the blood on his hand with dismay. "What the hell did you do *that* for?" he asked, a trifle plaintively.

"I don't like to have my head pushed into the pillow, thank you. I'm afraid of suffocating. The Desdemona Complex. I've told you that before."

"You like this, you like that. What d'ya think I am? A gigolo?"

"No, darling. I think you'd need a little more refinement to succeed as one."

He stared at her angrily. "Ah, the hell with it," he said at last, and stamped off to the bathroom, slamming the door behind him. She had no doubt that he was in there washing down his scratches and dabbing antiseptic on them.

She reached for her cigarettes on the bedside table, lit one, then fumbled around until she found her glass and gulped down what was left in it.

Harry was right, she told herself. Loving Marty was bound to lead to trouble, all the more so since he probably didn't want to be loved. Still, there it was. She hated every moment when she was away from him, even when she was onstage, and she hadn't felt that way about anyone since the early days of her affair with Robby. She was amazed that she could feel anything of the sort with Marty Quick——of all people! He was the wrong person in every way, yet it didn't matter. Or perhaps it was what *did* matter.

She rummaged through the mess on the bedside table looking for an ashtray among the evidence of Marty's insomnia —books, papers, memo pads, half-completed crossword puzzles. . . . He did not seem to have either the skill or the patience to finish the *Times* puzzles, and she was tempted to do some for him. She picked one up, quickly completed a word, then drew a circle around it. She turned the circle into a heart, before she even realized what she'd done.

Dr. Vogel had been fascinated by doodles, which he compared to "visible dreams," but her own were too simple to require much interpretation. Marty, she was interested to see, would have engaged Dr. Vogel's attention fully—*his* doodling was apparently richly complex. Sheet after sheet of Claridge's expensive gray notepaper was covered with elaborately intertwined dollar and pound signs, along with carefully drawn nudes, some of which, she was mildly pleased to see, resembled her. Quick, though no draftsman, had cleverly caricatured her face, the heart shape of it, the big eyes, and the mass of dark hair, and lavished a good deal of attention on her small waist and legs. He had not devoted much attention to her breasts, which had caused Si Krieger so many problems when she had first arrived in Hollywood. He had wanted them padded and she had refused point-blank.

Another notepad was full of sketches for *Don Quixote*. The figures were rough, sticklike, but recognizable. She flicked through it, impressed by Quick's unexpected skill.

A letter was folded in the pad. Thinking that it was probably another note from Sylvia or her replacement, she opened it with a smile, only to find that it was from a firm of solicitors, marked "Confidential." It amused her to read Quick's personal correspondence, but she had very little interest in his business affairs. She did not put the letter back, however, for in the middle of the page, underlined, she read "Re Robert Vane, Esq. and the Duke of York Theatre." She usually found legal letters boring and incomprehensible, particularly those from English solicitors, who seemed to have developed a Dickensian language of their own, expressly intended to puzzle the lay person. This one, however, was simple enough. A gentleman with a flowing and illegible signature was pleased to inform Mr. Quick of further details of Mr. Robert Vane's lease of the Duke of York Theatre. There followed a string of numbers that was meaningless to her, except that they clearly indicated the growing weight of Robby's debts.

She didn't have to guess that Marty was looking into Robby's financial affairs—particularly the theatre, which was his Achilles' heel.

She would have to find some way of warning Robby, she decided, already beginning to feel the ground moving a little under her feet. If she was going to have a lover, it would have been a good idea to pick one who wasn't trying to undermine her own husband!

She glanced at her watch impatiently. Really, she thought, anybody would think Marty had been bitten by a rabid dog! She swung herself out of bed, slipped into his dressing gown and walked to the bathroom door. Over the sound of running water, she could hear him talking on the telephone. She smiled. There were men who fell asleep after making love (Robby was in that class), men who had to light a cigarette, men who wanted to talk, and men who wanted to remain silent—but Marty always wanted to make telephone calls. Sometimes when they were in bed, she could see him cast a longing glance toward the phone when he thought she wasn't looking. She had taunted him mildly on the subject but had come to the conclusion that it was one of those things you couldn't change about Marty, if indeed you could change anything at all. It wasn't like him, however, to spare her feelings by going into the bathroom to make a call. Usually he was perfectly open about it—although if he was talking about some deal he had going, he would occasionally whisper to her, "You didn't hear that, okay?" accompanied by a ferocious scowl.

So far she hadn't heard anything that interested her much—it was hard to work up much curiosity about the details of motion-picture financing, or putting on ice shows. She stood close to the door, just about to tell him to hurry up, when she overheard him say, quite clearly, in a tone of voice that was at once matter-of-fact and threatening, "I don't care how the fuck long we've known each other, you'll do this or I'll break you." There was a pause. "Does the name 'Billy Dove' mean anything to you?" Another silence. "Don't screw around with me. You met him outside the Ritz. Since then you've been meeting at a pub, the Fox and Grapes, am I right? Stop acting, you can't lie to me. Because I've got *photographs*, my friend, that's why. . . ."

She backed away suddenly, tripping over the robe, which was far too big for her. Quick must have heard a noise, because he turned up the taps so that she could no longer hear what he was saying. She knew what the Fox and Grapes was, all right—it had been Robby who had mentioned it to her. As for Billy Dove, the mention of the Ritz Hotel finally reminded her who *he* was—the young man who had befriended her the night she ran from the opening of *Richard III* in the rain.

She could see him clearly in her mind, walking beside her in his shabby raincoat and his cracked shoes, his voice gentle and soothing. She suddenly remembered, all too sharply, that he had told her one of his clients was a great and famous actor.

She went into the living room, where she had seen the note about Billy Dove on Quick's desk, but it was gone. She opened the drawer and poked around. Nothing caught her attention except an expensive leather address book. She opened it and saw, stuck in the back, a fragment torn from a photograph.

She turned on the desk light and stared at it. It was a dark, grainy picture, obviously taken at night with a small camera, the kind of snapshot that most people would probably throw away. It appeared to be a picture of two men leaving a pub, their hands touching. One of them, his profile turned to the camera, was unmistakably Billy Dove, his features pinched and pale even in the poor light. The other man had his back to the camera. Her heart skipped a beat at the familiar double-breasted jacket, elegantly cut, the coat slung casually over the broad shoulders, the rakish fedora cocked to one side, the way he had worn it in the old days. She couldn't see the face, nor could she even make out the color of the hair, but something about the suit, the posture, the hands thrust deep in the jacket pockets, thumbs forward, and above all, the hat, reminded her of Robby.

She was not sure which horrified her more—the sudden realization that there was a reason for Robby's indifference over the past few months or the fact that Marty Quick was all too obviously attempting to blackmail him. She knew Quick's reputation included blackmail, but she had believed he would never do anything like that to Robby, or to her. As for Robby, he had lied to her about his relationship with Randy Brooks and continued to lie to her about himself— for he had never admitted what was all too obviously true.

She took the photograph, ran back into the bedroom and began to pull her clothes on as fast as she could, suddenly stricken with a terrible feeling of claustrophobia and nausea at the sight of the rumpled bed. She knew she couldn't stay here a moment longer, and yet there was somehow a part of her that didn't want to go, that same feeling she had had years ago with Harry Lisle, when she had wanted to run, or to turn and kill him, yet stayed, hating herself for it.

She grabbed her handbag, stuffed the photograph into it, and ran from the room, just as the bathroom door clicked open, releasing a cloud of steam and cigar smoke.

The noise outside was appalling as the ground crews ran up the engines of the big bombers, one after another, to full throttle, making the sheets of plywood that closed off the empty windows shiver and creak.

Randy Brooks held a hand over one ear while he pressed the receiver as hard as he could against the other to hear what Marty Quick was saying. Given his special status, Colonel Fruchter was more than happy to let Brooks use his office, but there was no quiet, not with a whole wing of B-17s just down the road.

Only the day before, while he had been taking a call from

his father-in-law, Leo Stone, from Los Angeles, the whole base had been rocked by a mammoth explosion that shattered every window. Brooks had narrowly escaped having his throat cut by the flying glass from Fruchter's windows and had assumed that a German V-bomb had struck the base, but it turned out that one of the ground crews had dropped a bomb from its shackles without having checked to see that it hadn't been fused.

Stone, who had jumped to the same conclusion as Brooks when he heard the explosion reverberating through his telephone seven thousand miles away, had immediately called the papers with the news, so there were headline stories all over America, describing how Randy Brooks, America's beloved comedian, had stuck courageously to his post in the middle of a German air raid. There were calls to award him a medal, a VFW chapter in Burbank announced that it would henceforth be named after Randy Brooks, a proposal was cabled to him from Si Krieger for a movie of his war exploits, as well as innumerable requests for interviews, all of which he turned down. "It won't do you any good," Fruchter had warned him solemnly. "You're just going to get yourself a reputation for being modest as well as a hero. Keep your mouth shut, and you can be the first Hollywood comedian to run for the Senate and win."

As for Fruchter, the sudden fame that had descended on him as Randy Brooks's commanding officer had given him a new lease on life—he was talking about having Sylvia, Marty Quick's ex-driver, transferred to the United States Army and commissioned. "If Ike could do it for Kay Summersby," he said, "why not?" There were even rumors that a star was in the pipeline for him.

Randy himself, however, had found the whole experience profoundly depressing. The terror of the explosion and the fear of being decapitated by glass shards were bad enough; worse was the sight of the crater, in which a huge four-engined bomber had simply disappeared, leaving only some blackened aluminum scattered round the site, together with grisly reminders of the frailty of human life—part of a leg, still wearing a G.I. boot, a hand, the fingers outstretched as if begging for help, with a high-school class ring on one finger, many small, unidentifiable bits and pieces of bone and flesh, which unlucky disciplinary offenders were busy collecting in tin pails. Brooks had long since come to the conclusion that sanity, like bravery, was a diminishing asset in war. Each man started out with a certain amount and used it up day by day until, eventually, everyone would end up as insane cowards, some, of course, before others. The explosion had used up what remained of *his* courage, and his instant acclaim as a hero, while the men who had died were gathered up in buckets, had used up, he felt, the balance of his sanity. He was in no mood to deal with an angry Marty Quick.

It was not that he didn't *believe* Quick. During the twenty years that he and Marty had known each other, he had learned to take any threat from him seriously, and as for his reputation, while he didn't care that much about it himself, he still wanted to preserve it intact for Natalie.

His reserves of laughter were burned up, too. Lately, his soldier audiences were dismayed by his tone, which was increasingly bitter and strident. He knew it, but there was nothing he could do about it.

As he looked out at his audiences, the young faces, so many of them destined to die, he wanted to cry, he wanted to tell them that he loved them, to comfort them the way a mother might have comforted her son, and, of course, he couldn't, which broke his heart. The boys sensed that something was wrong, and it made them uneasy—so much so that Fruchter had suggested he take a rest, or even go back to the States. The only person who would have understood was Robby Vane. Now here was Marty Quick, trying to make him threaten Robby!

"Threaten Robby with what, Marty?" he asked, though he knew the answer.

Quick's voice was low, as if he were obliged to whisper, and, mysteriously, there was the sound of running water in the background. "You know what," he snapped.

"Are you calling from Niagara Falls? What's all that noise?"

"Never mind the fucking noise. Just *try*, all right? Do it

in a friendly way first, that's okay with me. If that don't work—and it probably won't—turn up the heat a little. Tell him it's important to *you*. If the son of a bitch still won't come around, hint, just *hint* that you've kept your mouth shut for a long time about what happened between the two of you, so he owes you one."

"Nothing happened between us. He doesn't owe me a thing."

"Don't bullshit *me*, Randy! You do this for me, or else . . ."

"I'd do a lot of things to help you, but I'm not going to pimp for you, and I'm not going to blackmail for you, certainly not over a lousy movie, and that's final."

"I don't care how long we've known each other," Quick growled, the noise of water growing stronger, so that Brooks, who was only a few hundred feet away from four Wright Cyclone aircraft engines being run up, could hardly understand a word he was saying. "You'll do this or I'll break you."

Brooks knew, more than most people, the pressures that were on Marty. He knew some of the people Marty raised his financing from, knew them from the old days, killers and leg-breakers one and all. He hadn't the slightest doubt that one of them had passed the word on to Marty that if he didn't deliver what he had promised soon, his old friends would come gunning for him. Marty was drowning, however well he managed to hide it, and if he didn't get help he would pull as many people down with him as he could. Brooks tried, but he couldn't make himself care, one way or the other. "Forget about it, Marty," he said gently, his voice sad. "I'm not going to threaten Robby for you. That's final."

"Does the name Billy Dove mean anything to you?"

Brooks closed his eyes. He could predict every step of the conversation. He felt a sudden exhaustion come over him. "It doesn't ring a bell, no."

"Don't screw around with me. You met him outside the Ritz. Since then you've been meeting at a pub. The Fox and Grapes, am I right? Stop acting, you can't lie to me."

"I'm not an actor. I'm a comedian. And what's all this crap about not lying to you?"

"Because I've got photographs, so don't bother."

"Photographs! Who's going to care, Marty?"

"Every gossip columnist and studio, that's who. Even your father-in-law Leo won't help you. As for Natalie, she'll have your balls."

"She's welcome to them. She can always have them made into earrings."

"Don't get funny with me. I'm gonna put the squeeze on your little friend Dove, Randy. He's gonna tell his story, all about how you took him upstairs to your room and seduced him . . ."

Brooks sighed. Of course young Dove would say that. For one hundred pounds he would probably say anything, and who could blame him? Besides, Marty would presumably have found some way of terrifying him, as well as paying him, just to make sure. It was sad, really, he thought: Billy was a nice enough young man, in no way capable of resisting Marty Quick—another victim in a world full of more or less innocent victims.

He assessed the threat. Marty could certainly destroy his career, ruin his reputation, and make Natalie miserable, if he wanted to. He could deny everything, of course, but it probably wouldn't help much, since there had always been rumors about him, and anyway, denial wouldn't do him any good, once he was facing Natalie. He knew her unwritten and unspoken rule—no public scandal. So long as she didn't *have* to know, she was content.

He could hear Quick whispering hoarsely, a meaningless gabble of threats. All of a sudden, he simply lost interest. He felt in him the strength of knowing he no longer gave a damn. "Marty," he interrupted politely, "I have to go." He hung up and walked swiftly out of Fruchter's office before Quick could ring back.

He stood outside for a moment, eyes closed against the summer sun. Then he put his G.I. cap on and walked over to the nearby hangar, where the ground crew was working

on a B-17. A dozen young men, under the command of a
sergeant who could not be more than nineteen himself, were
getting the aircraft ready for another raid at dawn. They
looked like teenagers working on their hot rods. The sergeant,
a freckled-faced boy from L.A., waved at him from the cockpit. "Hey, Randy," he shouted, "how's the big star?" Randy
put his cap on sideways, stuck one hand in his tunic and
imitated Napoleon, then he took the cap off, threw it high
into the air, did a quick buck-and-wing, and caught the cap
on his head as it fell. The crew laughed and applauded. Well,
he told himself, you can't beat the old vaudeville routines—
they never fail. "Hey, Sarge," he called up, "any chance
of going on the mission tomorrow?"

"*You?* You wanna fly on a mission? What are you, crazy?"

Brooks made a few faces and did his idiot act, a piece of
bravura physical comedy which always brought down the
house in the old days, and didn't fail him here. He caught
his breath and shrugged. "I want to see what it's like."

"Like? I went out once myself. You wanna know what
it's like? You're cold, shit-scared, and somewhere along the
way you start praying, that's what it's like. Do yourself a
favor—don't. Take my word for it."

"I promised a friend in Hollywood I'd go, Sarge. Big
producer. He's making a war movie, needs my advice."

Hollywood, of course, was the magic word. Anything was
possible if it came from there; any notion, however crazy,
made sense if it involved the movies. The sergeant nodded.
"I'll ask the skipper," he said. "He's a nice guy, from New
York, he knows who you are, he'll be happy to have you on
board for the ride. Is it okay with Colonel Fruchter?"

"It's his idea," Brooks said, knowing Fruchter would
never be out of bed at dawn to see him go.

"Leave it to me. I'll fix it. We'll get you kitted out and
sneak you on the plane."

"Thanks, Sarge." Randy Brooks felt a great calm come
over him. All his life he had taken risks, so what was one
more? He looked up and saw for the first time the name of
the aircraft painted on the nose. "The Last Laugh," it read,

in white script above a row of bombs and a cartoon of a man slipping on a banana peel in front of a sexy blonde who was leaning against a lamppost and laughing at him.

The story of my life, he told himself.

For the first time in months he was looking forward to tomorrow.

"I never know where she is half the time," Robby Vane grumbled, as he poured a whiskey and soda for Guillam Pentecost.

"Cheers," Pentecost said. His long frame was jackknifed into an armchair which would have dwarfed most men, but looked like a piece of children's furniture with him in it. "I don't know how you put up with it."

Vane was so taken aback that he splashed soda water on his shoes as he made his own drink. "My dear fellow! Felicia *is* my wife. I don't think I can allow you to say that kind of thing about her."

"I didn't mean Lisha, Robby. I meant marriage."

"Ah, marriage . . . has it occurred to you that the only plays Shakespeare wrote about married couples are *Othello* and *Macbeth*? That says it all, I think. . . ." He sat down and sipped his drink. "So what *do* you think of our *Othello* at this point, with two days to go? You've been uncharacteristically reticent."

"Not reticent. Merely careful. I don't want to further offend Lisha. Once bitten, twice shy."

"You don't think she's any good?"

"Actually, I think she's rather splendid in her own way, but she's destroying the play, scene by scene, and *you* are letting her do it. She's all fire and action—all very well for Lady Macbeth, but a little out of key for Desdemona."

Vane sighed. He dreaded having this kind of conversation with Felicia, but he knew Pentecost was right. "I'll talk to her about it," he said glumly.

"I wish you would, Robby, if it's not too late. The two of you don't seem to be playing *together*, if you see what I mean. Frankly, I wondered if perhaps there was something —wrong."

"Wrong?"

"Between you."

"Good God, no, nothing like that!" Vane said indignantly.

"Forgive my asking."

"Not at all. In fact, Lisha seems to have more energy lately, constantly on the go, always in a whirl. I was rather pleased by the change, actually."

"Yes, but onstage too much energy is as bad as not enough, sometimes." His eyes strayed to the far wall of the Vanes' sitting room, and he whistled. "I say, what a lovely little painting!" .

Vane turned and glared at it as if he wanted to will it away. "It's Felicia's," he said frowning.

"She has superb taste. Of course one knew that already. Where did you say she got it from?"

"I didn't. Her uncle—that old rogue Lisle—gave it to her. Been in his collection for years, I gather." Vane's voice suggested a certain irritation. He was not much interested in paintings, and having brought Pentecost home he wanted to talk about the play. Pentecost was one of those Englishmen who seemed to be equally knowledgeable about every art, which Vane found useful from time to time, but was something he didn't share at all.

"Surely not?"

"Absolutely. She's admired it for years, apparently. Never told me about it, but then why would she? Lisle must be thinking about his own mortality to give it to her, but there's a time when that happens to everyone, I suppose."

"Yes. But you know, I *saw* that painting at Billy Ponsonby's, not three months ago. He was complaining that he was going to have to sell it because Moira had asked him for a divorce. Said he didn't mind losing her, but he was really going to miss the Renoir."

"Must have been one just like it."

"No, as a matter of fact. It's an unusual painting—very small, for Renoir, who usually liked a nice big canvas for his flowers." Pentecost unfolded himself from his chair like a man getting up on stilts, and stalked over to the painting. He examined it carefully, ran his fingers over the surface, then took it off the wall and looked at the back. "I'm not wrong," he said. "This is Ponsonby's Renoir all right. There's a sticker on the back from Christie's. I was there when it was auctioned, in fact. Went for thirty thousand pounds."

"Thirty thousand! To whom? To Lisle? He wouldn't spend that kind of money on a painting, then just give it away to Felicia."

"I don't imagine he would, no. But it wasn't Lisle who bought that painting, Robby." Pentecost looked gloomy, his huge simian eyebrows lowered, his deep voice lugubrious. "Marty Quick bought the painting, Robby. He was determined to have it—apparently didn't care what it went for. Frankly, it didn't seem to me his kind of thing. Didn't seem that way to Ponsonby, either. Afterwards I overheard him asking Quick what he was going to do with it—whether he would keep it in England or send it back to the States. 'Keep it, hell,' Quick told him. 'This is a gift for my girl.' Ponsonby was a bit taken aback by that. 'She must be some girl!' he said."

"And then?" Vane asked quietly.

Pentecost sighed. "And then he laughed. 'You bet your life!' he said. 'She's going to be all mine—and her husband isn't even going to know it!' "

Pentecost put the painting back on the wall. "I'm sorry, Robby," he said. "There may be nothing much to it, of course," he said haltingly, but then he stopped, because for the first time since he had hitched his wagon to Vane's star, Vane wasn't acting. He sat, hands clutching the sides of his chair, eyes sunk deep into his head, just like any other husband in the world.

It had never occurred to Pentecost before that Robert Vane was merely human.

He wished he hadn't found it out.

"What's so bloody urgent?" Harry Lisle asked Robby Vane petulantly.

"I thought you said you were coming down to London, anyway, for the opening."

"So I was. But I didn't appreciate being called late last night about your domestic problems. I've got my own, thank you very much."

They sat in a quiet corner of the bar in Lisle's club, looking out over St. James's Street. Although he was not, by instinct, a "clubbable" man, Vane was a member of the Garrick, where actors were welcomed, and was rather in awe of White's, which had never yet had an actor member. Once upon a time, when he was married to Penelope, White's had been one of his ambitions—and one that would have been realized, too, had he not left Penelope for Felicia. There was still a part of him that wanted to be a member here—what Felicia called his House of Lords side—but he was not about to show it to Lisle.

"The thing is, I'm worried about Lisha," he said.

Lisle looked wary. "Can't think why," he said. "She seems fit as a fiddle to me."

"Does she? I don't think so."

Lisle's hooded eyes showed his hostility, but that did not surprise Vane. "She's high-strung," Lisle growled. "A thoroughbred. You can't handle her like a farmer's nag."

Vane let the insult pass, along with the horsey metaphor. Like every English actor of his generation, he had been obliged to learn to ride, but he was a timid horseman, and loathed every moment spent on a horse—a fact which Harry Lisle had noticed, watching his films, and had pointed out to him, much to his annoyance.

"I *know* she's 'high-strung,' Harry. But never as bad as she's been lately. I can't help worrying about what's going to happen tonight. . . ."

"The first night of *Othello*? I assume she'll be fine. She seemed in good spirits about it when I talked to her last. She has a temperament, agreed, but surely that's one of the marks of a great actress? I'd think you were used to it by now. Nothing to do with me, anyway."

"Well, that's why I wanted to chat, Harry. It *may* have something to do with you. You remember that painting you so generously gave Lisha? The little Renoir she'd always admired so much?"

Lisle's expression was wary now. The hand that held his drink was shaking a little, Vane noticed. It seemed to be covered with age spots, which he didn't remember noticing before—in fact, Lisle, now that he looked more closely, suddenly showed all the signs of age. And about time, too, Vane thought uncharitably.

"The Renoir?" Lisle said vaguely. Like an actor who hadn't had time to commit his lines reliably to heart, he seemed to be searching hard for the next thing to say. "A nice little painting, yes."

"Did you have it for a long time?"

"Donkey's years, old boy. Bought it for a song in Paris in the late twenties, when the impressionists were going cheap."

"I never saw it when I was at Langleit."

"Well, you haven't been there often, have you? It hung upstairs, anyway, in Maude's sitting room, so you wouldn't have seen it."

"It's awfully decent of you to have given it to Lisha. I suppose it ought to be insured. How much would you say it was worth? Just for the purposes of evaluation?"

Lisle looked puzzled. He drummed his fingers on the table. "Thirty thousand pounds," he said at last. "Of course, you'll need an appraisal for insurance. Frankly, I wouldn't bother. An appraisal's a time-consuming business. Expensive, too."

"Yes," Vane said, a malicious gleam in his eyes, "but in this case, it shouldn't be too difficult. After all, we know what it sold for at Christie's, don't we?"

"Christie's?"

"Come off it, Harry. That painting was never at Langleit. I took the trouble of going around to Christie's to make inquiries, and they very kindly gave me the picture's pedigree, or whatever it's called."

"Provenance."

"Exactly so. Ponsonby bought it from Lord Wraith's widow, and Wraith bought it from a dealer in Paris named Meyerman in 1919, and before that it was always in France. *You* didn't give it to Lisha."

Lisle sipped his drink, his hand shaking so badly now that

he spilled a few drops on his tie. "Why don't you ask Lisha about it, old boy?" he said. "None of my business."

Vane stared at him. "Because in the first place she's avoiding me, and in the second place I have a play to open tonight, and having it out with her a few hours before the curtain doesn't seem clever. Anyway, what I want to know from you, Harry, is why *you* lied to me, not why Felicia did. That, I already know."

"I haven't a clue what you're talking about."

"Yes, you do. She lied to me, Harry, and you backed her up. Which was bloody silly, actually, because nobody knows Felicia better than I do. . . ."

Vane was struck silent by the sudden expression of hatred on Lisle's face. Feeble he might be, but his eyes were as venomous as a snake's, his mouth a thin, blue-white line, the lips sharply compressed. Dislike from Harry Lisle he was used to, and reciprocated, but this was something far different and sharper. "Know Felicia?" Lisle asked sharply. "You don't know a bloody thing about her, you poor booby."

The old man's sudden vehemence was almost Lear-like in his intensity. Lisle seemed no longer able to contain his rage and fury.

"Harry," Robby said, as calmly and gently as he could, like a man trying to quiet a maddened dog that appears about to lunge, "I've never known why you dislike me, but perhaps it doesn't matter anymore. All I wanted to know is whether Lisha asked you to lie for her, and I suppose I already know the answer to that."

"Dislike!" Lisle spat out the word. "I don't *dislike* you. I despise you."

Vane flushed, but continued patiently on. "That's going a bit far, isn't it? What on earth have I done that you should feel that? If I could have married Felicia sooner, I would have. Who could have guessed that Charles would make so many difficulties over the divorce, or that the war would get in the way? If it hadn't been for that, we'd have started a family long ago, and I suspect been spared a lot of grief."

"Family!" Lisle barked, so loudly that several men at the bar turned to stare at him. "*Family?* You bloody fool! You've got as much chance of having a family as I do of seeing twenty again!''

''What are you talking about?''

Lisle was trembling now. He leaned forward and in a deadly whisper hissed, ''She can't *have* children, damn you! She had a difficult time giving birth to Portia, surely you know that?''

''She told me, of course.''

''Of course!'' the old man said derisively. ''She told you that, but she left out the important part. The delivery was a nightmare. The doctors botched it. Portia survived, a bonny, healthy girl, thank God, but Felicia could never have another baby—the doctors made that clear to her. I don't think she was unhappy about it, frankly, not a bit. She had such a bad time that I don't think she'd ever want to go through with it again, but in any case, she can't. So if you were waiting for Felicia to produce your son and heir, you might have spared yourself the bother. Not, if my own guess about you is true, that you've been trying all that hard.''

All Vane wanted to do was to reach out and throttle the old man, but he could not make a public spectacle of himself. ''How do you know all this?'' he asked, but even as the words were out of his mouth, he knew the answer, as if all the pieces of a jigsaw puzzle that had haunted him for ages were suddenly falling into place. He was not talking to a man who was merely Felicia's uncle—the man before him was jealous as only a lover could be. What Harry had had against him all these years was simply that he had taken Felicia away from him. ''Harry,'' he said, very quietly, ''you loved her, didn't you?''

The old man's eyes softened, took on a grayish cast, filled with tears. '' 'Course I did,'' he said. ''She's my niece.''

''You loved her more than that, though, didn't you?''

Something of Lisle's old spark came back. ''More than *you* ever did,'' he snarled. ''Always have. Always will.''

''And Charles? Did you hate him, too?''

''Not in the least. Nice fella. Picked him myself.''

''Picked him yourself?''

Lisle snickered. "Well, she had to marry somebody, didn't she?"

"You're not saying there was a child between you, are you?" He felt a kind of horror creeping over him, paralyzing both his body and his mind. He wanted to shout, run, hit the old man, feel anger, revulsion, indignation, but he could do nothing. He was like the victim of some terrible accident. He wanted to learn more about what had happened, but the sound of Lisle's voice nauseated him.

Lisle nodded. "There was a child," he said. "She wanted to have it, you know. Wouldn't hear of having it taken care of, which was the sensible thing to do. A couple of weeks in Switzerland, at a clinic in Lausanne or Geneva, and bob's your uncle, but she wouldn't do it, God knows why. Well, no, I *do* know why, in fact. Her mother, you know, was a Christian Scientist. She died of appendicitis, in Nairobi, when the worst damn fool of a surgeon could have saved her easily. She frightened Felicia with stories of doctors, and of course the poor child believed her. Even when she grew up, she simply wouldn't have anything to do with doctors, so the result was that she was less frightened of having the child than of getting it removed."

Lisle gave a sigh. He seemed almost to be talking to himself now. "Her mother—now there was a *woman*! Too good for my brother, just the way Felicia is too good for you, frankly. I'd have taken her to the hospital, if I had to knock her out, tie her up, and *carry* her there, but of course my brother Ned believes in letting people do what they want to do, which is just another way of saying that he doesn't give a shit, and wants to be left alone to do exactly as he pleases, himself. I'll tell you something, Vane—something I've never even told Felicia. Her mother was the most beautiful woman I've ever known, the woman I wanted most of all. Threw away her life, *wasted* it, on Ned, when she could have had me for the asking—and she knew it. She loved me, too, you know. Oh, I'm not saying she didn't love Ned, but she loved me more. I've sometimes wondered if Felicia herself might be mine. . . ." He paused and shook his head, perhaps appalled by what he had been about to say to Robby Vane, of all people. "Well, but it's best *not* to wonder, isn't it?"

"Yes," Vane said firmly. "Much the best thing." He lit a cigarette, pleased with himself for still being able to carry out such a small, ordinary act. "Did Lisha tell you she was having an affair with Marty Quick?"

"Of course she did. Well, what can you expect, old boy? You haven't been paying much attention to her—so she says, anyway, and I believe her. And if you don't mind my saying so, you've never had quite the touch, when it comes to Lisha. She's a very hot-blooded girl, she is, just like her dear mother. You've got to give her a lot of attention." He leered. "In bed and out."

Vane felt overcome by a deep fatigue. He only hoped he would be able to go on tonight. "Why Quick?" he asked. "Did she tell you that?"

But Lisle's head was resting on his chin. He had been drinking steadily since Vane had arrived.

"I said, why Quick?" Vane repeated, more loudly.

Lisle opened one eye. He looked genuinely astonished. "Why, my dear fellow," he said, in quite an amiable tone of voice, "because he's not *you*, don't you see? He's totally the opposite—and totally wrong for her, too, so she's punishing you and punishing herself at the same time. Punishing me, as well, I shouldn't wonder." He gave a lopsided smile, causing Vane to wonder if he had had a stroke recently. "You're still the one she loves, Vane, that's the irony of it. She'd *kill* for you, my boy."

"You look like hell."

"I'm perfectly fine, thank you."

"You're cutting things rather fine. It's not like you to leave your makeup to the last moment. Particularly *this* of all times."

"Guillam, you're not my nanny. No, no, dear boy, I apologize. Is Felicia here yet?"

"Of course she's not, Robby. *She* doesn't need to paint herself black from head to toe, thank God!"

"Quite right. I don't know where my mind is. Guillam,

could you be a dear and ask somebody to get me something to eat?''

''*Eat?* Before an opening? It's nearly three o'clock. And you've just come back from lunch, surely?''

''As it happened, I didn't get anything to eat. A sandwich. Biscuits. Tea. Anything will do. Please. I'll get cracking.''

They were standing on the ornate wrought-iron circular staircase that led to the principals' dressing rooms, a contrivance that seemed designed to give the more important performers the maximum opportunity of ''breaking a leg,'' literally, before going onstage. The stairs were noisy, slippery, prone to rust, and made all but the most fearless of actors and actresses nervous, but they were original and authentic, so Vane had refused even to consider replacing them.

Neatly laid out on the table, in front of the mirror, harshly lit by bare hundred-watt bulbs, were the tools of his trade— sticks of greasepaint, jars of cold cream, putty, wax, rubber cement, powder. He inhaled the familiar smells. The electric fire in the old coal grate was glowing, giving off more light than heat. He went over and stood in front of it, shivering as he began to undress. Above the mantelpiece was his beloved portrait of Garrick, who had once owned this same theatre. Garrick had played Othello here, had prepared for it in this same dressing room, had gone down those same iron steps to make his entrance. Had *he* had troubles with his Desdemona? Surely nothing like mine, Vane told himself.

He stripped naked. He examined his body critically in the pier glass—an Englishman in his late thirties, fairly broad-shouldered, running a little to fat at the waist, not nearly so slim as he had been when he played the languid lovers of Guy Darling's hit plays long before the war, nor as muscled as he had been when he went to Hollywood and competed for athletic roles requiring a bare chest and lots of swordplay. I must get more exercise, he told himself, but he knew the flab was a consequence of the role. Exercise, like makeup, was a tool. If he were playing Hamlet, he would have slimmed down and fenced once a day, but Othello is an elderly man, no longer a soldier, a general whose days of hand-to-hand combat are behind him.

He stood quietly, his skin raised in goose bumps by the cold, rubbing on the first coat of body paint, a deep, rich brown, like dark milk chocolate. He dipped his fingers in the paint, and rubbed it over his genitals and buttocks, feeling a little foolish. He wondered as he did it just what it was that Felicia saw in Quick—and why, like the most buffoonish of cuckolded husbands, he had suspected nothing. Or had he simply ignored his suspicions? He had seen the signs all right, he thought bitterly—he had simply decided not to read them.

He stood for half an hour, seething with anger, while the body paint dried. What did she want from him? How often had he proved his love—turned his career inside out for her? And yet she had betrayed him, and with Marty Quick, at that! He tried not to think about the two of them in bed together and failed. He knew he needed his peace of mind, and he knew he was not going to get it.

The next task was even more tedious—he and Abel, his dresser, had to rub black shoe polish onto his body, then buff it with a damp rag until it gleamed. He might have been the priest of some bizarre religion, preparing for a sacrifice at the high altar. He was glad when it was over and he could slip gingerly into his stained robe and take a sip of tea. His face was still untouched—that would come last, along with pink palms, but at least the longest and most tedious part of the job was done.

"Is Miss Lisle in her dressing room yet?" he asked. Abel raised an eyebrow—a majestic gesture, perfected in a hundred minor roles in his own acting days. Normally, Felicia and Vane made a point of arriving at the theatre together; if his role required more time to prepare for than hers, she took a nap in her dressing room, or answered correspondence.

"I believe not."

Vane studied his face in the mirror. Guillam was right, he decided. He *did* look bloody awful. Where the hell was she? he wondered. A stupid question to ask—she was probably in bed with Marty Quick at this very moment. Or had Harry Lisle reached her to tell her that her husband now knew everything? She might be hysterical with guilt, wandering through the streets, suicidal. . . .

"Is Miss Lisle's understudy in the theatre?" he asked.

Abel's eyebrow rose even higher. "I believe so, sir," he said. "Shall I ask her to come up?"

"No. Just so long as she's here, and ready."

There was a knock on the door, not at all muffled this time, but full-blooded and self-confident. Felicia in a rage? He was unsure of how to handle the situation. With return anger and fury? But what would be the effect of his anger on her performance tonight? He was like a general making his last-minute preparations for a battle—like Othello himself, it occurred to him. He had confidence in his own ability to play his role no matter what was going on in his life— exactly the kind of thing that Felicia no doubt hated about him—but he had no such confidence in her, not since San Francisco. Still, if she was here, she would have to be faced. "Come in!" he shouted, and turned around to find that it wasn't Felicia at all.

Standing in the doorway, a sour smile on his suety face, was Sir Herbert Tarpon, trying to look as if he belonged backstage despite his civil servant's homburg hat, striped trousers, and black jacket, and the stiff white collar which seemed to have been starched into his neck. "Hope I'm not intruding," he said.

"Actually," Vane said, "this isn't the best of times, old boy. Perhaps later, after the performance. . . ."

Tarpon gave a small bow, to show he understood the artistic temperament and deferred to it. "I wouldn't normally have dreamed of butting in like this," he said unctuously, "but Lady Tarpon and I were on our way to an early meal before the show, and I had a piece of news I thought you might like to hear. I believe I bring good news," he said smoothly. "I think you may count on your name in the next Honors list."

Vane hardly knew what to say. Yesterday it would have been cause for rejoicing—not that he wasn't expecting it, but still, here it was at last, the youngest knight in theatrical history, the first theatre knight in decades! But he felt nothing except an urgent desire to get Tarpon out of his dressing room and be left alone to make up his face.

"Thank you," he said. "I'm speechless. Now, if you'll forgive me . . ."

"Of course, of course." Tarpon inclined his head as if he were offering a view of his bald pate as a kind of gift. "May I say how pleased I am for you—and of course for Lady Vane, as she soon will be."

"The honor is mine—*ours*."

"Just so," Sir Herbert said, straightening up. His expression was severe now, a schoolmaster about to give a warning following on praise. "One little caveat, my dear fellow, that I'm obliged to mention—these things are always *conditional*. If you run off with a barmaid"—he laughed, brimming with false heartiness—"or if there's anything the Palace might consider a scandal—oh, I know, it's not going to happen!—then I'm afraid the offer of a knighthood must be withdrawn." Tarpon blushed. "You do understand—it's normal to mention this. I need hardly say that it is not relevant to yourself and the delightful Miss Lisle—or Lady Vane, as we shall soon be calling her."

Vane nodded gravely. "It's quite understood. Thank you for putting it so tactfully."

Tarpon backed out to the door. "By the way," he whispered, as he opened it, "there'll be royalty in the audience tonight." He winked. "Forewarned is forearmed, eh?"

Vane nodded, as if he didn't care, but as soon as the door closed behind Tarpon, he opened the drawer of his table. He never drank before a performance, but in the circumstances, he decided, it was the only sensible thing to do. He poured a generous measure of single-malt whiskey into his tea and swigged it down, hoping it would calm him.

It didn't help a bit.

"Is she here?"

Vane stood perched on the iron staircase, arms outstretched so as not to smear his velvet robes. He had spent months trying to transform himself into a black man of overwhelming power and dignity, and here he was on opening night shouting like a hysterical fishwife outside his own dressing room. Toby Eden, villainously wigged as Iago, appeared below, forefinger pressed to his lips, and reluctantly mounted the steps. "Hush, old boy," he whispered. "The bloody audience will hear you."

"I don't care a damn if they do. *Is* Felicia here?"

"Of course she is. She arrived late and breathless, looking radiant, as always."

"I have been asking for her for an hour or more."

"She left word that she didn't want to be disturbed. My dear Robby, do be calm. It isn't the first time that Felicia has cut it fine." He leaned closer, an expression of astonishment on his face. "That isn't *whiskey* I smell, is it?" he asked.

"I had a little in my tea."

"*You?* I've never known you to touch a drop before going on."

"It seems to work well enough for you."

"Well, yes, but if you're not in the habit . . ." Toby rolled his eyes apprehensively. "Do be careful," he said.

"Of what?"

"The stairs, to begin with. Then yourself. How do you feel?"

"Splendid."

"Oh, dear!" Toby closed his eyes in anticipation of the horror to come.

Vane could hear the noise of the audience as it settled down. His mind was a total blank—he felt no fear, but neither could he recall anything of the Othello he had planned and rehearsed for so long. He needed to talk to Felicia desperately, but she was locked in her dressing room. He clung to the railing like a captain about to go down with his ship, while Toby, one hand on his arm, studied him. "You're walking Lear," he whispered anxiously. "An old man's shuffle. All wrong, old boy. This is the lusty Moor, remember?"

"I'll be all right."

"I hope so." Eden leaned closer. "A word of advice. Stop worrying about Lisha. Worry about yourself. It isn't *her* understudy who should be put on notice, it's *yours*."

Vane dismissed him and stood for a moment leaning against the ancient, stained brick wall, eyes closed, trying to forget about Felicia and to concentrate on the play. But he hadn't the slightest notion of how he was going to deal with Felicia for two hours.

"A *fellow almost damn'd in a fair wife*," he heard himself described onstage—and almost laughed, for it was far too true.

There was no point in waiting for her to come down, he knew that. She would stay in her dressing room until the last moment, and his entrance took place before hers.

They would meet onstage.

I can't face him, she told herself behind the locked door of her dressing room.

But she would *have* to face him, and shortly, despite the shame, guilt, and fear swirling inside her mind.

Her head ached. She had been trying desperately to reach Marty Quick, but he was nowhere to be found. Living as he did on the fringes of Supreme Headquarters, there was no office where she could find him, no secretary who kept track of his movements. Calls to American headquarters on Grosvenor Square were taken by men with strange American accents who refused to admit they had ever heard of a Colonel Quick and asked her for the password of the day. She *had* to see him, but he had vanished into the military machine, surely deliberately. To hide from her? Very likely, but somehow she *had* to stop him from blackmailing Robby. She couldn't let him destroy Robby's career.

She had ignored the frantic knocking on her door this past hour while she was making up and dressing—she couldn't face Robby—but she recognized that this was a different knock, discreet but firm, a signal, not a desperate appeal. "Five minutes," a voice announced. She said, "Thank you," and turned back to the mirror. She had dismissed her dresser—she wanted to be alone. She examined her face. For Desdemona she wore her hair long and loose, with simple makeup and a low-cut velvet dress with a tight bodice that emphasized her tiny waist and made her look younger. Desdemona, after all, was not much older than Juliet.

Not many women of thirty-five could pass themselves off as a seventeen-year-old even onstage, she told herself. Of course, if you looked closely, the eyes gave the game away. You could cover over the fine lines, push up the bosom, use greasepaint on the neck, but the eyes had simply seen more life than a young woman's, and where there should have been hope and joy, there was only fear.

Well, at least in the theatre, thank God, there was no such thing as a close-up. She rose and walked to the door, opened it. Her dresser, who had been waiting in the cramped hallway, fussed over the costume, dusted another quick layer of powder on her face, warned her fiercely to relax.

"Mr. Robert is on now," she said. "In good voice, from what I could 'ear. Got a very nice 'and for his entrance."

"Was he in good spirits?"

"Well, he seemed a little upset, poor man. Not like himself at all. Kept asking 'ow you were, dearie. I didn't 'ave the 'eart to tell 'im the news."

"*What* news?"

"Oh, dear, I'm not sure I should tell *you*, either. It's about a friend of his, you see . . . and yours. The American comedian, Randy Brooks."

"Go on, what about him?"

" 'E's *dead*, luv. Shot down in a bomber over Germany yesterday. It do seem a shame, don't it? Sending a talented young man like that off to 'is death, when the world is full of people who wouldn't 'ardly be missed."

Felicia stood backstage, willing herself not to think about Randy's death, listening to that great voice which was so large a part of her happiness, hardly even muffled by the scenery—

> . . . *Upon this hint, I spake:*
> *She lov'd me for the dangers I had pass'd,*
> *And I lov'd her that she did pity them.*
> *This . . .*"

A pause longer than anyone else would have dared, that set her spine to tingling even though she had heard it a hundred times before, in which the echo of his voice somehow swelled through the theatre, from deep backstage to the highest row of the balcony, so powerful a moment that the audience was not just silent but unable even to take a breath—

"only—"

Another shorter pause, preparing the way for the next majestic phrase—

"is the witchcraft I have us'd. . . ."

Her heart was beating so hard that she felt it might burst at any moment. Toby appeared, sweat pouring down his plump red face, with that unmistakably satisfied look of an actor who knows he has given his best. "They're *alive* tonight, old thing," he whispered to her. "A good audience —not a cougher in the bloody house. When Robby came on in his blackface you could have heard a pin drop! Are you all right?"

She nodded. "Fit as can be."

"Good, good." He leaned closer. She could smell the drying sweat, the greasepaint, the faint aroma of gin and pipe tobacco, comforting in their familiarity. She felt strangely at peace—*this* was her family, this was her home, this stage her equivalent of the marriage bed. Here were the people who trusted and loved her, not Harry Lisle, who had merely exploited her youth relentlessly, or Marty Quick, who hadn't an ounce of romance in his body, or Charles, who had been unable to understand what she felt, or even poor little Portia, who would never stand here listening to a man who could hold fifteen hundred people breathless, suspended by his voice out of their own lives and concerns. . . . "It's an important night," Eden went on. "Mum's the word, darling, but that pompous old swine Tarpon told Robby there's royalty in the audience. If all goes well, you're going to be Lady Vane before you know it."

The assistant stage manager pointed at her. She felt Toby grip her wrist. She could see his lips move as he wished her good luck, but she heard nothing as she stepped into the shadows at the edge of the stage and took a deep breath, like a diver about to plunge.

For a brief moment, she could see the audience before they could see her, row upon row of faces. The assistant stage manager nodded, but she didn't even see his cue—didn't need it any more than Robby did. Without even realizing she had moved, she was suddenly out in the glare of the lights, hardly even hearing the deafening waves of applause rising from the audience, her eyes fixed on Robby. . . .

She could not fail him now.

She had never experienced anything like it onstage before. The tension between them was so great that she was hardly even conscious of his exaggerated makeup. He was not *acting* his jealousy, his suspicion, his growing anger—he felt them genuinely, just as she, without any conscious thought, tried to appeal to him, to convince him of her loyalty, if not her love.

She felt his rage, as one might feel the wind or the tug of the waves at the seaside; for perhaps the first time in her life she did not consciously *play* the part, she simply *was* Desdemona—had never been anyone else. It was an exhilarating experience, one that left her dazed. For the first time she understood what *he* had felt playing Richard, and longed to share it with him. But he was too exhausted during the interval, as well as furious with her, and he wouldn't say why.

Could he have learned about her and Marty? she wondered. But how? The most she could get out of him was that they would talk later, which, coming from Robby, was a sure sign of trouble ahead—but now he had to change costume and rest his voice, as she did. The play imposed its own discipline, like war, and there was no ignoring it.

She went to her dressing room, he to his, and they did not meet again until they were onstage, by which time he seemed even angrier than before. If it had been anyone else, she would have put part of his fury down to drink, and indeed she thought she caught a trace of whiskey about him—but that was impossible, so she dismissed the idea.

The next interval found them both exhausted. She took a lit cigarette from one of the stagehands and tried to talk to Robby as he climbed the iron stairs to his dressing room—but as fate would have it, Toby Eden was standing there in costume, puffing on his pipe, and chose that moment to tell him about Randy Brooks's death.

She saw Robby grasp the railing as if he were about to fall. She reached up and put her hand on his, trying to tell him that she understood, but he simply stared at her as if she were a total stranger and made his way slowly up the stairs. She wanted to cry out that it was not her fault, that she would share his grief with him, but already her dresser was signaling to her frantically for her costume change.

The worst was yet to come, and the fury of his performance made her dread it more than ever. Now, for half an hour, she had to endure his accusing her of deceit, of having betrayed him, had to stand close to his rage like a daring traveler walking on the edge of a volcano. He was no longer acting —his own feelings, uncontrolled, were merging with the part.

She could smell his anger, a cold, hard smell that rose above the sweat and the greasepaint, and from the silence of the audience, she knew that her own performance was as real as his, that her fear was genuine. She looked at his face, hardly seeing the thickened nose and lips, the black skin, the curly white wig, seeing only his eyes, dark blue, flecked with gold, insane with grief and fury, the eyes of a cruel stranger—the eyes, it suddenly occurred to her in a burst of panic, of *death*. . . .

She fought hard to control herself, but she was shaking like a leaf, her voice trembling, sweat pouring down—she who hardly perspired even under the strongest lights!

The moment she dreaded was coming now, the moment when he would pick up the pillow to suffocate her. Even in ordinary circumstances it made her faint with fear, but tonight she was petrified, sure that his hands would drive it down hard on her face and choke the life out of her. His eyes seemed to her to have no life at all, as black and shiny as his makeup in the harsh stage light.

She knew his lines without hearing them:

> *"If you bethink yourself of any crime*
> *Unreconcil'd as yet to Heaven and grace*
> *Solicit for it straight. . . ."*

She stiffened as he pressed the pillow against her face. He pushed her down hard against the bed, one knee holding her, and as she struggled for breath she knew with perfect clarity that he was going to kill her now, here, onstage, in front of fifteen hundred people.

Her lungs were empty. There was a stabbing pain in her chest. She saw fields of bright multicolored sparks rush across the blackness in her eyes. There was a pounding in her ears as if she were drowning in the surf. She felt panic, and could do nothing to stop it.

She twisted, kicked, used her elbows on Robby, who backed away astonished and dismayed, dropping the pillow. Then, without even realizing what she was doing, or knowing how on earth she had found the breath for it, she let out a scream that echoed through the theatre, one that nobody could have confused with acting, and covering her face with her hands, ran from the stage.

She did not stop until she was out in the street, running through the blackout in costume, hearing only the sound of his voice calling out—

> *"She's like a liar gone to burning hell.*
> *T'was I that kill'd her."*

20

Felicia stood silently in her own drawing room as if she had never seen it before, still shaking with fear. The young man beside her eventually broke the silence. "If this was mine, I'd stay here forever," he whispered in awe.

"Well, it isn't yours. And I can't stay."

Fate had led her to Billy Dove again, standing in his usual place outside the Ritz Hotel. This time, seeing her in her costume as Desdemona, he knew who she was—and recognized her agony.

He had found her a taxi and helped her home, but she couldn't stay here—she realized that, the instant she was through the door. She had disgraced Robby and ruined her own career as well as his. By tomorrow, all of London would say she was mad, as perhaps she was.

How ironic, she thought, that she had been helped twice by the young man who had been, perhaps still was, her husband's lover. That no longer mattered to her. What did matter was that she needed time, and the longer she stayed here, the less there was. At any moment, Robby would come looking for her. She could not face him until she had put things right. She had ruined Robby's career. She could at least prevent Marty from ruining his life.

"Billy," she said, "I need to get away from here. Just for a night. I can hardly go to a hotel. It would be in every newspaper by the morning. Do you have anywhere I can stay?"

He looked startled. "Stay? *You*?"

"I need to think. You know my husband, don't you?"

Billy nodded. She thought of the photograph she had taken from Marty Quick's desk. Yes, she thought, you know him well. "We've quarreled," she said. "I don't want to be here when he comes home."

He looked hesitant. "I'll pay you," she added.

He blushed. "It isn't that. It's not exactly a—suitable—place for you."

"It will have to do." She rummaged through the desk drawer, found some money, and handed it to Billy without counting.

His eyes opened wide in astonishment, and he shrugged. "Anything you say, Miss Lisle. But don't say I didn't warn you."

"Wait." She ran into the bedroom, shed her costume and put on a dress. She put a scarf over her head, belted on a mackintosh, then dumped whatever she needed into a leather shoulder bag—the sleeping pills she was never without, cigarettes, what money she could find. On the way back through the living room, she paused at the desk for one thing more.

She looked at the clock. Any moment now, Robby would be here. He must not find her before she had done what she had to do—for him. "What's your address?" she asked Billy, scribbling it down quickly on the notepad.

She dialed Claridge's and asked for Colonel Quick.

"He's not to be disturbed," the operator said.

"This is Felicia Lisle. Put me through *at once*!"

There was a moment of silence. Even here in London the magic of Hollywood stardom always worked. "Yes, miss," the operator said meekly.

"Yeah?" Quick answered in an angry rasp.

"It's Felicia."

"I guessed. You ran out on me the other day. How come?" He sounded sleepy, as if he had been dozing.

"I've been trying to reach you."

"I was away."

"On military business, no doubt? With your charming young driver?"

"Get off my back, Lisha. We're not married. If you *must* know, I was collecting Randy's belongings to send home to Natalie. You heard?"

"I heard."

"They're giving him a medal."

"I'm sure Natalie will be pleased. I need to see you."

"Now?" He was suddenly alert.

"Now."

"Say, I thought this was the opening night of *Othello*. What happened?"

"Marty, I have to see you." She paused, then added, "I'm not going to let you get away with it."

"What are you talking about?"

"I warn you! Once I tell people what you tried to do, *nobody* will touch you, not in Hollywood, not here, not anywhere."

There was a moment's silence. She could imagine him lying there, frowning, the jet-black eyes glittering as he con-

sidered his options. "I'm on the way," he said at last.
"Where?"

"Twenty-two Shepherd's Garden, top floor."

"Where the fuck is that?"

"Tell your little sailor friend to find it."

She hung up.

The squalor was more than she had bargained for. In the
narrow streets prostitutes were busily accosting soldiers,
while touts for after-hours drinking "clubs" huddled at every
corner. The streets were so dark that people looked like shadows, only an occasional brightly painted face or glowing
cigarette to show they were alive.

Eighteenth-century London had been preserved here in all
its horror. A smell of rotting vegetables, old drains, cheap
perfume, and beer clung like a vapor to everything.

She gave Billy a pound note and let him pay for the taxi,
then followed him through the greasy cobblestone alleys,
aware that in almost every doorway there was a woman standing, whispering obscenely into the dark.

Billy's house was a narrow building that hadn't been helped
by four years of German bombing. It seemed to slouch villainously, the windows drooping at different levels, the upper
stories canted out over the street until they nearly touched
the house opposite, the plaster flaking away from ancient,
rotting beams. There was a woman lurking in the doorway,
her lit cigarette the only way of advertising her presence in
the blackout. Felicia smelled the cheap perfume that failed
to conceal the odors of an unwashed body, the stale cigarette
breath, the face powder, and recoiled.

"That isn't you, Billy, is it?" the woman said, drawing
on her cigarette. Felicia had assumed she was old, but in the
brief red glow, she saw it was a young girl.

"It's me."

"You? Wiv a *woman*? Don't make me larf."

"She's a friend, Vi."

"A *friend*? A girl? You?"

Billy pushed past her. Felicia followed him up the narrow
rickety dimly lit stairs. The house was full of sounds—

groans, shouts, the creaking of bedsprings, violent cursing. It seemed to Felicia to be pressing in on her, as if she had been buried alive. The higher they went, the narrower the stairs were, until they began to resemble a badly made, steep, shaky ladder. At the top was a door, thick with two hundred years of paint and grime, which Billy unlocked with an ancient rusty iron key. "Home," he said brightly.

One bare overhead bulb illuminated a strangely shaped low-ceilinged garret room that might have been a monk's cell, with its stained white walls, tiny leaded window, and sparse furnishings—a narrow bed, a chest of drawers, and two decaying easy chairs. The floor was bare linoleum, the only decorations pictures of movie stars, torn out of magazines and newspapers and pinned up neatly in clusters, as if to cover cracks and holes.

In the dim light it was hard to identify them, but she thought she recognized Mark Strong, Randy Brooks—who seemed to be one of Billy's favorites—and Robby himself, in a still taken from one of his Hollywood movies. Had Robby made love to Billy on this bed? She refused to think about it. She had made up her mind. She was going to wipe the slate clean—for him, perhaps for both of them—and nothing else mattered. She noticed several photos of herself, too. Billy was clearly a devoted fan.

She sat on the bed. It was as neatly made as a soldier's, or a prisoner's, the coarse, threadbare linen pathetically clean, the blanket folded with knife-edge precision. "This will do fine," she said.

"The lavatory is two flights down."

"I don't need the lavatory."

"There's a gas fire in the grate. You need a shilling. I'll start it for you." He put a coin in the meter and struck a match. The single row of gas jets flared a pale blue.

"Billy," she said, "I have to meet somebody here. I know it's your room, but can you leave me alone for a few hours?"

He looked worried. "Are you sure?"

"Quite sure."

She nodded. Once she had dealt with Marty, there would be no problem in buying Billy's silence. She waved him on his way and lit a cigarette, putting the match in the little jam-jar lid that served Billy for an ashtray.

She was still sitting there motionless, half an hour later, when she heard a knock on the door.

She did not look up. "You took your time," she said.

"The hell I did. This dump isn't easy to find." He looked around him and shook his head. "What the fuck are you doing here?"

"Putting right what you've done, Marty. Putting right what I've done, too."

He stood there, hands in the pockets of his pale nonregulation belted trenchcoat, cap pushed back on his head, a silk scarf wrapped around his neck, a cigar jutting out of the corner of his mouth. He was handsome, smiling, determined to take all this casually. "This looks like a set from *Stella Dallas*," he said. "Does Robby know you're here?"

"No. I suppose your little tramp of a driver is waiting downstairs with the other whores."

He shook his head. "I figured I'd come alone. I got a taxi. There are *some* things Amelia's better off not knowing. This looks like it could be one of them." He took his coat off, put it on the bed, folded the scarf, and sat down next to her on the bed. She smelled his familiar after-shave. He took a flask out of his pocket, unscrewed the top, and poured her a drink. She took it gratefully. "So what's the story?" he asked.

"I know who Billy Dove is," she said.

He looked startled. "Who?"

"The young man you paid a hundred pounds to."

"So?" He shrugged, as if it didn't matter.

"I saw the photograph you had taken outside the pub."

"Okay." He seemed puzzled now, as if he was wondering where all this was leading.

"I'm not going to let you get away with blackmail," she said.

"Blackmail? What's your problem?" He poured himself a drink and put his cigar down in the ashtray. "Look," he said, "I don't know why you're slumming. You wanna talk, let's go some place where we can talk."

"We can talk here."

He put his arm around her, exasperation on his face. "What's the matter, Lish? What's all this shit about blackmail? So I play rough? I've *always* played rough. It doesn't matter anymore, right? It's over. What's done is done."

"It can be undone. It *has* to be."

He was really puzzled now. "I don't see how. I mean, it's too late. . . ." He leaned over, holding her tight, and kissed her. "I'm sorry it happened," he said. "But it wasn't anything to do with me. I didn't make him get on the fucking plane. . . ."

She wasn't listening. She was shaking, not from fear, but from anger at her own weakness. She felt his hand on her thigh, moving up under her skirt.

She moved away, trying to regain control of herself, one part of her mind wildly contemplating the madness of what she planned to do, the other coldly preparing to carry it out. She trembled at the consequences—scandal, disgrace, punishment—but if it was the only way to save Robby, then so be it.

Shakespeare's women, she told herself, did not hesitate to finish what they had begun. Cleopatra, Juliet, Lady Macbeth—*they* understood grand gestures, great sacrifices. She knew exactly what to do—but still she felt an enormous weight of reluctance and doubt holding her back.

The room was so small she couldn't move far enough away from Marty to place herself out of his reach. She felt suffocated by his presence, his voice, the threat of his anger.

"I'm *talking* to you," he said, anger bursting out at last. He grabbed her wrist and pulled her sharply toward him.

She didn't resist—she let herself go limp. He pressed his mouth against hers, reaching around with his other hand to grasp her waist. "Christ," he muttered, "why'd you drag me all the way here? This bed's too small . . ."

She tried to push him away, but he only laughed. "Don't play hard to get with me, Lish." he said. "I know you better than that."

You don't know me at all, she said to herself. *I* don't even know me, not anymore. Her bag was on the bed behind her, only a few inches away. With a fierce effort of will, she plunged her hand into it and felt her palm begin to burn, as if she had just grasped something red-hot—then, as if she were trying to throw away whatever it was that had burned her, she straightened her arm, her eyes closed.

She felt a sharper pain run through her wrist, all the way up her arm. For a moment she thought she had dislocated her shoulder, but the feeling passed, leaving behind an aching numbness as if the arm had gone to sleep.

Marty did not move at all or make a noise. He had been pressing against her, pushing her down onto the bed with his full weight, but now he suddenly seemed to be slumping, his muscles relaxed, as if he had dozed off.

He shook his head groggily and rose to his knees. His eyes, for the first time since she had met him, showed not only surprise, but a kind of wonder. There was nothing hard about them, for once—they were the dark, tearful eyes of an injured child.

"Jesus!" he said. "What the *hell* was that?" He reached up with his right hand to feel his back, and what he found there made his eyes open wide in amazement and fear. "You crazy bitch!" he shouted—or *tried* to shout, for his voice was feeble and distorted, as if he were shouting underwater.

She was as startled as he was at the sight of the dagger stuck in his back.

He made an effort to rise, his hand flailing at the dagger, but he seemed unable to make his muscles do what he wanted them to, and he merely fell over onto his side clumsily, with a deep, muffled groan.

He reached out to her feebly, whether to hold onto her or to punish her, she couldn't tell. She moved a few inches farther away from him to the very end of the bed, away from the warm stickiness which she could feel on her skin, and sat there, legs crossed under her primly, just out of reach. It wasn't cold in the room, yet she was unable to stop shivering.

"Help me," he said, in a voice as thin and small as a child's. He was actually *begging*.

She shook her head. She couldn't help him. She couldn't help herself. She sat frozen to the spot on the pillow as if she were on a tiny island only big enough for one person, beyond which lay all the dangers of the deep and the dark.

"A doctor. *Please*."

She didn't—couldn't—move to help him.

He was crying now in earnest, tears rolling down his freshly shaven cheeks—he must have shaved quickly before coming here. "Why?" he asked. "What the fuck did I ever do to you?"

She didn't feel like talking. "It's not for me." she said, forcing the words out. "It's for Robby."

"Robby?" Marty was breathing noisily now, fighting for air. He coughed, a deep, liquid cough, and a trickle of blood ran down his chin. "Why? I never touched Robby."

"The pictures, Marty—of Robby with Billy Dove. I saw one! And I overheard what you were saying at Claridge's. You were blackmailing him."

Marty coughed again, this time a sound like none she had ever heard before. His eyes were wide open with amazement and fear. "*Randy*, not Robby! That was *Randy* with Billy Dove. . . ."

He lay silently for a moment, while she prayed he wouldn't cough again—then he laughed, a good laugh in the circumstances, as if the joke were on him. "You made a big mistake, Lish," he said, chuckling. "A big, *big* mistake." His breath was coming in deep gasps now, as if the effort to breathe was consuming his last strength. "I made—a big mistake—too," he said haltingly, still trying to laugh. "You live and learn, Lish, huh? Now *help* me. Please!"

She didn't hear him. All she could think about was that she had done all this for the sake of Randy Brooks. She put her hands over her eyes in horror, remembering suddenly the last time she had seen Randy, at her wedding reception, dressed identically to Robby, and how angry that had made her—had *always* made her. . . .

She took her hands away from her eyes and looked at Marty as if she were seeing him now for the first time. She had killed him, and ruined her own life—and all for nothing. She had sacrificed herself for Robby and done him nothing but harm—for there would surely be a trial, and a scandal of epic proportions.

Marty's eyes were fixed on her like a wounded animal's, but there was nothing she could do for him, or even *say* to him, that would make any difference now. The Shakespeare dagger was sticking out of his back, six inches of the blade buried in him. His hand grasped feebly at the hilt, but he hadn't the strength, and besides she knew it wouldn't have done him a bit of good. Her father had warned her never to pull a knife or a spear from a wound if it was deeply placed. "Leave it in and there's always a chance," he had said, as if this had been urgently important advice for a twelve-year-old girl. "Pull the bloody thing out, and you're dead. Never fails."

He had managed to get his fingers around the handle of the dagger, and was working it feebly back and forth.

"Randy, not Robby," he repeated, producing pink froth from his lips, then, more urgently: "Get this *out!*"

She knew she should stop him, but before she could, he managed to summon up one last burst of strength, and withdrew all but the last inch or so of the blade. "Oh, my God!" he shouted, his entire body jerking with the new pain. He closed his eyes. They opened again involuntarily a moment later, and what they showed her this time was death. Her father had been right.

She sat quietly at her end of the bed, while his blood dripped to the floor, creating a widening pool. All she could do was wonder what Robby would make of what she had done. Would he understand that the whole scene had gone wrong? Would he ever realize what she had tried to do for him, that this too was an act of love?

She had no strength to get up, find a piece of paper and write him a note; besides, all her life she had despised explanations. "Never apologize, never explain"—that ought to have been her motto in life. And see, she thought bitterly, where it had gotten her. . . .

She reached for the bottle of pills in her handbag. *"The*

bright day," she thought, was done—and *she* was *"for the dark."*

She began to cry, at last.

A lifetime of playing Shakespeare had conditioned Robby to bloody scenes of violence and death, but his knees were trembling at what he saw.

He had come as fast as he could, but not before significant delays. Desperate to find her, he had stopped at Claridge's for Marty, then sought Harry Lisle at his club, only to find that he had already left for the country. Since neither was available, he went home, his first port of call, hoping to find that she had returned. It was only then, two hours too late, that he had seen the scrawled address on the notepad by the telephone in the drawing room. He couldn't imagine what she might be doing at that unknown address, or who Billy Dove might be, but he did not need to ask what had happened here. It was all too obvious that Quick was dead.

Killed by Shakespeare's dagger. How could he deal with the horror? He made himself look at Felicia.

"It's going to be all right, darling," he said, with as much confidence as he could manage, but she gave no reaction. She was slumped on the bed, eyes closed, her breathing shallow and irregular. On the chest of drawers next to her was an empty pill bottle and Quick's pocket flask.

Barbiturates and scotch, he told himself—but how *many* pills, and how long ago? In San Francisco they had found her almost immediately, before the pills really had had a chance to work. Quick had been the first to guess what was going on, and had broken down the locked bedroom door of the suite with his shoulder. How he loved to be in charge of things, did Marty. . . .

Why had she done it? he wondered. A lovers' quarrel? He could imagine her killing in the heat of passion, certainly—only too well, in fact!—but why here? This squalid little room was an unlikely "love nest" for her, let alone Marty; and there was not a trace of either of them in its meager furnishings.

Had she *planned* to kill Marty in cold blood? Lured him here, for that purpose? That would make sense of much that could not be explained—she would hardly want to carry the act out at Claridge's, or in her own home. She had the cunning to do it, he thought, but did she have the nerve? He looked at Marty's body and shuddered. Clearly she did.

Had she done it for him? It was a possibility, far more disturbing than a lovers' quarrel. She would know better than almost anyone just how far Marty would go to collect his pound of flesh—certainly she knew better than anyone how precarious his own finances were, now that he owned a theatre. . . .

He wanted to make the scene before him disappear, but he couldn't. His heart ached at the sight of her, as beautiful as ever despite what she had done. What had he done—or neglected—he wondered, to make this happen?

It was too late for regrets. The only way to show her that he loved her now was to save her, if he could—and even then, he thought sadly, she might never know, for she seemed catatonic, as if it were *she* who was dead.

On the chest of drawers he saw an old-fashioned china basin and a pitcher of water. He dipped a washcloth in it and held it to her face. She blinked slowly. He decided there was hope.

He knew what he had to do next, but he hesitated. Then he sighed, and slapped her, hard, feeling his hand tingle. Her eyes opened. Her lips moved, and he leaned close to her. "*The stroke of death is as a lover's pinch,*" she muttered. He recognized *Antony and Cleopatra*. At least *some* part of her mind was functioning.

Whatever she had done, he was responsible for her. It was *his* fault that she had run from the theatre. He had lost control tonight on stage, overcome by his anger. He had almost choked her—certainly had frightened her out of her wits.

Was that the reason for this? He had no idea why she had killed Marty, but whatever the reason, she would not hang for it. The thought of Felicia being measured for the drop or having a noose placed around that swanlike neck was unbearable.

The image brought him back to the reality of their situation. Felicia had committed a murder, and merely by standing here he was becoming an accomplice to it, if only "after the fact."

Funny, he thought, how the phrase popped into his mind. He had once played a barrister—not to speak of a Scotland Yard detective. He knew the drill.

There was no time to waste—that much he knew. There were surfaces and doorknobs to wipe clean of fingerprints, evidence to be disposed of, the murder weapon to reclaim. . . .

Reluctantly, he grabbed the dagger's hilt and pulled, startled by the dreadful sucking sound it made as it came out the final inch or two. The hilt was as bloody as the blade. He wiped Shakespeare's dagger clean on Marty's Burberry, wrapped it in his scarf, then dropped it in Felicia's leather bag. Was that how she had brought it?

He would get no answers from Felicia, who seemed unaware that he was in the room.

He looked around the room and removed Felicia's cigarette butts, then carefully wiped the doorknob and every other surface he could think of with his handkerchief, as if he were playing a scene. The pill bottle and the flask he threw into the bag. Acting on instinct, he removed Marty's billfold and watch, to suggest robbery. Only then did he walk over to Felicia and pull her to her feet. "*Walk!*" he told her.

Her feet shuffled a little, but her weight was all in his arms. On her own she would have collapsed to the floor.

He tossed the bag over his shoulder, and pondered the next move. He did not think anyone had seen him come in, but even if they had, the sight of a single man entering this building would not arouse much notice. Leaving it might be another matter, however. He picked Quick's service cap off the floor and removed the cigar from the rusty little makeshift ashtray. In the dim light of the blackout, anyone who saw him might conclude he was an American officer taking a drunken woman home to his hotel—not an uncommon sight these days.

"We're going, Lisha," he said, gently. "Try to walk, darling, do."

Her feet still didn't move. He held her upright for a few moments, then tried the one way he knew to reach her. *"Beginners, please!"* he shouted.

He felt her stiffen. "The play?" she asked, trembling, her voice hardly audible, feeling panic for the first time at the prospect of failing him again.

"*Antony and Cleopatra*, darling. Listen. There go the trumpets! Don't you hear them?"

She nodded, but she was so weak that she could hardly do more than shuffle her feet.

He half carried her down the stairs, resting at each landing to catch his breath. By the time they reached the filthy downstairs hall, she was able to put one foot in front of the other—though he could tell how much the effort cost her.

In the dark, he saw the huddled figure of a woman. "Pissed, is she?" she hissed.

"Lay off, will ya?" Vane growled, clenching the cigar between his teeth. He hurried past her, using his best American accent to curse her. With any luck, he hoped, all she would have seen was an indistinct face, a cigar, and an American officer's cap.

Outside, the narrow alley was pitch-black. He pushed and pulled Felicia toward Jermyn Street, beyond the archway, wondering how he would make it to the cab stand—for even at this late hour, there were people on the pavements, and the familiar silhouette of a bobby on patrol.

He ditched the cap and the cigar, and, leaning over, whispered to Felicia, "Come on, darling! It's *your* scene!"

He felt her muscles begin to work, as if she were calling on some inner strength. Her feet began to move, and they made their way slowly, haltingly, toward the archway leading to the street, beyond which a row of taxis waited.

Then, as if the arch was the proscenium, she began to walk, head high, front and center, into the lights in which she had lived so much of her life.

21

All the way down Admiralty Row and around the statue of Queen Victoria, the flowers glowed in the sunlight of a perfect summer morning. The sky was blue and clear, unmarked by the tangled white contrails of airplanes and buzz bombs, as if the war were over. Of course it was an illusion—if you looked closely you could see the silver barrage balloons floating above the Thames, the occasional bombed-out house along Pall Mall, like a tooth missing in an otherwise perfect smile. The war had simply moved a little farther away; the climax of the last act was delayed, like a play that had gone on too long.

For a moment, Felicia almost imagined that if she closed her eyes and opened them again she might find that the sentries outside Buckingham Palace were back in their scarlet coats and bearskins, but of course it wasn't so—they were still in khaki, their sentry boxes protected by walls of sandbags, the policemen in front of the high gates still carrying gas masks slung over their shoulders, even though everybody else had long ago ceased to bother.

The sight of the policemen made her tremble slightly, despite the warmth of the day. Two months of enforced "rest" after her "relapse" onstage had kept her quietly out of sight—not that there had been any reason to connect her to the death of Marty Quick.

Still, even in the nursing home in Bath, the nurses talked about the news in front of the patients, and sometimes even left a newspaper lying around, though it was against the rules. She had followed the police inquiries into Marty's death, which were fortuitously swept off the front pages by the British breakthrough from Caen and the plot against Hitler's life.

With so many thousands of people dying every day, the

417

death of one showman in sordid circumstances could hardly be expected to hold the public's interest for long—nor even that of the police, particularly since Quick was an American officer, which, as usual, brought Scotland Yard and the United States Military Police into jealous conflict, ensuring that nothing would happen. Robby had been interviewed, along with almost everybody else who knew Marty, but the general opinion was that he had probably picked up a prostitute and had been killed when she—or her pimp—tried to rob him, a theory made more plausible by the fact that his watch and billfold were missing. The police had not questioned her. Why should they? They were told she was recovering from nervous exhaustion from overwork.

She had no complete memory of what had happened—or rather, her memory was clouded and imprecise. She could remember seeing Marty enter the room, she could remember the sight of his body, and she could remember Robby helping her to her feet, but mercifully she had no memory at all of holding the dagger. All the same, the sight of a policeman made her nervous, even when he was only directing traffic, and perhaps it always would, she thought. Guilt took strange forms and that perhaps was one of them. . . .

She felt Robby squeeze her hand. "We're almost there," he said. Then, after a long pause: "Are you all right?" His concern was obvious. He protected her from everything and watched over her like a mother hen these days.

"I shall be fine, darling," she said. "I was just thinking."

He frowned slightly. Thinking was dangerous—thinking about *some* things, anyway.

She moved closer to him. "I'm so happy for you," she whispered.

"For both of us, really."

She shook her head. "It's your triumph. But I'm glad we're together for it."

He gave her a quick kiss, holding her hand firmly, as if he was suffering from stage fright—which, she thought to herself, might very well be the case. "Don't worry," she teased. "You were wonderful in the rehearsals!"

He smiled. There were no rehearsals, of course, but there had been plenty of instruction and prompting, even for so skilled a performer as himself. "It's all over quickly these days, I'm told," he said.

" 'Slam, bam, thank you ma'am?' " she said, laughing.

"What?" he looked puzzled.

"Just a phrase, darling," she explained. "Something I remember from America." She had heard it from Marty Quick, in fact, who had told her it was what one of his girls had said it was like to be fucked by Leo Stone on his famous white leather casting couch.

She firmly pushed the memory out of her mind. Marty, sex, Hollywood—these were exactly the things she was supposed to avoid thinking about.

"They shortened the ceremony for wartime—made it less formal. Well, it's appropriate for this age of austerity, I suppose. Besides, I hear the King hasn't been feeling well at all, poor man."

"Really? But he's so very young? . . . ." She had to remind herself, too late, that the King wasn't Edward VIII, with whom she had once or twice danced and mildly flirted in more carefree days before the war, when he was still Prince of Wales, but his less dashing brother, George VI, who stuttered.

Robby raised an eyebrow. "Well, not all *that* young, surely?" he said, anxious to avoid contradicting her. "Of course, you're quite right that he's always *looked* youthful."

Her mind did that sometimes, skipping a decade or a year like a gramophone needle jumping out of the groove. The doctors said it was nothing to worry about, and really, she *didn't*. Memory was not high on the list of things she worried about at the moment. Forgetting was more important.

They held hands silently as their car joined the line waiting to enter the palace gates. She glanced at Robby, elegant in black morning coat and striped trousers, his hair cut short, *en brosse* ("crew cut," as the Americans called it), for *Titus Andronicus*. He was thin, his eyes more deeply sunken, there were deep lines on either side of his mouth. Hardly a trace was left of the young matinee idol he had once been, as if all that had been burned away—as, she supposed, it had. He looked older, but more handsome than ever.

Until a few weeks ago it would have been possible to imagine that he could play Romeo again, had he wanted to, but there was too much experience etched in his face now, too much sadness reflected in the depths of those dark blue eyes.

Her own face was unlined and unchanged. People told her that all the time, not just Robby—of course, they always said that to a beautiful woman, especially if she was a famous actress—but she could see in the mirror that it was still the truth. Only the eyes gave her away, and for that reason she had taken to wearing sunglasses like a Hollywood star, even on the darkest and most dismal of English days, an affectation which she had once despised.

She had chosen a pale lavender suit for the occasion—one of those tweeds that only the French know how to weave, so soft and delicate that they seem to have nothing in common with Scottish tweed but the name. She wore a small hat of violet velvet with a single spray of diamonds, her gloves, handbag, and shoes matching it perfectly. She had bought the entire outfit with Robby in Paris, to wear at the Elysée Palace for a luncheon in their honor given by the President of the Republic, before the war.

"Do you remember the day we bought this?" she asked.

"At Chanel? My God, yes. It cost an arm and a leg." He ran his hand down her leg lightly. "Afterwards we went back to the Ritz and made love," he said, with a smile. "The telephone kept ringing because Aaron Diamond was in the hotel and wanted to invite us to dinner, so I finally put a pillow over it. Do you remember? Aaron asked the concierge why the hell he couldn't get through, and what the problem was, and what they were going to do about it, and the concierge told him very elegantly, 'Ah, Monsieur Diamond, this is France—we don't interrupt a man and woman in the middle of the afternoon unless there's a fire or a war.' "

She laughed. Then, quite suddenly, her mood changed. "Will we ever live that way together again, do you think?"

His expression turned serious, the lines around his mouth deeper. He said, "I hope so." Then, more firmly, "Of course we will."

Did he mean it? She needed to believe he did, *believed* it, in fact. She felt tears forming in her eyes at the thought of how happy they once had been, and all that had happened to them since then. "Will I ever get used to being called 'Lady Vane,' I wonder?"

He shrugged. "I don't expect anyone who matters will ever call you that, darling. You'll always be 'Miss Lisle.' Here we are."

The car stopped in the courtyard; a liveried servant opened the door for them. There were a few cheers from the crowd beyond the railings, so she smiled and waved at them. She did not smile and wave at Harry Lisle, who was waiting on the steps, a flower in the buttonhole of his morning coat, top hat at a rakish angle, his weight bending his cane.

At first she had been horrified by Robby's decision to invite him, as well as surprised—for there was nobody she could think of whom Robby disliked more—but it turned out that Robby was thinking of *her*. He was allowed to invite two relatives to the ceremony, and since he didn't want to leave her alone, he thought of Harry to keep her company. As it happened, Harry was the last person she wanted to sit beside at Buckingham Palace, but she was not inclined to argue with Robby on the subject.

She held out her hand, and Harry raised it briefly toward his lips, a gesture more perfunctory than courteous. "You're looking as beautiful as ever," he said, his voice slurred. From a distance, he had seemed as perfectly groomed as ever, but now that she was close to him she saw the small signs of carelessness that even the best of valets couldn't hide. "Portia sends you her love," he said.

"How is she?" She took him by the arm, and helped him slowly up the steps. He didn't resist. He clung to her like a child, as if their roles had been reversed at last.

"Fit as a fiddle," he said, pausing for breath. "Jumping fences that would have made *me* hesitate, before I hung me spurs up. Girl's a natural rider," he mumbled. "Don't know who she gets it from." He winked.

She controlled herself. This was not the time, nor the place, to quarrel with Harry Lisle. The three of them followed a servant into the palace, and down a long corridor, the walls of which were covered with red silk and hung with large, gloomy Dutch masterpieces. When they reached the far end, Robby left them, to wait with the other knights-bachelor-to-be. He gave her a kiss. "Thank you again," he said.

She and Harry were shown into a big room, all gold and white, lit by chandeliers, with a raised, carpeted dais at one end, and a lot of those flimsy little gilt chairs like the ones on which *clientes* perched uncomfortably at Paris couturiers'—in fact, seeing those familiar little chairs, the stage, and the well-dressed crowd, she was reminded of an opening at Molyneux or Chanel in the old days, except that there were more men than women here, and a throne—really hardly more than an elaborate armchair in gilt and red damask—was placed at the center of the dais. Guests were seated at the back of the room. Felicia and Harry were shown to their seats, each marked with a small pasteboard gold-edged card, with beautifully inked calligraphy that read, "Mrs. Robert Vane"—not even a famous actress would be called by her maiden name here—and "Lord Lisle."

They sat, in Harry's case with obvious relief, while the family members of others on the Honors list seated themselves like the audience for a matinee. "He got you here, I see," Harry said gruffly, polishing his monocle with trembling hands. Age had finally accomplished a revenge which she had been unable to carry out. She could even feel pity for him—the emotion he most despised. .

"In a way, Harry, I got *him* here. But never mind about that."

Harry stared at her through the monocle, which merely magnified the signs of age. The eye was watery, unfocused, obscured by a pale gray, opaque film. "Been a hell of a time for you," he said, with what might have passed for sympathy if she hadn't known him too well. "Marty Quick's death— that must have come as a shock?"

She nodded, biting her lip. Get on with the ceremony! she thought.

"Extraordinary thing, wasn't it? What do you suppose a fellow like Quick was doing in some dingy Shepherd's Market bed-sitter? And that chap what's-his-name? Dove? How do you suppose he and Quick met? Bloody fishy story, Dove's. Some woman paid him a fiver to rent his room for the night, and when he came home in the morning, she was gone, and there was Quick, dead on the floor." He laughed. "Not bloody likely, eh?"

She shrugged, as if the subject were of little or no interest to her. "The police believed him, I seem to remember, Harry."

"Oh, I don't think they *believed* a word, dear girl, as a matter of fact. They simply couldn't disprove the blighter's story, that's all. Obviously, this woman, whoever she was, simply scarpered and took the murder weapon with her. . . . A cool customer, wouldn't you say?"

"I wouldn't know."

He gave her a sly smile. "I should have thought you'd take an interest. You and Quick were—close. I'm surprised the police didn't want to interview you."

"Why should they have? I didn't really know him all that well, in fact."

"Oh, come on! This is Harry Lisle you're talking to, lass. You told me yourself that you and Quick were lovers."

"You're imagining things, Harry," she said coldly. "It happens, at your age."

His face flushed. "I think you know more about what happened to your Mr. Quick than you're letting on."

She put her face closer to his and gave him a merciless stare. "I know nothing, and there's nothing to know, Harry." Then she smiled sweetly. "I don't know who killed Marty, and I don't care. But I *do* know this, Harry, darling: anyone who could stab him to death in cold blood must have had a good reason for it—and could probably do it again, I should think, if it was a question of saving herself."

She paused. "Or himself," she added, delighted to see that there were beads of sweat on Harry's forehead.

"You're surely not threatening me?" he asked, blustering—but there was fear in his voice.

She felt a sense of triumph. "Certainly not!" she said sweetly. "But if I were, I'd have learned how to do it from you, Harry, dear. You were my teacher." She plucked the silk handkerchief out of his coat pocket and dabbed his face with it gently. "You should be more careful," she said. "At your age, it's not a good idea to upset yourself."

He blushed, blinked, and coughed. "Quite," he said. "I daresay you know best. Glad to see you're over your 'breakdown.'"

"Thank you," she said graciously. To her relief, there was a bustle of activity at the far end of the room, around the throne.

Harry stared toward the throne. "Then"—he muttered huskily, hardly more than a whisper—"it all worked out for the best in the end?"

There was a moment of silence. Everybody stood, as the King, looking weary beyond his years, entered from a door behind the throne. He was wearing the uniform of an Admiral of the Fleet, with all his ribbons. It seemed much too large and heavy for him. His aides stood behind him in uniform, most of them tall, broad-shouldered, towering over their sovereign, who nevertheless managed to command the full attention of the room without apparent effort.

There was a bustle and a low murmur as everybody sat again, then the voice of the Lord Chamberlain—to her surprise she recognized Sir Herbert Tarpon, despite his long white wig and black robes of office—calling out the name of the first knight. Clearly he, too, had risen in the world.

She sat back and closed her eyes. Robby, of course, would be the last, unless there was one whose name began with X, Y, or Z.

"Yes," she said firmly. "It all worked out for the best in the end."

"Mr. Robert Gilles Vane!"

She heard his name called and saw him approach the King—his walk stately, measured.

King George VI nodded as Robby's services to the theatre were read out in curiously formal terms. One of the aides behind the King gave Robby his cue, a quick nod, and, as he had done before, so many times on the stage, Robby dropped to his knee, head bent, while the King touched his shoulder gently with a sword. She shivered involuntarily at the sight of the bright shiny blade.

"Arise, Sir Robert," she heard the clear, slightly high-pitched voice proclaim. Somewhere in the middle of the progression of knights, the King had seemed to her to tire and falter, but the sight of Robby had restored his spirits, perhaps because Robby reminded him of so many evenings in the theatre in happier days, or because Robby's bearing was theatrically perfect.

George VI leaned forward and placed a ribbon around Robby's bent neck, the enameled insignia of a Knight Bachelor hanging from it, then, in a simple gesture, one Englishman to another, shook his hand while they exchanged a few whispered words. Robby laughed, gave the required bow, backed four steps away from the King, and turned to take his place with the other new knights. He gave her a quick wave and a wink. She had never seen him happier.

"The poor, *dear* chap," Harry said, grasping her hand as hard as he could. Tears were running down his cheeks now, and his lips were beginning to tremble, to her amazement, for she had never seen him cry before. Then she realized he was crying at the sight of his sovereign. Of course. Even the most unsentimental of Englishmen went to pieces in the presence of their King, and Harry Lisle was no exception.

She herself was crying, but, loyal as she was to the throne, for very different reasons. She dried her tears.

Holding Harry's arm, she helped him out into the sunshine of the courtyard, where Robby waited.

"The King asked after you," Robby said as they posed, a little stiffly, she thought, for the photographers. "Said the Queen's favorite play was *Mayfair Madness*, and that she wanted to know how you'd managed to stay as beautiful as ever."

"What did you tell him?"

"I said, 'Sir, it simply isn't so.' 'Isn't *so*?' His Majesty asked, rather shocked. 'No, Sir,' I said, 'Miss Lisle is *more* beautiful than ever!' "

"Flatterer!"

"Not a bit of it."

One of the photographers called out, "Give us a kiss."

Robby, who had been giving them his most serious expression as England's first theatrical knight in decades, frowned as if he found the request mildly impertinent, but Felicia didn't hesitate for a moment. She flung her arms around him as hard as she could, looking up at him with that expression that so many actresses had envied over the years, but had never done so well, eyelids three-quarters closed, lips parted just enough to show her perfect teeth, neck gracefully stretched like a swan's. . . .

It was a face that demanded to *be* kissed—"a stunning exercise in erotic submission," in the words of one critic, "the embodiment of the fact that the female of the species is more deadly than the male," in the words of another; and to hell with them both, she thought, because what did *they* know about it?

She had prepared herself for his kiss as Juliet, chastely; as Lady Macbeth, voluptuously; as Cleopatra, passionately; as Desdemona, fearfully; and he had not failed her—nor did he now.

He lowered his head, smiling, and kissed her on the lips gently—the perfect close-up, fade-out kiss, so perfectly that she almost expected to hear applause.

"That one was for the reporters," she said, and kissed him passionately, while the flashbulbs popped all around them. "This is the real thing!"

She stared into his eyes now as she had done so many times before, and arm in arm they turned to face the cameras, smiling "radiantly" (as she knew the captions would read tomorrow).

They walked the gauntlet of the press toward the gilded wrought-iron gates, Harry shuffling along behind them, snarling at the reporters, whom he despised, having been brought up on the principle that a gentleman should only have his name in the newspaper when he is born, married, and dies, and even then, only in the *Times*. "No, I am *not* her bloody father," she heard him growl, "nor *his*."

She knew it didn't matter. Half the papers—the ones most people read—would get it wrong anyway. Nobody *ever* knew the truth about other people's lives—most of all when they thought they knew it all.

She clung close to Robby as if they were Siamese twins, while the reporters and the crowd surged around them. Waiting on the pavement were Guillam Pentecost, smiling as if he himself had arranged all this, Toby—whose turn it would be next, she guessed—and Philip, making a monumental effort to hide the envy he must surely feel.

They all stood together for a few moments in a group, while the photographers snapped them. She felt Philip, who was standing beside her, take her hand. "Are you all right?" he asked softly.

"Never better, darling," she said firmly.

"One hears rumors . . ."

"I needed a rest. People do."

Chagrin's expression was haughty, his head held high, as it always was in the presence of the press. If a stranger had been asked which of the men standing here was the knight, Chagrin would certainly be the first choice—he managed to make everyone around him seem a little vulgar, except her. "*People*, perhaps," he sniffed, keeping his voice low. "Actresses of your quality, *no*! The stage *needs* you, darling. More important, you need the stage!"

"The doctors don't want me to work just yet, Philip. They're afraid of the stress."

The corners of Chagrin's mouth turned down sharply. "Fiddlesticks!" he snapped. "The only stress that can hurt an actress of your caliber is *not* working. *That's* the killer, my girl—you mark my words!"

At the word "killer" she went pale. It was something she simply couldn't control. Well, you couldn't control *everything*, could you? She could see the alarm on Philip's face.

She pulled herself together—she was getting good at that, she thought—and took a deep breath, which was supposed to help, but usually gave her an instant headache instead. "Soon," she said. "I promise."

"I shall hold you to that," Chagrin said, with the look of piercing authority that he always did so well.

Robby guided her toward the waiting car. "What are you going to be doing next, Sir Robert?" a reporter asked, pushing his way close to them.

Robby gave his Great Man of the Theatre, thin-lipped smile. Well, she thought, God knows he had earned the right. "*Henry the Fourth,*" he said. "Parts One and Two."

"And will Lady Vane be in it?"

For a fraction of a second she wondered who "Lady Vane" might be, then she gave a brilliant, happy smile, and laughed. "Sir Robert and I don't have any plans for working together at present," she said. "We thought we'd try *living* together instead, for a change."

Robby laughed. "Lady Vane always had a way with exit lines," he said. Then, taking her by the arm, he helped her into the car. The chauffeur shut the door. She waved to Philip, Toby, Uncle Harry, the reporters, feeling rather like a royal personage herself.

Beyond the reporters was a vast crowd of people. She waved at them, and they waved back. Many of them, she saw, were carrying photographs of her, some of them even hand-lettered signs that read "Get well, Felicia!" or "Felicia, we love you!" It was *his* day, but in some strange way, the crowds were hers, as perhaps they always would be. *He* was the great actor, but she was the star, perhaps the brightest that England had ever produced.

"Thank you for today," Robby said with a sigh, leaning his head back against the seat. "And for much else."

She took his hand. "Robby," she said, "whatever I did, I've always loved you. Perhaps we shall never work together again. Perhaps we *shouldn't*—perhaps that's where the trouble began. Perhaps not being with you onstage, ever again, is my punishment. But even if we never do, will you still love me? Can you tell me that, if it's so? And mean it?"

She could see that he was beginning to cry, the dark blue eyes welling with tears. It was a curious fact, known perhaps only to herself, that Robby had never been able to cry on cue. *She* could produce tears whenever they were called for, as most actors and actresses did, but he required every possible artifice, from special eyedrops to a prop man chopping up an onion in the wings for him to inhale. He could fake many things, but never tears.

"I promise I will love you forever," he said. "To my dying day." He had never sounded more fervent, or more sincere.

She nodded and sat back against the soft leather, convinced that he was telling her the truth. He would love her as he would never love anyone else.

"Thank you," she said.

She would have to learn how to stop thinking about the past, hard though that was.

She tried to think about the future. That was even harder.

She closed her eyes.